The
Jump Off

The Jump Off

Doug Dixon

KENSINGTON PUBLISHING CORP.
http://www.kensingtonbooks.com

DAFINA BOOKS are published by

Kensington Publishing Corp.
850 Third Avenue
New York, NY 10022

ISBN 0-7582-1356-5

First Kensington Trade Paperback Printing: August 2006
10 9 8 7 6 5 4 3 2 1

Printed in the United States of America

This book is dedicated to
My loving parents Fred and Leola Dixon,
my brother Desmond Dixon, my sister Deirdri Brown,
and to the late Mrs. Cora Anderson,
my spiritual advisor who taught me how to walk
in the confidence of God in troubled times.

Acknowledgments

First and foremost I would like to thank God for each and every blessing that He has put in my life.

Special thanks to my consultant Chandra Sparks Taylor for your continued encouragement and patience.

To Nicole Bruce for giving me the opportunity to become a part of the Kensington family.

Thanks to the fellas Tracey Clarke, Kenneth Allen, Dwayne Butler, Darryl Portis, Cedric Perryman, Gerald Westry, Damian Collins, and Michael Rawls for always being there through this long process.

Thanks to Archie Wesley, Hampton Simmons, Terrance Marshall, Eric Goshay, and the rest of the BZ 'nupes' for all of your support.

Also, thank you Greselda Collado, Victoria Jackson, Vernetta Perkins, the Mobile clique Kim Collins, Dyra Louis, and LaTonya Robinson for being true friends.

Last but not least I'd like to thank the boys back home for being there as well. Your support has been greatly appreciated.

CHAPTER 1

Breaking News

It was a Thursday evening, and I was on my way to Copeland's to meet my fiancée, Jennifer Stevens, for a late evening dinner. Copeland's was a Cajun-style seafood restaurant where Jennifer and I would meet for dinner and drinks, on the corner of Airport Boulevard and Hillcrest Road in Mobile, Alabama.

Since I had missed lunch, my stomach was growling like crazy, so I was in a hurry to get there. It was rush hour, and I had the music blasting to Ludicras's song "Move" Get out the Way" and I was doing just that. I was speeding down the street trying to move everyone the hell out of my lane as I zipped through traffic.

I worked as an applications engineer for Norwood, Cook & Allen, a large engineering consulting firm in downtown Mobile. I'd been there for a little more than three years where I designed billing software on an application called Billright for clients. This application allowed our clients to process their customers' billing statements and print them on paper. Our clients consisted of corporations such as banks, utility companies, and telecommunication companies. Because this was a consulting firm, I worked under short-term or long-term contracts based on the workload of the firm. I was currently finishing up the first year of my two-year contract at which time a new one might be offered.

The first three years of my career I lived in New Orleans, Louisiana, before moving back to my hometown of Mobile, following my career path. I had hopes of one day starting my own engineering firm once I got more experience under my belt. That's when I met Jennifer Stevens. Yeah, my girl. She was an attorney for Collins & Clarke, a small black law firm in Mobile, where she practiced criminal law. She was originally from Pensacola, Florida, a city about fifty-five miles outside of Mobile.

We had first met two and a half years ago in Pensacola. I was walking down the beach one summer afternoon checking out the honeys and passed her as she sat alone on a towel reading a novel by Michael Eric Dyson, *Is Bill Cosby Right?*, as she enjoyed the nice weather. From the moment I saw her, I knew she was someone special. There was something that came over me that told me not to leave until I approached her. Nevertheless I kept on combing the beach, trying to get as many numbers as I could.

See, I was used to having three or four women on standby, and this was the day to add and delete. You know, add another honey to the list and delete the ones who were getting too boring or trying to hook me in a serious relationship.

Me, serious? No way. I just couldn't picture it. I could never see myself being with the same girl each and every day for the rest of my life. But, for some reason, my mind was set on meeting the girl sitting there all alone.

For most of the afternoon I kept trying to get her to notice me. Because she was all into what she was reading, she didn't even bother to look up at a brother. This went on far too long, and it was time for me to just make some kind of move. I had to say something before it got too late or before she decided to leave for the day, and then I might not ever see her again.

The thing that intrigued me first was her body and how fine she was. The swimsuit she was wearing was not too revealing, unlike with the other women on the beach, but for the most part it kept my attention.

As I began to get closer I must have scared her, because she looked up at me like I was a thug brother coming up to strong-arm her or something. I just stopped in my tracks and smiled at her to let her know that everything was cool. While standing there ready to introduce myself the craziest thing happened, I froze up. I mean my mind went completely blank. *I've been hollering at honeys all day, so why has this one got me all frigid?* She just sat there looking up at me staring at her like I was crazy.

Finally she stood, grabbed her towel along with the rest of her things, and began packing them up. I wanted to say something but I was too stunned to open my mouth.

I could tell she was getting kinda nervous by the way she was frowning at me from the corner of her eye as she dusted the sand off her legs. She finally turned and looked at me again.

"Is there something wrong with you?" she asked as she continued to gather her things.

"Uh, no, baby. I just thought you were someone I knew, that's all," I replied nervously.

"No, I don't think so," she said as she began to walk away.

"Hey, wait!" I said as I walked up to her. "Uh, I really came over to ask you your name, that's all. No harm intended."

"My name," she replied.

"Yeah, your name."

She paused, still staring at me. "Well, it's Jennifer Stevens."

"Hi, Jennifer, my name is Troy Sanders, and I didn't mean to run you off. I just wanted to meet you, that's all. Uh, can we talk awhile or do you have to leave?"

She took a deep breath. "Well, uh, I guess I can stay for a few minutes."

That day we spent the next thirty minutes laughing and talking before finally exchanging numbers and then parting ways in opposite directions. On my way out, for some reason, I tossed all those other numbers I had collected and really just thought about her.

Within two months we started going out. On the weekends I was able to get away, we went to the movies, out to dinner, even to the casinos in Biloxi, Mississippi. We did almost everything together. All that traveling back and forth pretty much ended my days of playing honeys, and I seriously considered being faithful.

As time grew, so did our feelings for each other, and we fell in love. Our love was so strong that Jennifer ended up leaving the district attorney's office in Pensacola to work with Mckellon & Horton in Mobile, Alabama, to be closer to me. Two years later we got engaged.

As I got to the parking lot of Copeland's I didn't see Jennifer's car, so I parked and headed inside to grab a table. Jennifer was very dedicated to her work, so it was no surprise that she was late.

While I sat there waiting, I had three drinks. My favorite was cognac, Hennessy, Courvoisier, whatever. I just loved the smooth taste of it on the rocks.

I drank two kinda fast and sorta sipped my third one, still waiting patiently for her. By the time I made it halfway through that one my buzz kicked in. At that point I sat there fumbling with things on the table or just watched as other couples ate their dinner, which made my stomach growl even louder. Pretty soon the liquor started working on my kidneys, so I jumped up and headed to the restroom. While inside I checked myself out in the mirror, making sure I was tight. I brushed off my neatly trimmed beard and checked my nose to make sure the coast was clear up there and made sure my clothes were in order. Seeing that I was cool, I headed back to my chair.

As I tried to sit down, I was rudely pushed aside by two extra-large honeys not looking where they were going who caused me to knock my drink off the table, and it spilled all over my pants and shoes. *Damn*, I thought, as I quickly grabbed a napkin and bent over to dry myself off. No excuse me, I'm sorry, or nothing, just run me over. I was pretty hot and was ready to cuss someone's ass out when all of a sudden I felt this soft touch on the back of my neck. Surprised, I looked up and saw that it was Jennifer standing over me.

"Hi, baby. What happened here?" she asked, looking down at me.

"I was just trampled by those women sitting over there," I replied, still drying off my pants.

She laughed. "Boy, you so silly. So, how was your day?" she asked.

"It was cool. I'm just hungry as hell right now," I replied as I got up to help her to her seat.

I looked her up and down as I walked her to her chair. She was wearing this black business suit that complemented her cocoa-brown skin, her shiny black hair hanging below her shoulders. As she turned her head to thank me, I could smell the sweet scent of her perfume. The scent was so fresh it followed me back to my seat.

I sat down and handed Jennifer a menu while I ordered her a glass of her favorite merlot. We sat there looking over the menu, trying to find something new to eat, but as usual, we both got the same old thing. I ordered the bowl of gumbo with the seafood platter while Jennifer ordered the cup of gumbo, fried shrimp, and crab cakes in a cream sauce.

While waiting on dinner, like always I started talking about our wedding, kids, and having wild and crazy sex all night, making her laugh out loud. For some reason she wasn't into the conversation. It was like her mind was somewhere else. Seeing this, I reached over and grabbed her hand.

"What's wrong, baby? Is everything okay?" I asked.

"Yeah, I'm okay," she said with her head slightly tilted, rubbing her thumb against my hand.

"You sure? 'Cause you don't look okay," I said.

"No, I'm all right."

"Guess what?" I said with excitement.

"What?" she replied.

"I found this great three-acre lot the other day for sale overlooking the city that fits perfectly in our budget."

"Oh, really?" she said, not showing much excitement.

"Yeah, that means we can build the house we've talked about so much, you know, the two-story with the pool," I said, excited.

"Uh, yeah, but—"

"And now we can have the wedding we always wanted and the reception at the ballroom of the convention center. Isn't that great, baby?" I said.

She gave me a hard smile as though she was forcing it.

"Baby, what's up? You don't seem excited. I thought this was everything we wanted."

"Well, Troy, I am happy for you, but to be honest, it's not everything that I wanted."

"What do you mean? This is what we've been talking about since last year."

"No, this is everything that you've been talking about since last year, Troy. Look, I like Mobile a lot, but I feel stagnant here. I feel like I'm doing the same thing day after day, and it's beginning to take its toll on me."

"Where is this coming from? I thought you were okay being here. You have a good job, you make good money, *we're* together, so what's the problem?"

"Well, I don't feel like I'm growing here anymore. I want to get out and explore more options with my career, not just deal with the same thing every day, you know, someone beating his wife, drug dealers, and deadbeat dads. It's the same crazy thing over and over and I'm just tired of it," she said emotionally.

"So what are you saying? I mean, what do you want to do about it?" I asked.

"Well, I was going to surprise you with my good news, but you caught me off guard with yours. For the past month, I've been on the phone with this huge law firm in Atlanta about a job. They've been impressed with my background and because I'm bar certified to practice law in Georgia, they want me to work for them in Atlanta."

"Atlanta," I said, surprised.

"Yeah, and today they made me an incredible offer."

"Offer. What kind of incredible offer?" I asked.

"Well, they want to almost double my salary, give me a bonus every quarter, and if I do well, I could be up for partner in the next two years."

"Well, have you given them your answer yet?" I asked nonchalantly.

"Well, I told them yes."

"Yes?" I replied, shocked. "Oh, so this is about you now? I can't believe you did this without even thinking about talking to me."

"Well, I was going to tell you before you surprised me with your news, Troy. Besides, they needed to know right away or they would have extended the offer to someone else. I had to give them an answer."

I shook my head in frustration. "Are you serious, Jennifer? You told them you'd take the job?" I said, looking directly at her.

"Yes, Troy, I'm dead serious, I put them off too long, and they pretty much extended the last offer to me. I had to say yes," she replied.

I looked off. "When do they want you to start?" I asked.

"Well, they want me to report in about a month."

"A month. Damn," I said. "What about us? What about the wedding and everything we've planned?"

"We can still get married. Can't you just pack up and come along with me?"

"Girl, you know I can't just break my contract like that. I still have one year left. Besides, even if I did break it, I couldn't afford to pay back all of the bonus money they gave me last year. It's all tied up in investments. That'll blackball me for sure in this field. I'm sorry, I'm stuck here."

"Well, what do you want to do?" she asked.

"Hell, I don't know. It seems like your mind is already made up on what you want."

"Well, maybe we can just put our wedding off until you move there with me."

I chuckled in anger. "Oh, so it's that simple for you, huh? Just like that. Do you think I can be without you for an entire year? I barely see you enough as it is."

"The only difference will be that we won't be in the same city for a while, that's all."

"That's not the point, Jennifer. You really don't understand what I'm talking about here, do you?"

"I do, Troy. I just want you to understand what I'm talking about and how I feel. This shouldn't be about just you. It should be about us. Shouldn't we both be happy in this relationship?"

"Why do you think I've been working my ass off so much, Jennifer? To get you the nice house, to have a beautiful wedding, to keep you happy."

"I know, Troy. But I feel that moving to Atlanta will help me grow in my career."

"I just wish you would've told me about this a lot sooner so that we could have worked something better out with our situation. Damn! I can't believe this shit. One minute I feel like I'm on top of the world and now I feel like I just got kicked in the groin."

There was silence.

"What are we going to do, Troy?" she asked with concern in her voice. "I don't want to lose you over this."

"What do you mean what are we going to do? Are you suggesting that we break up?"

"Oh no!" she quickly responded. "I wouldn't dare break us up over this. If this makes you that unhappy, I can call them first thing in the morning and tell them I don't want the job," she said with disappointment in her voice.

I looked her in the eye as she turned her head to keep from showing her emotions. I couldn't dare let her turn down something she truly wanted to do. I composed my anger for a moment.

"You know I love you, right, and I only want you to be happy? And, well, if this is going to make you happy, then I guess I have to accept it. When do they want you to start?"

"They would like for me to report to work in about a month so that I can start this big case."

"A month, huh? That damn soon? I just don't believe this shit is happening. Can you at least put *that* off for a while?"

"I wish I could because this is so sudden, but I have to find a place to stay and pack all of my things. I just have so much to do in so little time."

As she continued to talk, my anger made her voice fade as I thought about how it would be without Jennifer with me. I felt like someone had just taken my stomach and tied it into knots. I started thinking about how I could keep us together and how I was going to change my schedule so I could visit regularly. As my anger started cooling I could hear her clearly again, talking about all she had to do before she left for Atlanta. I grabbed her hand and pulled it closer to me.

"Do you love me?" I asked.

"Yes, baby, with all my heart, why?" she replied, looking concerned.

I took a deep breath. "If you love me like you say, then I guess we'll have to make this work," I said with somewhat of a doubtful tone.

She smiled as tears started to build in her light brown eyes.

By the time we got our food, neither one of us was in the mood to eat. We just nibbled and sat there in silence, occasionally making small talk. Jennifer finally suggested that we leave.

With everything that had taken place I didn't realize that it was after nine o'clock. We got the waitress to box our leftovers, paid the check, and started out the door. I walked her to her car silently holding her hand. We embraced and kissed before she got in her car and headed in the direction of her apartment. I got in my car and drove around town trying to clear my head after hearing such heartbreaking news. I stopped at the liquor store and bought a half pint of Hennessy and drank it straight out of the bottle as I rode around for about an hour. When my cell phone started ringing, the first time I didn't answer, but about a minute later it started again.

"Hello," I answered.

"Hey, baby, where are you?"

"I'm on my way home."

"I called you but no one answered, so I got worried."

"I'm fine, I just had to clear my head for a minute, but I'm cool now."

"Are you sure?"

"Yeah, I'm cool. I know it's late, so just go on to bed. I'll call you tomorrow."

"No, I want to make sure you make it home okay."

"Baby, I'm fine. Just go to sleep. You have to work tomorrow."

"Well, promise me you'll go straight home."

"Yeah, I promise."

I hung up the phone, and it hit me that Jennifer was actually leaving. That's when the alcohol kicked in and started talking.

What if she met another guy and dumped me? What if I couldn't get a job in Atlanta or it took longer than a year for me to find something? What if she just didn't want to get married and this was her way of getting out of it? What-ifs just kept running through my mind until finally I snapped out of it and realized that it was time to take my ass home.

CHAPTER 2

Turning Point

Two weeks had passed and my attitude about Jennifer leaving was starting to get a little better. I guess I had to come to grips with the fact that she had to go and understand that she was only trying to do what was best for the both of us in the long run.

One afternoon Jennifer called me at work to let me know that she found several apartments online and wanted me to drive her to Atlanta to view them. We both agreed to drive down on Saturday. I could hear the excitement in her voice as she talked about Atlanta and her new job. Every day it was something about Atlanta. It was really starting to bug the hell out of me the way she kept talking about it. I knew she was excited but damn, give me a break for a while. I was finally able to cut her off when I noticed that it was time for me to meet the fellas for lunch. I hung up from her and headed out the door to Mammie's. Mammie's was one of the best soul food restaurants in town, located about two miles from my job.

When I arrived I noticed a line damn near out the door. I got out of my car and walked slowly through the parking lot looking for one of my boys' cars. I was kinda anxious to see them because I was ready to vent again about this Atlanta shit.

When I got to the front door I saw them sitting in the back, waving me over. After making my way through the crowd, speaking to everyone I knew, I sat down. My seat was facing the door and my back was near the kitchen where I could smell all that good food cooking. Mammie's food tasted like what my grandma used to cook back in the day, you know, smothered chicken and gravy, collard greens, and real corn bread, not that Jiffy mix stuff. My favorite dish was the oxtails with gravy over rice, and macaroni and cheese. Yeah, this was the spot all right. Everybody and their mama knew about Mammie's, including white folks.

I was greeted by my boys, Michael Smith and Rick Walker, as I sat down, ready to eat. Mike was a detective with the Mobile Police Department. He was a deep chocolate brother who stood six-three and every bit of 240. He'd been a police officer for about ten years and was proud of that fact. Mike was married with two daughters who looked just like his ass. He was also the one in the group with the most sense. Every time Rick and I got into arguments, Mike was the one who reminded us how stupid we sounded, or if there was a dilemma in our lives, he was the one who could help us see a better side. Rick, on the other hand, was just the opposite. He was a high-yellow brother who stood about five-eleven and was 165 pounds of nothing. He was a branch manager at one of the local banks and the type who always tried to impress the ladies with the fact that he made over fifty thousand a year and drove a convertible sports car. He also lied his ass off about how much lay he got on the weekend and how many women he had running after him. He did mack the women, but sometimes he overexaggerated a lot. If a woman was not making at least forty thousand a year he wouldn't give her the time of day, unless she was fine and he just wanted some quick trim. But that was my boy. I didn't think I saw Rick settling down any time soon, because the average entry-level salary in Mobile ranged from thirty thousand to thirty-five thousand.

Since I was running late Mike had ordered for me. Yep, he got my oxtails. He looked at me as I tried to get comfortable in my seat.

"You're late again," he said, shaking his head in disbelief.

"Yeah, man, I was on the phone with Jennifer."

"How is she doing, by the way?" he asked.

"She's cool. Just every other word that comes out of her mouth is something about Atlanta. I'm telling you, man, that shit is about to drive me crazy."

"So what, man? She's excited. You need to be excited with her," Mike said.

"Forget that, man, she needs to stay home and you know it," I replied.

"No, man. Put yourself in her shoes. What if you had a dream, wouldn't you want to pursue it?" Mike continued.

"Yeah, but I would also think about my girl in the process and how it would affect us."

"She *is* thinking about your sorry ass, man. All she's trying to do is make a better life for the both of you. Name one law firm in Mobile that will give her the opportunity she's gonna get now. See, that's your problem, you're always thinking about yourself."

"I just hope she don't fuck up, that's all," I said.

"See, man, you already going into this wrong. You messed over so many honeys you think they're all like you. Just 'cause she's not around you all the time don't mean she's messing around on you. Get that out of your head and concentrate on what's gonna happen when you move up there."

Mike had a point but I didn't let him know it. Jennifer *was* the first girl to whom I had ever been faithful. In all of my past relationships I cheated. I slept with married women, white women, and Asian women. You name the nationality, and I slept with it. Meeting Jennifer was like a blessing, and her leaving had me thinking that I was being punished for all of my dirt.

At that time Rick started in. "In other words, Troy, Mike is telling you to shut up and accept the shit. If it were me, I would say 'go ahead and take your ass to Atlanta. But if you go, then we're through.' I betcha she would think twice about leaving then," he said.

Mike looked at Rick with a frown of disgust. "Shut the fuck up, man. You've already had two honeys leave you for saying that dumb shit. Two good women at that. What, one went to California, and the other joined the army on your ass?"

"Hey, that's all right though. They were broke, and I didn't want their asses anyway. Didn't none of that stop me from living, you know what I'm saying? When you look at it, they did *me* a favor," Rick said.

Mike looked back over at me. "Look, Troy, you know what I mean, man. I know you feeling messed up inside right now, but just give it a chance before you judge the situation, that's all I'm saying."

I looked at Mike, nodding to show that I understood.

At that moment the waitress brought our food. We said our grace and started eating. The rest of our lunch we spent talking about sports and old times, growing up in the hood.

After lunch, still thinking about what Mike had said, I called Jennifer to offer my support. I could tell she was relieved, because she started back again with Atlanta, telling me about all of these different places she wanted to go to that she heard about once we got there. I listened for about ten minutes before having to politely cut her off again.

"Baby, baby, baby, we can do whatever you want once we get you there, okay?"

"Thank you, Troy."

"Okay. Now let me get back to work and I'll see you tonight."

"Okay, bye. Have fun at work," she said before she hung up.

"Bye, baby."

After work as usual I was at Jennifer's house or she was at mine. The days spent together brought us even closer to each other. We were inseparable.

Saturday finally came, and we both got up at around five. Jennifer went into the kitchen and cooked this big breakfast. We had grits, eggs, bacon, toast, and washed it down with big glasses of OJ. After eating two helpings, I was ready to hit the road. Since we were only going to be gone for one night, we each packed a change of clothes, something to wear at the club, and a shit-load of bottled water. We put what we had in the car and jumped on Interstate 65, heading north. The first hour into the drive was boring as hell. All we saw were a bunch of trees and miles of land everywhere. It looked like something out of a Clint Eastwood western.

Since I traveled a lot throughout Alabama, I was used to seeing miles of forest. Normally, if I was alone I would listen to my CDs, but when I had someone else traveling with me, I usually talked. In this case talking was out. About an hour into our trip I looked over at Jennifer and her ass was knocked out. Every now and then she would mumble something crazy. I put in a CD, got comfortable, and continued.

Another hour into the ride I saw a sign that read MONTGOMERY, 25 MILES. This meant Atlanta was only another two and a half to three hours away. As soon as we got into Montgomery I had to stop and run to the bathroom. I guess it was because of all of the water I drank on the way. You know how you feel when your kidneys are so tight that if you laugh, sneeze, or bump into something it's all over? I did what I had to do, and we got back on the road. By this time Jennifer was wide awake. Since she had gotten her rest she was ready to sing every song on the radio. I just shook my head and kept on cruising up the highway. As we continued she sang and sang all the way to Atlanta's city limits. When she saw this, her whole demeanor changed. It was like looking at a little kid at Christmas getting ready to open her gifts. Jennifer looked all around like we were on the moon or something and everything around her was new. She then looked over at me with this big smile. Seeing her so happy, I couldn't help but smile.

"You're home, baby," I said.

"Nope, you mean we're home. Remember, we're in this together," she replied.

I looked at her with surprise, nodding. "That's right," I said. "We're home."

She reached down and grabbed the map of the entire city of Atlanta that she had bought.

"Do you know how to get to Dunwoody?" she asked, all confused as she looked at the map.

"Yeah, I think it's off 285," I replied.

"You think?" she said with a silly grin.

"Well, I know," I said with assurance.

"Good, because these directions don't really tell you much."

"Don't worry, baby, I got your back. I don't use maps, I go by memory."

"All righty then, let's do the damn thang," she said as she put the map away.

We got on GA 400 and followed it all the way to Dunwoody, which was the exit of one of the apartment complexes on her list, and followed the road to a stoplight. Over to the right you could see a bunch of apartment units that faced the highway. The apartments stretched so far down the interstate that they almost looked like another city. Finally after waiting about five minutes for the light to turn, we maneuvered through more traffic before finally making it to the front gate of one of the complexes. I was really impressed with the way the building was made. There were security cameras all around the outside, and the community was gated with card access. Inside, there was real nice landscape. It was tight.

We pulled up to this box where you could ring the front office for them to let you in. When I pushed the button a voice came across the speaker.

"Can I help you?" it said.

"Uh, yeah, we're here to view a unit that we called about sometime last week."

"Okay, come right in and follow the arrows to the leasing office," the voice replied.

"Okay, thank you," I answered.

A few seconds later the gate opened, and we followed the arrows right to the leasing office.

When we got out of the car, we were met by this fine-ass sista. She walked out of the door with this big smile on her face like she was happy to see some blacks interested in the complex. As she got closer I couldn't help but look at her and the way she walked. She was a brown-colored sista who had these nicely toned thighs that showed her muscles through this tight pantsuit. I tried not to stare but I couldn't help it because she walked with such grace. She had her long brown hair pulled back in a ponytail that hung down her back. Damn, she was sexy.

She finally made it over to us with her hand extended to greet us. "Hi, I'm Lisa Phillips. Welcome to the Summits."

Jennifer smiled and extended her hand in return. "Hi, I'm Jennifer Stevens. I think I spoke to someone in your office about viewing an apartment last week. Oh, and this is my fiancé, Troy Sanders."

I extended my hand. "Hi, Lisa. Nice to meet you."

"Hi. Nice to meet you as well," she replied. "So when are you looking to move in?" she asked Jennifer.

"Well, I'm starting a new job, and I was hoping to get something today so I can move in next week," Jennifer explained.

"Are you looking for a one-, two-, or three-bedroom?" Lisa asked.

"I'd like a two if there's one available," Jennifer replied.

As their conversation continued on, I stood back and had a complete view of Lisa's body. This sista was definitely fine. Every inch of her looked like it was molded to perfection.

Lisa wrote some information on a card before walking us around to a golf cart. As she walked, her ass jiggled like Jell-O; every move she made her bottom just bounced in rhythm. I stared for so long I damn near got hypnotized.

We all climbed into the cart and started riding.

While Lisa and Jennifer sat in the front seat talking, I was in the back looking around at all of the brothers and sistas who lived in the complex. I didn't think I had ever seen so many fine sistas in one place. Of course they couldn't compare to my Jennifer, but it made a brother think. Whew, if I was a single man and living up here, shiiit, I could do some serious damage. My boy Rick would lose his mind. Every time I turned my head, I saw a sexy sista walking or riding by. I was looking around so hard that when I looked forward again all I saw was Jennifer staring dead in my face with this mean look. I played it off by glancing at my watch and fumbling with my shirt like I had a stain on it or something. She quickly turned her head back around and continued talking to Lisa.

Finally we made it to the unit where the apartment was and got out of the cart. Jennifer quickly reached over and snatched my hand, pulling me alongside her as we walked. Lisa, noticing it, kinda laughed to herself.

The apartment that we viewed first was on the top floor. We started up the stairs and walked inside. I couldn't believe how big it was and how new everything looked. From the front door we walked right into this huge den. Jennifer was so impressed and anxious that she let my hand go and moved around to really get a good look at what I knew was her soon-to-be new place. To the left was this huge kitchen with all of the latest appliances. Everything looked new, from the stove and dishwasher down to the refrigerator. To the right was a sunroom with a patio door that led to the balcony that overlooked

the pool, the tennis courts, and one of the fitness areas. The bed-
rooms were in the back. As we started down the hall to the first one,
Lisa stopped to show us the alarm, air, and heating system. As she
made a sudden stop, my head was turned, and I walked right into
her. My manhood sank right into the middle of that soft ass of hers.
Even though it was only for a second, it felt like minutes. Instantly I
got a hard-on. I had to fake a cough just so I could turn around before one of them noticed. I know Lisa felt it because she turned her
head and gave me this big smile after I composed myself. Jennifer
was so excited about her new place she didn't notice anything. I
thought, *I'd better walk in the front with Jennifer before I get myself
caught in some shit back here.*

We continued down the hallway to the master bedroom. It clearly
was the biggest room in the apartment. There was a large vanity outside the bathroom right next to this huge walk-in closet. As we continued forward, we entered into the bathroom, which had a lot of
mirrors around this huge garden tub and a glass shower on the side.
I must admit, the place was nice as hell, and for the most part it
seemed safe.

As Jennifer walked out of the closet, I reached and grabbed her
arm. "So, what do you think?" I asked.

"Oh, I love it," she said, excited.

"Me too. I think it's perfect for you."

Lisa smiled. "This unit is available right now."

"Okay, I'll take it," Jennifer said.

"Okay, let's head back down to the leasing office and take care of
the paperwork and you'll be all set."

Jennifer smiled, grabbed my hand, and we walked out the front
door. We got back in the golf cart and headed toward the leasing office. When we got there, Jennifer and Lisa continued to discuss more
details before going into the back room to sign the papers. I waited
in the lobby where I grabbed a couple of magazines and chilled out.

About a half hour later, I heard the door open and saw Jennifer
and Lisa shaking hands and smiling, which meant everything was
done. Jennifer walked toward me, wiping her eyes, yawning as she
grabbed my hand and led me to the door.

"Are you okay? You look a little tired," I said.

She turned to me and smiled. "Yeah, I don't know what's wrong with me, but I'm exhausted."

"Exhausted," I said, laughing. "You slept halfway here."

She gave me an innocent frown.

"Okay, well, as soon as we get to the hotel, you can take a nap."

"No, baby. I thought we were going to tour the city today."

"Don't worry about that. We can do it some other time."

"Are you sure?"

"Yeah, besides, you can rest up for tonight."

Still walking, she looked over at me. "Troy, thank you for everything, okay? I really mean it. You have been wonderful during all of this, and I really appreciate you."

"Didn't I tell you I'm there for you? I'm supposed to look out for my girl, right?"

She put her head on my shoulder as we continued on to the car.

We drove out of the complex and started toward Sandy Springs, another small area outside Atlanta, to check into the hotel room we had reserved. We drove around for what seemed like hours, fighting through Saturday traffic, until we finally made it into the hotel parking lot. I got out of the car and grabbed our bags while Jennifer checked in. By the time I got everything out and into the room Jennifer was lying across the bed asleep. Her clothes were half off, legs all spread apart like she just fell out while trying to undress. I reached over and pushed the rest of her body into bed. I started to undress and jump in with her but remembered that I needed to find the nearest shopping center and pick up a few things for that night, namely condoms.

I walked outside, jumped back in my car, and got into the busy traffic to fight my way to the nearest store. I must've driven another forty minutes before seeing a Wal-Mart about two blocks down on my right. When I parked and went inside, I was met by a mob of people trying to shop. I looked over at the checkout lines and there were so many folks that the lines stretched damn near down the aisles. *Damn*, I thought, *is everything in this city like this? It seems like every place in this city is crowded and uncomfortable.* I shook my head in disgust and began walking around, trying to find what I came in to get so I could get the hell on.

Almost every aisle I went down was jammed. I maneuvered around baskets, whining kids, slow-walking old ladies until after finally walking around the store twice I got all of the items I needed.

Since I had been in the store for a while, I just knew the lines had gone down so I could just check out and go. But once again I was wrong. This time they seemed even longer. I was so mad I started to put all my shit back and walk out the door. The hell with it though. I was there so I might as well stay 'cause it could be worse somewhere else.

I got in line and for the first ten minutes I think I moved about an inch. After that I was at a standstill because someone needed a damn price check on some shit that cost about two damn dollars. I was so mad I started to buy the shit for them myself just so the line could move forward. After that little ordeal took place the line started moving again and this time I made it about three people closer to the register.

All of a sudden something happened. Out of nowhere I had an ordeal of my own. My bladder starting messing with me. All that water I had drunk earlier started to kick in again. I looked around and spotted the bathroom and thought, *Good. As soon as I check out I'm going straight there. Besides, I'm only three people away from the register, no problem.* Standing there with my legs together, I glanced around at what the people in front of me had in their baskets, to kind of give myself some mental relief as to how long it would be before I could go. Still sure that I could make it, I closed my eyes and blocked out the pain that was starting to come. I hummed to myself, gritted my teeth, and even looked over at some magazines. Everything was fine until I heard the cashier say something about checks.

I leaned over and looked at the people in front of me and my kidneys felt like they were adding a few more pounds of pressure on me. Every one of the people in front of me had their checkbooks out. Damn, what bad timing. Gritting my teeth and kinda stepping in place, I thought, *Why me, Lord? Why now!* My kidneys were so full I could feel the pain all in my lower back. I squeezed my legs real tight to try to keep the pressure off my kidneys, but that wasn't working. Still, I felt I could hold it a little while longer. Out of nowhere the cashier left the register and walked over to one of the managers. Seeing that added another pound of pressure. I couldn't help it, I had to break and fast. Finally, I darted out of line and headed for the bathroom. People watched as I streaked past them. I was running so fast when I made it to the bathroom door I almost knocked it down.

When I got inside I couldn't believe my eyes. There was a line in there too. "Oh, shit, oh, shit," I yelled as I pinched the head of my prick to keep from pissing on myself. Suddenly, I yelled out, "Please can I jump in front of someone? 'Cause I am about to burst open." Nobody said anything. I asked again. Still, not one person said a word; they just looked at me like I was crazy. Before I knew it, I said out loud, "Fuck it!" There was only one sink open, so I ran over to it and starting peeing like crazy. I was peeing so hard that it splattered all over the mirror in front of me. I could hear the people behind me mumbling aloud, but I didn't give a damn, I just kept on pissing. I could feel the relief it gave me and the pressure that was lifted off my kidneys.

After I finished I didn't even bother to turn around, 'cause I knew people were still looking. Instead I leaned over in the same sink, cleaned it out with liquid soap, washed my hands, and ran out the door to try and get my spot in line. When I got there I noticed that there was only one more person in front of where I was standing. I pointed to my basket that was still where I left it and gestured to the lady behind it to let me back in. I could tell she was annoyed, but she moved back enough for me to get my spot. I stood there relieved while reading the headlines in the gossip magazines as I waited on the guy in front of me to check out. I felt much better. I would never have been able to explain to Jennifer how I pissed on myself.

It suddenly hit me that people were looking at me. Everywhere I turned my head I saw people looking and whispering. *Hell, I'm from Alabama. These people don't know me and probably won't ever see me again,* I thought. It didn't bother me until I saw this man talking to the security guard, pointing in my direction as the cashier starting ringing up my items. I looked over toward the security guard again and he was talking on the radio to someone while walking in my direction. I thought, *Damn, my ass is getting ready to go to jail for pissing in the sink.*

When I paid the cashier and got my receipt I started heading for the door. At the same time the guard starting briskly walking toward me. I started to walk a little faster as I headed for the door when I heard him yell out, "Hold it." At that time I stopped in my tracks and got into a defensive stance in case he tried to grab me. All of a sudden the guard ran past me and tackled this husky white guy who was trying to run out of the store with a portable CD player. It seemed security had been watching him for a while and it just so happened he was in the line next to me. *Whew. Let me get back to my room before some more crazy shit happens,* I thought. As I walked to my car, laughing, I looked at my watch and noticed it was now 5:30 PM. I had just enough time to get back and rest a little before we went out. Plus, I had a special thing planned for Jennifer.

I jumped back in the car and headed for the hotel. When I opened the door to the room, I noticed that Jennifer was still asleep, so I decided to set the mood.

I must have bought at least twenty-five red-berry-scented candles, so I hooked the room up. I put most of the candles in the bathroom. I had them on the floor, on the vanity, and all around this huge garden tub. I had the wine chilling in this plastic wine bucket I bought. I took out our matching red body wraps and placed them over the towel rack in the bathroom. I started running the bathwater, adding bubbles and a cherry-scented gel that turned the water bright red. After a short while the scent from the candles started to fill the room. I turned on Luther Vandross, got undressed, and got in the bathtub. I could hear Jennifer wrestling around in bed. She giggled out loud over the sound of the music. A moment later the bathroom door slowly opened and Jennifer was standing there totally naked. As she stood in the doorway I could see the lights from the candles making her beautiful body glow. Her hair folded over her shoulder, barely covering her right breast. She slowly placed one leg at a time into the water and sat facing me. I reached over, poured her a glass of wine, and watched her slowly move the glass to her mouth to take a sip. As she brought the wineglass down I leaned over and kissed her, tasting the sweet berries of wine. She slowly lay back against the wall of the tub as we sat face-to-face. I began to gently caress and kiss her feet. As I did, I could see her nipples get hard.

While Luther played on, my hunger for Jennifer grew more and more. She leaned in, and we engaged in a long, intense kiss. I was so turned on my manhood was sticking straight out of the water. She reached down and gently caressed it, sending pleasure through my body. Minutes later we moved from the bathtub to the bed with my erection at full blast as I watched her lie on her back with a look of desire in her eyes. I gently began to suck each of her beautiful toes while letting my hand gently stroke the back of her legs. I worked my kisses up her ankles to the top of her thighs as my throbbing erection followed. By the time I got to the inner part of her thighs, her legs slowly opened, signaling that she wanted me to put my face in the center of her rose bed. I obliged and began slowly and gently moving my face until I could hear her breathe deeper and harder from my touch. The faster I went, the deeper she breathed.

Suddenly Jennifer lifted her legs and wrapped them around my head and used her hands to push me in deeper. As she did that I could hear her breaths turn from light moans to whimpers. I could tell that she was about to reach her point. Her hips started to twist and turn while she continued to push my face deeper and deeper until she screamed out, *"Troooy, oh, baby, I lov-lov-love yooooou"* as every muscle in her body gave out. When I looked up at her face, she had tears of passion in her eyes as she stared down at me long and hard. I moved to her side and pulled her close, feeling her heart thumping rapidly from the intense moment of passion. Jennifer reached over and stroked my face.

"Damn, where did that come from? I've never felt like that before," she said, sounding exhausted.

"It's always been here," I said, smiling. "Every now and then I have to show you that all the time is not about me."

"Whew. Well, in that case we don't have to go out. We can just stay in bed the rest of the night so I can return the pleasure."

"Nooo, we have plans. I want to take you to Puffy's Restaurant, Justin's, and then I want to take you dancing. I want our first night to be more than just sitting in a hotel room."

Jennifer smiled. "Well, okay, I guess I can go without it for one more night."

I laughed.

"What time are we leaving?" she asked.

"Well, it's about eight now, so I think we should get up and get dressed."

We both hurried to the shower.

Jennifer wore this black dress that stopped right above her knees and hugged her body. She was looking too fine. I started to ask her to wear something else, seeing how it revealed her figure. I wore this brown suit that was fitting me like it was tailor-made with a tan mock-turtleneck shirt. My goatee was trimmed just right. I was looking sharp. Jennifer stared me up and down, giving me this look like she wanted some more of what she had gotten earlier.

I smiled as I grabbed my keys.

"Don't give me that look," I said. "Let's go before I change my mind."

"What look?" she replied, smiling.

"You know what look. Don't trip."

We both laughed and headed out the door toward the car.

CHAPTER 3

Having a Fit

We left the hotel and got on Peachtree Street. According to the map, this would take us straight to the restaurant a few miles down the road. I reached into my pouch and grabbed my Jay Z CD and started jamming it to kinda get the night started right. Jennifer and I started rocking to the beat and rapping along with the music. People who drove past my car were looking at us like we were crazy. We just stared right back at them as we continued. After a few more miles I could see the restaurant coming up on my right. I had been hearing so many good things about Justin's that I couldn't wait to get inside.

We pulled into the lot and saw that they had valet parking. I was really impressed. We got out of the car, and I gave the keys to the valet and started walking toward the door. From far away the restaurant looked kinda small. But as we got closer, I was surprised to see it was actually bigger. When we walked inside, Jennifer and I both were shocked at how elegant this place was. It was classy the minute you hit the door.

"Baby, look at all these people in here. Do you think we'll be able to get a table?" she asked.

I looked around until I saw the hostess. "Yeah, I see a hostess taking names at the podium straight ahead. Let me reserve a table," I said.

As I headed up to the podium, I noticed all these honeys checking me out. They smiled and looked a brother up and down. Hell, I knew I was sharp. But they were looking at me like I was chocolate candy and they had a serious sweet tooth. This one honey had on this dress that stopped maybe two inches below her butt cheeks. When she saw me looking, she kinda bent over just enough so that the bottom of her ass stuck out. She had brothers all around her, too, each one in her ear trying to get her attention. I didn't entertain her by staring, I just turned my head and kept walking.

This other honey sitting at this table eating had this tight shirt on that pushed up her big breasts. I swear if she sneezed, they would have fallen all in her plate. Again I laughed as I continued on.

When I got to the podium, the line was kind of long so I just stood there until I was able to get to the front. I continued to look at and listen to all the bullshit brothers were talking just to impress these women. I heard this brother behind me talking about how he was Jermaine Dupree's cousin, and that he worked for So So Def records, looking for girls to be in an upcoming video. It seemed like an honest story, but the brother had an ID badge hanging off his pants, and the badge didn't say So So Def. From what I could read it said something about a meat-packaging company. I dropped my head to laugh. I couldn't believe that some of the women were falling for that. They were all crowded around him like *he* had a platinum album.

I must admit though the women in the restaurant were tight. I saw some sistas who pulled up in Jaguars, E-class Mercedeses, and BMWs. These honeys walked past brothers trying to holla at them and didn't crack a smile. I guess they were just out trying to grab a drink or maybe get a bite to eat or something. Whatever they were there for they came to do just that and not for no bullshit. They waved brothers off before brothers could even get close to them.

After I reserved a table for two, I turned and began walking back to Jennifer. I saw her through the crowd looking around still admiring the way the place was laid out. I made it to her, grabbed her hand, and guided her up to the podium so that we could be together when they called us for our table. We had stood there waiting for about thirty minutes when our name was called.

We followed this tall honey to a table near the back by a piano.

The seating area was perfect because you could see almost everything that was going on in the restaurant. The hostess gave us menus, then started telling us about the meal of the day. As she talked I scanned the drink menu looking for the Hennessy. Ah, there it was. I ordered it straight up, and Jennifer as usual ordered her merlot. We looked at the food menu until the waiter came back and brought us our drinks. It was hard to decide what to eat because everything on the menu sounded good. They had pork chops, chicken, shrimp, gumbo, as well as a whole lot of other good choices. Finally I ordered the beef ribs, collard greens, and mac and cheese, while Jennifer ordered the pork chops, candied yams, and collard greens. We handed the menus back to the waiter and sat back in our seats looking around at everyone's plate and enjoying the view.

"This is our first dinner in Atlanta, and I think we're starting off right," she said.

"I know. Didn't we pick a nice place?" I replied.

"Yeah," she said. "The people here seem really professional and the place has a lot of class."

"Yeah, I guess. You know, I was listening to how pathetic some of the brothers were spitting game at these ladies in here. Have you checked that out yet?" I asked, smiling.

"Yeah, while you were gone this guy came up and started talking to me."

"Guy? What guy?" I asked.

She started scanning the restaurant. "I don't see him now, but when you left he came up and told me some BS about working for So So Def and that Jermaine Dupree was his cousin."

"No shit!" I said, laughing.

"Yeah, but what was funny to me is that when I looked down he had a badge that had some other company's name on it. Plus, his fingernails were dirty and his shoes were all scuffed."

I laughed loudly as she continued.

"I politely brushed him off, and he walked away," she said.

"You know, I saw that same brother when I was making our reservation, saying the same thing to a group of girls in the corner. He said that he was looking for someone to be in the next video. Shit, they even gave the brother their numbers."

Jennifer shook her head in disbelief. "They'll be in a video all right," she said, chuckling.

"Yeah, but ass won't be shakin', it'll be getting drilled," I said.

Jennifer burst out laughing, almost spilling her drink. "Oooh, Troy, you are wrong for that," she said as she continued to laugh.

At that time the waiter brought our food. After saying grace, we both anxiously started eating. Neither of us said a word until we had tasted everything on our plates.

"Wow, this food is good," I said.

"Uh-huh. It sure is, and it's seasoned really well," Jennifer said.

"Let me taste some of your pork chop," I said, still chewing on my greens.

"Okay, 'cause I want to taste your beef ribs," she said with a mouthful of yams.

Jennifer and I ate, drank, and laughed until we were full as hell. We enjoyed it so much we didn't realize how much we had drunk. The waiter came back and brought us the bill as he cleaned the table. *Damn,* I thought, *I drank five Hennessys and Jennifer drank four merlots.* By this time I was buzzing and ready to hit the club to get my dance on. I wasn't a real good dancer, but that night who cared?

We paid the bill, got up, and started out the door. The valet brought us the car and we left. Our next stop was the club. According to Rick, Vegas Nights was the spot on Saturday nights, so that's where we headed. Jennifer pulled out her map to try to navigate us, but once again we got lost. I guess the good thing about her directions was that at least they got us to Marietta, on the outskirts of Atlanta, where the club was located.

We stopped at a convenience store where a man gave us directions that led us right to the front door of the club. At first I thought we were at the wrong place because it was so huge. But as we got closer you could see the sign in lights as plain as day.

We pulled into the lot and had the valet park the car. I grabbed Jennifer's hand and started to the door. There were two lines of people outside the club waiting to get in. One line seemed to be moving faster, so we walked up to it trying to figure out why. There was a security guy standing against the wall who walked over to us as we stood there trying to figure out what to do.

"Can I help you?" he asked with his chest all puffed up.

"Yeah, man, is this the line?" I replied, looking around.

He looked at us strangely.

"Yes, sir, that long line down the parking lot is where you have to go," he said in a cold tone.

Damn, we are going to be out here for a while, I thought.

"Do you have VIP passes, or anything like that?" he asked.

"No, man, this is our first time here," I replied.

"Well, if you purchase VIP tickets for ten dollars more, you can get into this line," he said, pointing at a shorter line by the door.

"Ten dollars more? How much is the regular cover charge?" I asked.

"The regular cover is ten dollars, sir," he said.

"Well, uh, yeah, let me get two of 'em then, 'cause I ain't trying to stand in line all night," I said, reaching for my wallet.

The security guard guided us to the short line of people near the counter where we bought the passes. We went through the security scanners and walked down the hallway to the main part of the club. I could see brothers leaning against the wall checking Jennifer out, slapping hands, and talking to their boys under their breath. At first it bothered me, but as we continued to walk I just ignored it because, after all, she *was* with me.

The club was huge. There was an area upstairs where you could look down on the dance floor. Because we were already buzzing from Justin's, Jennifer and I decided to skip the bar and walk downstairs to the dance floor. When we got there, we had to walk through a mob of people. I grabbed Jennifer's hand, and we made it to the stage area. Ja Rule's "New York" was playing. Jennifer and I danced and danced and danced. I was trying to be cool and just rocked from side to side to stay with the beat, while Jennifer, along with the people around us, danced like she was on *Soul Train* or something. Girls were dancing with girls, showing off new moves like they were in a contest. They weren't gay or anything; they looked like they were just teaching one another new moves.

The deejay was off the chain. I think it was someone called DJ

Chip or something with Frank Ski from V-103. They kept jamming, playing hits like 50 Cent's "In Da Club," and Bone Crusher's "Never Scared," as more people packed the dance floor. About five songs later, Jennifer and I were drenched in sweat. We both signaled to each other that we needed to rest for a while and started walking around the area near the corner of the club. As we continued I noticed a door in the back where people were going in and out. As we got closer I could see females coming out wearing bikini swimsuits. *Damn, what's going on out there?* I thought.

Trying not to let Jennifer notice me looking, I kinda turned my head as though I was trying to find a gap in the crowd for us to go through, but I was trying to sneak a peek at those girls' bodies. By the time I found a gap in the crowd and started to walk through it, Jennifer pulled me back, telling me she had to go to the restroom. I had to stop in my tracks and look for the girls' restroom. I struggled, looking over the large crowd until I found one. It just so happened it was over near the door where the girls were coming out with bikinis on.

Still holding Jennifer's hand, I guided her in that direction until we made it to the restroom. She slowly opened the door and went inside. While I waited, I walked up to the door to see where all these fine honeys were coming from. I slowly opened it and peeked outside. Man, I saw about twenty girls in a pool, just jumping around, splashing water everywhere. There were other honeys just sitting around on chairs just chillin' like they were at the beach. When I looked near the back I saw a brother on a grill cooking hamburgers. I really tripped out then. *Damn, what kinda club is this? 'Cause they got it going on up in here,* I thought. I mean these girls were wearing thong bikinis, wow, bikinis, at the club. I had never seen anything like it in my life, especially in Alabama. I opened the door a littler wider to get a better look until I saw Jennifer from the corner of my eye coming out of the restroom and walking over to where I was standing. I quickly played it off, frowning in disgust as I eased the door closed.

"What's going on in there?" she asked.

"Oh . . . uh . . . nothing, I was . . . uh . . . just wondering what was in there, that's all," I said.

"Uh-huh, yeah. I saw some girls in the bathroom changing out of their bathing suits. Is that what you were looking at, Negro? Is that what you were trying to get an eyeful of?" she asked with a frown.

"No, I just wanted to see what was going on out there," I answered in an innocent tone.

"Come on, boy, before you get hurt up in here," she said as she pulled me away.

We started walking back upstairs to get a seat and to rest for a minute before dancing again. Once more we had to walk through a mob of people to get to the stairway. As soon as we got to the top, I heard a loud male voice yell out, "Jennifer! Jennifer Stevens! Hey, Jennifer, over here."

We both stopped in our tracks and turned around to see where the voice was coming from.

"Who the hell knows you up here?" I asked as I continued to look around.

"I don't know. Maybe there are two Jennifer Stevenses at the club tonight," she replied, looking confused.

"Shiiit, better be," I said.

This clean-cut, high-yella brother came out of a small crowd on the side of the stairway and was walking our way with this big-ass smile on his face. He stood about six-two and was wearing a light gray suit with a white shirt. You could tell he thought he was cool by the way he was pimp-walking over to us.

Jennifer smiled back, letting my hand go to walk over and greet him. "Robert Wesley," she said with excitement in her voice. "Hi."

"It's me, baby," he said, smiling.

He quickly grabbed Jennifer and gave her this big hug and kiss on the cheek. He was so loud that everyone around us stopped what they were doing to see what was going on.

I felt like a punk at first because after the people looked at this fool all up on my lady they began to stare at me as I stood behind Jennifer like I was a flunky or something. I tried to step up a little closer to her so that she could introduce me, but this brother was talking so much she couldn't get a word in.

"What are you doing here? I haven't seen you in what, two years?" he said.

"Well, I—" she said before being interrupted.

"You look so beautiful," he said, looking her up and down. "You haven't changed a bit."

"I just—" she said.

"I can tell you still work out. You know you broke my heart when you left, don't you? Where are you sitting? Let me buy you a drink."

Jennifer stepped back and grabbed my hand. "Robert, I want you to meet my fiancé, Troy."

His big-ass smile completely disappeared when he heard the word *fiancé*. He just stepped back and gave me this fucked-up look like, *what do you see in his ass?*

Being the man that I am, instead of trying to start some shit, I reached out to shake his hand. He paused for a minute, still disappointed at the news, but then obliged. The handshake lasted about a half second as he quickly dropped my hand and turned his head toward Jennifer again and started running his mouth.

"Are you still practicing law?" he asked.

"Yeah. I'm moving here. I'll be working for Collins and Clarke," she replied.

"Collins and Clarke. Damn, that's one of the top law firms in Georgia," he said, smiling.

"Yeah, I start in a few weeks, right after I get settled," she said.

"Well, where are you staying? I can come by and help you move your things."

Jennifer looked over at me, and she knew by the look in my eyes that I was fed up with this motherfucker.

"Well, thanks, but I got all of that taken care of. My fiancé is doing all of that for me."

"Oh, okay," he said with disappointment in his voice. "Well, if you need anything else, let me know. But you look good, girl. Now that you're here I hope this time we keep—"

"Yeah, thanks, Robert. Well, you take care. It was nice seeing you again," she said.

He looked at me, sensing that Jennifer was trying to cut him off.

"Yeah, sure. Okay, well, I hope it doesn't take another two years before I see you again," he said, giving her another hug.

I walked up close to him with my hand extended again, and said, "No, it won't be two years, brother. You can always come to the wedding."

He looked at me, nodding as if to say, *whatever, nigga* and walked back over to his friends.

I looked at Jennifer. "Who was that?" I asked.

"Oh, he's just a friend from college. Just nobody," she replied.

"Nobody, my ass," I said. "The way he was all in your face, he's more than nobody."

"Baby, he is nobody like I said, just a friend from college, and nothing more."

"Oh, so that's all I get? Some brother is all in your face and all of a sudden he's nobody. Bullshit!" I shouted.

Suddenly people started to stare.

"Troy, calm down. Please, not here, okay? Look at me. He's a friend from college. I don't have any type of history with him other than him being a friend from school. So please let's drop this and enjoy the night."

I looked around at people as they continued to stare and dropped it for the moment, but you can believe that this shit would come up again until I could get some closure. *Don't no dude walk all up in your lady's face kissing her and he's nobody. That's bullshit,* I thought.

Jennifer and I walked upstairs onto the balcony and found a table. I sat there looking at her to see if she was going to look for this guy with her eyes or do something that would give me an excuse to drill her again about this guy. I was ready, and my mind was cocked like a pistol to shoot all kinds of questions.

As I sat there thinking about what to do next, my boy Mike crossed my mind. *Mike wouldn't give this brother the pleasure of seeing him all shaken up over him talking to his girl. He would just play it off and enjoy the rest of the night,* I thought. Finally I just shook it off and concentrated on something else.

From where we were you could basically see the whole club. I was kinda glad to be sitting down, 'cause it looked like the club was filled to capacity. The dance floor was full, the balcony was full, you could even see people struggling to get through the crowds. I sat there for about twenty minutes watching until I started getting a little thirsty from all that dancing earlier. I got up to get us two bottled waters to cool us off. When I stood up to head for the bar, I spotted Robert on my far left almost on the other side of the club. He looked straight at me as I walked to the bar. Again not giving him the satisfaction of thinking that he had gotten to me, I walked with this confident stride and look just to let him know that I wasn't at all worried about my girl giving him any kinda play. Inside, though, I must admit I was suspicious as hell about what was going on in Jennifer's head after not seeing him for two years.

I walked over to the bar in the back corner and got in line behind a crowd of people waiting for drinks. I made sure I was still in full view of Jennifer to see if any type of eye contact was being made. I stood there for about five minutes until I noticed Robert walking in her direction. I could see him looking around trying to find me in the crowd near the bar. As he got closer I could see him reach inside his coat pocket. He pulled out something that appeared to be a wallet and began looking into it very thoroughly as he got closer to her.

"Yo, who's next?" the bartender called out.

I quickly turned my head in the bartender's direction. "Oh . . . uh . . . it's me," I replied as I walked toward the bar, still trying to keep my eye on Robert. "Let me get two bottled waters and a glass," I said, trying to rush my order. I quickly turned my head again to see what was going on, but there were so many people around the bar, I couldn't see between them. I tried looking around them, but I still couldn't see clearly.

The bartender placed the waters on the bar and handed me the glass. I gave him the money, quickly grabbed the bottles, and headed through the crowd again. When I finally got a good view of Jennifer, Robert was nowhere in sight. As I continued to walk toward her, I scanned the club trying to find out where he was. *I can't believe he disappeared this fast,* I thought. *I wonder what he gave her. I bet it was his phone number or a business card or something. Shit, wait a minute. I know Jennifer. If he tried to play her like that over me, she would probably freak out or something. Or would she? The way they carried on a few minutes ago . . . I don't know now, makes me kinda wonder. Look at her over there, all smiling and shit. I wonder what's going on.*

When I made it back to the table I started pouring her water in the glass, still looking around to see if there was any sign of that motherfucker close by. When I finished pouring, I handed her the glass. As she reached for it, I focused on her hand to see if she had his card somewhere balled up. Because I rushed over so quickly, I really didn't give her time to reach down and put it in her purse. Or did I?

She looked at me, puzzled. "Are you okay?" she asked.

"Uh . . . yeah, I'm cool. Why?"

"I don't know. You're just acting strange."

"Strange," I replied. "Girl, you tripping."

"Well, to me you are," she said, as she sipped her water.

I shook my head and sat down. She wasn't tripping. You damn right I was acting strange. I wanted to know what was going on up in here. I knew he gave her something. I really got pissed then. I didn't make it obvious though. I was just starting to feel uncomfortable, so uncomfortable that I couldn't sit still. I sat there moving to the beat, still trying to find Robert in the crowd, but I couldn't because the place was packed.

The deejay started playing Luther Vandross's "A House Is Not a Home."

"They're playin' your song. Let's dance," I said.

"Oh, baby, I would but my feet hurt," she replied.

"Come on, baby. Let's get one more dance in and we can leave."

"No, baby, I feel kinda tired right now," she said as she looked at her watch.

"Are you ready to go?" I asked.

"Yeah, I'm all partied out for now," she said as she yawned.

I was so pissed off, all I could do was grit my teeth to keep my cool. I started thinking all kinds of crazy shit then. I don't know what had been said or done when this Robert came over, but whatever it was changed Jennifer completely. I was ready to go off, I was so mad. Instead I took a deep breath and calmed down a little so that my anger wouldn't be noticed.

"Okay. Let's head on out," I said dryly.

I helped Jennifer out of her seat, and we started for the door. I took one last look around the club as we walked to the front exit. But still there was no sign of him anywhere.

We got outside the club and the valet brought the car around. We both got in and started for the hotel. During the ride Jennifer didn't say a word; she just stared out the window the whole time.

"Are you okay?" I asked.

"Yeah. Why do you ask?" she replied.

"It's just that you are so quiet over there."

"No, I'm fine, just ready to get into bed and sleep," she said with a deep yawn. She reached over and grabbed my hand. "Thank you. I really had a good time tonight."

I looked at her strangely, wanting to say something. But I couldn't show my anger no matter how hot I was. Instead I just forced a smile, sat back, and concentrated on the road.

When we got back to the hotel it was really late. We both had just enough energy to go to our room, get undressed, and go to bed.

Sunday morning crept on in as the rays of sunshine pierced through the window shade in our room and woke me up. I rolled over and held on to Jennifer as she slept. As I gently stroked her hair, I noticed that the clock on the nightstand table read 9:45. I moved around, feeling a little sluggish from the night before with the bad taste of liquor still in my mouth. Dragging myself out of bed and into the shower, I stood under the hot water, letting it run down my naked body as I slowly started coming back to life, feeling more energized. I got out of the shower, brushed my teeth, got dressed, and headed downstairs to get breakfast for us.

When I opened the door to our room, I could smell fresh-cooked bacon all down the hallway coming from the restaurant area below. I was so hungry that my stomach started growling as I followed the aroma. When I walked inside the restaurant, I could see lots of people standing in line to fix their plates while others sat at tables with their family enjoying their food. I grabbed a plate and got in line behind this big ole fat man. His plate was so full that the food was hanging over the sides as he struggled to hold it steady. I was all ready to eat, too, until I saw him lick his fingers and put his hand all over the food on the serving trays. He leaned over to reach for a biscuit and the grits from his plate ran on to the pancakes. His nasty ass licked his fingers again and moved the pancakes out of the way with his hands, trying to pile more on his plate.

At that point I thought, *Oh, hell no! I am not about to eat this shit. Look at this nasty motherfucker over here.* I got out of line mad as hell, and headed back to the room.

When I got inside, Jennifer was up and in the shower. I walked over to my suitcase and started getting my things together. Instead of folding my clothes, I just threw them inside my bags and placed them on the floor by the door. I noticed Jennifer's purse neatly placed on the table close to the bathroom. I stared at the purse for about a minute, thinking this would be a good time for me to look inside to see if she put Robert's number in there. I slowly eased my way toward her purse with my arm extended, ready to grab it. As soon as I touched the strap, the door to the bathroom swung open. I was so shocked that I quickly jumped back, almost tripping over her shoes, which were in the middle of the floor. Jennifer looked at me with a strange expression as she walked out of the bathroom, drying herself off.

"I thought I heard some noise out here. What are you doing?" she asked.

"Oh yeah, it's me. I thought you were in the shower, so I started packing my stuff," I replied, trying to compose myself.

"I *was,* but when I heard a noise I jumped out to see who it was," she said.

"Who else could it be but me?" I asked.

"It could've been the cleaning lady or something, I didn't know."

"Well, it's just me so you can go on back in there now," I said.

"Oh, I'm finished. I just have to turn the water off. You just startled me, that's all. You can't be too careful. Besides, you never know what goes on in hotels," she said.

Damn, that was a close call. I almost got caught over this shit, I thought.

Jennifer started getting dressed while I sat there watching TV.

"Are you hungry? 'Cause I'm 'bout to die over here," I said.

"I can eat a little something. I'm not that hungry," she replied.

"Well, we're gonna have to stop at a McDonald's or some place along the way, unless you want to go to the Waffle House or something."

"No, McDonald's is fine," she said. "Don't you want to grab something downstairs?"

"Hell no. Those people are nasty down there. They're licking all over their fingers and shit, touching the bacon and pancakes. I can't eat that. I bet some of them were even digging in their ass before they got there and touching all over everything."

Jennifer laughed out loud.

"You know I'm telling the truth," I said, laughing. "If you want, I can go down there and make you a bacon and ass sandwich."

"Troy, you are so nasty," she said, still laughing out loud.

About an hour had passed, and we were ready to get back on the road. I grabbed the bags while Jennifer checked us out of the hotel. After I got all of the bags in the car, I went around front and picked her up, and we found the nearest McDonald's before heading back to Mobile. The ride back seemed a lot longer than the one coming. I guess it was because my mind wasn't on anything but what had happened the night before. I thought about asking Jennifer more about her relationship with Robert, but I knew it would lead to a big argument, which was the last thing I needed with such a long ride home. Finally I just concentrated on something else and before I knew it we were back in Mobile.

I dropped her off, put her bags inside her apartment, and headed home. I couldn't wait to call my boy Mike. This shit was bottled up inside so tight I had to talk to somebody.

"Hey, Mike. What's up? This is T," I said, having called him the minute I dropped Jennifer off.

"Troy, what's up, man? When you get back?" he asked.

"I've been here for about thirty minutes now, man."

"How was the trip?"

"It was cool, until we got to the club last night."

"What happened at the club?" he asked.

"Man, Jennifer ran into some brother she went to school with. I think she used to date him or something," I replied.

"How do you know she used to date him?" he asked.

"Well, I don't. It's just the way he was looking at her and the way he grabbed her and kissed her on the cheek and shit. I know something happened," I said.

"Aw, man, that ain't nothing to worry about. It's just a friend from the past, that's all. Don't you hug honeys you haven't seen in a while?"

"Naw, it wasn't that kinda hug, man."

"C'mon, dog, I know you ain't tripping over no damn hug."

"Well, why did he wait till I left before he went back over there all in her face?"

"Man, that's still nothing to worry about," he said.

"Well, why didn't he do the shit when I was there? Naw, the sneaky motherfucker waited on me to leave."

"Did you ask her about it?" he asked.

"No. I started to go off on him, but I didn't want to ruin the night, so I just chilled."

"You did right. You know Jennifer wouldn't pull no shit like that, man. You know her better than that."

"Yeah, I guess. But still, I just don't feel right inside. You know, I even tried to look in her purse while she was in the shower, but she came out right before I could get my hands on it."

"Man, you're losing it, dog. I thought you were going to tell me something more serious than that shit. I think you just trippin' 'cause she's leaving in two weeks."

"Whatever, man," I said.

I heard Mike's wife in the background trying to get his attention.

"Hey, Troy, let me hit you back later. I've got to step out for a minute. In the meantime, man, stopping trippin' over that simple-ass shit," he said before he hung up the phone.

I was getting close to my apartment. I picked up my cell phone again and called Rick.

"What's up, Rick?"

"What's up? You back already?" he asked.

"Yeah, man. We got up this morning and hit the road," I replied.

I wouldn't dare tell Rick what was going on because I knew how he would have reacted. Everything with him and trusting honeys was so negative. I just stuck with the small talk.

"How was it?" he asked, all excited to hear some dirt.

"It was great. Man, they have a lot of bad honeys there. I'll tell you, man, you would lose your mind in Atlanta."

Rick started laughing. "For real, dog? I bet a lot of them had sharp cars and shit, huh?" he asked, anxiously waiting on a response.

"Oh yeah. I'm talking about Benzes, BMWs, and Jags, and they were beautiful, professional women, not boogie bears."

"For real, dog? I can't wait to get there and meet me a honey like that instead of these tired-ass honeys here," he said.

"Yeah, man. It's straight real in the ATL."

He laughed.

"Well, dog, I just wanted to let you know a brother made it back all right. I'll hit you back later."

"Cool," he replied before he hung up.

When I finally made it home, I spent the rest of the night in bed watching TV.

CHAPTER 4

We Shall See

For the next two weeks, Jennifer and I were together almost every night. I couldn't believe how fast time passed. All we did was take apart furniture, pack boxes, and make love. It kept me from thinking about a lot of negative shit and focused on everything we'd built together.

After our last night of making love, I held her in my arms and just didn't want to let her go. Every now and then I would look up at the clock. Before we knew it, the sun was out. That morning was unlike any other we'd spent together. When I opened my eyes it was hard to look in Jennifer's direction without feeling sad. I think she felt the same way, because we both just lay there not saying a word. I guess we both finally realized that this day had to come sooner or later and we had to make the best of it.

About ten minutes later she turned, and our eyes met. We stared directly at each other like our lives were coming to an end. Suddenly out of the blue, Jennifer just exploded into tears. She held on to me as tight as she could and just let go of her emotions. Seeing that got to me. I tried to hold mine back, but it was hard. All I could do was grit my teeth and comfort her, trying to convince her that everything was going to be okay. Hearing this just made it worse as she held on to me like she was never going to see me again. I just held on, whispering in her ear that everything was going to be all right, promising her that we would see each other every weekend.

I guess hearing those words made her feel a little better, because the tears stopped and a smile took over. She slowly got up out of bed and headed to the shower. I started to join her, but I wanted her to have that time alone to get herself together.

We both finally got dressed and headed out the door. We had to stop by her apartment to make sure the movers had gotten everything out and for her to turn her key in to the front office.

The law firm had movers come down and pick up all of Jennifer's things, including her car, so all she had to do was catch her flight. Me and the guys were going to drive up later in the week to unpack the heavy furniture and everything and put it all together.

We left the complex and grabbed some breakfast before heading to the airport. When we got inside we checked her bags in and walked over to the security checkpoint. This was the farthest I could go through the airport without a boarding pass. In an instant I started feeling this knot in my stomach. Reality had set in that Jennifer was actually leaving. I could feel her squeezing my hand as we got closer to the security checkpoint. She turned to me as tears flowed from her eyes and gave me a big kiss.

"Well, baby, this is it," she said in a soft voice.

"I know, just 364 more days and I'll be there with you for good," I said.

"Yeah, only 364," she said, laughing as she turned to keep from crying some more.

"I know we'll be just fine. I'll call you every day," I said.

"And I'll be there waiting on your call," she replied, sniffing and wiping her eyes.

More people started lining up behind us to go through the security checkpoint.

We embraced and shared one last kiss before she turned and walked through. I stood there watching every step she made as she slowly faded into the crowd. I felt so weak in the knees that I walked over to the sitting area and slammed myself in a chair near the window where I could see a line of planes waiting to take off. I knew she was flying Delta, and there were three of their planes lined closely together waiting to be boarded. Several minutes later, all three Delta planes started backing up and heading for the runway. My body was so numb I just got up and walked away without looking back until I got to my car. I heard the loud engines roar over my head as each plane left the airport and slowly disappeared into the clouds. As I opened my car door to leave, I could still smell the sweet scent of Jennifer's perfume lingering in the air. I slowly sat down, trying to gather myself before actually starting the car. In an instant I lost it; tears started flowing from my eyes and down my cheeks. All I could do was to put my head down and let it go. I felt like I was coming apart and about to lose control of myself. Minutes later, I sat back in my seat and began pulling myself together.

The drive home was lonely and quiet. I didn't want to listen to the radio or anything. Mobile just didn't seem the same.

Later that day Jennifer called to let me know that she had made it in safely and that everything was delivered okay. I could tell by her voice that she was still hurting inside but was trying to hide it by thinking of things to say. I was pretty much feeling the same way. I talked about everything except the fact that she was gone. We ended the conversation by saying we would talk again in a couple of hours when she got herself situated.

I didn't want to be alone that day, so I went over to Rick's for a while and chilled. When I got there he had just finished cleaning up from one of his wild nights and was sitting there watching a baseball game.

"What's up, man? Come on in and grab a beer," he said.

"Who's playing?" I asked.

"The New York Yankees are playing the Florida Marlins," he said.

"What's the score?"

"It's one to zero Yankees, in the second inning," he replied with his eyes glued to the TV.

"Have you heard from Mike today?" I asked as I walked into the kitchen to get a beer.

"Yeah. He's supposed to be on his way. I called him right before you came over," he said. "So, did your girl make it okay?" he asked with concern.

"Oh yeah. She called to let me know she was cool," I said as I walked into the den and sat down on the couch to watch the game.

"Now that she's gone, you got a chance to get some new ass," he said, smiling.

"Naw, man, I ain't even thinking 'bout nothing like that," I replied.

"Man, please. Your whorish ass. You trying to fool everyone like you're all dedicated to your relationship, but remember, I know you. Remember all those honeys we had back in the day? And what about all them honeys at your job? I know you popped at least one," he said.

"No, it ain't like that, man, and you're right, that *was* back in the day. But this is now, and to me, Jennifer is different. I can't go out like that this time, man."

"Man, I ain't saying fall in love with them. All I'm saying is just get you a little bit on the side every now and then. What's wrong with that?"

"I ain't like you, man. I want to build something now. For once in my life I want to go all the way in a relationship instead of keeping secrets and having to hide all the time when I go out. That cheatin' shit is played."

"Played for who? Damn sure not me. Look, man, you're not married yet, and until you are, go out there and cut up, have fun. Then when you get married you can be Ward Cleaver," he said, laughing.

"Brother, my uncle told me once, you have to practice to be married before you get married. Michael Jordan played basketball, the game he loved, he practiced it until he was good at it. You don't see him playing soccer, running track, or playing football. No, he is dedicated to one sport, basketball, and his dedication made him the best player in the game. That's how I want to be, the best at my relationship, which is why I have to practice being faithful, but you . . . you want to play every sport and not dedicate yourself to just one, which is why you don't have a steady lady now. You play too many women."

"You're right. I'm gonna play until I can't play no more, because I'm an all-around player like Bo Jackson and Deion Sanders. And I get MVP, Most Valuable Penis, every night that I'm handling my business," he said, laughing.

"Okay, man, but I'm just saying maybe you need to slow your roll just a little."

"Look, Troy, I hear what you're saying, man, but I just don't see myself settling down. Every day I meet a new honey who looks better than the other, and I don't know what it is but I just have to have them."

"Okay, man, I'm through with it then. I can see you're you and I'm me, so I'll leave it alone."

Rick leaned over as we slapped hands. "All I'm saying is don't let her get your mind, man. Look at you with the long face all sad that she's gone. Relax. Don't act like—" Mike came knocking at the door, interrupting. "Like this brother," Rick said, pointing at Mike. "I called him more than three hours ago, and he's just now showing up. You know why? 'Cause his wife would've kicked his ass if he had left that early," he said, laughing.

"Man, I had yard work to do," Mike said. "Plus, I knew you wasn't doing nothing anyway."

"I ain't doing nothing but getting fucked up all day, that's all," Rick said, laughing harder.

"Did your girl make it okay?" Mike asked me as he walked to the kitchen.

"Yeah, she's straight," I replied.

"When are we going to Atlanta to help her with her things?" Mike asked.

"Well, today is Saturday, so how about this coming Wednesday? And come back the following Friday, if that's cool," I said.

"Cool," Mike said, opening his beer.

"So, after we move all her stuff around, are we gonna hang out?" Rick asked.

I looked over at Mike with a grin, shaking my head.

"Yeah, man, that's the plan. We're gonna hang out," I said.

"I mean are we gonna hang out hang out? Not that bullshit like going to happy hour at a restaurant watching honeys walk around all night. I want to see some asses shake. I know where a few strip clubs are that we can check out," Rick said

"That's cool too," I said with a smirk.

"Strip club? Man, I ain't hangin' out in no strip club all night. I want to go to a jazz club or something," Mike said.

Rick shook his head. "See, man, that's what I'm talkin' about. You two henpecked motherfuckers are scared to even look at a different piece of ass. What's the matter? You scared your love ain't as deep as you think?"

"Hell no, man, I don't mind going. I'm just saying I ain't hanging out there all night."

"Look, I don't care what we do. I just want the fellas to kick it in the ATL. Let's do both. First we'll do the jazz club and then we'll do the strip club," I said.

"Yeah, man, 'cause the honeys there get butt naked, and I want to see it all," Rick said.

Mike nodded. "Yeah, let's just kick it."

We watched the game until it ended around three o'clock, then sat around for a couple of hours before Mike and I headed home. I was buzzing so bad that when I got home I just jumped into bed and slept the rest of the day away.

Wednesday came and around 7:00 AM Mike and I met at Rick's apartment since it was closest to the interstate. As usual Rick wasn't up. When I got there I knocked on the door for about ten minutes before he opened it. Rick slept with the radio on all night and because he had it so loud he couldn't hear anything else. While we waited, Rick got himself together and packed his things in the car, and thirty minutes later we finally left.

The first half of the ride was quiet. Since it was so early in the morning no one said much of anything until we got to Montgomery. That's when Rick wanted to stop at Alabama State University to see the girls hanging out on the campus. Ignoring him, I just kept straight on down the interstate until we made it to Atlanta. That's when Rick started again.

"Hey, man, let's hurry up and get Jennifer fixed up so we can hang out. I want to go downtown to get something to eat. I heard a lot of women work downtown."

I looked over at Mike as he sat there shaking his head. "Man, is that all you think about?" he said. "On the way here you didn't say a word. Now we can't get you to shut up."

Rick laughed. "That's all right, man. You won't hear a sound out of me tonight 'cause I'll be too busy working my game."

Mike looked at Rick. "Whatever, man. I can't wait to see you in action tonight. Remember, this is a different city out here. The honeys here don't fall for that simple shit you talk like they do in Mobile."

"Oh, it doesn't matter about the city. Honeys are all the same. You just have to flow with the situation, that's all. See, women like a man who is well dressed, who looks good, is professional, and who is able to have a decent conversation."

"Decent conversation? Well, that eliminates you right there. I've heard some of your weak-ass lines before, and if that's all you got, then I can't wait to see how the honeys dog you tonight," Mike said.

"Okay, okay, man. We'll see," Rick replied, nodding with confidence.

"That's right, we'll see," Mike said, laughing.

As we entered Jennifer's apartment complex, I used her pass code to enter the gate since I didn't have card access. The first person I saw was that fine-ass girl Lisa who had shown Jennifer and me the apartment.

As we pulled in she stared at the car with a puzzled look, so I stopped.

"Hi, Lisa. Remember me?" I said.

She stared with a frown. "Uh, oh yeah, you're the one who got the apartment a couple of weeks ago, right?" she replied.

"Well, actually it was my fiancée, but yeah, it was a couple of weeks ago."

"I haven't seen her since she moved in. So how does she like it so far?" Lisa asked.

"She loves it. As a matter of fact, I'm here with my boys to help put her furniture together."

Lisa walked over to my side of the car and leaned over to speak to Mike and Rick. As she bent over, her breasts were just hanging in my face. "Hi, guys," she said.

Rick and Mike spoke almost simultaneously. "Hey, what's up?"

She looked in my direction, almost catching me looking down her shirt. "Well, I hope to see you again soon."

"Oh, I'm sure you will," I said, trying to keep my eyes from wandering all down her body.

Lisa turned and walked away. I hesitated for a moment just so I could see her bottom shake in those pants. She got a few feet away and quickly turned around almost like she was trying to catch us looking. I turned my head so fast trying to look away that I almost sprained my neck.

In the backseat I saw Rick staring like he was in a daze.

"What do you think?" I said.

Rick shook his head in disbelief. "Damn, man, I didn't think they made honeys that fine anymore. She's fine. Troy, you're gonna get in trouble up here. I saw how you were flirting with her."

"No, man. All I did was look. Like I said before, I look but I don't touch, that's my word."

"You can't tell me you wouldn't hit that if you had a chance, man," Rick said.

I laughed as I drove away. "Yeah, I ain't gonna lie. I thought about what it would be like, but that's all I did was think. See, man, you have to think about the consequences too. Yeah, she's fine and all, but she could also be a low-down trick who would try to fuck my shit up, and you know I can't lose what I have over a new piece of ass."

"Man, fuck that shit you talking. The only thing I would think about afterward is hittin' that ass again."

Mike laughed. "That's why this fool always stays in shit. He always lets his little-ass head run his life."

"Man, shut up," Rick said. "I saw you slobberin' at the mouth too when she walked away, so don't give me that shit."

Mike laughed even harder but didn't respond.

Rick shook his head. "See, I knew he was up to no good, always trying to preach to me. Do I need to teach you boys the game? See, the key is, when you hit it you have to get her to do some freaky shit like give you head or put her on tape. That way you know she'll keep her mouth shut. If she tells, she knows that it's her ass too."

"Damn, man, is that what you do, tape honeys?" Mike asked, looking disgusted.

"Sometimes, yeah. You have to have backup when you playin' the ladies, my brother. Why you think I get away with so much now?"

"Man, you are a lowdown," Mike replied. "Damn, you a lowdown," he said with a disgusted chuckle.

"Call me what you want. It works though."

When we got to Jennifer's apartment, we unloaded our things and walked upstairs. Because Jennifer was at work, she had left the key under her doormat. I opened the door and went inside.

When I walked in, there were boxes and paper everywhere. I got kinda upset.

"Damn, it looks like they just took everything off the truck and threw it in the apartment. They better be glad I wasn't here. I would've made them pick this shit up and do it right."

Rick looked at me. "Man, shut up and let's put all this stuff together. I ain't tryin' to waste time listening to you bitch about some boxes."

Mike and I laughed.

"Quit cryin', man. You just cranky 'cause you don't feel like doing any work," I replied.

"Come on, let's get started, man," he said as he put his bags by the door.

For hours we opened boxes and put furniture together. I couldn't believe Jennifer had all this stuff packed away. We opened one box after another, putting things together while sweating like pigs. Around six we had finished everything and organized it how I thought Jennifer would want it. When she came through the door, her face lit up as she walked toward me.

"Wow! I can't believe you guys got all of this stuff put together in such a short time," she said as she kissed me on my sweaty cheek.

"Yeah, baby, we set up every room in the apartment."

"Yeah, *we* sure did," Rick joked.

Mike and Rick walked over and gave Jennifer a hug. To them Jennifer was just like their sister. Even though Rick was crazy about her he still felt as though I was running after her all the time. Personally, I think he just wanted me to run the streets chasing honeys with him every night.

Jennifer walked to each room in the apartment checking out

everything we'd set up. "I have some cold beer in the refrigerator for you guys if you're thirsty," she yelled from the back room. We got up and grabbed the beers out of the fridge. Mike and Rick went back into the den, but I walked into the back where Jennifer was.

"How was your day?" I asked.

"It was great. I have to go to court for this big civil case next week. I can't believe they added me to the team so soon. I feel like they really have a lot of confidence in me."

"That's great, baby. I know you'll do fine 'cause you know your stuff," I said.

"I just hope I don't get too nervous on my first big case here."

"No, I think you'll do just fine. So how do you like it here so far?" I asked.

"Oh, I think I'm going to love it here. They have all these malls everywhere. I can just shop for days. I even found a church called New Birth not too far from here," she said with excitement. "I can't wait till you're able to move out here. You'll love it, baby."

"Yeah, it seems like a nice place to live. I'm just glad you like it."

"Yeah, I think this was the right move for me and you," she said after pausing for a moment. "Well, I'm gonna change and relax for a minute before looking over these papers I brought home."

I gave her a kiss and walked out of the room, closing the door behind me, and headed back into the den with the guys to watch TV and drink more beer.

Later that night we were all ready to hang out. Rick was especially excited because it had been a while since he visited Atlanta.

Before we left I went into the back to give Jennifer a kiss good night since we were gonna be out kinda late. When I went into her room she was sitting in the bed with papers scattered everywhere, concentrating on her work. Instead of interrupting her, I just gave her a kiss on the forehead and headed out the door. As I turned around to walk out she got up and caught me at the front door.

"You guys are leaving now?" she asked.

"Yeah, we're out, baby," I replied.

"Hey, well, you guys be careful. This is not Alabama."

Rick and Mike smiled.

"Oh yeah, we'll be all right," Rick said as he walked to the car.

She turned and looked at me. "Troy, please be careful out there, okay?"

"Yeah, we're just going to a couple of places and we're coming straight home. We'll be okay."

"Okay, I love you," she said.

"Yeah, I love you too," I said before I closed the door and walked to the car.

It was around seven, which gave us time to stop some place for drinks. I recommended Justin's because I knew Rick would love it. I didn't tell him at first because I wanted to see his expression when he saw all the women.

When we pulled into the parking lot you could see all of these beautiful women getting out of their cars walking to the door. Even Mike had to comment.

"Damn, Troy, you know, I don't think I've seen an ugly woman since we got here."

Rick nodded. "See, man, I told you that you got married too soon. Look at those honeys. Troy, hurry up and park," he said, anxious to get inside.

"Calm down," I said. "This ain't nothing. Wait till you get inside."

I gave the car to the valet, and we walked to the restaurant. The minute we hit the door Rick started freaking out. "Damn," he said. "Lord, have mercy, I must be dreaming."

Mike and I slapped hands.

"Troy, you think you'll be able to handle yourself when you move up here, dog?" Mike said.

"Oh yeah. All I'm doing is window-shopping, that's all, just window-shopping," I replied, laughing.

We got some drinks over in the bar area and stood in the corner for a while and just looked around at all of the honeys coming in. Rick walked over to this redbone honey sitting near the corner of the bar all alone. He was all in her face just talking away. Apparently she liked what she was hearing, because Rick sat down next to her.

Mike looked in amazement. "Rick jumped on a honey already," he said.

"Yeah, you know how he is," I said.

We stood there watching, impressed, at the way he handled his game. Suddenly we saw Rick stand up and gesture for us to come over. As Mike and I headed in his direction, Rick and the girl started walking to an empty table. As we got closer to the table, two more females walked in front of us, heading in the same direction. I turned and was like *damn* as I directed my attention to them. They stood between five-five and five-seven. One had on a short black dress that stopped at the knee. When she walked, the dress clung to her shape, showing off her sexy figure. The second female had a nice blue pants outfit. She looked more businesslike, as the pants she wore hugged her firm, tight bottom, showing just a hint of a thong print.

My eyes jumped from one ass to the other as they continued to the table where Rick and his new friend were sitting. We looked at Rick as he stood there smiling at us to signal that his game was intact. He then turned and introduced us to his new friend.

"Gina, these are my boys, Troy and Mike," he said, pointing to us. "Fellas, this is Gina."

Mike and I shook her hand.

"Nice to me you, Gina," we each said.

She smiled as she reached out to honor our handshake.

Rick pointed to some chairs behind us. "Could you guys bring those chairs over here for her girls to sit here with us?"

I looked behind me and grabbed one chair as Mike grabbed the other.

"Oh, I'm sorry," Gina said. "These are my girls Ginger and Louise."

"Nice to meet you also," Mike and I said as we exchanged handshakes with the women.

"Nice to meet you as well," they both said.

Since I was standing close to Louise, I helped her into her chair and Mike did the same for Ginger, who was near him. Mike and I, who were still amazed, looked over at Rick and he continued to lay his rap on Gina, basically ignoring the rest of us.

"So, where are you guys from?" Louise asked.

"They're from some place called Mobile, in Alabama, girl," Gina replied, trying to hold in laughter.

"Alabama! Really! I've never been to Alabama," Louise said. "What's it like? I mean do you guys have like cows and chickens running all across the front and back yards?" she asked, giggling.

"What? Cows? Hell no! I don't know where you got that from," I replied defensively. "Mobile is a recognized city in Alabama."

"Well, I've never heard of it," Louise said.

"Have you heard of Mardi Gras?" I asked.

"Well, yeah," she replied. "Hasn't everyone? We went to the one in New Orleans."

"Well, did you drive or fly?" I asked.

"We flew, why?" she asked, confused about the question.

"Well, had you driven, chances are you would have gone through Mobile to get there . . . and believe it or not, Mobile is where Mardi Gras originated."

"Yeah, right. Everyone knows Mardi Gras started in New Orleans," Louise said.

"Well, Louise, now that he mentioned it, I remember seeing something on TV about Mardi Gras starting in Alabama. Something about when the French would come home, the people celebrated by having parades on the streets downtown, and when some of them settled in New Orleans they kept the tradition going," Ginger said.

"That's right," I said proudly. "Now where are you from?" I asked sarcastically.

"Oh, I'm from Detroit, baby," Louise replied.

At that time Mike jumped into the conversation. "Detroit! I know you can't talk. We may have chickens but y'all got a city full of chicken heads," he said as Rick and I laughed.

"Wait a minute! Have you ever been to Detroit?" Louise asked, offended.

"Yeah, that's why I can talk," Mike replied. "I've been there too many times, that's why I live in Mobile."

"So you're saying my girl is a chicken head?" Louise joked.

"Noooo, I'm just saying if she wants to go there about my city, let's go then. She started with all that 'do you have chickens in the yard?' jive," Mike said.

"Well, they do raise chickens in Alabama," Louise said.

"I'm sure *they* do, but *I* don't," Mike replied. "I don't raise chickens, nor do I have a tractor or live on a farm."

"Hey, I heard you don't have stop signs, you have whoa signs down there," Gina said, leaning over to Louise, laughing.

"Oh, so now *you* want some," Mike said.

"Damn, Mike, they're dogging you out, man. You gonna sit there and take that?" I said, smiling.

"What do you mean dogging me out? They're talking about you too," he said.

From that moment we all continued to joke back and forth.

I was surprised Rick didn't get into the action. I guess it was because he was trying to impress Gina.

"Hey, let's order some drinks," I said as I signaled for the waitress.

When she came over, she was smiling. "You guys are off the chain over here. People were cracking up at how you guys were jonesing on each other."

We began to place our orders. When the waitress got around to Mike, Louise started on him again. "Mike, you know you have to drink out of a real glass in here. They don't serve liquor in jelly jars like they do in Alabama," she said, laughing.

Laughter erupted once again. Even the waitress started cracking up.

"Oh, so you're back with the jokes?" Mike said as he looked over at Louise.

"No, no, I just had to get that last shot in to get Mike back," she said, smiling.

Mike smiled and nodded. "That's cool. I'll let you have that one."

I could tell that Louise was feeling Mike. Her conversation with him shifted from joking to flirting. Mike kept his cool though. Unlike Rick, Mike was talking more about what was happening around the city of Atlanta than about getting into Louise's drawers.

Ginger started flirting with me. Her legs were crossed, revealing her peanut-butter-colored thighs. The black dress she wore moved farther and farther up as she drank. She had brownish red hair and green eyes that seemed to change color with each sip of her apple martini.

Louise was a caramel-color sista with long, thick, curly hair down her back with a cute black mole near her chin. I think that was the sexiest thing about her.

Gina was light skinned, a true redbone with jet-black hair. She could almost be mistaken for Spanish or something. She had full lips and an innocent-looking smile that would melt a man's heart, which was why Rick was all in her face.

We continued eating and drinking until around nine, when Rick, who had been mackin' all night, finally spoke out.

"Hey, let's go somewhere where we can dance or something. I'm tired of just sitting at the table eating and drinking," he said.

"Yeah," Gina replied. "Let's go to the Velvet Room or some place."

"Yeah, I haven't gone out dancing in a while," Louise said, looking over at Mike.

"What's the Velvet Room?" Mike asked, looking confused.

"Just follow us. Trust me, you'll like it," Louise replied, getting up from her chair.

Gina and Ginger walked to the restroom. The waitress came over and put the bill on the table. As I reached over for it, Louise grabbed it.

"No, I got it," she said.

"What? Noooo," I said, looking surprised, "I got it."

"Yeah, I got it. Let this chicken head pay the tab," she said, pulling out her credit card.

"No, we can't let you do that," Mike said.

"It's already done," she said, smiling as she handed the waitress her credit card.

Rick walked over to Mike and me and put his arms around us, pulling us into a huddle. Louise walked away, heading toward the bathroom.

"Let her pay for this, man. I know I drank and ate about sixty dollars' worth of shit myself, and I ain't tryin' to give my money up if I don't have to."

I looked at Mike and said, "Man, don't listen to Rick, he's low-down."

"Look, if she wants to pay, then let her ass pay," Rick said, laughing.

I paused. "Let her pay," I said as I walked off, agreeing with Rick.

Mike just followed us laughing as we walked to the front door of the restaurant.

When we got outside, there were a few people waiting to get their cars from the valet. The girls handed the valet their ticket. Apparently Louise was a regular because she just walked up front while everyone else had to wait in line. The valet disappeared in the crowd of cars in the back. Minutes later as we continued to wait, this black Mercedes-Benz 500 series came out from the back. It was sharp as hell with chrome rims and a light tint on the windows. It was so nice that everyone standing in line was staring it down in amazement. The valet got out of the car, opened the door, and gestured for Louise. She walked all sophisticated-like with her purse swinging from her arm and slowly eased down into the driver's seat. Right before she slid down in her seat, she looked up at us and winked to let us know she had it going on. Mike raised his eyebrows and shook his head at her. Gina and Ginger got in, and the women pulled over to wait for us.

Finally my car came. Yeah, my little-ass '95 Maxima. Not that a car makes a person, it's just that after all that shit we talked inside I really felt like I *was* in a tractor compared to Louise's Benz.

When we got inside my car, Louise gestured for us to follow them. We pulled out of the parking lot, heading to a club called the Velvet Room, which was located a few miles up the street. On the way, we saw the girls bouncing around to some music, shaking their heads, having a good time. In my car Rick was in the backseat running his mouth as usual.

"Man, check that ride out. You know, birds of a feather flock together. Those are corporate women up there, real high-class sistas. See, Troy?" He looked over at me. "Those are the type of women I deal with."

I looked back over at him with disbelief.

"Man, just because she's in a Benz doesn't mean she got shit," I said.

"What? What? Man, that's a brand-new Benz. The cheapest one on the lot costs at least seventy thousand. Mike, you better tell him something."

Mike laughed. "Man, a car doesn't mean nothing to me. I'm all about the person."

Rick shook his head in disbelief. "I don't believe this shit. I know one thing, though, I'm not letting Gina get away." He paused for a moment and started back again. "See, while you two were over there jonesing with Louise and Ginger about that Mardi Gras shit, I was checking out Gina real hard. See, guys, a playa is very observant. Just like women check us out, we have to check them out too. See, I was scoping Gina out when she looked in her purse."

"What, man? What you doing looking in the girl's purse?" Mike asked.

"Wait, man, let me finish. When she looked in her purse I saw a stack of business cards with her name on them. I could only read part of it because she had her hand in the way, but I did see where it said Gina Wells, executive something." He chuckled. "You hear that? Executive, my brothers, top shelf, money, that's what I'm talking about," Rick said, laughing out loud, waving his arms around. "That's right, I got me a big-time executive honey. Hell, I might be moving up here my damn self and let her take care of me. Man, I'm telling you it's a gold mine up here. Whew, Troy, it's not too late to change your mind, boy. You may need to hoe around a little bit more before you commit yourself."

I looked in the rearview mirror at Rick. "No, man. I'm happy with my setup. Forget that shit you're talking."

"All right, all right," he said in a calm voice. "Don't say I wasn't there for you trying to help you out." He looked over at Mike. "And you, my brother, why you up there all quiet?" he asked. "You having second thoughts about your relationship?"

"Hell no," Mike replied. "I'm just trying to drown you out. I ain't thinking 'bout those girls, man."

"Yeah, right. Don't think I didn't see you all up in Louise's face."

"What?"

"Yeah, I saw you. But, hey, it's cool. I'm just glad to see you back in action again."

"You know what, Rick? I'm not gonna even entertain that bullshit you talkin'."

Rick laughed out loud again as we continued down the street.

CHAPTER 5

Call 911

We arrived at the Velvet Room. Louise gestured for us to park next to her on Peachtree Street. When we pulled into the parking lot, Rick quickly jumped out and walked over to the side of the car where Gina was sitting and helped her out. I just looked over at Mike in disbelief. When I finally parked, Mike and I got out and met up with Louise and Gina, who were waiting for us at the door of the club.

After being checked by security, we made it inside by the bar. I was impressed from the moment we walked in. The atmosphere was great. The club was sort of upscale and catered to the twenty-five and older crowd, which I thought was cool. As we walked around looking for a table, there were people packing the dance floor trying to get their groove on. The deejay kept jamming, and the host was another local deejay from V-103 FM. He was cracking on people and had everyone rolling with laughter.

Finally, after making our way into the back, we found a table near the dance floor and seated the ladies. The waitress who was standing next to us took our drink orders as we continued to enjoy the music while Rick was still all up in Gina's ear, giggling and flirting, until he heard his song come on by Mystikal, "Shake Ya Ass." He grabbed Gina and headed to the dance floor. Louise and Ginger started rocking in their seats as they bounced to the music. Seeing this, Mike and I stood and gestured for them to follow us to the dance floor.

We all started jamming to one song after another. It was so packed that by the time the third song started we all were drenched in sweat. Mike and Louise couldn't take it and went back to the table. Ginger and I danced one more song before sitting down. Rick and Gina were still going at it. Song after song after song they continued to dance. Rick was dancing so hard that you could see the sweat flying off his face. Gina just danced along with him, wiping his sweat off with her napkin. This went on and on for almost an hour before they finally decided to take a break. They would dance until they got tired, rest for a while, then get right back on the dance floor.

I looked at my watch and noticed that it was 1:00 AM.

"Wow, it's getting late. I think we'd better be heading out," I said.

Louise looked down at her watch. "Yeah, we better get going too," she said.

Rick and Gina were still going at it on the dance floor. I walked over toward them and got Rick's attention.

"Yo, let's head on out. It's getting late," I said as I pointed at my watch. Rick nodded and grabbed Gina by the hand to walk off the dance floor. By the time they made it halfway down, a slow song came on by Maxwell. Rick stopped in his tracks and pulled Gina out to dance again. I just shook my head as we all stood there watching as they held each other, rolling and grinding to the beat of the music. I was so tired and ready to go that I started to run up and snatch Rick's ass off the floor and drag him outside. But instead I chilled and let my boy get his groove on.

After the song ended, Rick grabbed Gina's hand and guided her over to where we all were standing. We finally got to the car and everyone started saying their good-byes.

"Well, guys, we had a wonderful time," Louise said.

"Yeah, I really enjoyed myself, I haven't done this in a while," Mike said.

Louise leaned over and hugged Mike. "You can tell your wife you've been a good boy tonight," she said as she smiled.

"Oh yeah, all the time," Mike said.

Ginger looked over at me. "So what's your story?" she said with her arms folded.

"Well, uh, I'm happily engaged, baby," I replied, smiling.

"I thought something was wrong, the reason you didn't pick up on my signals," she said.

"Noooo, I picked up on them. I just couldn't send you any back," I said.

"I can respect that," she said as she dropped her head.

Rick and Gina surprisingly gave each other a kiss on the lips. Louise saw this and started to giggle. "Well, what's going on here?" she asked.

Rick looked up. "Oh, I'm just saying good night to a beautiful lady," he replied, licking his lips.

Gina looked up and smiled, blushing.

"What's up for tomorrow?" she asked Rick. "Can we have lunch or something?"

"Well, yeah, I guess if I'm able to get away," he replied.

She reached in her purse. "Here, I'll give you my business card. Give me a call if you're available."

Rick and Gina exchanged business cards. As Rick looked at the card, his big smile changed to a frown of confusion.

"Hey, let's all exchange cards and keep in touch," Gina suggested.

We all pulled out business cards and exchanged them. When I looked down and read Gina's card, I couldn't help but chuckle to myself. I stood there looking at Mike, waiting on him to read the card, 'cause I knew he would look over at me. He held the card for a second before looking down at it. I watched as he fought to hold back his laughter when he looked at me. Louise and Ginger both exchanged cards with us as well. I looked at each one of their business cards and then looked over at Gina's again to make sure I had read it right.

The card read:

Gina Wells
GingerLo Day Care
Executive Office Receptionist

I looked over at Rick, who was standing there with his mouth wide open in disbelief. I looked at the business cards from Ginger and Louise. They were the owners of seven GingerLo day-care centers in Atlanta, and Gina was the receptionist who worked for them. I just stood there still trying to hold in my laughter.

Finally the girls got into the car. Gina leaned over and gave Rick another big kiss before finally driving off. I noticed that one wasn't as sweet as the one he got before. I walked over to my car and pulled out my keys, biting my lip, trying to keep from laughing. Rick, who was still standing there with his mouth wide open, glanced over at me with this goofy look on his face.

I couldn't help it. I burst into laughter. I laughed so hard that the gum I was chewing flew out of my mouth. When Mike heard me he lost it too. He laughed so hard that tears started flowing down his face. My laughter continued until my side started to hurt.

Rick walked toward the car still looking disgusted. He had thought Gina was this big executive who had all this money he was going to spend. Rick was still in a state of shock as he sat in the backseat, frowning. That's when Mike started. "So, uh, Rick, when are you moving up here again?" he asked sarcastically.

"Fuck both of you," Rick said, trying not to laugh. "I can't believe I wasted a whole night with this broke-ass girl, man. I should have known something was wrong when she kept asking me what kinda work I did and shit like that, you know, questions broke people ask your ass. Every time I opened my wallet she would look down in it trying to see what I had. I can't believe out of all the women in Justin's, I had to pick the one with no money."

Mike and I were rolling with laughter again.

"Man, I can't believe this," Rick kept saying over and over.

"Well, at least she was nice, man," I said.

"You damn right she was nice. Wouldn't you be nice if you were trying to reel a brother in?" he said.

"There's nothing wrong with her being a receptionist, man," I said. "You just let looking at that body throw your weak-ass game off."

"I didn't say anything was wrong with working as a receptionist. I'm just saying I have certain standards that I'm looking for in women, and from looking at this card, she can't even get an application from a brother like me."

"Oh, so if Louise would have given you some play, you would have jumped at the chance, huh?"

"Hell yeah. I would have jumped, leaped, flown, whatever I had to do to get with her. *She is paid.*"

"I finally see it now. Rick, you are truly a dirty motherfucker," Mike said.

"Yeah, call me what you want, but I'll make sure I'm a paid motherfucker too."

"Forget it, Mike. You know this brother ain't gonna change. No matter what we say he won't listen. He'll just have to find out the hard way," I said.

"I know you ain't talking, Troy, the way you was all up in Ginger's face tonight. I know you ain't tryin' to judge me."

"All up in whose face?" I asked. "Man, I told Ginger what the deal was with me. Ain't that right, Mike?" Mike nodded in agreement. "I had a good time, but I knew how to handle my business, unlike you," I continued.

"Yeah, whatever, man," Rick replied. "I'm through with this shit anyway. Let's go to Strokers so I can see some naked ass."

"Man, it's one-thirty in the morning. Strokers is out for tonight," I said. "I'm going home to be with my girl. We can do Strokers tomorrow night."

Rick gave me a hard look and a deep sigh. "What, man? You gonna let me go out like this? First, this shit with Gina and now my boy won't even take me to Strokers, man, damn."

"Man, just chill. I said we'll hit Strokers tomorrow," I said.

Rick thought for a moment. "Yeah, you're right. Let's just take it on in. Maybe I'll have better luck tomorrow."

By the time I got to the gate at Jennifer's apartment Mike and Rick were both knocked out.

"All right, get your asses up, we here," I yelled as I parked the car.

Startled, they jumped right up and got out of the car. When we got inside, Jennifer was stretched out on the sofa asleep. When she heard us come in she woke up and headed to her bedroom.

"Good night, guys," she said in a soft, tired voice.

"Good night," they replied.

I grabbed the blankets from the closet and placed them on the couch.

"Okay, who wants the couch and who wants the bed?" I asked.

Mike looked at Rick. "I think you should have the bed, my brother, seeing that you had a rough night and all," Mike said, chuckling.

"No, I'll take the couch. I'll sleep anywhere right about now," Rick replied, wiping his tired eyes.

"Well, whatever," I said. "I'm going to bed."

I walked down the hall to Jennifer's room and closed the door behind me. I stood there for a moment and stared at her curled up in a ball, sleeping like a baby. I put my pajamas on and eased myself next to her, pulling her close to me. It felt so good having her in my arms again. Before I knew it I was sound asleep.

The alarm went off the next morning at around six o'clock. When I rolled over I saw Jennifer jump out of bed and start getting her things together for work. I could hear her walking around the room mumbling, as she collected the scattered papers she had left on the floor the night before. Still tired, I just reached over, grabbed her pillow, and put it over my head, slowly falling asleep. About twenty minutes later I was awakened again, this time by the sweet scent of her perfume as it filled the room. I knew she was close to being ready for work. I yawned and stretched as I slowly opened my eyes. When my vision cleared, I saw her standing in front of the bathroom mirror, leaning over, brushing her hair wearing nothing but a black bra and a black thong. Instantly I got hard as a brick. There was something about the way her sexy body looked in a thong, especially when it was black, that got me horny.

As I looked up and down her body I started pulling my pajamas off until I was butt naked under the covers. Noticing this, she gave me a half smile. I turned over and reached down in my bag, which was near the bed, and grabbed a condom. Slowly I got up and walked over to her as she continued to brush her hair. She turned and looked down.

"Baby, what are you doing?" she asked, still looking at my hard-on. "Uh, I can't do anything now. I'll be late for work," she whispered.

Without saying a word I softly started kissing her on the back of her neck. She just turned and dropped her head, giving in to my touch. I dropped the condom on the floor next to her feet as I slowly began rubbing all over her soft breasts. As I caressed them I could feel each nipple get harder. Her heart was racing fast and she was breathing heavily with uncontrollable desire from my touch. Slowly I moved my hands down her back and around her waist until I felt the lining of her thong panties. Still kissing her softly on her neck, I began to slowly move my kisses down her back while gently pulling her panties down her legs. Before I could get them to her ankles she lifted her legs one by one and stepped out of them. I reached for the condom and slowly put it on as she watched through the mirror. By the time I got the condom on Jennifer's legs were slightly parted, waiting on me to take her from behind. I could feel her body tense. She reached back and grabbed my waist, pulling me in just a little deeper until I reached her spot. Her deep breaths turned into soft moans with every stroke. I watched her body move as we continued our motion for several minutes.

Suddenly, I could feel her about to reach her point. She was starting to breathe and moan even louder. Because she knew that Mike and Rick were in the next room, she bit down on her lip to hold in her passion. I felt myself about to reach my peak, so I wrapped my arms around her and started moving faster and harder. Jennifer started losing control. She reached over and grabbed a towel that was lying next to the sink and put it over her mouth. When she reached her point she screamed into the towel as loud as she could. When I heard her I lost control and reached my point. I let out a loud moan as I squeezed her body tight. I know Mike and Rick heard me, but at that point I didn't care. It was feeling so good that I had to let it out. We were so weak that we got back into bed and just held each other. Jennifer lay there with her head on my chest with her eyes closed, rubbing my shoulders.

"Hey, why don't you go in late today?" I said, rubbing her hair.

She smiled as she opened her eyes to look at the time. "Um, I wish I could, baby," she said in a breathless whisper. Realizing she had to go, she got up, staring at me with a smile, shaking her head in disbelief. "Damn, Troy, my body is still tingling," she said as she walked toward the bathroom with a towel wrapped around her body.

I laughed. "Well, how about another round?"

Right before she got to the door, she stopped and let the towel unravel from her sexy brown body. As it hit the floor, I threw the covers off and headed toward the bathroom after her. When I walked through the door, she was bending over turning the water on for the shower. I reached for her, pulling her back toward me. She grabbed my hand, pulling me closer. We both got in the shower and quickly washed off.

She got dressed, looking good as usual, and headed for the door. As we both walked through the den, we looked over in the corner at Rick, who was on the couch with his mouth open sounding like a broken chain saw. Jennifer gave me a kiss and walked downstairs to her car. I had closed the door and started toward the kitchen to get some breakfast when all of a sudden Mike appeared from inside the second bedroom.

"What's up? You getting ready to hook up some breakfast?" he asked, scratching his head.

"Yeah, some Froot Loops," I replied, reaching for a bowl.

He laughed. "Well, get me a bowl too," he said as he walked to the table.

Rick rolled over, yawning loudly. "What you two doing up so early?" he asked, stretching.

Mike looked over at the clock on the wall. "Early? Get your ass up, man. It's damn near eight o'clock in the morning."

Rick sat up on the sofa. "You can get up early 'cause you slept in a comfortable bed. I had to sleep on this hard-ass couch. Man, my back is killing me."

I looked over in Rick's direction with a mouthful of cereal. "You didn't act like your back was hurting the way you were snoring this morning."

Rick laughed. "I wasn't snoring, man. I was yelling in my sleep 'cause I was in some agonizing pain on this cheap couch."

Mike and I laughed as we continued eating our cereal. Rick got up and headed for the bathroom in the hall to shower. Mike and I finished eating before going into the den to watch TV.

We had sat there flipping through channels for a couple of minutes trying to find something to watch when we heard a phone ring. We both looked around the room trying to figure out where the ringing was coming from. After about the third ring Mike noticed that it was coming from Rick's bag and reached in it and picked up his cell phone. Quickly Mike ran up to the door where Rick was showering and yelled out, "Hey, Rick, your phone is ringing, man."

"What?" Rick shouted back.

"Your phone . . . it's ringing," Mike shouted again.

Rick yelled back, "Well, answer it then, man. Can't you see I'm in the shower?"

Mike shook his head as he answered the phone. "Hello . . . Hi, how are you? . . . Yeah, I had a good time too. No, this is Mike. Rick is in the shower right now . . . Okay, well, I'll have him give you a call back … Okay, take it easy, and I'll talk to you later. Bye." Mike laughed.

"Who was that?" I asked.

Mike looked at me, smiling. "That was Gina, man. She wanted to speak to Rick. I guess she wants to know if he's going to meet her for lunch."

I shrugged. "Man, you already know what his answer is."

Mike nodded. "Yeah, you know Rick. The least he can do is meet her for lunch. Hell, it won't hurt anything if he does that."

"Yeah," I said. "We can drop him off at some place close to her job for about an hour and pick him up later."

"You know Rick ain't going for that," Mike said.

Rick came out of the bathroom with his jeans and throwback Barry Sanders jersey on, spraying cologne all over his shoulders and neck. "What's up? Are you two ready to hit the streets?"

I looked in his direction. "Yeah, let me put my shoes on first."

Mike jumped up and walked toward the bathroom. "Wait, man, let me shower before we leave."

Rick walked toward the kitchen. "Okay, man, but hurry up. I'm gonna eat some breakfast. Hey, if you're not done by the time I finish eating my cereal—"

"If I'm not through by the time you're finished eating, then your ass will just have to eat another bowl," Mike said.

Rick laughed. "Okay, play if you want. You come out, me and Troy will be gone. Ain't that right, Troy? Mike, man, you take a shower like a little old be-itch."

"Just for that, I might take a bubble bath instead," Mike shouted as he closed the bathroom door.

Rick laughed as he poured the milk on his cereal. "Okay, keep playin'."

I sat in the den still flipping through stations until I got to the Weather Channel. I quickly sat up on the edge of the couch in excitement.

"Rick, come here, man. Hurry up. Look at Lisa Mozer on the Weather Channel."

Rick jumped up with his bowl in hand and milk dripping from his mouth.

"Damn. See, that's the kinda girl I want. She's beautiful, sexy, and making paper."

"Yeah, you're right about that, she *is* sexy," I said, staring at the TV.

Rick stood about two feet away from the screen still crunching on his cereal. "You know what I noticed about her, man? She never turns around so you can see her ass."

"Yeah, 'cause she's got a body," I replied.

We stood there watching, waiting for her to turn around so we could see how fine she was.

"Come on, baby, turn to the side so I can see what that body looks like . . . Come on, baby. Come on," Rick said, focused on Lisa Mozer. "Come on, just one time, baby."

We were both focused on the screen. I don't think we heard a word she said the whole time. All we wanted her to do was turn around.

Finally, I got tired of waiting. "Man, she ain't gonna turn around. Every time I watch her she never does it. She probably knows brothers like us are waiting to see how fine she is."

Suddenly she turned around with her back facing us. Her suit was fitting every inch of her body, showing the curves of her hips and bottom.

Rick shouted. "Look! Look! Look! Troy, see, see how fine she is? Damn, Lisa Mozer, where can I hook up with you at around here?"

I shook my head as I got up from the couch. "She *is* fine, man, but I tell you this, she ain't got shit on Rosalyn Sanchez, the honey in *Rush Hour 2*."

Rick quickly turned his head in disbelief. "What? Man, you must be out of your mind. Do you know how sexy Lisa Mozer is?" he asked.

"Yeah," I replied. "All I'm saying is that Rosalyn Sanchez is the finest in my book."

Rick shook his head. "Man, you *must* be crazy. She ain't got nothing on Lisa Mozer."

"C'mon, man, I can't believe you even said that stupid shit. Rent *Rush Hour 2*," I said.

"Yeah, well, it ain't on now, so you need to keep that to yourself until it comes on, instead of trying to put down Lisa Mozer. Now, if you really want to go there, I'll take Janet Jackson over all these honeys."

I dropped my head. "Oh, here you go. Every time a brother mentions a fine honey's name, you have to mention Janet Jackson like that's a period at the end of what I got to say. I still would take Rosalyn Sanchez over Janet Jackson."

Rick laughed. "Man, you sick. Over Janet Jackson?"

I looked at him with assurance. "Hell yeah, over Janet Jackson," I said. "I'll take Alicia Keys over Janet Jackson too."

Rick stared at me in disbelief. "Now I know you're crazy."

"What's wrong with that?" I asked. "I'll take those two honeys over Janet Jackson any day."

Mike came out of the bathroom dressed in his jeans and Sean John shirt, holding his towel and shaving kit. "What are you two fools talking about?"

Rick quickly turned to Mike. "Mike, this fool said he would take Rosalyn Sanchez over Janet Jackson. Can you believe that shit?"

Mike looked at me, puzzled. "Who is Rosalyn Sanchez?"

"Man, you know, that Spanish honey in *Rush Hour 2*," I replied.

Mike answered with a confused look on his face. "Oh yeah, I know who you're talking about. Yeah, she *is* fine, but I don't know about Janet Jackson. That's a tough one, dog."

Rick responded, "What do you mean a tough decision? Janet

Jackson is the epitome of fine, man. You two are crazy as hell. Well, who would you take out of the two, Mike?"

Mike looked at Rick. "I'm married to my Janet Jackson and Rosalyn Sanchez, so leave me out of that. I'll take my wife over any honey out there," he said as he walked away.

Rick looked away. "Aw, there he goes. Every time we talk about honeys he always has to break the conversation down by bringing his wife into the shit."

"Well, if you ever stop looking at dollars and look at a person's heart maybe you'll feel the same way one day," Mike said.

"Yeah, whatever, man," Rick said. "Are y'all ready to go yet?"

I looked over at Mike, laughing, while I grabbed my keys. "You are the only one who can shut him up, man."

Rick looked at me. "Oh, he didn't shut me up. He just wanted to reassure himself of the fact that he's married. He knows damn well if Janet Jackson walked in here and gave him some play, he would drop everything he had to get with her, including his wife."

Mike just laughed as I opened the door.

"Man, come on, let's go. You made your point," I said to Rick.

"All right, you don't want me to talk about you, do you?"

I laughed. "Man, get down those stairs before I kick you down."

We all walked outside and got in the car. As usual Mike sat in the front and Rick sat in the back. As I began to back up to leave the complex, Rick's phone started to ring again. Mike quickly looked over toward me as Rick answered it.

"Hello . . . Oh, hey, Gina," he said, frowning. "Uh, well, we're on our way to the Home Depot to pick up some things for Troy's girl . . . Well, uh, I really don't know if I'll be able to make it to lunch today, and we're leaving tomorrow . . . Uh, I don't know if I'll be able to make dinner either . . . Well, okay, just call me later. Okay, bye." Rick hung up the phone. "Damn! Something told me not to answer the phone."

I looked in the rearview mirror to see Rick's expression. "What's up, man?" I asked.

Rick ignored me and looked at Mike. "Was that Gina who called me this morning?"

Mike nodded. "Yeah, I forgot to tell you, that was her who called while you were in the shower."

"What did you tell her?" Rick asked.

"I told her just that you were in the shower."

Rick looked out of the window. "Man, she wants to meet for lunch today. I just told her we were too busy. I don't feel like being bothered with her ass today anyway."

I looked through the rearview mirror again at Rick. "Why, man?" I asked. "You can at least have lunch with the honey."

Rick shook his head in frustration. "Hell no, man. That's out."

Mike turned toward Rick. "Why don't you just go by there and see her before we leave tomorrow? That way you don't have to stay long."

"Well, I guess I can do that, 'cause I ain't trying to spend my last night up under her broke ass, and that's for real," Rick replied.

"Why don't you call her back and let her know that?" Mike said, turning back around.

"I'll call her later. In the meantime, let's cruise around town and catch those corporate honeys going to lunch or something. Or, Mike, maybe we could head to the malls in Buckhead. Who knows, we may run into Janet Jackson," he said, laughing.

As Rick continued to talk, I leaned over and turned the radio up to drown him out. It was obvious that he wasn't thinking about Gina. To me, though, she had a lot of potential. She was cute, fine, and seemed to be a nice girl too.

CHAPTER 6

Shhhhhhhh

As the hours continued to pass by, I managed to take care of every-thing I wanted to do to get Jennifer's apartment in order. We stopped at about five different stores and even had time to grab some lunch before heading back to the apartment. Rick was pissed off because Gina kept calling him every two hours to see if we were having trouble getting around or just to hear his voice. I think that kind of spoiled his afternoon, because all he did was complain about how much she was bugging him. The only thing that was on his mind was hanging out later.

We finally made it back to the apartment and settled in. Mike and Rick sat around drinking beer and watching TV while I cooked a little something for Jennifer to have when she got home. It was nothing fancy, just a little lasagna and bread sticks with a small dinner salad on the side along with her favorite wine. I called her a few times to see how things were going, but each time she was unavailable. I figured she was having a hard day, so the least I could do was have her come home to a decent meal.

By the time the bread sticks were done she was walking through the door.

"Hi, guys. What's up?" she asked as she walked in. "Oooh, something smells good."

Rick and Mike threw up their hands and waved as they continued to watch TV.

I smiled as I walked over to give her a hug. "Hey, baby. How was your day?" I asked.

"Busy, busy, busy. I spent most of it in the courthouse," she replied as she put her briefcase down by the front door.

"Are you hungry?"

"Oooh yes. We were so busy today the only thing I had to eat was some crackers and a soda. Oh, and I did get your messages, but I couldn't get a free moment to call you back."

"That's cool," I said.

"So, what did you cook that smells so good?"

"Oh, I just hooked up a little lasagna and a salad for my baby."

"Um, I can't wait to eat," she said. "Let me see, I think I have a bottle of wine somewhere in here."

"I got that covered, baby. You just go put on something comfortable while I get your dinner for you."

Before going to her room she walked into the den by Mike and Rick. "Hey, guys. What's up?"

Rick stood and gave her a hug. "What's up, Jen Jen? Girl, you looking good today."

Jennifer smiled. "Boy, I look good every day, you didn't know?" she joked.

Rick laughed and looked over at Mike. "See how Troy's arrogance is rubbing off on her already?"

Mike laughed, too, as he leaned over to give Jennifer a hug.

Jennifer headed down the hall into her bedroom and closed the door behind her.

"What's on TV?" I asked.

Mike looked in my direction. "Oh, we're watching *Vampire in Brooklyn*," he replied.

"Oh yeah? Did it just come on?" I asked.

"Yeah, about thirty minutes ago," he said.

"Hey, man, what time are we heading out?" Rick asked.

"What, man?" I replied, looking at him as if he was crazy.

"What time are we getting out of here, man? You heard me."

"Damn, man, let me make sure my girl is straight first. The club ain't going nowhere."

"I'm not trying to rush you. I just want to make sure we're still going out, that's all," Rick said.

"Yeah, man. We're still hanging out," I said.

"Go on and do your thang, man. You all in the kitchen cooking like you Emeril Lagussi, Lugas, or whatever the hell his name is," Rick said.

"It's Lagasse, motherfucker, Emeril Lagasse."

"Yeah, him . . . Hey, are we all still gonna hang out at you know where?" he asked as he looked back to make sure Jennifer wasn't around.

"Oh yeah," I replied, nodding. "We're still going there. I just want to eat dinner with Jennifer before we go."

"Cool. In that case take your time, 'cause it stays open all night."

Rick's phone started to ring again. He reached over to answer it with an irritated expression. "Damn," he muttered under his breath.

"Is that Gina again?" Mike asked.

"Hell yeah. Man, she's about to run my damn battery down with all of these phone calls."

"Are you going to answer it?" Mike asked.

"Hell no, man. I've already told her I wasn't gonna get with her tonight. I don't know why she keeps calling," he replied.

"Look, man, why don't you tell her you'll stop by tomorrow before we leave? Then after that you don't ever have to worry about seeing her again. If not, she's going to call you all night."

Rick answered the phone. "Hello . . . hey, how are you? Yeah, I'm doing fine . . . Yeah, I was going to call you but we've been busy all day trying to get things together for Troy's girl . . . No, I won't be able to see you tonight . . . Yeah, I will definitely see you before I leave tomorrow . . . Yeah, I'll call you tomorrow . . . Well, let me go, and I'll call you in the morning . . . Okay, I'll talk to you later. Bye."

After Rick hung up he took this deep breath. "Man, this babe is about to drive me crazy. I can see why she doesn't have a man. She's too worrisome. Hell, I've only known her for one day and I'm already sick of her ass."

"Look at it like this, dog, you only have one more day to deal with it," Mike said.

Rick shook his head. "Yeah, you're right about that, man, 'cause after tomorrow, I'm through with her."

Jennifer came down the hall and sat at the dinner table. She had on sweatpants and a T-shirt with her hair in a ponytail, looking sexy.

"Oooh, baby, this looks good. Are you going to eat with me?"

Before I could say anything Rick jumped into the conversation as he walked toward the table. "We all are going to eat with you tonight, baby." He looked over at me. "Hurry up, waiter, and fix all of our plates. Can't you see we're starving over here?" he joked.

Everyone laughed.

Mike and Rick washed up and joined us.

After we said our grace we all dug in. For the first five minutes no one said a word. All you could hear were forks scraping the plates and lips smacking.

"Troy, this lasagna is hitting, boy," Rick said with his mouthful of food.

"Yeah, man, you put it down today," Mike said.

Jennifer smiled. "Yeah, my baby knows he can throw down when he wants to."

I just smiled and kept on eating. I must admit, the food was off the chain thanks to my own secret herbs and spices.

Jennifer ate one helping and was full, but me and the guys continued eating.

She looked over at Mike. "How's Gail?" Gail was Mike's wife. She and Jennifer were good friends. They hung out a lot before Jennifer moved to Atlanta. I guess that's why Mike was always trying to keep me from messing around, because of the relationship our girls have. Gail was real religious and pretty much a homebody. But she was really sweet and perfect for Mike.

"Oh, she's fine. I talked to her earlier today. She told me to tell you hi and to call her," he replied.

"Oh, okay, I'll do that. And how are the kids?" she asked.

"Oh, they're fine, just bad as hell. Mya just learned how to walk and is tearing things up around the house. And Michelle, she thinks she's grown. The other day I caught her in Gail's purse trying on makeup. I know I got my hands full."

"Oh, that's so sweet. I really miss them," she said as she looked over at Rick.

"Hmm, I don't know who to ask you about," she said, giggling.

Rick looked up. "Oh, you know what to ask me."

"Oh, really, and what's that?"

"Hey, Rick, how are your ladies doing?" he said, laughing.

"See, Rick, you're wrong for that," she said, giggling. "I wish you could find one woman and just settle down."

"Settle down? Noooo, baby. I'm not ready to do that yet. Speaking of ladies, though, are there any nice sistas at your job?"

"Boy, I'm not even gonna go there with you. I ain't trying to get no one caught up in your mix."

"Aw, c'mon, Jennifer, just introduce me to one girl, that's all I'm asking."

"Why? So you can lead her on and break her heart like you did the last girl I introduced you to? Oh no, not this time, my brother."

"See, that was different. She had some jacked-up feet. Her bunions were so bad her big toe was pointing in the direction of her little toe."

We all laughed.

"Boy, you're crazy," she said. "See, that's your problem. You're too damn picky."

"No, all I'm saying is that I like certain things about a woman, and pretty feet are definitely one of them."

"Well, I guess," she said, looking confused. "Well, who knows, you might just meet someone tonight. Speaking of tonight, what are you guys gonna do?"

Not expecting that question, we all paused for a moment, each waiting on another to answer.

Finally Mike spoke. "Well, I think we're going to shoot some pool tonight somewhere downtown."

"Oh yeah, that should be fun," she said. "If I didn't have to go to work tomorrow, I'd join you guys."

Rick's eyes got extremely wide. "Yeah, uh, too bad you have to work," he said.

"Well, you all better be careful out there. This is not Mobile, you know."

"Yeah, baby. We'll be all right. We're just gonna go to the ESPN Zone or something."

"Yeah, you'd better enjoy this night out with the boys, 'cause when you come back next weekend, you belong to me," she said, smiling.

"And you know that, baby," I replied as I leaned over and gave her a kiss.

"Aw, hell. Mike, hurry up and get me out of here, 'cause they're about to make me sick with that lovey-dovey stuff," Rick said.

"Boy, please," Jennifer said, laughing.

We all finished our dinner, put the dishes in the dishwasher, and headed into the den to chill out for a while. Jennifer sat with me for a few more minutes before heading to the back room.

"Well, I had a long day, guys. I'm about to go to bed. You all have a nice time."

Both Rick and Mike said good night as Jennifer closed the door to her bedroom.

Rick grabbed his bag and headed to the bathroom to freshen up while Mike and I grabbed another beer. About fifteen minutes had gone past when Mike got up to see what was taking Rick so long.

"Hey, man, what are you doing in there?" he asked, knocking on the door.

"Hold on, man. I'm just trying to get myself together. Leave me alone and sit your ass down somewhere," he replied.

"Well, hurry up, man."

Mike walked back into the den and sat down. A couple of minutes later Rick came out of the bathroom smelling like someone had broken a bottle of cologne over his head.

"Hey, man, what the hell did you do in there?" I asked, looking at him strangely.

"Nothing, man. I just had to freshen up. C'mon, let's just get out of here and go to the club."

Rick and Mike headed outside to the car while I went into the back to let Jennifer know that we were leaving.

We left the complex on our way to find Strokers. Rick, who again sat in the backseat, was the navigator. Listening to him got us lost so many times we started to forget about Strokers and find another club in Buckhead or something since we were more familiar with the area. Mike, being a police officer, suggested that we get the attention of a cop the next time one passed by and get directions. Sure enough, we saw a black DeKalb County police officer sitting in the parking lot of a nearby shopping center and pulled up next to him. Mike got out of the car, showed the officer his badge, and got the exact directions to the club. When we turned the corner of East Pounce Street, all we saw was this big neon sign directly in front of us that read STROKERS. A smile lit up Rick's face as we pulled into the parking lot.

There was a line of cars in front of us waiting to park. We rode around a few times until we finally found a spot near the back of the club. I was ready to check out the honeys I'd been hearing so much about. Georgia was different than Alabama. In Georgia the girls get butt-ass naked, showing off everything. All we got in Alabama was G-string and pasties on the breasts, so you know I was hyped.

When we got to the door of the club, the security guys were checking IDs and making sure no one had any weapons. We took out our IDs, made it through the line, and went inside. As soon as the door opened, our mouths dropped. There were butt-naked honeys everywhere, all around the bar, near the pool tables, even standing up having casual conversations with people. There were women all over the place. Security was tight. They had brothers about six-six, three hundred pounds of solid muscles who didn't crack a smile. While we stood by the door, one of them came up to us with this hard frown like someone had just slapped his mama. Before we could say a word he spoke.

"What's up, fellas? That will be ten dollars," he said as he pointed in the direction of the counter.

We all walked over, paid the lady at the counter, and continued into the club. As we went farther to the back, we saw this big stage, and on it were about six naked girls dancing. On the floor I could see about ten or fifteen more naked honeys walking around, some giving lap dances and some walking on top of the bar. We just stood there in total disbelief that so many fine honeys could be in one place at one time, naked.

Finally, Rick walked off and found a table in a dark corner in the back and signaled for us to come over. Mike and I walked through the crowd, bumping into a few naked honeys making our way to the table, and sat down. Before we could get comfortable in our seats, out of nowhere this honey walked over. She was about five-two with a pecan color. She had a shape like a Coke bottle. I mean fine legs, tight ass, firm breasts, and she looked like the kinda girl you would take home to your mother. She leaned over and looked at us all.

"Hey, guys, would you like a private dance?" she asked.

Rick, being a regular at strip clubs, leaned over in the girl's ear and said, "No, maybe later. We just want to get a few more drinks in us first." The girl quickly walked away and went to the next table.

After we'd been in the club an hour, my buzz had me feeling kinda right. Mike was sitting next to me drinking his beer while Rick was up near the stage throwing money to damn near every girl who danced. I was looking at him, laughing my ass off, watching him act a fool just to get the women's attention. Suddenly the music stopped and the deejay yelled out, "Finally! What you've all been waiting to see! Welcome to the main stage . . . Chocolate and Vanilla."

These two girls came out onstage dressed like the Lone Ranger and Tonto. They must have been the house special or something, because every guy in the club ran up to the stage with his money out. These honeys were fine, too, I mean real fine. The girl dressed up as the Lone Ranger was slightly bowlegged with this nice dark brown skin. She was glistening in oil from head to toe. As she danced, you could see the muscles in her thighs flex. She had a plump, round ass that looked like it was sculpted to perfection. All she had on was a gray thong, a black vest and mask, and a white cowboy hat. The girl dressed like Tonto was fine too. She was high yella and had an Indian band around her head. Her hair hung to the middle of her back. She wore a brown suede thong, a brown vest with tassels, and a brown mask. She also had a real firm ass, but her legs were what stood out the most because they were thick with tattoos on each thigh.

Their show was off the chain. They came out on Kool Moe Dee's "Wild, Wild West," and they rocked the stage. I got as close as I could before being stockpiled by all of these drunk brothers trying to get to the front of the stage.

When the strippers started taking their clothes off, the men went crazy. Rick was throwing dollar after dollar at them. When Tonto came over by Rick she bent over and started making her butt cheeks jiggle and clap together. He was all into it too. He just grabbed a handful of money and tossed it all over her back. She reached down and picked up one of the dollar bills and slapped it against her bottom, making it stick.

The Lone Ranger grabbed a bottle of chocolate sauce and poured it on her neck and let it run all the way down between her legs. She then reached down between her legs, caught some with her finger, and started licking it off. The room went wild as brothers continued to push their way to the front. Finally, I'd had enough. I forced my way through the crowd and headed back to my seat with Mike.

"Man, did you see those fine-ass women up there?" I asked.

"Hell yeah," he replied. "I was just tripping off how Rick is throwing all of his money at them."

"Yeah, he must have spent more than three hundred dollars already," I said.

"Well, that's Rick. You know he's gonna have a good time no matter what," Mike said.

After about three songs the girls got off the stage and started walking around the club. Rick came and sat down. "Man, this is a live club," he said, almost out of breath.

"Yeah. It's just too many brothers in here. You can't even get to the honeys to see them dance," I said.

As soon as I said that, this girl walked up to the table and stood in front of Rick.

"Hey, you want a private dance?" she asked.

He looked at her, licking his lips. "Hell yeah, baby, but can you get some more girls over here to dance for my boys?"

"Yeah, hold on one second," she replied, nodding.

While she turned around and gestured for two other girls to come over, I grabbed my beer and drank the last drop, waiting in anticipation. When I looked into the direction she was pointing, out of the crowd popped the Lone Ranger and Tonto. I scanned their bodies until they got to us. The Lone Ranger had the prettiest toes I had seen in a while. The closer she got to me, the more excited I became. When the Lone Ranger finally reached me, she leaned over and grabbed my hands.

"Hey, baby, can I dance for you?" she asked.

I looked at her like she had just asked the dumbest question in the world. "Oh yeah, baby. Let me see you work it."

She leaned over to my right side and whispered in my ear, "Would you like a private dance or just a floor dance?"

As I was turning my head to answer her, I felt her hot tongue circle the outside of my ear. It felt so good that it made my back quiver.

"Uh, I'll take a floor dance, for now," I replied, trying to compose myself.

"Are you sure about that?" she asked as she rubbed her finger between her legs.

"Hell no, I ain't sure," I said, licking my lips, "but for right now I better get the floor dance before I get myself caught up."

I wanted a private dance bad as hell. But I didn't want to get it in front of my boy Mike. I didn't mind getting it in front of Rick, 'cause Rick didn't give a damn. But Mike made you feel guilty about things sometimes.

With my heart racing with excitement, I whispered back, "Let me see how you do it."

As soon as the music started, the Lone Ranger broke into a move. She was dancing to R. Kelly's song "It Seems Like You're Ready." As she turned her back to me, she began to make her butt cheeks jiggle one at a time to the beat of the music. She then started to slowly bend over and grabbed her right ankle with her right hand while her left hand reached back to caress her left butt cheek as her body continued to the music. She started caressing her butt in a slow, sensual motion. She then began reaching back with both hands on her ass, spreading it apart to show me everything she had. I started feeling my hard-on growing through my pants. With both cheeks spread apart she began rocking her hips oh so slowly to the beat of the song. What really got me was as she stood there with all of her ass in both her hands, she bent over in a doggy-style position, turned around, looking me straight in my eyes, and slowly started licking her lips.

I was so turned on by this dance she was giving me I just started getting into it with her. I started licking my lips and sat up, staring right in her eyes. Still in a doggy-style position, she started rubbing herself all over as she continued licking her lips like her body tasted so sweet. She then turned around and slowly started walking up on me until my head was about two inches from her body. Because I was sitting in a chair, her big, beautiful breasts were bouncing around my face. She lifted her left leg and placed it on the edge of my table. Instantly my hard-on began throbbing like crazy. With her leg still in the air she begin to move her hips in slow motion like she was grinding on an imaginary person. One finger rubbed her neatly trimmed brown bush. I could hear the song was about to end, because R. Kelly was singing his famous hooks at the end of his tracks, so I realized that this dance would end soon. To keep my woody from being noticed, I reached in my pocket and pulled out some money and gently placed it on her thigh, which was still on the edge of the table. I was so into the dance she had given me I didn't even notice all these guys standing behind me enjoying the show too. Knowing this, I felt my woody going down in an instant. When the song was finally over she put the money in a little pouch, leaned over, and whispered in my ear, "Thank you for letting me dance for you."

I looked her in the eye. "No, baby, thank you. Hey, take off the mask so that I can see your beautiful face," I said.

"Noooo," she replied, "that would give me away. Besides, I'm not a regular here. I work at another club. No one knows who I am here but the owner. Well, I'll see you later."

I watched her sexy ass walk to the back room where all of the girls went to change. After that dance and seeing all that fine ass in my face, I was ready to go home and wake Jennifer up and put a hurting on her. Looking at the time, I noticed it was getting pretty late.

I leaned over toward Mike. "Hey, man, you about ready to go?"

"Yeah, man, I've seen enough ass for one night," he replied. "Besides, that honey you had was the finest thing in here."

"Yeah, I know. She had a serious body."

I looked over at Rick to see if he was ready to leave, but he was all in some other honey's face. I got up and walked over to him. "Hey, man, you about ready?" I asked.

"Hell no! Man, come on, let's stay another hour. I'm trying to get one of these honeys to leave with us."

I looked at him like he was crazy. "Man, c'mon, let's go. I may have to ride home with the window down as it is to get this strip club smell off me."

Rick laughed. "Oh yeah, I forgot you do have to sleep under Jennifer tonight."

"Sleep, hell. After what I've just seen tonight, I might have to wake Jennifer up tonight."

We slapped hands as we laughed. "Okay, man, let's head out," Rick said.

We all got up and walked toward the door. As we walked out, we saw the same muscle-bound brother who was checking IDs at the door. As we passed him, he looked over and grinned like he knew we had a good time.

"Take it easy, brothers, and come back again," he said, smiling.

Mike reached over and shook his hand as we exited the club. When we got outside, there was still a line of people trying to get in. We passed them all by and got in the car, heading back to the apartment. On the way home, I rolled down the window so that I could let the wind blow some of that strip club smell off my clothes. In the meantime Rick was running his mouth about how he could have had a couple of women follow him out if he only had enough time to work his game. He talked about that for so long that Mike fell asleep. I just turned up the music and ignored him until we made it back to the apartment.

We parked next to Jennifer's car, got out, and walked upstairs. Because it was after one o'clock, we slowly opened the door and quietly walked in so we didn't wake Jennifer. She had set up the couch for one of the guys to sleep on. Rick noticed the setup and laughed softly. "Hey, Mike, there's your bed," he said.

"I know, man, just hurry up and get your ass out of here so I can sleep," he said.

"Oh, don't worry about that, my brother, I'm on my way," Rick replied.

I softly walked to Jennifer's room. As I slowly opened the door I could see her sound asleep with a bunch of books scattered all over the bed. I gently walked into her bathroom and started taking off my clothes. I grabbed my face towel, put a little soap and water on it, and washed my face, arms, and neck. When I thought I smelled a little fresher, I walked over to the bed. I reached over and grabbed all of the papers and books and stacked them in a pile on her dresser. I then eased myself into the bed next to her and fell fast asleep.

The alarm went off around 7:00 AM. Again Jennifer jumped out of bed and headed for the shower. I was so tired from the night before that all I could do was roll over and fall back to sleep. I think I faded off again when she closed the door to the shower or something, because the last thing I heard was her turn on the water. From that point the only thing I remembered was Jennifer kissing me before she left for work, telling me to call her before I left. When she opened the door to walk through the den area I could hear the TV on. I knew then that Mike was wide awake and ready to head back to Alabama to see his wife. I lay in bed for another fifteen minutes until slowly forcing myself out. I walked into the bathroom, ran my water, and jumped in the shower. I got dressed and gathered all of my clothes so that I could start to put them in the car. I walked out of the bedroom to the den where I could hear Mike and Rick talking and laughing out loud as they watched TV.

"What's up, man? You about ready to go?" Rick asked.

"Yeah, we can start putting things in the car right now if you're ready," I replied.

"Yeah, I'm ready. I've got all of my things right here at the door," Rick said as he got up from his chair.

"Here are my keys. Go ahead and put your stuff in the car while I get me some breakfast. Are you two hungry?" I asked.

"No, man. Mike and I already had about two bowls of cereal. As a matter of fact I think we ate it all," he said.

"What do you mean you think? Either you did or you didn't," I said.

"Well, man, I guess we did. You know how Mike's big greedy ass is." They laughed.

"Well, I guess I'll have to grab something on the way out," I said. I locked up the place, and we all loaded our things in the car and headed out.

"Remember, Rick, you have to see Gina before we leave," I said as I backed out of my parking space.

"Aw, man. I thought you forgot about that shit. I was hoping we could just hit the road and head on home."

"Come on, man. You told that girl you would see her before you left today," Mike said. "Don't be an asshole and a liar."

Rick shook his head. "Okay, okay. Let's go so I can get this over with."

As we left the complex I grabbed my cell phone and called Jennifer at the office. I knew she would be in court all day, so when I got her voice mail, I just left her a message that we were heading out.

When I made it to the gate, I stopped, waiting on directions.

"So where are we going, Rick?" I asked.

"Yeah, man, how do you get there?" Mike asked.

"How the hell should I know? Let me give her a call so I can get some directions from her," Rick replied.

Before he could dial Gina's number, his phone started ringing. He looked at the number of the incoming call and dropped his head. "Damn. She won't even give me a chance to call her ass, man. Let's hurry up and go over there so I can get the hell back to Alabama." He answered, "Hello. Yeah, we're just leaving now . . . How do you get to the day care? Wait, hold on one second. Troy, what area is this we're in?" Rick asked.

"Oh, this is Dunwoody," I replied.

"Yeah, Gina, we're in Dunwoody. Okay . . . Okay . . . All right. I got it. If we get lost I'll call you at the office. Bye."

"So where to?" I asked.

"Here are the directions," he said, placing them in Mike's hand.

We followed them exactly as they were written, which led us right to the day-care center in Stone Mountain, which was about twenty miles away. When we pulled up in the driveway, there stood this red-brick two-story building in the middle of what looked like around seven acres of land surrounded by a twelve-foot privacy fence. We came up to the gate where you had to buzz in to enter the premises. Since Rick was the guest I drove close enough for him to talk through the intercom. Rick leaned over and pressed the button.

"Hi, may I help you?" a voice asked.

"Uh, yes. Is Gina Wells in please?" he replied.

"Yes, may I ask who's calling?"

"Yeah. This is Rick Walker."

"Okay, Mr. Walker. Hold on for just one moment please."

After waiting a couple of minutes, Rick got frustrated. "See, man, she knew we were on our way. She could have at least had her ass at the door. That's why I should have gotten with Ginger or Louise, you know, someone with some clout. I bet if I was with one of them we could've driven straight in."

Mike and I just sat there. We let Rick continue on with his petty gripes about Gina. I wasn't really in a hurry, and as soon as he closed his mouth to take a breath, someone buzzed us in.

I looked at Rick's face as we drove up to the center. He was still kinda pissed about coming. But this could've been avoided if he would just have met Gina the day before.

His demeanor changed after he saw Gina run outside wearing this real nice pantsuit that gripped her body.

Rick got out of the car, and Gina met him with a big hug and a kiss on the cheek. They stood there for about five minutes hugging and giggling before she even noticed Mike and me. After seeing us sitting in the car, she signaled for us to come in. We got out and followed her inside. I was impressed from the moment we walked through the front door. These girls had it going on for real. The place had a big TV room, a playroom, a sleep area, and a nursery with two nurses on duty. As we walked farther down the hall I could smell something sweet being baked, like cookies or something. We walked into this really nice cafeteria. It reminded me of high school or something, a bunch of long tables with benchlike seats that were bolted to them.

I was so hungry my stomach started growling like someone was moving furniture around in it.

Gina took us upstairs and showed us around. I saw an accounting department, a snack area for employees, and a video room with monitors everywhere that covered the entire property. As we walked to the back part of the upstairs, we came to Gina's cubicle located between two huge offices in the back corner. It was a nice size with a desk and two chairs on each side of her cubicle. Still amazed at the layout of the area, I began looking around as I stood on the outside entrance of Gina's cubicle.

"Oh, those office areas in each corner belong to Louise and Ginger. They're both out today," Gina said.

"Wow, they look nice," I said, nodding my head.

"C'mon, let's go in Louise's office where it's private. She won't mind," she suggested.

We all followed Gina into Louise's office as she took a seat behind Louise's desk. Being inside impressed me more. It had a cherry-colored oak desk and matching computer tables and chairs. She had a lot of contemporary black art on all the walls and a lot of potted plants near her window, which faced the front of the building.

"Sit down and make yourself comfortable," Gina said.

We all sat down, still looking around the office admiring Louise's exquisite taste.

"So did you guys have fun last night?" she asked.

"Yeah, it was cool. We did the guy thing, you know, just club-hopped a little bit," Rick replied.

"So where did you all go?"

"Well, uh, we just played a little pool and had a few beers at a couple of spots in Buckhead, nothing big."

"Good, but next time you come, you have to let me take you to some real nice spots around town," she said.

"Yeah, that's cool," Rick said.

Rick and Gina kept their long, boring-ass conversation going on for about twenty minutes while Mike and I just sat through it. My stomach started growling again. This time it caught Gina's attention.

"Dang, Troy, you hungry over there?" she asked, concerned.

"I ain't gonna lie. I'm starving. I started to walk into your cafeteria on the way in and grab some of those cookies or whatever that was cooking in there."

She laughed. "Well, let me get one of the ladies down there to make you a sandwich."

"That'll work," I said, relieved.

"Rick, would you and Mike like anything?" she asked.

"No, I'm cool," Rick replied.

"Me too," Mike said.

She picked up the phone and called the cafeteria and had some-one make me a ham-and-cheese sandwich. She also asked for some potato chips and a fruit drink. I was so happy that my mouth started watering just from the way she ordered it over the phone.

"It'll be up in just a minute," she said.

"Girl, I don't know how to thank you right about now, but I really appreciate it."

"No problem," she said.

She and Rick talked for another ten minutes until they were inter-rupted by a heavyset woman dressed in a white uniform, who came to the door with this big white container and a fruit drink in her hand.

"Excuse me, Gina. Here is the sandwich you ordered."

"Oh, thank you, Miss Jackson," she replied.

I quickly got up and walked toward Miss Jackson to get my sand-wich, which I had longed for since Gina picked up the phone and or-dered it. When I reached for the sandwich, Miss Jackson kinda pulled back the container and looked at me with an evil look in her eyes, like she was going to whip my ass if I touched it. I played it off by looking over at Gina, waiting on her to tell this crazy-ass woman to give me my damn food. Gina caught my signal and quickly responded.

"Oh, Miss Jackson, the sandwich is for him. Thank you."

Miss Jackson then gave me this pleasant smile as she handed me the container. I gave her a hard look in return.

When I turned around, I saw Mike and Gina laughing like they read my expression.

"You must be mighty hungry, baby," she said.

"Oh yeah. For a minute I thought me and Miss Jackson was about to tussle up in here. She just don't know, it would have been ham and cheese all up in this office."

We all laughed out loud.

"Where can I go to eat this?" I asked.

"You can sit right here and eat," she said, clearing off some space on the desk. "Grab that chair and bring it over here."

"Are you sure? I can go downstairs in the cafeteria and eat."

"No, don't be silly. Come sit right here."

I quickly sat down in the area she had cleared on the desk and began to chow down. Everyone was staring at me, but I didn't give a damn. When I swallowed that first bite, I swear you could hear it hit the bottom of my stomach.

I sat there for about five minutes and ate everything in the container. Rick kept giving me an ugly frown for me to hurry up 'cause he was ready to go. As soon as I finished the last bite he jumped up and grabbed Gina's hand.

I wiped my mouth. "Thank you. That sandwich hit the spot."

"Oh, it was no trouble," she replied.

"Well, Gina, I think we'd better be going now, 'cause Mike has to hurry up and get back home to take care of something with his job. I just wanted to stop by and see you before we left," Rick said.

Mike, caught by surprise, looked at Gina. "Uh, yeah, I have to go by my office and review some papers for this crime I'm investigating," he said.

"Oh yeah, I understand. I'm just glad you guys were able to come by before you left," she said.

Gina, looking disappointed, got up and led us back downstairs and out of the front door to the car. While Mike and I sat inside, Gina and Rick gave each other another big hug and kiss on the lips before Rick got into the car with us. We all said our good-byes and headed out of the front gate of the day-care center.

"Man, I'm so glad that's over. Now we can finally hit the road," Rick said.

Mike looked into the backseat in disgust. "Man, quit lying, the way you two were carrying on in there. Your ass is tripping."

"Aw, man, I didn't want to be rude to the honey, so I just made up things to talk about so I could get out of there. It was working, too, until Troy's greedy ass had to get him a sandwich."

"You damn right. That's what you get for eating all of the cereal. Besides, I was hungry and wasn't about to turn down a free meal. But for a minute I thought I was going to have to whip Big Miss Jackson's ass for my sandwich," I said.

We all laughed.

"I don't think you could've handled that," Mike said, laughing. "She was a heavyweight. You're too light in the ass for all that meat. Oh yeah, Rick, why you always have to keep me in the mix of your shit, talking about we gotta go 'cause Mike has work to do for his job?"

"It worked, didn't it? We're on the road now, right?" Rick replied.

"Okay. One day you gonna get caught up in some lie you can't get out of."

"Yeah, yeah, yeah, man. Just turn up the music, turn your ass around, and let me enjoy my ride home," Rick said as he got comfortable in the backseat.

As we got on the 285 expressway, I put some Trick Daddy in the CD player, and we started on our journey back to Alabama.

After a four-and-a-half-hour drive, we made it back to Mobile. I pulled into my apartment complex where the guys had left their cars. Because they were so tired they just grabbed their things and headed home. I was tired as well, so I just went inside, tossed my things on the floor, and sat on the couch to watch TV. While sitting there I noticed the light flashing on my phone, signaling messages. I got up on my way to the kitchen, grabbed the phone, and checked it. Everyone had called except Jennifer. I wasn't mad, just disappointed that she didn't at least return my call from earlier. I just walked back over to the couch with a beer and got comfortable again. Minutes later the phone rang.

"Hello."

"Hi, baby. Did you have a safe drive home?" Jennifer asked.

"Yeah, it was cool. How was your day?"

"Busy, busy, busy. Still trying to get things in order. The only break I had today was lunch at Houston's. Oh yeah, do you remember Rhonda Johnson, my old classmate from college? Well, I ran into her at the restaurant and we exchanged numbers. She started telling me about all the people that were up here from college and how they keep in touch and meet for lunch."

"Well, that's good. Now you have people to hang out with."

"Yeah, I told her maybe we could meet for drinks one day to catch up on old times or something."

"Yeah, you need to get out and see more than just the courtroom and the highway. I told you before not to let your work consume your private life."

"Yeah, I know, but I just want to let my boss know that he didn't make a mistake by hiring me."

"He knows how valuable you are, so don't think like that."

"Yeah, I guess," she said.

"Where are you now? Are you home yet?"

"No, right now I'm on my way to the law library."

"See, there you go."

"No, I just have to look up something and then I'm heading home."

"Okay, if you feel that's what it takes, go for it."

"I won't be gone too long. Well, let me go, baby. Traffic is starting to build up, and I don't want to get in an accident while on the phone, so I'll give you a call later tonight, okay?"

"Okay, I'll talk to you later," I replied.

"Okay, Troy. Love you."

"Yeah, I love you too."

I felt better hearing her voice. I just didn't like the fact that she was always on the go. I knew Jennifer loved her job, but somewhere you had to draw the line.

CHAPTER 7

Contemplation

After a grueling six months had passed, things for the most part were still good between Jennifer and me. The first three months were the toughest. She still worked constantly, which didn't allow much time for us to see each other. But she did call when she had a spare moment. As for me, I only had a little more than five months left on my contract before I could receive my transfer to Atlanta. Because of that, I worked on various projects that required me to travel a lot. I was in and out of the office during the middle of the week, which made it difficult to visit Jennifer like I wanted to on the weekends. The times I stayed home, I was usually hanging out with Mike and Rick. We would get together for drinks or go to the gym and work out or just chill at someone's place. Mike's wife was pregnant with their third child and Rick, well . . . he was still Rick.

I had just arrived home late one Thursday from a four-day trip from Norfolk, Virginia. I had to sit in on meetings all week trying to design a simulated Billright database for one of our clients. This was the third week in a row that I was out of town, which meant this was the third weekend in a row that I was unable to visit Jennifer. Sure, we talked on the phone, but it wasn't the same as being there. I still remained committed to our relationship, though, and never once cheated despite the pressure from Rick to do so. I was beginning to doubt our future, by the way things were going. I felt like Jennifer stopped making the effort and only called to keep the routine going. I really started missing her a lot and thinking crazy thoughts that made me feel insecure. Maybe God had put us in this position for a reason. After all, Jennifer didn't really like living in Mobile, and since she had moved to Atlanta, she wasn't really making the effort to come here to visit me. It just wasn't the same anymore. I knew I still loved her, but did she still love me?

My alarm went off around 6:00 AM. Still struggling from the after-effects of my trip, I forced myself out of bed, brushed my teeth, and started toward the kitchen for some cereal. With bowl in hand, I walked to my closet to find something to wear. Since it was Friday, I decided to dress kinda casual, you know, a mock-turtleneck shirt, pants, and my Kenneth Cole shoes, which I had just polished.

I got to work a little earlier than usual. I needed to finish some projects I was working on before I had left for Norfolk.

When I entered the building, I walked straight to the break room to get my usual thirty-two-ounce cup of water and also to get my mail, which had been sitting there for about a week. I opened it and began walking toward my office door, concentrating on what I was reading. When I got to my door I was startled by a noise coming from the office next to mine. It was strange because that office had been empty for almost seven months and also because I didn't think any-one else was in the building.

Curious as to what was going on, I put my briefcase down and softly walked to the door to listen further. The door was cracked just enough for me to peek inside and catch a glimpse. I leaned in and glanced around, but I could only see the corner of the desk and some old boxes on the floor. I heard the noises again. This time it sounded like someone opening and closing file cabinets. I gently pushed the door just a little to get a better look when all of a sudden it swung open and I heard a loud scream. Not only did it scare me but I jumped back so fast that I dropped my mail and spilled my water all over the floor. When I looked up to see who in the hell it was who screamed, there, standing in the doorway, was this girl, her mouth wide open. She stood about five-five and had long, silky black hair down her shoulders with a high-yellow complexion that was turning redder by the second. She had one hand on her hip like she was pissed off and the other hand was on the knob of the door.

"Who in the hell are you, and why are you sneaking around my office like this?" she asked in an angry tone.

I bent down to one knee and started picking up my mail. "Well, uh, I heard a noise, and I was wondering what was going on inside the office since it's been vacant for so long," I replied, looking embarrassed.

"Well, why didn't you just knock? Don't you think that would have been the polite thing to do instead of scaring the hell out of me like that?"

"Yeah, you're right, and I apologize for that."

"Well, can I help you with something?"

"Uh, no. Like I said, I was just curious, that's all. I'll be out of your way in a minute."

Still frowning in anger, she stared down as I struggled to get my mail out of the spilled water.

"Wait," she said in a short, firm tone. "I have some extra paper towels you can use."

"Oh, uh, thanks," I said, looking back up at her.

When she turned around, I couldn't help but to look at her. Her long, silky hair whipped around. She was wearing these light-colored jeans that fit her thick, athletic build perfectly. With each step, her ass tightened in the rhythm of her stride. When she made it over to the corner of her desk, she leaned over slightly to reach for this big roll of paper towels on her desk. As she stretched for them I could see her big round breasts jiggle with every motion of her arm. Trying not to be obvious, I quickly dropped my head in the direction of the spill. I could hear her tear sheets of the paper towels off before she walked back to where I was kneeling. When she got about two feet in front of me she leaned over and handed me the paper towels. As I reached for them, I couldn't help but to notice her hand and that she didn't have a ring on any of her fingers that signaled marriage or some kind of engagement. With that in mind I began to converse.

"Thank you for the help," I said with a grateful smile.

Her anger faded. "Well, it's the least I can do. I guess I did have a part in making the mess."

"Yeah, I guess you did," I said jokingly.

She smiled, looking down at me with her hands on her hips.

"So who are you, by the way?" she asked.

I dropped the towels and stood out of respect to shake her hand.

"I'm Troy, Troy Sanders. I work in the office next door."

"Well, Troy, I'm Dana, Dana Suarez."

"Suarez," I said, surprised. "Are you Mexican or something?"

"No, I'm Puerto Rican," she quickly replied.

"Oh yeah, you speak Spanish and stuff, huh?"

"I speak Spanish and French," she said.

"Oh yeah, cool. So you'll be working here, huh?"

"Yes, I'll be here for a while, I guess," she said.

"So what project will you be working on?" I asked.

"Oh, I'll be working on parts of the Ingles project," she said.

Ingles was a huge telecommunications company with whom our firm had a contract. Since we had so much work to do for them our firm brought employees in from other offices around the country.

"So, when do you report to work, or have you started already?" I asked.

"Well, I don't officially start until Monday, but I decided to come in today to get my office in order. That way all I have to do is concentrate on work once I get in on Monday."

"Yeah, I can see you hooked it up," I replied as I looked around. "You must have been here kinda early this morning."

"Yeah, I still have a few more things to do before I leave, but for the most part, this is it."

"Well, I'll let you get back to what you were doing, and I'm sorry if I frightened you."

After I cleaned as much of the mess up as I could, I grabbed my things and started toward my office. "Well, welcome aboard, and it was nice meeting you," I said, walking off.

She turned and gave me this sexy half smile. "Okay, Troy. I guess I'll see you around."

I walked into my office, put my things away, and turned on my computer. I couldn't help but smile to myself at what had just happened. I was thinking about how fine this woman was and the fact that she would be working right next to me.

I sat down, gathered myself, and got to work. By the time I really got into what I was doing, I was interrupted by the sound of other people coming into the office. The smell of fresh coffee filled the air, and the constant ringing of the phones made it hard for me to get back into what I was working on. Seeing that my door was halfway opened, I got up with papers in hand and walked over to close it. By the time it shut completely I heard a soft knock. Still concentrating on what I was reading, I slowly opened it. When I looked up, I was surprised to see that it was Dana standing there with a huge cup in her hand. "Hi," I said with a smile.

"Hi," she replied. "I want to apologize for being rude earlier, and as a gesture of good faith, I brought you another cup of water."

My eyebrows rose. "Well, thank you but you didn't have to do that."

"Well, since we'll be working together I didn't want you to think I was a bitch. You know, first impressions are usually the ones that last in a person's mind."

"No, you never came across like that, but I appreciate your gesture of good faith anyway."

"Well, that's all I wanted," she said, looking confused as to what else to say. "You have a nice day. I have to go home and finish unpacking my things."

"Unpacking," I said. "What office did you come from, by the way?"

"Oh, I came from the one in San Francisco," she replied.

"San Francisco! What made you want to come to Alabama of all places?"

"Well, I have family here that I don't really get a chance to see that much of, and I thought by coming here it would give me a chance to get closer to them again."

"Well, that's thoughtful."

"Yeah, I think so. Well, anyway, I'll let you get back to work, and I'll see you on Monday." She slowly turned, giving me another smile before walking away. As she walked I watched her as she disappeared down the hall near the elevators. It was about time the firm brought in an attractive woman to this group. All the other girls they brought in were either heavy or nerdy-looking with thick-ass glasses and shit.

Well, at least the last four were like that. I chuckled to myself as I closed my door and walked back to my desk.

As I tried to concentrate on my work once again, it was hard. Dana had really made a good impression. She seemed cool and laid-back, not stiff like most of the people at my office. Plus, she was fine as hell and working right next to me.

Suddenly I started feeling a little guilt about the way I was analyzing this girl. I picked up the phone and called Jennifer. Since it was still early, I would have a chance to catch her before she got busy at work.

Jennifer picked up. "Hello."

"Hi, what's up?"

"Hi, baby. I was just thinking about you. How is your morning?" she cheerfully asked.

"Oh, everything is good so far. I just have a lot of work to catch up on, that's all. How about you?"

"Well, right now, I'm on my way to the office to get some documents, and then I'll be in court the rest of the day. What happened to you last night? I called you but I kept getting the answering machine."

"Oh, as soon as I put my head on the pillow, I was out like a light. What time was it when you called?" I asked.

"Around one my time, so it had to be midnight there."

"Oh yeah, I was definitely asleep. So, what are your plans for tonight?"

"Well, I'm supposed to meet Rhonda and some more college friends for dinner, and after that, I'll be at home working."

"Well, if you get some time, give me a call. I don't think I'm going anywhere tonight. I'm still a little worn out from my trip."

"Okay. I'll just call you later on tonight then."

"Cool. Have a good day."

"Okay, baby. Bye."

I got off the phone feeling much better. Just hearing Jennifer's voice seemed to put me in a better mood. The little guilt I was feeling started to go away. All I had done was look at an attractive female. What was the harm in that? Hell, it wasn't like I was trying to get with her or something. With that in mind, I quickly wrapped myself up in my work again. I was so into what I was doing that three hours passed by before I knew it.

When my cell phone rang, I thought. *Damn, another interruption. At this rate I'll never get any work done. It's probably Rick.* He usually called to see if we all wanted to meet for lunch.

I reached over and grabbed the phone. "Hello." It was Rick just like I had guessed.

"Hey, man. What's up? What are you doing for lunch?" he asked.

"Nothing. I think I'll work through today," I replied.

"C'mon, man. You mean you don't want to get out?"

"Not today, man. I have too much shit to do."

"All right, man, do your thing. Hey, you know, Gina's crazy ass has been calling the hell out of me all morning."

"Man, I ain't in the mood to hear that shit about you two today. Why don't you be straight up with her and tell her you're not feeling her?" I said.

"I thought about it, man, but I don't want to hurt her feelings like that. I just don't want her to expect anything else from me but friendship," Rick said.

"What?" I replied. "You getting kinda soft there, ain't you, brother?"

"No, it's just that she's been kinda cool these last few months and helped me through some shit. You know, advice about things here and there."

"Well, then, brother, stop complaining."

He laughed. "Well, anyway, you gonna just chill today, huh?"

"Yeah. Maybe we can all get together at the gym tomorrow or something," I suggested.

"Cool. Well, let me call Mike and see what he's doing and let him know about tomorrow."

"Okay, man, I'll holla at you later," I said.

"Peace."

I hung up the phone, shaking my head. Rick knew I was tired of hearing about that shit between him and Gina. He just liked the fact that she was running behind his ass and wanted us to give him all this attention like he was running things. Personally, I think he was kinda digging her but didn't want to lose some points with the fellas about his playa status.

Gradually I got back into my work, and several hours later I had completed two major tasks on my project. I leaned back in my chair and glanced over at my clock on the wall. It was now 4:45, and I was ready to get out of the office and enjoy my weekend. I gathered my things, turned off my computer, and headed for the door. While outside my office I glanced over at Dana's office one last time. Instantly I chuckled to myself as I thought about this morning, before I walked out the door.

CHAPTER 8

Cooling Out

After an hour of fighting through traffic, I made it home. I dropped everything at the door and headed to my bedroom to get out of my clothes. Since I wasn't going anywhere that night I took off everything except my boxers. I made a sandwich and sat on the couch watching TV. Just as the sandwich was getting good, the phone started ringing.

I got up, ran over to look at the caller ID to see who it was. *Damn, it's Rick's ass,* I thought. Something inside said not to answer it, but I knew if I didn't he would call me on my cell phone until I did answer.

I picked up the phone. "Hello," I said with a mouthful of food.

"What's up, man? Whatcha doing?"

"I'm trying to finish this sandwich. What's up with you?" I replied.

"Well, Mike and I are headed to the Jazzy Blues Café."

The Jazzy Blues Café was a real nice adult club that played jazz on the first level and on certain nights played hip-hop or blues on the second floor. About twelve different styles of chicken wings were served, and the place always stayed packed. This was one of the main spots we normally hung out on Fridays after work. Tonight, though, I just wasn't feeling it.

"I'm in for tonight, man," I replied.

"What? There's gonna be some bad honeys down there."

"Yeah, I know, but I'm gonna have to pass tonight."

"Are we still on for tomorrow at the gym?" he asked.

"Oh yeah. I'll meet you guys there around noon."

"Cool."

I hung up the phone and attacked my sandwich again. I ate every bite and was still hungry. I got up and headed for kitchen and poured me a glass of Hennessy. I gulped the first glass down and quickly poured another and headed back to the den to watch some more TV. Before I knew it I was sound asleep.

I was awakened by the stiffness in my neck. I jumped up and headed for the bed. It felt really good to be able to have some peace and quiet for a change and just rest. Within minutes I was again out like a light.

The next morning I was awakened by the chirping birds outside my bedroom window. I pulled the covers over my head and nodded on and off for a few more hours before finally getting out of bed. I looked at the clock and noticed it was 9:35. Still dragging around the apartment, I brushed my teeth and showered. As I was getting dressed, I thought, *Damn, I wonder why Jennifer didn't call me last night.* I reached over, grabbed the phone, and dialed the first three digits of her telephone number before hanging up.

Instead of sweating that shit I just headed out the door to get my workout on. On my way to the gym, I started thinking long and hard until shit started bothering me. I felt like I wasn't a priority anymore, like if Jennifer wasn't going to make an effort anymore, then why should I? All I was getting were broken promises. Hell, if you say you're going to call, then call. If something comes up, just pick up the fucking phone and say that. What's so hard about that shit?

I had this issue in my mind the entire way to the gym. By the time I got there, it was about eleven o'clock. I thought I'd get warmed up with the weights before the fellas got there. I walked over to the bench, placed some weights on, and started doing bench presses. I got in about three sets before Mike came in and stood over me, laughing.

"Man, I know you can lift more than that light-ass weight," he said.

I put the weights back on the rack and looked up. "Light, my ass. That was my third set. I'm just trying to get warmed up before I dog y'all's asses out on the court." I got up laughing as we slapped hands.

"Where's Rick?" Mike asked.

"Man, you know his ass is probably still in bed," I replied.

Mike just shook his head in disbelief.

I grabbed my towel, and we walked to the basketball court in the back of the building. When we got there we noticed that there was a game going on already and another group had next on the court. Mike and I called game after them and went to a corner and stretched while we waited our turn. Moments later, Rick came walking through the door. We watched as he walked around the gym looking for us. Finally after having no luck in the front of the facility he headed to the back where we were stretching. Seeing us, he came over.

"Sorry I'm late, man. I had a rough night last night," he said with a tired look in his eyes.

Mike looked up. "Rough night. Man, I was with you all night. What do you mean rough night?"

"Man, you left at ten. I left the club and headed to this wild-ass party this white chick that I knew was having. Man, honeys were all over me as soon as I hit the door. I'm talking blondes, brunettes, redheads, all kinds of honeys. I started to call Troy, but I knew he wouldn't be down for it."

"You're right. I just wanted to chill. I wasn't in the mood to hang last night."

Rick leaned over to Mike and whispered, "I bet all he did was sit at home talking to Jennifer on the phone."

They both laughed. I heard his ass, but I didn't think it was funny, especially with the way I was starting to feel, so I played it off and kept on stretching.

I started thinking again, this time giving Jennifer the benefit of the doubt. Maybe she and her friends stayed out kinda late or maybe she just went home like I did and crashed. Whatever her reason was for not calling, I just had to wait and see and not let it get to me.

We sat there and watched the other guys play until it was our turn. When we did get the court we ran it for about an hour before losing. The run felt good.

The Hennessy I had drunk the night before made it hard for me to really play like I wanted. But we still had a good run anyway.

Mike and Rick were good basketball players. Because Mike was a cop he was in good enough shape to run all day. But me, I was exhausted after the second game, though I held my own out there.

We left the court and headed up front to get a drink. While at the water fountain, we watched as the sistas in the aerobics class twisted and turned their asses to the music. They looked up at us and tried to really show off. Even the white girls with no asses kept trying to shake them for us, and the other men who watched.

I was about ready to head back home. I noticed the time and that it was a little after four.

"Hey, guys, I'm about to head home," I said, as I grabbed my bag.

Rick grabbed his things. "Yeah, man, me too. What's up for tonight? Are y'all gonna hang out?"

Mike shook his head. "No, man, I'm spending time with my wife tonight."

"I might do something," I replied. "Give me a ring. What's going on tonight anyway?"

"I don't know. Let me make some calls and see what I can find. I know something's happening," Rick said.

"Yeah, well, hit me up when you find out," I said.

"Okay, I'll do that," Rick said as we both headed out the door. Mike stayed so that he could hit the weights before going back home. I left and headed to the market to get some things to cook for dinner since I had a feeling Rick wasn't doing anything tonight. I picked up a couple of steaks and potatoes and went by Blockbuster to get me a couple of movies. Since I hadn't seen *The Brothers* in a while I decided to rent it again.

I got home, jumped in the shower, and relaxed for about a couple of hours before putting on my steaks. While everything was in the oven, I grabbed a beer and chilled out on the couch. After my steaks started to cook, I heard a knock at the door. When I looked through the peephole, I saw Rick standing outside frowning. I opened the door, chuckling. "So what happened to this party you were talking about, man?" I asked.

"Man, ain't nobody doing anything tonight," he said with disappointment in his voice.

"Well, the night is still young. Can't you make some calls later?"

"Man, I have been calling honeys since we left the gym. There ain't nothing going on tonight."

"What about Jazzy Blues Café?" I asked.

"I went there last night. I don't want to hit it two nights in a row. Man, I wish I was back in Atlanta so that we could hit Strokers again."

When he said *Atlanta,* instantly I thought about Jennifer and walked to the back to call her. I could still hear Rick in the background talking about how bored he was while I dialed her number.

Since it was in the evening I figured she was at home. I let the phone ring and hung up when I got the answering machine. When I called her cell phone she answered. All I could hear were people in the background like she was around a crowd or something.

"Hello!" she yelled.

"Hello," I replied.

"Hello. You're going to have to speak louder," she said.

"Hello," I yelled again.

"Troy?" she yelled.

"Yeah. Where are you?"

"I'm at a baseball game. Wait, let me call you right back. I can't hear you clearly."

I hung up the phone, puzzled. *What is she doing at a baseball game?* I thought. Minutes later the phone rang. This time I could hear her more clearly.

"Hello," I said.

"Hi. Sorry about the noise."

"Where are you?" I asked.

"I'm at the Atlanta Braves baseball game."

"The baseball game," I said in disbelief.

"Yeah, Rhonda's cousin plays and gave her some tickets."

"Oh yeah? Are you having fun?" I asked.

"Yeah, it's okay. We met her cousin and he introduced us to some of the other players and coaches. I thought it was pretty cool."

"Well, that's good. I'm glad you're having fun."

"Yeah, we may hang out after the game, so I'll call you when I get in."

"Oh, just like last night," I said sarcastically.

"I didn't get in until late, and I just fell asleep, but I'll call you tonight, baby," she reassured me.

"Okay, well, have fun," I replied.

"Thanks. Talk to you later."

We hung up, and I headed back into the den with Rick.

"What's up, you on the phone?" he asked.

"Yeah, I called Jennifer."

"Oh yeah? What's she up to?"

"Nothing much. She's out with some friends at the Braves game."

"Braves game," he said, surprised. "Man, the Braves are playing the New York Yankees. How did she get tickets? That game was sold out at the beginning of the season.

"Oh, her college friend's cousin plays with the Braves and gave them some tickets. She sounded like she was having fun. They got a chance to meet the players and coaches before the game."

"Her friend's cousin plays with the Braves?" he asked.

"Yeah," I replied. "That's how they got the tickets."

He gave me a hard look. "Man, I ain't trying to be funny, but you need to watch that."

"What do you mean, man?" I asked.

"Man, Jennifer's a homebody, and now she's hanging out at a Braves game meeting players and shit."

I looked at him strangely. "What are you trying to say, Rick?"

"Man, Jennifer don't know a home run from a homeboy. That's what I'm saying. You'd better watch her friends, man. She's gonna fuck around and get herself caught up in some drama."

"Aw, man. She's just hanging out with her old college friends, and that's it."

"Okay, if you say so. I'm just saying she needs to be careful, that's all."

I walked into the kitchen and pulled the steaks out of the oven. Rick did make sense. Jennifer had never been interested in baseball enough to go to the games. What if those players were trying to get with her? She was attractive, she was a lawyer. What if what Rick said was true? Maybe I did need to watch out.

"Hey, man, what are you doing in there? You're missing the game," Rick shouted, breaking my concentration.

"Oh, my bad. I'm just getting this food out. You hungry?" I asked.

"Yeah. What you cook?"

"I just cooked up some steaks and potatoes."

"Steak and potatoes," he said. "Hell yeah, I'm hungry."

I fixed the plates and headed to the den. After the game ended, nothing else was really on so I put in the movie, which later turned out to be a big mistake. The whole time Rick kept bringing up stuff to get me to see his point about Jennifer being at the game and around the players. He would compare Jennifer and me to the characters in the movie, trying to make his case. After a while it started to annoy me, but I didn't let him know. Instead I just concentrated on the movie.

After dinner I poured me a glass of Hennessy while Rick drank beer. Still, he kept on talking. But it was strange, the more I drank, the more his shit started making sense. Some of the things he was saying could very well happen. Especially the part at the bachelor party for Shemar Moore. Jennifer could be at a party with all those baseball players and get caught up in some drama, or she could hang around one and fall in love with him or something. Rick had a point. I just sat there not even paying attention to the movie anymore. Instead I was sitting there pissed that Jennifer was at a baseball game. I got up and went into my bedroom to call her again but changed my mind when I picked up the phone. What was I gonna say? I couldn't really get mad over something that hadn't happened. Instead I went back into the den and finished watching the movie.

When it finally ended Rick was tired and headed on home. I was tired myself, so I went into the bedroom and lay across the bed, looking up at the ceiling until my eyes began to get heavy. I rolled over on my side staring at Jennifer's picture on my nightstand until I dozed off.

CHAPTER 9

What Next?

Sundays were sort of a busy day for me. I would spend my mornings in church and the rest of the afternoon over to my parents' house for dinner. This morning I wasn't in a really good mood. As I got out of bed and looked over at Jennifer's picture, I got pissed off because it reminded me that she didn't bother to call like she said. I wanted to call her to find out what had happened, but I knew it would lead to an argument, and I didn't want the angry spirit in me on my way to church.

After a long sermon that I really didn't pay much attention to, I went over to my parents' house, which was where my aunts, uncles, and cousins usually were after church. My mother cooked a big Sunday dinner, and we all sat around talking and watching the baseball game on TV. We had fried and smothered chicken and gravy, macaroni and cheese, collard greens, corn bread, broccoli and cheese, rice, and barbecued ribs.

I usually ate more over at my parents' house than I did at home the entire week. And like mothers do, my mama would always pack me a huge to-go plate that was fit for three or four people.

Since I was the only child, and never really saw much of my cousins during the week, this was the day I looked forward to where we could really bond and catch up on family things.

We normally ate and watched TV until all the games were over. By the end of the day most of us were either asleep or stretched out on the floor from all the food we had eaten.

It was getting late and I was ready to head home. When the last game ended I got up and went into the kitchen where my mama was, thanked her for everything, and kissed her good-bye for the night. Seeing that I was leaving, my dad got up and walked me to the car.

When I got home, I put the food away and changed into my house clothes, you know, shorts and an old T-shirt, and lounged around the house looking through magazines that I had ordered until the phone rang.

"Hello," I said.

"Hi. I know you're mad I didn't call last night, but we all went out to this restaurant in Buckhead and had dinner and drinks, and time just got away from me. I know you're pissed."

"Well, as long as you had a good time," I said, trying to hold back my anger.

She paused for a moment. "You mean no lectures?"

"Nope," I replied nonchalantly. "If I was on your mind you would've called, that's all."

I heard her inhale deeply and let out a hard breath. "Troy, that's just not true."

"Look, baby, I'm glad you had a good time. No big deal," I said, knowing damn well I was fucking pissed.

I could tell Jennifer sensed something was wrong, so she tried to avoid starting an argument.

"So what did you do all day?" she asked.

"Oh, nothing," I replied.

"Nothing like what?"

"Nothing. Just hung around at my parents' house after church."

"How are they doing? I need to call them."

"They're cool."

"So what did you do after that?"

"Nothing. I came home. What's with you and all these generic questions?"

"We haven't talked, and I just wanna know how your day was."

"Oh, so now you want to know about my day?"

"What do you mean? I always ask you about your day. Why is that so unusual?"

"I don't know. Maybe I'm missing something here. I don't hear from you, and all you want to know about is my day. To me that seems fishy."

"Fishy how?" she asked, concerned. "I think you're making a big deal out of nothing."

"Yeah, okay, whatever," I said, frustrated.

We went back and forth all night. Even though I was upset I didn't let it get me to the point of cussing her out. Instead I continued to make my point of letting her know how disrespectful she was for not calling like she said.

While we talked, Jennifer's phone kept ringing like crazy. Her call-waiting was beeping every couple of minutes, interrupting the conversation.

I'd had enough when she kept me waiting for about five minutes. When she came back, I just said, "Look, I'll talk to you tomorrow. Apparently someone needs to talk to you real bad, so I'll let you go."

As usual she tried to explain that it was either friends or job related. Whatever the case, it was still out of the norm for her. When I got off the phone I started analyzing our situation. Before, I didn't have to worry too much about anything. Now it seemed like I wasn't comfortable with our situation and Jennifer wasn't doing anything to reassure me.

I woke up Monday feeling kinda sluggish. I had been tossing and turning all night and didn't really sleep that well. When I got to work I stopped by the break room, grabbed my water, and headed to my office as usual. While sitting at my desk I could hear Mr. Ford, the VP of the company, introducing the new girl, Dana, to the other project teams in our office. By the time they made it to my office, I was already into my work. I heard a knock at the door.

"Hey, Troy, you got a minute? I'd like you to meet our new project member."

I stood and walked over to them. "Hello again," I said.

Mr. Ford turned to look at Dana, puzzled. "Have you two met before?"

Dana smiled. "Yes, we met Friday."

Mr. Ford smiled with surprise. "Well, good. You know, Troy is one of the team leaders on our Ingles project."

"Oh," she replied.

"Yes, and I would like for you two to work together on this new task that they have given us. Is that okay with you, Troy?"

I nodded. "Yes, that's fine. I'd be happy to work with Dana."

"Good, I'll leave now and let you two get started."

Mr. Ford left us standing at my door. I quickly glanced at Dana while she watched him walk away. She was absolutely beautiful. She wore this business suit with a skirt that stopped below her knees. Her look and body reminded me of Regina Greer, aka Piggy on *The Steve Harvey Show*.

"Well, we meet again," she said with a smile.

I smiled back. "Yeah, this time the situation is more pleasant."

"So, when do we get started?" she asked.

"Well, let me get a copy of the project and I'll meet you in your office."

"Okay, I'll see you in a minute."

Dana walked back to her office, and I grabbed some folders off my desk and started going through them, trying to find the papers I needed to get her started. After I got what I needed, I walked over to her office and sat in one of her chairs near her desk, and began going over the details of the project. At first it felt kinda awkward being around a fine honey concentrating on something other than her body, but after a while I started to relax. Dana was very professional. She thoroughly wanted to go over every detail of the tasks we needed to work on. A few times, though, I caught her checking me out when she thought I wasn't looking. I couldn't blame her. After all, I was looking kinda sharp, if I must say so myself.

We worked together all morning. Dana had great ideas that complemented the direction in which I was trying to go. We finalized some things and decided to take a break.

"Well, what are you doing for lunch?" she asked.

"I don't know yet. I thought about going to my spot not too far from here for some soul food. What about you?" I asked.

"The only place that I know about is the McDonald's up the street."

"Noooo. Let me take you to this spot that I go to. I think you'll like it."

"Sure, I'm game," she said with excitement.

We continued working until around noon and left the office, going to Mammie's Restaurant. As usual it was packed. We waited several minutes before getting a table near the front entrance. We sat down, and I handed Dana a menu.

She looked at it and around the restaurant.

"Do you need some help? You look kinda confused," I said.

"Uh, yeah. What would you recommend?"

"The oxtails are good," I replied. "You ever had them before?"

"Oxtails, eeeww," she exclaimed.

"You mean you've never tried them?" I asked, looking surprised.

"No way. An oxtail? You've gotta be kidding," she said.

"No, they're good," I said.

"Whatever," she said as she continued looking over the menu.

"Well, I'll order the oxtails. You can order something you're familiar with, and I'll let you taste mine. I bet you're gonna like them."

She laughed. "I guess I can handle that. It won't hurt to try them."

We ordered and talked as we waited for our food. I noticed Dana kept staring around the restaurant. I guess being from California you don't see too many real soul food restaurants unless you're in the hood.

"Are you okay?" I asked.

"Yeah. It's just that I can't believe how packed this little placc is," she replied.

"Oh yeah. Everyone comes here to eat."

"Yeah, all of the food I see on people's plates looks good. I can't wait to try it."

Minutes later we got our food. Dana looked at my plate and frowned as the waitress put it on the table. I had oxtails, collard greens, and mac and cheese covered in oxtail gravy, and she had smothered chicken and rice.

I grabbed her hand and said grace. Surprised, she looked and bowed her head along with me. As I said grace I could feel the firm grip she had on my hand, like she was really feeling my words. When I finished, we both kinda paused a little, still holding hands like we were waiting on each other to let go. Slowly I released her hand, grabbed my fork, and dug into my meal. Dana paused as if she was waiting on me to give her the okay to eat. She waited until I sampled my food before she dug into her plate.

"Um, this is delicious," she said as she slowly chewed.

"You like, huh?" I said with a smile. "Well, if you think that's good, taste this."

"Okay."

Without hesitation, she reached over with her fork and scooped a piece of the oxtails from my plate. She took in the food and held it in her mouth.

"What's the matter?" I asked.

She shook her head.

"Go ahead, chew it. It's good."

She started frowning as she slowly began to chew. I sat there waiting on her to respond before I continued to eat. Soon after, she started to chew faster.

"Well, what do you think?" I asked.

"You know, this is really good. I mean really, really good. I'll have to get this next time I come," she said.

"See, I told you the food here was the bomb."

Nodding, Dana began to eat her chicken and rice.

We sat there and enjoyed the rest of our lunch, laughing and talking. She continued from time to time to eat more of my oxtails. At first, I didn't feel comfortable with her reaching all in my plate, but after a while I didn't really pay it any attention.

We finished lunch and headed back to Dana's office to work. I had eaten so much food that for the rest of the day I was getting tired and fighting sleep. Plus, the fact that I had tossed and turned the night before didn't help much either. Noticing I was having a hard time staying awake, Dana gave me a funny look.

"You okay?" she asked.

"Yeah. It's just that I didn't get much sleep last night, and that big lunch didn't help."

"Do you want to call it a day? After all, we did get a lot done."

"You don't mind? I'm about to keel over on your desk if I don't get some sleep."

"No, I'm kinda tired too. We can just finish up tomorrow."

On that note I grabbed my things and left. That was the advantage I had working as a contractor, you could sometimes leave early. The only thing the company was concerned about was you completing your projects on time.

When I got home I was so tired that I just dropped my things at the door and crashed on the couch for most of the night. At around two in the morning I got up, showered, and got in bed. I didn't even think about Jennifer not calling me, I was just that tired.

Tuesday was cool. I went in to work full of energy. I had gotten the kinda sleep that I needed, and I was ready for a full day. Also I only had a few more days before I was supposed to see Jennifer. I walked into my office and right away I began to work. On my way in I noticed that Dana hadn't made it in yet, so I thought I'd get an early start on our project. Soon after I started, my cell phone rang.

"Hello," I answered.

"Hi, baby."

It was Jennifer. Surprised that she called, I stopped reading.

"Hey. How's work?" I asked.

"I'm at home today. I'm not feeling too good so I stayed home."

"Really? What's the matter?" I asked, concerned.

"Oh, I think I have a stomach virus or something. I ate out again last night and whatever it was tore my stomach up."

"Oh yeah? Why don't you cool out on that take-out food for a while? You really need to have a home-cooked meal."

"I know. It's just that I'm on the go so much that I don't have time to cook."

"Well, when I get there this weekend, I'll cook you a nice meal."

"Promise?" she said, slightly moaning in agony.

"Of course I will."

As we continued to talk, there was a knock at my door.

"Hold on, baby," I whispered.

I looked up in the direction of the door. "Come in," I shouted.

The door opened and Dana appeared. "Good morning," she said, full of energy.

"Oh, good morning," I replied.

I held my hand up to signify that I was on the phone, and Dana stopped in her tracks.

"Jennifer, I have to go. I'll call you later and check on you."

"Okay," she said. "Have a nice day."

Dana had turned to walk out the door.

"Hey, come on back," I said before she got there.

She turned back around and walked toward me. "I'm sorry. I didn't mean to interrupt."

"That's cool. What's up?"

"Well, I came to see if you were ready to work."

"Yeah, come on in and have a seat."

"Okay," she said as she sat at my desk.

Dana worked exclusively with me the entire day. At noon, we broke for lunch to separate locations and resumed our work until late that evening. This was pretty much our routine throughout the rest of the week. Dana would always come in early and would stay late if it helped our progress. We attended meetings and conference calls together and even managed to squeeze in a few lunches from time to time. She never got too personal and always stayed professional. Her work was neat and to the point. Mr. Ford would check on us from time to time and give us good reviews for our performance. I must admit, when I first saw Dana I didn't take her seriously. I thought she was just another pretty woman who got by on looks alone. But I was wrong, dead wrong. She was very talented.

CHAPTER 10

It's About to Go Down

By late Friday I was headed for Atlanta to see Jennifer. She was over her virus and was back to working her crazy schedule again. It had been weeks since we'd seen each other, so I was excited.

When I got to Atlanta I stopped by a Publix Super Market and picked up some fresh salmon and wine for dinner. I wanted to surprise Jennifer with one of her favorite meals before she got home. When I got to the apartment I called her and let her know I had made it and that I was preparing dinner. I had everything laid out. I had set the dining room table and had the salmon all seasoned when I heard Jennifer coming through the door. She had this big smile on her face as she dropped her things and ran into my arms. We kissed, I mean we really kissed, for a long time. It felt so good that I was ready to skip dinner and head to the bedroom. Instead I slowly moved my kisses from her lips and worked my way to her neck as we embraced in a tight hug.

She slowly pulled away, as she looked me up and down, still smiling. "Baby, I have missed you so much. I can't believe it's been three weeks since we've seen each other."

"Yeah, you look absolutely gorgeous, girl," I said, looking her over. She reached over and kissed me again until I had to break away and check on the food.

"What's for dinner?" she asked as she followed me into the kitchen.

"Well, I made baked salmon with dill sauce, rice pilaf, and green salad."

"Oooh, that's my favorite. Let me get out of my clothes and shower before we eat, so I can relax."

As she walked into the bedroom, I heard her scream with excitement, "Oooh, Troy, these roses are beautiful."

"You like 'em?" I yelled back as I walked toward the bedroom.

"Yeah, I like 'em. I'm taking these to my office on Monday. Oooh, baby, they are *so* beautiful. I'm really glad you're here," she said, her eyes full of tears as she reached for me.

"I'm glad you like them, baby. You don't know how hard it is to be without you."

"I know," she said with her head buried in my chest.

"Now, hurry up and shower 'cause dinner will be ready soon."

"Okay, let me change," she said, giving me one last kiss before going into the bathroom. While she showered I finished cooking and fixed our plates. Just as I finished putting everything on the table she entered the room.

"Damn, baby, you look great," I said, dumbstruck.

"Thank you," she responded, smiling.

Her glow was magnificent as she walked to the table to eat. She had on this red satin nightgown that stopped right below her knees. Her hair was pulled back in a ponytail, and her face was glowing with excitement.

I got the wine out of the fridge and poured us both a glass.

"Everything is so perfect. How can I top this?" she asked, looking at the way the table and food were prepared.

"Oh, well, I can think of many ways tonight," I replied.

"Okay, I tell you what, since you made dinner, I guess dessert is on me."

I took a moment to look her up and down, thinking about what she had just said. I was just imagining my dessert and how it was sitting at the table wrapped in red. All of a sudden I put my wineglass down and rushed toward her and began to kiss all over her face and neck. I then pulled her to her feet and guided her to the bed. We kept on kissing, both of us breathing hard, both our hearts racing. Before I knew it we were taking clothes off and throwing them everywhere. I got down on my knees and worked my way from her feet up to her mouth, licking every inch of her body like I was a madman. All I could hear was her moan with every stroke my tongue made across her body. I pushed her onto the bed, still sucking and kissing her. The next thing I knew we were making love. I mean we were going at it all rough in the bed. We rolled around so much we both fell to the floor. Still, that didn't stop us. We switched to different positions and I loved every inch of her. Finally I reached my point as I moaned loud and hard. Jennifer dug her fingernails into my back as she reached her climax and screamed with desire.

"Oooh, Troy, God, how I missed you, baby," she said, licking her lips as her body quivered.

"Yeah, baby, I don't think I can let another three weeks go by without being with you," I said as I tried hard to catch my breath.

We lay there on the floor for a few minutes and just held each other until we exhausted all our desire. Slowly I got up and pulled her off the floor and led her to the shower. We washed up and headed to the den to finally eat dinner. I reheated everything, poured us fresh glasses of wine, and we began to eat.

After dinner we just hugged up on the couch and started watching TV. Every once in a while during a commercial Jennifer would squeeze me or give me a kiss on the neck. This went on throughout the night until we both drifted off to sleep.

The next morning we got up and had a nice breakfast before Jennifer had to run by the office for a while.

"Hey, would you like to come to work with me? I have to pick up some files to look over."

"Yeah, that's cool. I haven't had a chance to see it yet."

We got to her building and went up the elevator. The place was really laid. It was glass from the fifth floor on up to the tenth floor. As we rode up I could see downtown Atlanta and all of its big, beautiful buildings. The elevator stopped on the seventh floor. When we got off, there was a big receptionist area that you had to pass before getting to the area where the lawyers worked. We walked down a long hall with dark hardwood floors that led us to the back where Jennifer's office was located.

When we got inside, I was impressed. Jennifer had this huge office that had oak everything in it. There was a sitting area that had leather furniture with an electric fireplace on the right side of the office. Her desk was the width of a queen-size bed, and her computer had a twenty-inch monitor on it. On the left side of the office was this tall bookshelf that was filled with books.

Jennifer walked behind her desk and booted up her computer.

"This won't take long. I just have to print out some papers," she said.

"Oh, take your time. I'm still tripping on how nice your office is."

"Aw, boy, it's okay," she said, shaking her head in disbelief.

"Yeah, right. This is more than okay. I wish I had something like this."

She logged into her system and started printing pages. I stopped counting after about ten and focused on something else.

"Hey, I'm gonna go down the hall and make some copies. You want to come?" she asked.

"No, I'll just sit here and check out the view. Go ahead and handle your business."

She headed down the hallway while I stared out of the window, checking out the huge buildings and watching as cars raced down the expressway. The skies were so clear that I could see a large part of downtown. After I had seen enough, I sat down at Jennifer's desk, leaning back in her chair before realizing her computer was on. I thought, *Yeah, I could play hearts until she gets back.*

I opened up the hearts game and started playing the computer. I played about three games in a row and lost all three. Determined to win, I played one last game. I started out good, but the computer was starting to come back on me. I was only leading by one point and felt that I could end the game with the hand that I was playing. I clicked the mouse to play a card when all of a sudden an e-mail notification popped up on the screen and broke my concentration. *Damn,* I thought, *just when I was feeling this hand, this had to happen.* When I finally got around the e-mail notification and looked at the score I realized that I made a mistake and played the queen of spades and lost the game.

I leaned back in frustration and turned the game off. When the game icon closed, I noticed Jennifer's e-mails were up on the screen. Just as I was about to get up from the chair, I noticed the name Robert Walker with a big happy face next to his name. My heart started racing with nervousness and anger. This was the same mother-fucker from the club, the one all in Jennifer's face. I reached for the mouse and clicked the e-mail open and read it.

> Hey, what's up?
> Have you talked to Rhonda about the game?
> Let me know,
> Rob

"What the fuck is this shit," I said out loud.

I began to search all of Jennifer's e-mails one by one, looking for Robert's name to see how long this shit had been going on. I started scrolling down, finding a few more e-mails from Robert dated days apart.

I began to open and read each of them, still pissed off.

> Hey, what's up? It's your boy Rob.
> Give me a call today.
> Peace!

> Hey, what are you doing for lunch?
> Let me know.
> Peace!

As I continued to read, my anger started to kinda fizzle a little. Each e-mail was kind of general and didn't give me much to bitch about. I was still pissed because it let me know that they still had some type of contact. My first instinct was to run down the hall and cuss Jennifer's ass out and head back to Mobile, but I couldn't base that just on these e-mails alone. As I read all of them I wasn't bothered too much by the first four. It was the last one I read that made me wonder, and it was dated two days before.

> Hey, I really need to talk to you. Call me at my office if you can. It's very important. I just need to get this off my chest. I need you to know this before it's too late and I regret it.
> Rob

I quickly closed the e-mail and felt this huge lump form in my stomach. *Finally,* I thought, *the shit is starting to add up.* I dropped my head in disgust and tried to figure a way to confront this shit head-on. *Is she fucking him?* I thought. I couldn't tell by the e-mail. *I should just walk in there and cuss her ass out. . . . No! Wait,* I thought. I still didn't know what was going on. I needed more to go on. After all, I'd invested too much in this relationship to have someone like Robert fuck my shit up.

I got up from the desk and started pacing the office. Still confused, I plotted more and more. I decided to call my boy Mike. Of all the times I needed him, it was now. I pulled out my cell phone and called only to get his voice mail. *Damn,* I thought, *where is he?* I just left a message.

I continued to pace the room in confusion. I took a real deep breath that relieved the lumps in my stomach. *Let me just cool out until I talk to my boy,* I thought, *I'm so messed up in the head right now that I may just go off.* At that time Jennifer came walking into the office all giddy.

"Hey, you about ready to go?" she asked.

"Sure. Whenever you are," I replied.

She walked over to her computer and logged off. I paid close attention to every move she made while logging off, but for the most part I didn't see anything suspicious.

She gathered her things and we left. In the car I wasn't saying too much, and at the same time I wasn't too quiet either. I didn't want it to appear like something was bothering me so Jennifer would ask a lot of questions. Every now and then I would look over at her and wonder what was going on inside her head. When she would catch me looking I would play it off by rubbing her hand or just giving her a short smile, you know, do things I would normally do.

We drove around town for minutes, much farther away from her apartment.

"Where are we headed?" I asked.

"Oh, I have to stop by the mall and get a few things before we go out."

"Oh," I said, "where are we going tonight?"

"Well, I was going to surprise you, but there's a play that I have been dying to see, so I thought it would be great if we went tonight."

"Oh yeah, a play? What's it called?"

"*What a Woman Wants, What a Man Needs.*"

"Is that right?" I said sarcastically.

"Yeah. I heard it's supposed to be really good," she said with excitement.

I looked over at her with a frown. "So can you tell me what a woman wants?"

"Well, I can't speak for all women, but all I want is you, baby," she said, smiling.

Yeah, whatever, goddammit, I thought. Just hearing her response made me cringe. I felt like it was a crock of shit. Instead of responding out loud, I just leaned over, turned up the radio, and stared out the window.

After a long ride down 85 North we made it to this huge mall called the Mall of Georgia. When we first pulled in the parking lot it looked like a small town or something. When we got inside all you could see were stores everywhere. I mean stores I'd never even heard of were packed with people. Jennifer guided me to the direction of Nordstrom's, a real classy department store that had a lot of nice gear.

When we got inside it looked even bigger than it did on the outside. Everything was neatly shelved and placed on the clothing racks. The salespeople were all polite and eager to assist us. There was even a guy playing the piano in the middle of the store while you shopped.

Jennifer stopped in the women's section and tried on clothes. From there she tried on shoes, then went over to another department and tried on suits. With all of this going on I looked at the time and realized that hours had passed. Still not satisfied, she looked a little while longer before finally buying something. We then headed for the food court. It was lit up like an amusement park or something. There were people lined up around every restaurant there. I stood in line for Chinese food while Jennifer was over in the section with the burgers. After another long wait we got our food and sat down in the dining area and ate our lunch. Again I tried to pick her brain.

"So where are all of your friends you hang out with?" I asked.

"Oh, most of them are probably at home or out, I guess."

"What about calling them and having them meet us at the play? I'd love to meet them."

"Hell no. This is the only time I get to see you. I don't want them around spoiling that. Besides, they're too messy anyway. This is our night tonight," she said.

Yeah, good-ass answer, I thought. *You may look and sound convincing, but you gotta do better than that shit to throw me off.*

We sat there and finished off our lunch before heading back to the apartment.

Later that evening we got dressed and headed to this place called the Fox Theater where the play was being held. The outside was lit up like a Las Vegas casino. The front box office was packed with people waiting to get in. We parked in the theater lot across the street and walked inside. The place was really classy, and you could see black folks lining up to be seated. Once inside we made it to our seats in the first balcony directly in front of the stage. Jennifer was excited as she sat anxiously in her seat while I sat back leaning away from her. My mind stayed on the situation that had occurred in her office. I could remember the e-mails like I wrote them myself.

What's really going on? I wondered over and over in my mind. How could I let myself slip up and let this man manipulate my woman like this? Maybe if I had gotten his number out of her purse that day I would have had a lead on his ass.

Suddenly, my concentration was broken by the sound of the

music signaling the start of the play. Jennifer, still excited, grabbed my hand and held it tight. The lights dimmed, the curtains opened, and the play began.

From the moment the play began it had my complete attention. I watched as the actors came out and started doing their thing. The play was about lies and deceit in a relationship among three people. Throughout the play Robert's face would pop up in my mind. He was trying to fuck up my relationship just like the character in the play. I would look over from time to time to see Jennifer's reactions. Because she was all into it, I couldn't pick up any signs. Instead she would react by gently squeezing my hand or by looking quickly over in my direction to see if I was paying attention to certain scenes.

After the play ended, we made our way through the large crowd and to the car. Jennifer was so full of energy that she talked the whole time.

"So, what did you think about the play? Wasn't it great?"

"Yeah, it was tight. I really enjoyed it," I replied nonchalantly. "So what's next?"

"You know what? Let's just get a movie and a pizza and head home. I just want to spend the rest of the night, just the two of us cuddled up watching a movie."

"Why?" I asked. "Don't you want to head somewhere for drinks?"

"No, I just want us to be together alone."

Again my brain started to send me signals that she was trying her best to stay inside and keep us from being seen. And again I held back my anger.

"Okay, let's go to Blockbuster, get a movie, and call it a night," I said.

Smiling, she leaned over and turned up the music as we drove to the video store. When we got inside, Jennifer walked around to the new releases. I looked for old movies like *Let's Do It Again* and *Uptown Saturday Night*. As I continued, I stumbled on the movie *Love Jones*. *Good,* I thought, *this is the perfect movie for the shit that I'm dealing with*. I grabbed it and walked around trying to find Jennifer. She was in the corner of the new-release section with a movie in her hand.

"Let's get this one," I said.

She turned around and looked down at the movie. "What's that, baby? *Love Jones* . . . What's that about?"

Surprised, I said, "You haven't seen *Love Jones*?"

"Well, no. Is it good?

"Girl, yeah. It's one of the best love movies out there. I've seen it at least four times, and each time I learn something new about the movie."

We walked past the new releases and on to the next aisle. I walked on ahead to find more movies I thought would be interesting. Minutes later, Jennifer walked up behind me, lifting her hand, and showed me the movies she picked out.

"Do you want to see *The Best Man* or *Baby Boy*?" she asked.

"I've seen those movies, too, but if you want to get them we can."

"Well, let's just get yours and one of mine," she suggested.

"Okay. How about *Baby Boy*?"

"That's fine," she replied.

We checked out the movies, got home, and made a little pallet on the floor. I lay on my back with my head propped on a pillow with Jennifer's head on my chest.

The first movie we watched was *Love Jones*. I picked this one because I wanted to get a reaction from her and also make her feel a little bit guilty about all the shit that was going on in her private life. During the movie I would look down and check out her expression or say something to hear her response.

"Damn, that's messed up how she gave it up and didn't even know the brother," I said.

Without looking at me, Jennifer responded, "Well, you see, she tried to talk to her fiancé about their relationship, but all he wanted to do was concentrate on his career. I don't blame her for leaving his ass."

I got kinda hot. "Oh, so you would fuck around like that because your man was trying to give you the world?"

She looked back at me with confusion. "No, that's not the point I'm trying to make, Troy. All I'm saying is that they had two different goals and were heading in two different directions. That's probably why she wanted to break up."

"Well, is that a good enough reason to fuck around on him?"

Jennifer sat up. "She didn't *fuck* around on him. The relationship was over, and she gave him back his ring. What she does from that point on is her business."

Quickly I sat up. "No, I don't buy that at all. Let's say that was us."

"Don't put us in this. First of all, I would talk to you if I were feeling like I needed to move on. I wouldn't just all of a sudden start messin' around. You have to look at the pattern of their situation and what brought them to their breakup point."

"No, let's just say—"

"Troy, I don't play those games. I don't let a movie influence me in any way. I look at the person I'm involved with and judge him by the pattern of our relationship, not by what I see on TV. What we have is reality, not some shit that people put together to make money."

I knew I had her ass cornered. She seemed like she was trying to defend something she was dealing with in her mind. I knew that I had to find out what the hell was going on. With that in mind I reached over and put a finger over her lips to get her to stop talking and to calm down.

"Okay, I get the point. Don't get all feisty tonight. It's cool."

She gave me an evil look and turned her head in frustration. I reached over and put my arm around her and pulled her close as we sat back and watched the rest of the movie in silence. When it ended she got up and headed to the kitchen to get a drink of water.

"You want to watch *Baby Boy* now?" I asked as I grabbed the movie.

She paused for a minute and gave me a strange look before she responded, "Yeah, that's fine, if we don't have to make an issue out of it like the last one."

"All right, I promise, not a word," I said.

We cuddled up and watched the movie in silence. I must admit, though, there were some scenes that almost made me hit her with a few more questions. But, instead, I just let it pass and chilled out the rest of the night.

The next morning I got up kinda early. I had so much on my mind that I tossed and turned until the sun came up. I looked over at Jennifer still sleeping beside me and decided to ease out of bed and cook breakfast while she slept. I tiptoed out of the bedroom and into the den, closing the door behind me. While on my way to the kitchen, I noticed her purse hanging on the arm of the dinette chair. My first thought was to grab it and start looking through everything, but I didn't want her walking in behind me and catching me in the act, so I continued toward the kitchen. I opened the refrigerator door and got out some bacon and eggs and placed them on the counter a few feet from where her purse was hanging. Because it was still early in the morning and so quiet I had to be very careful not to make any unusual noises that would wake her up. I cracked the eggs and began whisking them in a bowl while walking close to her bedroom door making the whisk bang up against the bowl, seeing if this would wake her.

Finally after making my way back toward the kitchen I grabbed her purse. I put it on the floor next to my foot as I stood in front of the stove. I put the bacon in the pan and turned the fire on low so if she walked in nothing would seem odd. Slowly, I bent down and opened the flap of her purse to get inside. I pulled out her wallet and noticed that she had a lot of small pieces of paper at the bottom of her purse that had numbers on them. I grabbed all of the papers and started looking through them, throwing them back in her purse as I finished. After looking at the first ten papers I thought, *These are numbers in Mobile to all of her friends*.

I then began looking through the smaller compartments in her purse but still couldn't find anything with Robert's name on it. Finally, I opened her wallet and started searching through it. I removed the papers she had neatly arranged, and placed them next to my knee as I continued to look. The only thing I came across were bank statements and more numbers like Rhonda's and a few other females but still nothing with Robert's name on it. Suddenly, out of nowhere, there was a loud knock at the front door. *Oh, shit,* I thought. I still had almost everything in her purse on the kitchen floor. I quickly started stuffing things back inside while trying to listen for any sound in the bedroom. I started grabbing the papers near my knee, trying to put them back in the order I got them out of her wallet.

I heard a sound like Jennifer was getting out of bed or something.

With my attention focused on the noise, I started dropping things around me. As I struggled to pick them up I started smelling burned bacon. I looked up and saw a small cloud of smoke coming from the frying pan. I jumped up and turned the gas off and put the pan on the back burner. There was another knock, this one much louder than the first one. Finally I just grabbed all of her shit and stuffed it in her purse. I leaned over to put it on the arm of the chair as the bedroom door swung open. I quickly dropped the purse on the floor by the chair as Jennifer came storming out of her room.

"Troy!" she shouted as she walked to the front door. "Why don't you answer the door? I know you heard it because I could hear it from the back room, and what are you burning up in here?"

I grabbed some eggshells and threw them on the floor. "I was trying to clean up this mess I made and by the time I got up to answer the door you came storming out of the room," I replied nervously.

Jennifer opened the door and politely started talking to some man with a really deep voice. As she did this, I slowly eased over and placed her purse back on the arm of the chair. Feeling relieved I didn't get caught, I walked over to the front door where she was standing.

The guy was some messenger who was dropping off a package or something from Jennifer's job. As she stood there signing papers I went back to the kitchen and continued to cook breakfast. Seconds later Jennifer closed the door and walked toward me.

"What's up with you this morning?" she asked.

"Nothing, why?" I answered.

"That loud noise almost scared me to death, and here you are in the kitchen just standing there like you didn't hear a thing."

"I was trying to clean up these eggs that fell while I was trying to get to the door. Why are you making such a big deal—"

"Okay, okay," she said. "It's no big deal. I'm sorry if I seem cranky this morning. Maybe I need coffee."

She placed her packages on the floor next to the table and headed back into the bedroom to shower. Still shaken by all of this craziness, I got her purse and neatly put her papers back in order before continuing to cook breakfast.

Later that afternoon I packed up and was headed back to Mobile. The ride home didn't seem as long this time. Maybe it was because of all the shit that I had running through my mind that kept my attention elsewhere. When I got home I just unpacked and chilled watching TV. It seemed like all that riding and thinking just wore me out. I didn't even want to really talk to Jennifer. I just called to let her know I made it home and spent the rest of the night on the couch.

CHAPTER 11

Fighting the Urge

That Monday I worked alone for the first part of the day. I was glad, too, because I wasn't in the best of moods considering my weekend. I was a nervous wreck, not knowing if I was coming or going. I quickly pulled out my Bible to read my favorite scripture, Psalm 37, to calm me down. I spent fifteen minutes in deep meditation before reading the entire scripture. Instantly I felt better. Reading this passage made me feel stronger. From that moment, I put my energy into my work and kept my focus until noon. I had lunch with the guys and worked the rest of the day with Dana. By now I had really become good company. Dana apparently had a good weekend, because she was full of energy and talked constantly about shit that really didn't interest me in the least. For hours she talked about California and her last job until she got on the subject of relationships and trust. Right there was where she got my attention.

"So you didn't tell me about your weekend," she said. "What did you do?"

Thinking about the question, I paused for a second or two. "Well, my weekend was all right, you know, nothing much to talk about," I replied.

"What's all right? What did you do?"

"Well, I just went out of town to visit my fiancée," I said.

Her eyebrows went up. "Oh, so you're engaged?" she asked.

"Yeah, I thought you knew that," I said. "Didn't I tell you?"

"No, I don't think you did. I would have remembered something like that. So when is the wedding?"

I paused again. "Well, that's the thing, I really don't know."

"You're engaged and don't know when the wedding is? What's up with that?"

"Well, she moved to another city, and it just kinda put things on hold for a while, that's all. It's really no big deal."

"Oh, so that's why you have the long face. You miss your little ol' baby," she said, laughing.

I cringed at the sound of the word *baby*. For the first time I didn't feel like Jennifer was 100 percent mine anymore. The more Dana questioned me, the more unsure I felt about Jennifer and me. Finally I just stopped answering her altogether. Seeing that I wasn't really into talking, Dana quickly cut the questions short.

"Well, I wish you two the best."

"Yeah thanks," I replied in a dry tone.

"Well, when you do get married I want an invitation."

"Oh, sure, no problem."

From that point we pretty much kept our conversation on work for the rest of the day.

The next morning I didn't feel any better. I tried to call Jennifer throughout the night but kept getting her machine. I even tried to call my boy Mike, but he was still working all those crazy hours and didn't have time to call me back.

I walked into my office looking pretty much like how I was feeling, you know, slightly torn. I just sat at my desk trying to figure out what to do next. Dana was out of the office that morning, so I was able to at least have that time alone to contemplate things. I pulled out my Bible where I had dog-eared Psalm 37 and began reading it again. I sat there in a daze, staring at the clock, watching the second hand move around and around. I was staring so long and hard that it looked like the clock was trembling right before my eyes. I took a deep breath. "Fuck this," I muttered. "Look at me sitting here like a punk worrying over this. Shit, I can hardly sleep, I'm having headaches, even my appetite is being affected by this shit. Enough is enough. It's time to find out what's really going on."

As I reached to pick up the phone, Dana burst into my office with a big smile on her face, holding a plant.

I leaned back into my seat, slightly startled by the fact that she just walked in without knocking.

"Hi," she shouted.

Forcing a smile, I responded, "Hey, what's up?"

"Well, I was out this morning and I thought I'd bring you a plant and a card to cheer you up."

"Uh, thanks, but you didn't have—"

"And I would like to take you to lunch."

I thought for a moment about how I'd said I wasn't going to let my situation control me like this and was about to refuse, but instead I agreed and took her up on her offer.

"Cool, let's do this," I replied.

"Good, I'll drive," she said.

"You're driving too? Wow, this is new."

"Yeah, today is my treat."

We left the office, got into Dana's Land Rover, and rode over to the bay area to the Original Oyster House Restaurant, which was known around town for its delicious seafood. Every dish was prepared from fresh seafood from around the Gulf of Mexico. The restaurant sat on the edge of a fishing pier that overlooked the entire Mobile bay area. It was best known for its fried soft-shell crab sandwich and seafood platters. I was surprised Dana even knew about this restaurant since it was sort of out of the way for her. But without hesitation she drove us right to it. When we got inside there weren't too many people, which was good because I was kinda hungry.

Inside, there was a bar with a TV mounted in the corner so people could watch sporting events or the news as they got their drink on. Dana and I sat in the dining area overlooking the water.

On the walls of the restaurant were pictures of celebrities who had once visited, along with pictures of fishermen who caught huge fish and crabs during the fishing rodeo each year.

Once seated, I grabbed the menus and handed one to Dana.

"Oh no," she said. "I already know what I want." She pushed the menu away.

"Oh, really?" I asked.

"I sure do."

"By the way, how is it that you know about this place?" I asked. "You must live nearby."

"No, I live on the other side of town. I just drove around one Saturday and just happened to stumble on to it. I'm glad I did because the food is great."

"Oh, I know. You don't have to tell me. If we didn't have to go back to work I would have you taste their Long Island iced teas."

"Oh, really, are they good?" she asked.

"Are they good?" I said. "They will knock you clean on your ass if you're not careful."

We laughed as I continued to look at the menu.

"Well . . . uh . . . I'm game if you are," she said.

Still caught up in the menu, I replied nonchalantly, "Game for what?"

"You know, Long Island iced teas."

Surprised, I looked up at her with a grin.

"Well, what do you say? I won't tell if you won't."

"What do you know about drinking?" I asked, chuckling.

"Don't worry about that," she replied, also chuckling. "Are you down for a Long Island iced tea or what?"

At first I wasn't down for it, but she presented it to me like a challenge or something so I couldn't seem weak and turn it down. "Let's do it," I said.

"To answer your question, I know a lot about drinking, especially wine," she said.

"Wine, that's weak. Drink something real like Hennessy."

"Hennessy?" she said. "What's that?"

"That's my drink, Hennessy on the rocks. It's a cognac that's really smooth."

"No, thanks," she said. "I'll stick to wine. But right now I want to try this Long Island iced tea."

The waitress came over and took our order. A few minutes later she came out with two twenty-ounce glasses of Long Island iced tea with straws.

"Well, this is it," I said. "Go ahead with your bad self."

Dana raised her straw to her lips and began to drink. I watched as she took a big sip and put her glass on the table.

"Oooh weee," she said. "This is good. It really tastes like tea with a little kick to it."

"Oh, you haven't felt the kick yet," I said. "Just try to drink it slow, 'cause it'll sneak up on you."

She grabbed her glass and took another sip, and I grabbed my glass and started drinking mine.

We sat there for about five minutes drinking and talking until our food arrived. I had the gumbo, which was excellent, by the way, and Dana had the steamed shrimp platter.

By the time she made it through her fourth shrimp, Dana's eyes got really glassy. I could tell that the alcohol had kicked in. I looked at her glass and it was barely halfway empty.

"Are you okay?" I asked, concerned but trying not to laugh.

"Sure. I'm fine. Why?"

"Oh, I'm just checking 'cause you look a little fried in the eyes."

She started to drink again. This time she took a big sip like she was trying to wash her food down. I had already finished my drink and was eating the last bit of gumbo in my bowl.

"Are you going to get another one?" she asked.

"No. I think that's it for me. Besides, it's the middle of the afternoon. I'll be asleep before two o'clock if I try to drink another one of these."

"I am really buzzing like crazy. You were right. These things are strong as hell."

"Well, let me get you some water so you can dilute the alcohol. Maybe that'll help."

"I hope so, 'cause everything around me is starting to spin."

The waitress brought some water and I had Dana drink it and eat some crackers. She drank so much water she started twisting and turning in her seat like she had bad hemorrhoids or something.

"Damn, what's wrong with you?" I asked.

"I really have to run to the bathroom, but I'm trying to hold it until my head stops spinning."

"Well, you better get up before you wet your pants."

"No, I'll be okay," she said, still twisting and turning in her seat.

I just laughed until finally she couldn't take it anymore.

"Okay. Where are the restrooms?" she asked.

I pointed in the direction of the entrance.

Dana looked over and started frowning. "You mean way over there? I don't know if I can make that."

"Well, you'd better do something and quick," I said, still laughing.

She pushed up from her chair to get out of her seat. I watched as she struggled to walk straight. I looked over at Dana's drink and had the waitress take it away. If not, Dana would sit there and try to finish it just because it was there.

While I waited on Dana, my phone rang. It was Mike.

"Hello," I answered.

"Hey, what's up? I got your message but I wasn't able to call you back."

"Man, I got some shit to tell you about what happened this past weekend."

"What happened, dog?" he asked, concerned.

"Man, do you know Jennifer still keeps in touch with that Robert motherfucker?"

"Robert?" he replied. "Who the hell is Robert?"

"You know, man, the guy I told you about when Jennifer first moved to Atlanta. He was the guy at the club that night."

"So, and what's up with that?"

"Man, I was—" Just as I was about to go into detail Dana came stumbling out of the bathroom on her way back to the table.

"Hey, Mike, let me hit you back later."

"Why, man? What's up?"

"Nothing. I can't talk right now, so I'll hit you up later."

"A'ight, peace."

By the time I hung up the phone Dana was sitting back in her seat.

"So are you okay now?" I asked.

"Whew, I feel a lot better. Sorry I took so long but I was having a rough time in there."

"Are you about ready," I asked, "or do you need some more time?"

"Yeah, I'm ready, but I don't think I'm gonna stay at work today. I am really buzzing over here."

"I told you that drink ain't no joke," I said with a grin.

She looked at the table. "Hey, where's my drink?"

"Oh, I had the waitress take it away. You are officially cut off."

"I just wanted to get one last sip before we left."

"Oh, hell no," I said. "The way you're struggling, one last sip would have really put you on your ass."

We laughed as we got up from the table and walked over to the register. Dana pulled out her credit card, paid the bill, and we headed out the door. I watched as she struggled to walk a straight line, almost slipping to keep her balance. When we got to her truck, she started walking toward the driver side, pulling her keys out of her purse.

"Dana, you'd better think again," I said, standing in front of the truck.

"What? Oh, I'm okay," she said.

"No, you'd better get over here on this side of the truck. I'm not gonna let you ball my ass up in some car crash."

She laughed as she handed me the keys and walked over to the passenger side of the car. We got in and headed back to work. While driving I looked in her CD case and put in some Maxwell. The music was so smooth and mellow that it put Dana to sleep. *And she thought I trusted her to drive,* I thought.

Moments later "This Woman's Work" came on. As Maxwell sang the first verse, I just bobbed my head to the beat. As I was starting to get into the song, I came up to a red light under the overpass of the interstate. I glanced back over at Dana. She was sleeping with her seat back, which made her look like she was sitting in a recliner. Her arms were folded so tight that they pushed her breasts up. *Damn, she has a fine body,* I thought. As I scanned her body, looking between her legs, I frowned with disbelief at how sexy she was. Her legs were spread slightly and her skirt was high on her thighs. I leaned over slightly to see if I could get a closer look, playing it off like I was turning up the volume. Her legs were firm and muscular all over and in between. I tried to look deeper between them, but I couldn't without making it obvious. Instead I sat back and looked at her breasts once again. This time the button on her blouse was undone, showing just a little bit more of her light-colored skin. I turned my head slightly to the side to get a better look. When I did this, a smile came on her face all of a sudden and her eyes were wide the fuck open, looking right at me.

Oh, shit! I thought as I quickly looked forward, trying to play it off.

"Are you okay?" she asked.

"Uh, uh, yeah. We're almost there," I replied, embarrassed and nervous. "So did you enjoy your catnap?"

Nodding and raising her seat, she said, "Yeah, it was cool, but I wasn't asleep."

Shocked, I played it off by laughing. "Shiit, I heard you snoring over there."

"Oh yeah? When was I snoring? Was it when you put in the CD and were listening to 'This Woman's Work' or was it when you looked over at me?"

Embarrassed, I said, "Yeah, uh, I looked over 'cause, uh, I wanted to make sure you had your seat belt on. You know, I was drinking, too, and you never know, right?"

"Yeah, you're right, you never know," she said with a slight smile.

I told her how impressed I was with her truck and the way it handled. Since we were much closer to work, I continued to make up shit until we got back to the office.

"Thanks for lunch," I said. "I really enjoyed your crazy ass."

"Yeah, it was interesting," she replied as she grinned. "I just thought you needed to get out of your office at least once this week."

"Yeah, it did me some good to get out for a minute," I said, nodding.

We both headed back to our own offices. Dana closed her door, probably to get some sleep, while I sat at my desk and worked a little the rest of the day. On my way home I called Mike back to finish our conversation.

"Hey, what's up?" I asked.

"Hey, man. Where you at?" he replied.

"Oh, I'm on my way home from work. Did I catch you at a bad time?"

"No, I just patrolling out west near the mall."

"Yeah, like I was saying earlier about this Robert dude. Man, I was in Jennifer's office last week playing on her computer when an e-mail from him comes popping up."

"Oh yeah?" he said.

"Yeah, so I opened it, read it, and deleted it."

"What? You mean you read it?" he asked, surprised.

"Hell yeah, I read that shit. You think I didn't?"

"See, man, you don't trust her, that's your problem. She's not like you, Troy. You have to give her space to fuck up. Every little thing she does, you question it, and that's not cool."

"Fuck that, man. I just want to know what the hell is going on. I remember when I spied on other girls I dated and found out they weren't shit either."

"See, man, there you go again judging her like those tack heads in your past. Hell, I told you they weren't shit when I first met 'em and you didn't listen."

"Yeah, whatever, man," I replied, shaking my head in disgust.

"So what next?" he asked. "I know you got a plan to do some more underhanded shit."

"You know, Mike, I really don't. I started to go off when I first saw the e-mail, but instead I just chilled. I ain't gon' lie, I was, and still am, pissed off. But instead I just chilled because I'm really trying to make this work. That's another reason I wanted to talk to you."

"Well," he said, sighing, "what I think you should do is just appease her for a while with her work. You always say that she's on the go all the time. Why don't you just help her by telling her things like you're proud of her and keep up the good work or maybe even plan a trip somewhere other than Atlanta? And if she has to take her work with her, then so what? Help her through it. Another thing is to surprise her during the middle of the week and cook dinner or go by her office. Don't send her flowers anymore. I know she is tired of that, 'cause I'm tired of hearing about 'em. Do something different, man."

"Yeah, that sounds like a good idea. Maybe she needs to just get away for a while."

As we continued to talk, I got another call.

"Hold on, Mike. Let me get this call."

"A'ight," he said.

I clicked over. "Hello."

"Hey, baby. What's up?"

I was so surprised to hear Jennifer's voice that a big smile appeared on my face.

"Hey, baby, hold on. Let me hang up from Mike." I clicked back over. "Yo, Mike, that's Jennifer. Let me hit you back."

"Okay, man, but remember what I said. Don't say anything stupid."

"Yeah, okay, dog. Let me go," I replied before I hung up the phone.

"Hello," I said as I clicked over to Jennifer.

"Hey. What's Mike up to?" she asked.

"You know, just work, that's all. What about you?" I asked.

"Well, we just won the case I've been working on all this time, and I'm so happy that I wanted to share it with you, and tell you that I miss you."

"Yeah, I miss you too. So let's celebrate this weekend."

"This weekend?" she said. "Well, I have to go to New York for the next two weeks to work on this new case they have me on. That's another thing I wanted to tell you."

"New York," I said, confused. "Why do you have to go there?"

"Well, a team of us are going there to represent one of the firm's largest clients. Remember when the messenger brought the packages that morning? Well, it contained my plane ticket and briefs for the case."

"Why are they making you go when they have other people to send?"

"Well, they're not making me go. I requested to go."

"You requested it?" I asked sharply.

"Yeah, I'm trying to make partner soon, and I need to do everything I can to show them that I deserve it. Besides, we'll be okay. It's only for a couple of weeks, that's all. By the time you move here I won't have to go through all of this to make partner and we can be together like we always wanted."

"There you go again, basing things on when I get there. What about now? We barely talk. When I do see you we always have to work around your schedule. Now look, there you go, taking the little time we do have away. How do you think that makes me feel?"

"What do you mean?" she asked.

"It's like you don't care about anyone but yourself, or you don't care about me. I do everything I can to work my schedule around yours just so that I can be with you, and you can't do the same for me?"

"Well, stop doing that," she said. "Don't adjust your schedule for me. I told you before that we'll make it no matter what."

"Forget it then. If you have to go, then go. Now I see where I stand with you. I guess I'm the only one who truly cares about this relationship."

"Troy, it's not fair for you to say that," she said. "You know I put just as much effort into this relationship as you, so please let's not go there." Just as I was about to respond she received another call. "Hold on, Troy," she said.

As I waited for her to come back, I was feeling numb with anger, and reality started setting in that Jennifer didn't give a damn about us. Here I was, doing everything I could for her ass, and she didn't appreciate it.

She came back on the line, giggling. "Hey, Troy, I'll call you back tonight, okay?"

"What?" I replied. "Tonight?"

"Yeah, I have to take this call, and I know I'll be a while."

"Yeah, whatever," I said as I hung up the phone.

I really got suspicious about her ass. All that stuff Mike was talking about went in one ear and out the other. It was time for me to find out what the hell was really going on.

When I got to my apartment, I decided to run me a hot bath and just soak while I thought about what to do. In the midst of all this thinking, I decided to take action my way. I knew Mike meant well with all that shit he told me to do, but that didn't apply in my situation. It was time for me to deal with Jennifer's inconsistencies my way. With that in mind, I lay back in the tub trying to get my thoughts together and figure out my next move.

CHAPTER 12

Torn to Pieces

The next day I felt like a totally different person. I had a calmness about myself that almost made me seem like I was high or something. Before walking out the door to work, I noticed that I had a message on my phone. I looked on the caller ID and saw that it was Jennifer, who had called around midnight central time. All she said in the message was that she wanted to tell me good night before she went to sleep.

As I walked to my office I passed Dana, who was holding a bunch of documents, looking good as usual but not fazing me this time.

"Hey, good morning," she said with a pleasant smile.

"Good morning to you too," I replied coldly.

She followed me to my office with a curious look in her eyes. "Hey, are you okay?" she asked with concern.

"Yeah, I'm cool. Why?" I said.

"No, you're hardly cool. What's up?"

"Nothing. Don't worry about it. You probably wouldn't understand anyway," I said.

Dana sat down in the chair near my desk. "If you want to talk, you know I'm here, right?"

"I know, Dana, but normally I don't share my personal life with people I work with."

As she was about to respond, Mr. Ford knocked at the door and walked into my office.

"Hi, you two. I'm glad I found you together. I just stopped by to let you know how good a job you're doing. Also, I wanted to know whether you both were free this weekend."

Dana and I both looked at each other and back at Mr. Ford, nodding that we were free for the weekend.

"Good," he said. "I want you two to join me and a client for dinner this Saturday. We're going to discuss a major contract, and I want you two to head the project."

"Sure," we both responded.

"Okay. Well, I'll see you two at Ruth's Chris Steakhouse this Saturday night at six," he said, smiling as he walked out of my office.

Forgetting what Dana and I were talking about, we looked at each other kind of shocked.

"What was that all about?" Dana asked.

"I don't know, but whatever it is he's excited."

My cell phone rang, and Dana signaled that she was leaving and headed back to her office.

"Hello!"

It was Mike. "Hey, man, what's up?"

"Nothing, just chillin'," I replied.

"I just wanted to see if you up for Mammie's today."

"No. I have to catch up on some things here. I've got a big project coming up. What about Rick?" I asked since neither of us had talked to him that much lately.

"Man, Rick is out of town again. His job has him everywhere, mostly in Dallas though."

"I know he hates that."

"Well, actually he likes it, man. He's supposed to be traveling every weekend for the next month, he says."

"That's a lot of traveling."

Mike quickly changed the subject. "You calm down about this Jennifer stuff?"

"Yeah, I guess it's cool."

"I told you, man, if you do what I said, everything will turn out all right. Just go up there one day during the week and surprise her or something."

"Yeah, you're right. I'll do just that," I said, not giving the idea a second thought.

Not really wanting to continue about Jennifer, I quickly cut the conversation.

"Yo, Mike, let me hit you back later. I got to finish up some things before the end of the day and I haven't even started yet."

"Okay, I'll holla at you later," he said.

I hung up the phone and began to ponder more about how I was going to get to the bottom of what I believed to be lies from Jennifer. I stared at my desk as I went into deep thought, planning everything in my mind. I began to get knots in my stomach as I thought about the worst thing that could happen. Could Jennifer be seeing this Robert guy for real? Why was she always in a hurry to get off the phone with me? *What's going on?* I kept thinking. I pulled out my Bible and held on to it tight as I thought about the words in Psalm 37: *Fret not thyself because of evildoers . . . for they soon will be cut down.* My concentration was broken by a knock at my door. I looked up to see Dana gesturing for me to follow her. I got up and walked toward her.

"I've completed this project and wanted to know if you needed to review it before I turned it over to the client."

"No, it's cool. I don't need to check it," I said. I paused for a moment. *Completed the project,* I thought as I looked at Dana. "Oh, shit, I forgot to give you my part of the project," I said nervously. "It's not complete unless I give you the flowcharts on the process."

Smiling, she looked up at me. "Troy, don't worry about it. I took care of the flowcharts for you. Everything's fine."

"You did?" I asked. "How did I forget that?" I turned my head in embarrassment. "Thank you, Dana. I know you think that was unprofessional of me, but—"

"Troy, don't worry about it. I know you have a lot on your mind. We're a team. We work together, right?"

Looking back at her, I smiled in agreement.

"Well, I'll make it up to you," I said. "Just let me know and I got you."

"Deal," she replied as she walked away to her office with a grin.

I headed back to my desk, feeling like shit. I couldn't believe I was letting my work slip over this bullshit. I knew it was time to take some action and *now*.

For the rest of the day I worked, I mean I worked until ten that night, trying to make up for not completing that project. If Dana hadn't helped me I could have lost thousands for our company. I couldn't let that happen again. Before I knew it I had completed my tasks on every project I had, including those that weren't due for weeks.

Exhausted, I grabbed my things and headed home.

Finally the weekend had arrived. It was Saturday and I was getting dressed for the dinner at Ruth's Chris Steakhouse with Mr. Ford, Dana, and the new clients. My mood and attitude were still the same about Jennifer, despite the fact that we had spoken a few more times before she had flown to New York.

I really didn't want to go to this dinner, because I wasn't in a social mood. But I had to go. After all, I did tell Mr. Ford I would be there.

I put on one of my best suits. It was navy blue and I paired it with a white shirt with a red-and-blue Italian silk tie and cuff links. My black Kenneth Cole shoes were so polished you could see the light from my lamp beaming off them.

As I walked out the door, I sprayed on some of my French cologne and headed to the restaurant.

I looked at my watch when I arrived and realized that I had gotten there forty-five minutes early. Since I had time to kill and because I wasn't really up for the night I drove around the corner to the liquor store and bought a half pint of Hennessy to mellow me out a little.

When I returned to the restaurant, I saw Dana sitting in her truck, which was parked near the back. Since there were so many cars in the lot, I flashed my high beams to get her attention. She looked suspiciously in my direction before noticing it was me and responded by flashing her high beams back and heading in my direction. She parked next to me in the back, facing the street with a good view of the front door of the restaurant. We both rolled down our windows and started talking.

"So, how long have you been here?" I asked.

"Not long. I guess about five minutes or so. You just getting here?" she asked.

"Not really. I was here earlier but I left to make a run real quick."

"A run?" she asked, looking puzzled. "What kinda run?"

"You know, a run to the liquor store. I just needed a little something to kinda mellow me out before we went to this boring dinner listening to corny-ass jokes and shit."

She laughed. "Oh, so you've been to one before?"

"Not just one, several, and they are all the same. A group of white people will be talking about their boring-ass life in the business and shit. But not this time. This time I will be so mellowed out I'll just laugh at anything tonight."

"So what did you get?" she asked.

"Oh, I just got a half pint of Hennessy. You know, just enough to get me inside to order one along with Mr. Ford from the bar. You want a hit?" I asked.

"No way. You know what happened when I drank that Long Island iced tea the other day. No, I think I'll pass on the Hennessy."

"Okay," I said as I unscrewed the top. I took a big swallow. I could feel the strength of the liquor go down my throat as I gulped it. "*Whew, ahhh*," I moaned with a tight face.

"Are you all right?" she asked, giggling.

"Oh yeah. It's just that I'm used to having my liquor cut with some ice."

"Is it good?" she asked curiously.

"Yeah. You want to try a little?"

"Noooo."

"You sure?"

"Well, uh—"

"C'mon, you know you do. Here, take just a sip."

"Okay, just a little," she said as she exited her truck and got in on the passenger side of my car. She grabbed the bottle and tightened her face as she took a quick sip

"Oooh, shit. This stuff burns. *Uuuh*. How can you drink this stuff without Coke or something like that?"

I laughed out loud. "You drank it too fast. You were supposed to take a sip. That was a gulp."

"*Oooh*. I don't want any more of that nasty stuff. I thought it would at least be sweet or something."

"Oh no, this is pure liquor, baby, not a wine cooler."

We both sat there and continued to talk. I took a couple more sips before putting the bottle under the driver's seat of my car. By now I had reached my mellow point and was feeling kinda right. Not drunk, but calm. I looked over at Dana and she was buzzing off the sip she had. I could tell because she had the giggles about everything I was saying. Finally, we saw Mr. Ford pull up in his S-series silver Benz.

"Hey, there's your boss, Mr. Ford," I said, pointing.

Still giggling, Dana looked over in the direction I was pointing and reached for the door handle. I got out of the car and grabbed a mint out of my pocket to freshen my breath.

"Hey, do you need a mint?" I asked.

"Oh yeah. I need two 'cause I know my breath wreaks of alcohol."

We walked toward the door and into the restaurant beside Mr. Ford and his wife, who were standing in the lobby. He greeted us with a smile. "Hi, you two. Good to see you."

"Hi, Mr. Ford," I said as I reached to shake his hand. I turned and greeted Mrs. Ford. "Hi, nice to see you again."

Dana was standing behind me and greeted the two in the same order as me.

We got our reservations confirmed and the hostess led us to our table. When we sat down I was still feeling mellow. I was worried about Dana though. She only had a sip, but she couldn't handle her liquor, and I didn't want her doing anything fucked up to embarrass herself because of me.

We all talked for a few minutes until I saw Mr. Ford stand and gesture for a group of people to come over to us. I began to gather myself and stood to greet them as they approached our table. When I looked up, I was completely shocked. *Damn, they're black,* I thought. Noticing my surprise, one of the gentlemen looked back at me and smiled.

"Hi, I'm Carl, Carl Banks, and this is my brother, Walter," he said.

I reached over and shook both men's hand. "Hi, I'm Troy, Troy Sanders."

Dana stood and extended her hand to greet them. "I'm Dana Suarez. Nice to meet you both."

We all took our seats and got right down to business before ordering anything to eat. Thirty minutes into the meeting I got up and politely went to the bathroom because my kidneys felt like they were about to burst. Before leaving I looked over at Dana, who was sitting there spaced out with a blank look. When she noticed me looking, she quickly turned her head in my direction and started giggling.

Oh, shit, I thought, *she's about to start tripping in front of everyone.* Because I had to piss like crazy, I had to chance her acting a fool rather than my pissing in my pants.

When I returned to the table I saw a waitress leaning over serving drinks to everyone. I looked over at my seat next to Dana and noticed two glasses filled with liquor that looked like Hennessy placed just in front of my chair. I sat down, and Dana quickly pushed one of the drinks over to me.

"What's up?" I asked.

"While you were gone we ordered drinks," she whispered.

"Oh yeah, what's this?" I asked, holding my drink.

"Oh, it's Hennessy on the rocks. Isn't that how you like it?"

"Yeah, but what's in your glass?" I asked.

"Oh, everyone ordered so fast, I didn't know what to get, so I ordered the same."

I politely leaned over to Dana's ear and said, "Hey, I don't think it's a good idea to be drinking this in front of the man. You know you can't hold your liquor that well."

"Boy, would you stop worrying about that? I'm fine."

"Okay. I'm just trying to save you from some embarrassment."

Instead of commenting she just leaned over and joined the group's conversation.

I just chuckled to myself and joined in as well.

Mr. Ford and the Banks brothers opened their briefcases and pulled out papers to discuss the details of what we could offer each other. Dana and I joined in from time to time to cover the technical aspects. We all were so involved in the meeting, and before we knew it an hour and a half had passed by before we all reached an agreement of each other's terms.

I noticed that I had drunk three Hennessys on the rocks and was feeling really good. Dana, on the other hand, had had two drinks and her eyes showed it. When the Banks brothers began to sign the papers, my stomach started growling really loud. Walter Banks looked up as he reached for the last contract.

"Was that your stomach or mine?" he joked.

"No, I think it's mine. I'm starving over here."

"Well, let's eat," Mr. Ford said as he handed everyone a menu.

Dana stood and grabbed her purse.

"You okay?" I politely asked.

"Yeah, I'm fine. I just need to go to the bathroom," she replied with a giggle.

"You know what you want to order for dinner?"

"Uh, not really. I have to look at the menu again when I get back," she said as she began to walk off.

"Okay," I said as I continued to look over the menu.

The waitress came over and began to take our orders for dinner. Since Dana was gone, I waited on her to come back before giving my order. While waiting I ordered Dana some iced tea to try to balance the effects of the alcohol. I could tell she was ripped or close to it.

About five minutes later Dana came back over to the table and sat down. As she got situated, the waitress came back over and placed the iced tea on the table in front of Dana.

"Are you guys ready to order now?" the waitress politely asked.

"Uh, yeah. Dana, do you know what you want or do you need another minute?" I asked.

"No, I'm ready," she replied, looking at the menu. "I would like to have the salmon over rice with a salad. Oh, and could I have a Long Island iced tea with that as well?"

I leaned over to her ear and whispered, "I ordered you this sweet tea that's next to you."

Giggling, she responded, "Man, I don't want no sweet tea. I want a Long Island iced tea, you know, the kind I had at the Original Oyster House."

"Okay, okay," I replied.

Instead of going back and forth with her, I just nodded at the waitress to bring Dana the drink.

"And you, sir?" the waitress asked.

"Yes, I'd like to get the rib eye, medium well, with a loaded baked potato and green beans," I said.

The waitress softly repeated my order as she wrote it down. "Okay, will that be all?" she asked.

"Yeah. I think that'll do it," I said, nodding.

We all started different conversations at the dinner table. I continued to watch Dana closely just to make sure she wasn't making a fool out of herself. When the waitress started bringing out all of our food and drinks, I reached over and passed Dana her utensils, which were over on my side.

"Why, thank you, Troy. You're such a gentleman," she said giddily.

"Yeah, no problem," I said, staring at her.

After we said grace, the first thing Dana reached for was the Long Island iced tea. She took a gulp so big that she looked like she was trying to drink the whole thing in one swallow. All I could do was look around to make sure no one else noticed.

While we ate, no one said a word. The food was just that great. I kept looking over at Dana to make sure she was okay despite all of the alcohol she was drinking. I looked at the Long Island iced tea and noticed that she had drunk nearly all of it. Instantly she started acting different. Her words began to slur, and her giggles turned to chuckles and loud laughter. I think Mr. Ford noticed, because every time he took a bite of food, he would look over at Dana, trying to figure out if something was wrong. It's not like he could've said much, because he had taken down a few drinks himself.

Finally, I just struck up a conversation to throw his attention off Dana and on to what I was saying. This pretty much went on throughout dinner. When everyone finished eating, Mr. Ford suggested that we all have coffee. The clients declined since it was getting kinda late and because we were finished with all of the details of our business meeting. I ordered a cup for me and Dana, who was wide open, talking louder than usual and laughing at almost everything people talked about at the table.

We all stood up as the Banks brothers shook our hands and thanked us for dinner. Dana leaned all over me as she extended her hand to the brothers. I could feel her breasts press up against the back of my arm as she shook each one's hand.

I played it off by sliding to the side just enough for her to move in front of me. As she did she stepped on my shoes but managed to keep her balance.

Mr. Ford walked the clients to the door of the restaurant and talked for a few more minutes before coming back to our table.

I noticed as Mr. Ford walked back toward us that he had a blank look on his face, which concerned me. I knew it had to do with how much Dana had had to drink. Before he sat down Dana got up one last time to use the restroom. Mr. and Mrs. Ford watched her closely. I knew she was wasted, but somehow she managed to walk without stumbling or tripping on something. I started another conversation.

"So, Mr. Ford, how did we do?"

"Oh, I think we did very well. In fact, we did better than I had expected."

"Great," I replied.

"I must say, Troy, I was very proud of you two tonight. You make a great team."

"Thanks. I'm glad that I have someone in my corner like Dana to work with."

"By the way," he asked, "is Dana okay?"

I got worried with that question and really didn't know what to say. It was obvious that she had drunk a shit-load of liquor and couldn't handle it. With that in mind I quickly lied.

"Uh, yeah, she wasn't feeling well earlier today, and it wasn't until after a couple of drinks, she realized she had taken some medicine."

"Oh my. I bet she feels awful," he replied with concern.

"Oh, I'd better go in and check on her," Mrs. Ford said.

"Well, I think she just has an upset stomach now."

"Yeah, I noticed that something was wrong. Poor girl, I admire her dedication to her job."

"Yes, sir. She *is* dedicated. That's why she thought it was important to stay at the meeting, no matter what."

"Well, can you make sure she makes it home safely? I think we are about to leave. Let her know if she's not feeling better by Monday to just stay home and rest."

"Sure, I'll let her know. Well, you guys drive carefully."

Mr. and Mrs. Ford got up from the table and headed out of the door. Minutes later, Dana came back to the table, walking slowly and wobbling from the alcohol.

"Are you okay?" I asked.

"Yeah, but my head is still spinning like crazy."

"Here, drink some coffee."

"Coffee? I don't want coffee. That'll make it worse," she said, frowning.

"No, just trust me on this. I've been drunk plenty of times. I know this will work."

"No, I don't want it. I just want to go home and get into bed."

"Yeah, that's really where you need to be."

She reached over and grabbed her things but stumbled a little.

"Do you think you're driving home like this?" I asked, looking at her like she was crazy.

"I can make it. I only live a few minutes down the street."

"Girl, give me those damn keys. I'll make sure you get home safely."

"I'm okay, Troy. You don't have to do that."

Ignoring her, I grabbed her keys, and we started out of the door to my car.

"I'll take you home tonight, and tomorrow I'll come and get you so that we can pick up your truck."

"I don't want to leave my truck, Troy," she said, staring at it out the window.

"Whatever. Just tell me how to get to your place."

Seeing that I wasn't trying to hear her, Dana just slumped back into her seat and directed me to her apartment. When we made it to her door, I helped walk her upstairs and waited as she unlocked it.

"You want to come inside for a minute?" she asked.

"No, I'd better go. I just wanted to make sure you made it home safely."

"Aw, come on in. I won't bite."

"Shiiit, I ain't hardly worried about that."

"Then come on in, I'll make us a drink."

"A drink? No, I'm cool. I have to drive home."

"C'mon, just one drink, and then you can go."

I went inside, and Dana walked into her kitchen to make us a drink. It was cool. I figured maybe one drink and her ass would pass right on out and then I could go. I sat in her den and admired the way her place was decorated. Her entire den was ivory from the entertainment center to the sofas and coffee table. Her kitchen had a long bar that separated the two spaces. I watched as she poured the liquor in the glasses and walked over to me.

"I made your usual," she said.

"Oh yeah, and what's my usual?"

"You know, boy. Hennessy."

"Hennessy," I responded, surprised. "What are you doing with this?" I asked.

"Well, when I went out to buy some wine one night I got this and bottles of other liquor and never opened them . . . Let's see what's on TV," she said.

"Yeah, sure, that's cool," I said as I sipped my drink.

She grabbed the remote and turned on the TV, searching for something to watch. We both were sitting on the couch. Dana had taken off her shoes and was sitting Indian style in the corner of the couch facing the TV. Her feet were well manicured and beautiful. She let her hair down and let it drape across her shoulders as she continued to flip the channels.

"Oooh, let's watch *Training Day*," she said with excitement.

"Yeah, that's cool," I said as I continued to sip my drink.

"Have you seen it yet?" she asked.

"No. I was gonna rent it, but it's out on cable now."

"Yeah, me either. I always catch the end of it every time it comes on."

"Hey, Dana, I can't stay long. I really need to get going soon, you know."

"Aw, c'mon and hang with me for a little while. I don't know anyone around here outside of my family, and pretty much all I do is sit at home. Please, Troy. C'mon," she pleaded.

Looking at her drunken eyes, I knew it wouldn't be long before she passed out, so I decided to hang for a minute.

"Well, okay, I'll stay for a little while longer."

"Good," she said, smiling.

I finished my drink, and Dana walked into the kitchen and brought the whole bottle into the den. She was still staggering a bit but not as much as before. When she sat down she handed me the bottle. I poured me another drink and continued to watch the movie.

About an hour had passed. It was now about 1:30 AM, and I was really buzzing. Dana still had the same drink in her hand. I could tell she had reached her limit, because she was very quiet and her eyes were half shut but still she was up watching the movie. She had her legs stretched out close to me, and the Hennessy bottle was almost empty.

"Hey, can I use your restroom?" I asked.

She looked up as though she was in a trance. "Yeah, it's down the hall to the right."

As I got up I could feel my buzz intensify. I staggered a little as I started toward the bathroom. When I got inside I noticed Dana's bedroom was across the hall. She had a king-size bed with a canopy around it. The curtains on the bed were slightly open and a stepladder was on the side. There were candles in every corner of her bedroom on long-stemmed candleholders. She had a lamp on her nightstand that was on dim, which set a very romantic mood throughout her bedroom. I was about to walk into her room to get a more detailed view until I heard Dana get up from the couch and start down the hall. I went inside the bathroom and closed the door.

A few minutes later, I walked out heading back toward the den. I took a quick look back at the bedroom and noticed that the door was slightly closed. I saw a silhouette of Dana bending over. Curious, I tiptoed back to her bedroom door. When I leaned in, I saw Dana standing with her back facing me changing out of her clothes. I leaned back a little, trying to remain out of sight as she undressed.

I saw her slowly pull her skirt down and toss it on a nearby chair. Her blouse covered her entire ass. She flung her hair over her shoulder and slowly took off her blouse, tossing it on the chair. What I saw next blew me away. Dana was standing there in a red thong and a red bra. Her body was cut to perfection from top to bottom. Her ass was nice and round without a single blemish. Her thighs and calf muscles were also perfectly shaped. Because her back was facing me I couldn't get a look at her breasts.

She turned around slightly and reached for something. I stepped back to keep from being seen. Rather than try to peek, I quietly turned and started walking back to the den. My manhood was so hard that I quickly sat down to keep it from being noticed. Minutes later, I heard Dana coming down the hallway. She walked back to the couch wearing a sweatshirt with baggy shorts. Before she sat down, she reached over, grabbed the bottle, and poured the last of the Hennessy into my cup.

"Oh no. I think I've had enough. My head is fucking spinning like crazy," I said as I watched her pour.

"Here, I'll pour some in my glass too."

"Nooo. I don't think you need any more either."

"I'm at home, so I can drink."

"Yeah, but I'm not. I still have to drive across town."

"Well, if you want you can stay here tonight."

I looked at her with a frown. "Oh no, you know I can't do that. It wouldn't be cool with me being engaged and all."

"What does that have to do with you staying here to keep you from going to jail or even killing yourself? I don't understand you people from the South. You mistake kindness for being offensive. Plus, you have to take me to pick up my truck in a few hours anyway. It just makes sense."

In a way she did make sense, but after what I'd seen, I knew I wouldn't feel comfortable in her apartment. I couldn't help but think about Jennifer and how she had been acting lately. *Fuck it,* I thought, *it's not like Jennifer gives a fuck about me anyway*. Because I was still upset at Jennifer, I agreed to Dana's offer to stay.

"Okay, I'll stay the night and just crash out on the couch."

"Good. I'll get you some covers and a pillow."

As she got up and walked toward the back, I watched as her ass jiggled in the shorts she was wearing. I instantly got another hard-on.

Dana came back into the den and handed me the covers.

"Are you about to go to bed?" I asked.

"No. I thought we could watch another movie now that you're staying. But if you're tired, then I can just go on to bed."

"No, I'm fine. We can watch another movie if you're up for it."

"Yeah," she replied as she smiled. "Are you sure you're okay?" she asked again.

"Yeah. I'm just messed up off this Hennessy."

"Oooh, me too. How much do you have left in your glass?"

I reached over and grabbed my glass and held it up. "I have a little bit left," I said.

"C'mon, let's drink it all," she said, holding up her drink next to mine.

"Wait. I don't drink like that."

"C'mon, let's do it together. It'll been fun," she said, smiling at me.

"Okay," I said, giving in.

"Okay, ready, one, two, three."

At the same time we drank every drop that was in our glass. The Hennessy was so strong it felt like all of my food was about to come up. "Ahhh," I said as I brought the glass down from my mouth.

"Whew," she yelled, fanning her mouth.

"That was a killer," I said with my face still twisted up from the strong drink.

"Yeah, that was strong. I feel totally ripped, man," she said as she put her glass on the table.

"Okay, now let me get comfortable and watch the movie," she said as she sat with her legs crossed Indian style again in the corner of the couch.

The movie we watched was *Ali*.

"I heard this movie was good," I said.

"Yeah, me too. Will Smith played the hell out of this role," she said.

Minutes into the movie, the television started watching me. All I could remember was hearing the voice of the crowd as they cheered for Ali. Next thing I knew I was out like a light. I moved from sitting in the corner of the couch to being stretched out on it. My head was buried into covers as I held on to the pillows for comfort. While I was still buzzing, my thoughts and dreams began to set on Jennifer and how much I missed her. I could feel a slight smile come over my face as I slept. *I wonder what she is doing right now,* I thought. I remembered the way I rubbed her body in the middle of the night and how she would position herself against me and just really turn me on. I really needed that at the moment. Right away I got a hard-on as I squeezed the pillows tighter and closer to my face. My dreams started to feel so real that I could almost feel myself touch her. The covers that surrounded me felt like her hands all over my body. My pillows felt like her soft breasts against my face. I pressed my face even more into them as I slept.

Damn, it was starting to feel like Jennifer was right next to me. The covers felt as soft and silky as her long hair as I continued to rub all the way down to the end.

Wait a minute! Long, silky hair? Jennifer doesn't have long, silky hair, I thought.

I quickly opened my eyes and noticed that I wasn't lying on pillows or covers at all. I was lying on the couch with Dana in my arms pressed up against me with a look of passion in her eyes. With our faces a few inches apart, I could hear the deep breaths she made as she rubbed her hand on my chest. My hard-on became intense as I felt her body pressed against mine.

"Oh, Troy, this feels so good," she moaned in a soft breath.

I reached over and completely grabbed around her soft ass. I glanced down at her body and noticed that the only thing she had on was her bra and thong set. My mind was in a dilemma. Part of me wanted to turn into the dog I used to be and hit that ass good, but the other part wanted me to get up and take my ass home. I thought momentarily as my hard-on started throbbing.

"Fuck it," I said as I pulled her closer and began kissing her on her neck with heated passion.

"Yeah, let me give you what you want, *papi*," she said while gently stroking my hard-on.

Hearing this, I felt my body starting to tingle like crazy. I was ready to give her the fuck of her life. We adjusted our bodies to get more comfortable. As I reached down to unzip my pants my knee hit the remote control, turning the TV on with a loud roar that broke the mood and snapped me back into reality. I rose up from the couch and mentally checked myself. *Troy, what the fuck are you doing?* I thought. The tingling I was feeling turned into an intense nervousness. I felt my way down by my knee, trying to grab the remote to turn down the volume, but I was struggling with it. Finally Dana sat up and grabbed the remote, turning the TV off.

"Now, where were we?" she said softly.

Feeling guilty as hell, I sat back in the corner of the sofa and looked over at her sitting there staring at me. I was still buzzing from the alcohol, but my senses were a lot clearer.

"What's the matter?" she asked.

I just sat there in silence as she began to move closer to me with her eyes focused on mine. Seeing this, I stood and looked down at her.

"Look, Dana, I'm sorry but I can't do this," I said.

"What's the matter? C'mon, let's finish what we started," she said, reaching for my hand.

"No, I don't think that would be cool, Dana. I mean, I want to and all but I just can't," I said as I moved out of her reach.

She moved closer to me, rubbing my hard-on. "Are you sure you don't want to? 'Cause this is saying something else."

I reached over and gently pushed her hand away. "Hey, like I said, I can't do this. I just can't go out like this. You don't understand what I stand to lose here."

"Stand to lose? Troy, we're both adults here. No one will know but the two of us. Hell, no one even knows you're here, so what are you gonna lose?" She stood and put her arms around me and began to whisper in my ear. "Troy, put your hand between my legs and feel how wet I am. I want you inside me right now."

I stood there listening to all she was saying, trying to fight the urge to screw her brains out, but I just backed away slowly, still eyeing that fine-ass body of hers. Not saying a word, I hurried toward the bathroom and closed the door behind me.

I turned on the water and ran my hands through it and across my face as I stared into the mirror contemplating what I was going to do. I was still hard as a brick and horny as hell, but I couldn't do Jennifer like that.

I was trying for the first time to be faithful to my woman and look at what was distracting me. Here I had this fine-ass woman in the next room ready to do anything I wanted, and I was trying to figure out if my girl truly loved me. Shit, what should I do? I took a deep breath, still thinking long and hard. Flashes of me all over Dana along with flashes of Jennifer appeared in my mind.

Fuck it, I thought. I walked over to the toilet, pulled out my hard-on, and began stroking it with my hand. I stroked and stroked for about five minutes until I came. I came so hard that my heart was beating fast and I was out of breath like I had just run a marathon. I walked back and leaned over the sink as I tried to catch my breath. Normally I don't go out like that, but I figured this was the only way to keep me from cheating on my girl. I grabbed some tissue from the box next to the towels, wiped myself clean, and headed out of the bathroom door with a changed mind.

When I walked back to the den, Dana was sitting on the couch under the dim lights still looking as good as ever with her legs open. But instead of admiring all that, I just walked past her to the table and grabbed my keys.

"So what's up?" she asked as she stood.

"What do you mean?" I replied as I stopped in my tracks.

"You know what I mean. Are we going to finish what we started?"

Since I had just jacked off in the bathroom I was full of confidence now 'cause the thrill was gone.

"Naw, baby, I told you I can't go out like that. I want to but I can't, so I think the best thing for me to do is leave."

"Leave? How can you just leave like that? Well, what about my truck?" she asked.

"Look, let me just go, all right? Here, I'll give you twenty dollars for a cab to take you in the morning."

"What! Money for a cab? You must be out of your damn mind. You know what, just take me to my truck," she said as she stormed toward her bedroom.

I stood by the door in silence and waited on her to get dressed. Minutes later she came out wearing some tight-ass jeans and a T-shirt with anger in her eyes. "I'm ready," she said as she snatched her purse off the coffee table and headed toward the door.

From the time we got in the car until we arrived at the restaurant, neither of us said a word. I tried to strike up a conversation, but Dana just ignored me and stared out the window with her head slightly tilted in disgust. When we got to where she was parked, she jumped out without saying anything and got in her truck.

I waited for a while, sitting in my car looking at my expression of guilt in the mirror. *Why should I feel guilty?* I thought. *Hell, I didn't do anything wrong. Even though I wanted to sex Dana I still didn't.* I guess it was the fact that I wanted to that fucked with my mind and made me feel like I cheated on Jennifer.

When I got to my apartment I checked my answering machine and found that there were no messages from Jennifer. My guilt was amplified and turned into nervousness. I was starting to feel confused and sensitive about things. Or was the alcohol making me feel this way? I still couldn't get over those e-mails that Robert had sent Jennifer. I was really confused. I picked up the phone wanting to call Jennifer just to reassure myself that she was at the hotel in New York alone in her bed instead of out there in the streets somewhere in the city. With the phone in my hand I climbed into bed trying to decide on what to do. Before I knew it, I was fast asleep.

I must have slept for about six or seven hours before the phone rang, waking me up. I was startled because it was in bed with me next to my ear.

"Hello," I answered, sounding exhausted.

"Hey, baby. How are you?"

"Hey. How is your trip coming?" I asked.

"It's okay. I'm just so busy. I haven't had time to do much of anything but work."

"Well, that's what you went out there to do, right?"

"Yeah, but I was hoping I could see a little of the city at least."

"Well, maybe you'll get a chance to get out before you leave."

"Well, I'm supposed to go to the baseball game to see the Yankees play tomorrow."

"That's good. At least you'll have a chance to do that if not anything else."

"I guess, but right now I'm just so tired. I have to go to the law library and do research, and after that I have to run around and collect documents. I just want to stay in bed. I wish I was back in Atlanta right now."

"Oh yeah, why is that?" I asked, stunned at her statement.

"I don't know. I guess it's the idea of being home or something."

"Yeah, I guess," I replied in a dry tone, still trying to figure out what she meant by her statement.

"Well, let me go. I just wanted to call and say good morning to you."

"Yeah, okay," I said dryly.

"Bye, baby," she said as she hung up.

After we got off the phone my emotions ran wild once again. I still felt like something wasn't right with us. Jennifer wished she were in Atlanta but not in Mobile visiting me. That to me was fucked up, you know, like she didn't want to be with me but with someone else in Atlanta. *Yeah, whatever*, I thought as I got out of bed.

As the day passed I just pretty much stayed at home doing nothing and often thinking about what had happened earlier that morning with Dana and how I was going to handle working with her. She seemed pretty ticked off about what had happened, or should I say what hadn't happened? Well, whatever the outcome, I would just take it like a man and deal with it.

CHAPTER 13

Who's Loving You?

The next day after sleeping for several more hours, I went over to my parents' house for dinner. Rick came over since he was back in town. My parents, especially my dad, loved Rick. I guess it was because he and Rick's father grew up together. We all sat out on the patio laughing and joking. My dad would often tease Rick about settling down just to hear all Rick's stories about the women he was playing around on.

"So, Rick, when should I buy me a new suit for your wedding?" my dad said with a goofy smile on his face.

"Oh no, sir. I think you'd better save your money on that one."

"Why not, man?" he asked, laughing.

"I just don't see myself doing that for a while."

"Well, have you got one in mind?"

"Not really. It's takes too many women to complete me. I haven't met one who is everything I need."

"How would you know, man? You keep playing around on them all. Don't you ever get tired of lying and carrying on?" my dad asked.

"Nooo, I don't have to lie to them. I just tell it like it is from the jump. Then it's up to them to stick around."

"Boy, you just like your daddy. He did the same thing until he met your mother and she got him straight."

"Yes, sir. You're right about that. But I don't even have marriage on my mind right now."

"All right, well, when you settle down let me know, 'cause I want to meet the woman who hooks you."

"Yes, sir," Rick replied, laughing and nodding his head in agreement.

Dad went inside to watch the baseball game. Rick and I stayed outside and continued to talk.

"So, how was your trip, man? Anything interesting happen?" I asked.

"Man, it was off the chain. I met this honey from Dallas who's bad. She has a big-ass house on the outskirts of Dallas with a swimming pool and everything. We hung out all night and went back to her place and sat by the pool and watched the skylight, all cuddled up. Man, it was tight."

"Did you hit it?" I asked, curious.

"No, but I tried like a motherfucker. I wanted it so bad I started to go down and eat it."

"What? Man, you tripping."

"No, man, this honey is fine. She is chocolate with a tight body. She's supposed to come visit me when she gets back from a business trip to Europe."

"Damn, she got it like that?" I asked, surprised.

"Yeah, man, just like that, with no kids and no drama in her life."

"Well, I heard that, my brother."

"So what's up with you and Jennifer?" Rick asked.

"The same. She's out of town right now for a couple of weeks."

"Oh yeah? Cool. Now we can hang out and go catch some freaks at these parties I know coming up."

"Hell no, man. I told you I ain't trying to go out like that."

"That's okay. When your nuts start to boil over, you'll come around."

"Yeah, whatever, man," I said, laughing.

My mother came out and called us in for some dessert. Her thing was peach cobbler, and it was delicious. She made it with fresh peaches that were really sweet, and when it baked in the oven the aroma filled the entire house. When we got inside, my dad and cousins were all around the TV watching the game.

"Hey, Mr. Sanders, who's playing?" Rick asked.

"Oh, the San Francisco Giants are playing the Los Angeles Dodgers."

"Cool. Let me get some cobbler and I'll join you guys."

"You better hurry. The game is getting good."

Rick and I got some cobbler and ice cream. He went back into the den and watched the game while I sat in the kitchen with my mother. As I ate my dessert at the table I could feel my mother watching me while she stood near the oven. When I glanced up, she was looking right in my eyes and smiling.

"So how are things with you, baby?" she asked.

"Oh, things are okay, I guess, you know."

"You guess," she replied. "How are things with Jennifer?"

I looked down once again, trying to gather my thoughts. When the guys asked that question I could immediately give them an answer so shallow that it pretty much satisfied them. But, with my mother, I couldn't do it as easily. Instead of lying, I just told the truth.

"I don't know, Mama. I just feel like I'm lost mentally."

"What do you mean?" she asked.

"Well, it seems like since Jennifer left, my life has been torn apart. All I do is think about her and what she's doing, and it's driving me crazy. I can't sleep sometimes, I hardly eat, I don't even feel like the same person inside. When I try to talk to her about it she blows me off like it's no big deal. I just can't take it anymore. I feel left out of her life."

My mother walked over to where I was sitting and sat down close to me.

"Look, Troy, you must think about yourself. You two have been together a long time and during that time has she ever given you any reason to doubt her?"

"Well, no, Mama, but I feel like she's giving me reason to doubt her now."

"And how is that?" she asked.

"She doesn't have time for me anymore."

"Troy, give her a chance. She's trying to accomplish her goals. If you set some goals for yourself, maybe you wouldn't just sit around and think about all the things she could be doing. Remember an idle

THE JUMP OFF 161

mind is the devil's workshop. Go out and set goals for yourself, baby. I think things between you and Jennifer are just fine."

The guys in the den started yelling and screaming. My dad came running into the kitchen with a big smile on his face.

"Hey! Barry Bonds just hit a grand slam to put the Giants ahead. Troy, you missed it!"

My dad went back into the den and sat down still excited and talking shit to my cousins, who were cheering for Los Angeles. I got up and kissed my mama on the cheek, thanked her for her advice, and headed for the den. I sat there and watched the rest of the game in silence as the guys continued to yell at the TV.

I started really focusing on what my mama was saying, and she was right. I didn't have any goals. All I did was sit at home waiting on Jennifer to call me.

What could I do to keep myself busy throughout the day? Hell, I'd always wanted to get into martial arts or something. Or maybe I could just get into a Big Brother program and help the kids. Yeah, something like that. I began to get excited. I had a feeling this would really help me take my mind off my negative thoughts about Jennifer and me while getting my sanity back.

Later that night I got home and looked through the phone book for different organizations that might be looking for men to be Big Brothers. I came across three places to call and wrote the numbers in my planner for the next day. After doing this I drifted off to sleep for about an hour before being awakened by the phone. Still delirious I leaned over and grabbed the phone.

"Hello," I answered in a tired tone.

"Hey. Are you sleeping?"

It was Jennifer. I was shocked to hear from her, because it was rare for her to call this late. She would normally wait until the next day or something.

"No, uh, I'm up. What's up?"

"Well, I think I'll be home Saturday night, and I was hoping you could come up. Baby, I miss you so much, and I need to see you."

My heart sank when she said that. She sounded like the old Jennifer, the one I fell in love with. A slight smile came on my face.

"Yeah, baby, I'll be there bright and early. What time is it now?"

"Oh, it's twelve-thirty your time. Sorry I called so late, but I had to tell you that I miss you."

"No, you know you can call me anytime. And I miss you too."

"Well, I'll call you tomorrow. I'm tired and I have to get up at six in the morning. I just needed to tell you that. Have a good night."

"Okay, baby, you too."

I rolled over with a smile, grabbed my pillow, and fell asleep.

The next morning I was in a really good mood. I got up early and bought the people in the office some Krispy Kreme doughnuts. When I walked into the break room they all saw the doughnuts and gathered around, waiting to dig. I put the boxes on the table and headed toward my office. I looked over at Dana's door, and it was closed. I walked into my office, closing my door behind me.

For most of the morning we had no contact with each other. Even though we were working on the same projects we didn't necessarily have to interact. I wanted to go over and say something, but I didn't know what to expect. As the hours went by I couldn't stand it. I picked up the phone and called.

"This is Dana," she answered firmly.

"Hi, it's me, Troy," I said.

"Uh, yeah, what can I do for you, Troy?"

"Well, I just wanted to know if I could come by your office and talk."

"Sure, that's up to you," she replied.

"Well, are you cool with that?"

"Sure, why not?" she said.

"Okay, I'm on my way."

I hung up the phone, took a deep breath, and walked over to her office. The door was slightly open this time so I just walked on in. She was standing with her back toward me looking out the window. Instead of wearing something sexy, she had on a pair of khaki pants with a white shirt that draped over her waist. Her hair was in a pony-tail that went down her back. Hearing me come in, she slowly turned and sat down at her desk, gazing directly at me with a blank look on her face. I sat down in the chair in front of her desk and stared right back at her with the same expression.

"Hey." I leaned over on her desk close to her. She looked up at me with her lips pressed together, trying to hide her emotions.

"Let's talk," I said.

She nodded.

I leaned back in the chair and began talking. "Well, I want to start out by saying I'm sorry. I guess the other night was hard for both of us. I, uh, think we let the alcohol get the best of our situation and we kinda acted without thinking. So, uh, I think we should—"

She dropped her head for a moment, then looked up at me again. "Troy, listen. First of all I need to apologize for the way I acted. I apologize for putting you in an awkward situation. When you left, I felt bad about everything. I guess us doing lunch and being together at work all the time affected my feelings in a way that it shouldn't have."

"What do you mean?"

"I don't know. I guess being new in town and lonely I just needed someone that night, and I reached out to you."

Not knowing what to say, I just shifted my eyes downward as she continued.

"Look, Troy, I just want us to be cool again and forget about the other night, but if you feel uncomfortable around me, then I understand and I can ask for a transfer to another project."

I quickly looked back up at her. "Dana, c'mon, it's not *that* serious. Nothing happened. It was just as much my fault as it was yours."

"You don't have to explain, Troy. We both know that it was a mistake the other night. So if we could just move on and forget about it, it would just make things a lot better."

I looked at her with surprise because I thought I was supposed to do the talking, but she basically said what I was feeling.

I got up and walked over to her and gave her a hug. "Dana, we're cool. I'm glad that we got this straight."

"Yeah, me too, and I hope we stay that way. I feel better now."

I smiled, nodding as I headed out the door. I must admit I felt better too. I really hadn't known what to expect when I walked in. I thought we would be fussing and fighting or something. But everything was cool. When lunchtime came, Dana called me like before. "Hey, you want to grab some lunch?" she asked, sounding like her old self.

"Yeah, that's cool," I replied.

"Okay, but let's eat light today," she said.

"What's light?" I asked.

"You know, burger or sandwich."

"A burger? That's not light."

"Well, it's lighter than usual," she said, giggling.

"All right, let's go."

I was glad we were back to our old selves again. I thought we really were true friends, even though we'd only known each other a few months. I guess we kinda grew closer over the weekend with our little episode and the fact that we were able to squash it peacefully.

During lunch we laughed like old times. I could tell that Dana felt really comfortable around me again too. We didn't bring up anything about that weekend. Instead we just ate lunch and laughed at each other's silly jokes.

When I got home later that evening I did my usual and just sat on the couch sipping my cognac. I grabbed my day planner and started organizing my week and weekend. In looking at the rest of the week I noticed that I was caught up with my work for the most part and had a few days to spare. Instantly I thought about what Mike had said about surprising Jennifer and having a really nice romantic time with her. In order for me to get my girl back I had to put forth an effort.

I got up and logged on to the computer and did a search for elegant places in Atlanta to eat and hang out in. The computer brought up about twenty different spots. I printed out the list and placed it in my planner to look over in detail the next day at work. I got up from my desk and headed into the den to watch some more TV.

I called Jennifer, who was in her hotel room working, just to say good night. She was so tired that I could hear it in her voice as she fought sleep. Instead of trying to keep her up all night in conversation, I just let her know how much I loved her and we got off the phone.

CHAPTER 14

Making Plans

The next day I was feeling pretty good about the morning. I slept well, I had a few days to spend with my girl, whom I hadn't seen in nearly two weeks, and I had my friend Dana back. I was really feeling great.

Dana came in a little after me looking like her old self. She had this real tight black business suit on that hugged her body with her hair and face made up. The guys in the office just stared at her with their tongues hanging out as she walked by.

"Good morning, Troy," she said in a cheerful tone.

"Oh, what's up, Dana?" I said.

"Nothing much, as usual," she said as she walked into her office.

I smiled as we passed each other in the hallway before going into the break room for some water. I got my mail and headed back into my office. I called the secretary and asked her to schedule me off starting Wednesday. I then picked up the phone and called Mike.

"Yo, yo, what's up?" I said after he answered the phone.

"Hey, T, what's going on, man? You sound all fired up this morning."

"Yeah, I been through some shit these past weeks, man, but I think I got my shit together now."

"Cool. Are we gonna try to get together for lunch today?"

"Yeah, I was trying to see if you and Rick were down for some Mammie's today."

"Yeah, it's cool with me. I know Rick is down."

"Okay, I'll meet y'all there around noon."

"Cool."

I got off the phone and began planning the weekend for Jennifer and me. I was gonna get to Atlanta on Thursday evening and clean up her apartment, making it fresh for her when she got home. Since she wasn't getting home until late Friday night I wanted her to come home to red roses everywhere and a nice hot bubble bath with candlelight and wine. Then while she was lying there, I was going to wash her entire body, all between her toes and all down her back and arms, then leave her alone to soak and wind down from her trip. When she was ready to get out, I would dry her off and dress her in a nice black sheer gown with a matching robe. I would then guide her to the bed and gently lie with her, making sweet, passionate love until we both passed out with exhaustion.

The next day I would serve her breakfast in bed with a carnation and take her to the Mall of Georgia and let her shop till she dropped and then end the night with a nice dinner at McKendrick's Steak-house. I was getting so excited that I couldn't sit still at work. I got up and walked over to Dana's office where she was sitting at her desk doing a crossword puzzle.

I knocked and entered her office. "Hey."

She looked up at me as I walked in. "What's up?" she replied as she closed her puzzle book.

"Hey, what are you in here doing? You know your ass is supposed to be working," I said, laughing.

"Aw, I finished that last night at home. What about you, what are you up to?"

"Shit, about the same. I'm taking the rest of this week off."

"Oh yeah, what are your plans?" she asked.

Since she and I had come close to having sex, I thought the question was a bit awkward at first, but she had this look on her face like it was sincere.

"Oh, I'm going to Atlanta for the rest of the week."

She smiled. "Oh, that's good. I think you need that."

"Yeah, me too. I think I need the time."

"So what are you guys' plans?" she asked. "'Cause if you need some tips, I can hook you up," she said, smiling.

"Oh no, I'm straight with that. I kinda just want to get out of the office for a while."

"Yeah, I think I'm taking some time off next week to go home for a few days myself."

"Oh yeah? Well, good," I said, trying to show the same emotion about her vacation as she did mine. "Well, what are you gonna do down in Cali?"

"Well, my cousin is getting married and I'm in the wedding."

"Oh, okay."

"Yeah, they've been living together for two years now, so I think it's about time they got married."

"Well, it should be fun going home since you haven't been in a while."

"Yeah, I guess."

"Yeah, you'll have fun," I said, smiling with reassurance. "Well, let me go. I just wanted to come by and holla at you for a minute."

"Okay," she replied as she got back to her puzzle.

I turned and headed toward the door.

"Hey, what are you doing for lunch today?" she shouted as I made it to the door.

I stopped and turned in her direction. "Well, I'm supposed to grab some lunch with the fellas today at Mammie's."

Hearing this, she looked away. "Oh, okay. Well, I think I may just head over to the bookstore or something."

"Well, uh, okay, I'll see you later on today then."

Still looking away, she nodded. I think she was waiting on me to ask her to join us, but instead I turned and walked out of her office. I wanted to invite her, but I kinda just wanted the fellas to hang out and do the guy thing.

A couple of hours had passed and it was time for me to meet the guys. I grabbed my keys and headed out the door for Mammie's. Dana had already left, because her truck was gone. Still, I kinda felt bad for not inviting her, but fuck it. It's not like she was my lady or anything. We just worked together, and I had to keep our friendship strictly business and not get her all into my friends and shit.

I pulled up at Mammie's around the same time Rick did. He walked up to my car as I parked.

"What's up, man?" he said as I got out of the car.

"What's up?" I replied.

We walked inside and saw Mike sitting in the back corner of the restaurant. It was still packed as usual, and as always you could smell the good food everywhere. We made our way to the back and sat down at the table where we greeted Mike.

"Damn, it's about time you two change your schedule to have lunch with a brother," Mike said, laughing.

"Yeah," I said. "I've been trying, but I've been caught up in so much work that I couldn't get out."

"For real," Rick said. "They had my ass flying all over the place. Man, I hated that shit till I started getting out and meeting honeys. Speaking of honeys," he continued, "man, I got a fine one now."

We laughed.

"Oh yeah?" I replied curiously.

"Yeah, man, I've been sleeping with this white girl we just hired at work," Rick said.

"Oh yeah, you got a white honey?" Mike said as he leaned in closer to listen.

"Hell yeah. You know me. I don't discriminate. I hollered at her for about a month, you know, laughing and joking with her, and the next thing I knew we hooked up and started kicking it."

Mike looked over at me. "I bet she's a scrub-looking honey. She's got to be to give this fool some ass."

"No, man," Rick replied. "This honey is tight, I mean all over. You know, strong ass, strong titties, big firm-looking calves. Man, she looks like a *Playboy* centerfold."

"What about the face, man?" Mike asked.

"I'm telling you, man. She has that black hair with a cute mole on her cheek. I'm telling you, she's fine," Rick said, all excited.

"Look at him, man. Watch, next month he'll be complaining about the chick," I said.

"Noooo, I may wait a little while longer on this one, my brother."

"Whaaaat? That's not like you, man. Normally you'll hit one or two times and let it go," Mike said, surprised at Rick's comment.

"What do you mean you may wait awhile?" I asked. "Damn, are you fucking the honey or making love to her ass?"

Mike burst out laughing. I could tell Rick didn't care much for my comment by his expression.

"Aw, fuck you, man. At least I'm getting some new pussy. Your scary ass is afraid to look at other honeys without feeling guilty."

"Scared?" I replied. "What do I have to be scared of? I ain't like you, Rick. I don't stick my dick in any woman with a big ass."

"Quit lying, man. Before you met Jennifer, you used to be out more than me, so don't give me that bullshit," he said as he slapped hands with Mike.

"He does have a point," Mike said, looking at me.

"You right, it was before I met Jennifer. You're still on that what-I-used-to-do shit."

"So what's the difference, man? You did the same thing I'm doing, so why you on me 'bout mine?"

"Man, would you two shut the hell up? You two always get into it about some dumb shit. Go on, Rick, I want to hear about this white chick," Mike said.

Rick looked over at me and took a deep breath before continuing. "So you gonna let me finish my story?" he said, looking at me with a grin.

"Yeah, go ahead, man," I said, shaking my head.

"Anyway, we started talking on the phone at work for a few weeks until one Friday I invited her over to my apartment for dinner. Man, when she walked through the door, I almost lost it. She had on these black capri pants with a white shirt with her hair all neatly hanging over her shoulders. When she came in, she reached over and gave me a hug so tight that my dick pressed up between her legs.

"Then we drank wine and ate dinner before sitting on the couch. We kissed a little while longer before I got up and made a pallet on the floor to make it more comfortable for us, but before I sat down, I went into the bathroom and took off my drawers and put on a condom."

"What?" Mike said, laughing. "You mean you walked out there with nothing on but a condom? Man, what you put a condom on in the bathroom for?"

Rick shook his head in disbelief. "See, man, you been out of the game too long. I put my pants back on. I just didn't have on any drawers under them. I just had a condom on. I did that for when we started kissing and rubbing all over each other. That's when the honey gets hot and lets you pull her clothes off. I ain't got time to run in the bathroom, put on a condom, and get back in the mood. I prepare in advance."

I was laughing loudly. It was like Rick had a science to this technique. Mike just shook his head in disbelief while laughing along with me.

"So when I came out of the bathroom she had her shoes off and was lying down facing me. I lay down next to her, and we talked another ten minutes before I made my move and we started kissing again. Man, she can kiss. She was moaning while sucking my lips and sticking her tongue all in my ear and shit. Then she started rubbing my arms and chest until she made her way between my legs. When she felt how hard I was, she started moaning even more. I started taking off her shirt and bra while she took off her pants. Before I knew it, we were both butt-ass naked. She rolled over and tossed her clothes on the couch and lay back down. Man, she had a body better than most sistas I've been with. I don't know what came over me, man. I jumped on her and eased myself inside. She cocked her legs up and clamped her heels on my back, and we started grinding."

"Damn, man," I said as he continued.

"She got in the doggy style, the missionary, and even cocked her legs behind her head. I mean we started on the floor and ended up in the bed until the next morning. We both woke up staring right at each other, smiling. She then looked down and saw that morning wood and started giving me head. Man, she sucked and licked all over my shit. After about fifteen minutes I came all over the place and she kept on going."

"Damn," Mike said. "You make me want to go home and put something on Gail."

"I think you've done enough damage to her. That's why she's six months pregnant now," I said.

We all laughed.

"That's seven months, man," Mike said. "So, Rick, did you go down on her?"

"Uh, what! Hell no. Man, you know me better than that."

Mike looked at me and we both laughed because we knew he was lying. "You a damn lie, man, I can see it on your face," Mike said.

"C'mon, man. You know I didn't go down on that damn girl."

"You did something you're not telling us about. That's why you can't look us in the eye," I said, still laughing.

Rick just shook his head and reached for the menu to ignore us. Mike and I grabbed our menus and we all ordered.

I went back to work full as always after a lunch at Mammie's. The door to Dana's office was open as she sat at her desk looking busy. I walked by and spoke.

"Hey, how was your lunch?" I asked.

"Oh, it was cool, I just went to the park and read my book. How was yours?" she asked.

"It was okay. Me and the guys just got together, that's all. Well, I'll let you get back to work."

"Okay," she replied as she continued with what she was doing.

I went to my office and worked the rest of the afternoon. At the end of the day, Dana stopped by before she left.

"Hey, have a good time, and I'll see you Monday."

"Okay, I said.

I felt good that I would be away from Dana for a while. I thought time apart would give us a chance to reassess our friendship and get any doubts out of our minds. Even though I would only be gone for a short while, a part of me would miss her because she was real cool and easy to talk to.

I got up and looked out of the window as she headed for her truck. I watched her until she disappeared down the street. In a way I felt sorry for her. Here she was, lonely and in a strange city. I knew she had family here, but still she didn't seem happy. I guess a part of me was concerned about that more so than trying to get with her.

CHAPTER 15

What the $%#$!

Thursday came, and I was so excited about going to Atlanta that I almost forgot to put my suitcase in the car. I went over everything again before leaving the apartment. I got on the road and headed up 65 North. On my way there I tried calling Jennifer on her cell phone, but it was off. Instead I just left a voice message on her answering machine at the hotel just to let her know I was thinking about her.

I made it to Atlanta and went straight to her apartment. When I walked inside, the place was just the way I thought it would be, a total mess. For the first two hours I cleaned the bathrooms, the den, and kitchen from top to bottom. I got the candles and placed them on candleholders throughout the apartment. After all of that work, I stretched out on the couch and took a nap for a few hours.

I got up and continued cleaning the rest of the house and decided to cook me something to eat. When I looked in her refrigerator I couldn't believe what I saw. It was filled with McDonald's and Waffle House bags, a gallon of water, a half-empty ketchup bottle, and other shit that was either spoiled or dried out. I looked in her freezer and all she had in there was a pint of ice cream, old-ass frozen chicken that I put in there months ago, and other shit that was wrapped in foil. *This is a damn shame,* I thought. I decided to jump in the shower and head to the store for some groceries.

After my shower I got dressed and headed out the door. When I walked to my car it started raining all of a sudden. Since I didn't have my umbrella I dashed to my car, which was parked near the stairway of Jennifer's apartment. It had gotten dark outside, and when I turned out of the apartment complex, the traffic around the area was starting to build up. When I got on the main street, it was bumper to bumper the rest of the way to the supermarket.

A few minutes later I made it to the parking lot and inside the store. I grabbed a shopping cart and began to go up each aisle getting a lot of canned goods, produce, and dairy items I knew Jennifer liked. I went to the seafood side of the supermarket and picked up fresh tuna, salmon, shrimp, and crab. I went to the meat section and got chicken breasts, chicken wings, and steak.

Finally I walked over to the wine section and bought two real expensive bottles for when she got home the next day. By this time my basket was almost full. I checked out and headed for the car. It was starting to thunder really bad, and lightning was streaking across the sky. People were standing inside the store waiting for the weather to calm down. Instead of walking outside, I decided to sit back and wait along with them.

About thirty minutes passed before the weather calmed down a bit. I rolled the basket to my car, unloaded my groceries in the backseat, and headed out of the parking lot. As I left I noticed a Blockbuster video on the corner. I decided to stop and get some movies since I had a universal card, which allowed me to rent movies anywhere in the country.

I turned into the parking lot of the Blockbuster and went inside. I walked over to the new-release aisle, looked around, and grabbed two action movies, *The Manchurian Candidate* and *The Bourne Supremacy,* before heading over to the drama section and getting the movie *Ray*. I figured I'd watch my two movies that night and watch the other one with Jennifer the next day.

As I got to the counter I looked outside, and it was pouring again. I couldn't wait on the inside this time because it was getting late and I was ready to get back to the apartment. I checked out and got back into the car, heading down the main street to the apartment. Still, traffic was bad. Even at eight o'clock at night it was bumper to bumper.

After cussing a few people out, I finally made it through the gate at the apartment complex. The rain was falling slowly but in heavy drops. As I turned in, I had to slow down because some big baller was in front of me in a chromed-out 7-series BMW with dark-tinted windows, taking his time getting where he had to go. It seemed like every turn the driver made I had to make, and at every speed bump he would almost stop before going over it. Seeing that I couldn't go around him, I just slowly followed. Finally I made it to the apartment. The rain started to fall a little harder, and I noticed my parking spot was still available. I waited on the baller to pass it so that I could park. Instead he turned on his signal and pulled into my spot. *Damn,* I thought, *now I'm gonna have to either turn around and park in the next unit's spaces or find one down at the end.* I drove ahead and turned around. I was pissed because parking this far from the apartment meant I had to take all of these groceries upstairs while getting drenched in rain. As I turned around, I passed the baller and found a spot about seven spaces from where I normally parked. I jumped out of the car to quickly get the groceries and run upstairs. I opened the door to the backseat and grabbed about four bags by the plastic handles and ran toward the apartment. When I got closer to the stairway the door to the baller's car opened, and as he got out of his car, he opened his umbrella, and walked to the passenger side. As he opened the door, a female was quickly getting out trying to get under his umbrella. When they heard me briskly walking and splashing water they both turned in my direction. As we all looked at each other I stopped in my tracks.

"What the fuck!" I said.

It was Jennifer. She looked at me with her mouth wide open. We were standing about ten yards from each other. She began to walk toward me with a look of total shock in her eyes.

"Troy, uh, baby when did you—"

"What the fuck is this shit?" I shouted.

I dropped the groceries and just stared at her while the rain poured down on me. My heart had sunk so low that my knees began to get weak, and I felt like I was about to fall. I was so filled with rage that my tongue began to tingle. Jennifer was standing with some big muscular motherfucker as he held the umbrella over her head.

"So, what the fuck is this shit? New York, huh! You lying bitch."

"Nothing, I was just—"

"So this is what's been going on since you've been here, huh? While I'm at home going crazy over your ass, you're here being a motherfuckin' ho."

"What?" she screamed.

"You heard me. Telling me you were away on fucking business. While you out here being a fucking slut."

"No, Troy, let me explain," she said, emotional.

"Shut the fuck up."

She walked closer to me and extended her arm, touching my shoulder.

"Bitch, get your fucking hands off me," I shouted as I pushed her hand away.

When I did that the baller came walking in our direction.

"Hey, man, don't put your hands on her like that."

"What? Man, fuck you. Who the fuck you think you talking to?" I said as I started walking in his direction.

"Troy, no. It's not what you think," Jennifer said hysterically.

"You heard me, man," the baller said, still walking toward me. Two more guys got out of the baller's car and ran over to him, holding him back. Jennifer ran and stood in front of me to keep me from walking toward him. I could hear the two guys talking to the baller saying I wasn't worth it, and that they should go.

Jennifer stood in front of me, begging and pleading with me. "Please, Troy, listen to me. It's not—"

"Shut up and get the hell away from me. I'm through with your trifling ass. I've got to be the dumbest motherfucker in the world to have believed all your bullshit this long. I knew it, I knew you were fucking around on me."

"No, no, Troy. Please just come inside and let's talk," she said, still crying and standing in front of me, cutting me off at my path.

"Go inside? Go inside? I ain't going no damn where. Is this the kinda nigga you want? Huh? Well, you know what? You got it. I ain't trying to fight over your trifling ass."

She began to cry uncontrollably. "Why are you talking to me like that, Troy? This is not what you think. Please listen to me."

I pushed her away from me as the baller struggled to get free from his two friends. Jennifer stumbled but didn't fall. Neighbors began to open their doors and run down to her aid as I walked off. I could hear her crying, begging me to come back. I just walked to my car with my head down as tears began to build in my eyes. I got the rest of the groceries out of my car and just threw them in Jennifer's direction, then got inside and drove off.

As I left I looked in the rearview mirror as people stood around Jennifer trying to hold her up as she cried.

The baller was standing near his car with his two friends staring at my car as I quickly accelerated away.

When I got outside the apartment complex, the tears flowed. Normally, I would have called Mike, but I was too hurt to talk to anyone. Instead I just jumped on the interstate and headed home.

The ride was in complete silence except for my cell phone ringing every five minutes. I knew it was Jennifer so I just turned it off. All I thought about was this guy being all up in Jennifer, and her making love to him like she did with me. This made the pain in my heart sting a little bit more.

I stopped in Montgomery, Alabama, because I was too upset to drive any more. I pulled into a package store and bought a liter of Hennessy and got me a room for the night. Since I had left all of my shit in Atlanta, all I did was lie across the bed and drink liquor straight out of the bottle. I drank and drank until everything around me was spinning like crazy. I would get up from time to time and look at myself in the mirror as tears ran down my face. *Damn. I can't believe this shit is happening to me like this. I thought this bitch was my soul mate, the future mother of my kids,* I thought. I believed all that shit about her loving me and missing me. I turned around and grabbed my cell phone to call her and cuss her ass out some more, but when I got to the last number, I just hung up the phone. I grabbed the bottle and started drinking again. I slumped back over in the bed with the bottle in my hand until I passed out.

I woke up the next morning looking and feeling bad. I had the worst taste in my mouth, and it made me sick to my stomach. I ran into the bathroom and threw up for about fifteen minutes. I was still buzzing a little, and so tired that I just sat with my back against the bathtub next to the toilet. I leaned over and threw up once more. This time it felt like my stomach was turning inside out. I got up, flushed the toilet, walked over to the sink, and rinsed out my mouth. I reached over and got the complimentary toothbrush and tooth-paste and began brushing my teeth. I was looking horrible. My eyes were bloodshot, my clothes smelled of liquor, and my stomach was still churning. I thought about grabbing my keys and heading home, but I was still too fucked up to drive. I started feeling alone. I started reliving the night all over again. I reached over and grabbed the bot-tle of Hennessy again, but the bottle was empty. I threw it on the floor and lay across the bed again. I could feel and hear my stomach as it growled and churned with emptiness. A few moments later I fell asleep again. When I got up it was close to six o'clock in the evening. I damn near slept the entire day away. I got up and grabbed my keys and walked to the front desk to check out.

As I passed people in the lobby, they just stared at me and frowned with confusion. I knew I looked fucked up but I didn't care. I got in my car and headed back to Mobile. I had a hangover like crazy. I really didn't care if I crashed into a wall or ran over the side of the road. I just wanted to get home in my own bed and just be alone.

I made it home around nine-thirty that night. When I got inside I walked straight to my room and sat down on the bed. Ten minutes later the phone rang. I looked up at the caller ID and saw that it was Jennifer. I just stared at the phone and let it ring until the answering machine picked up. I went into the kitchen and grabbed all the liquor I had and placed it on the counter. The only way I could deal with this shit was if I stayed drunk to numb my feelings. I pulled out a half gallon of gin, Canadian Club, Jack Daniel's, and Hennessy. Since I had started with Hennessy I grabbed it and headed back into the bedroom and began drinking like crazy. When I got my buzz on that time, it seemed like it depressed me even more. I grabbed the phone and called my boy Mike on his cell.

"Hello," Mike answered.

I paused for a moment, trying to gather my words together.

"Hello," he repeated.

"Uh, yo, what's up, boy?" I said, trying to sound calm.

"What's up, man? Where you at?"

"Oh man, I'm at the crib," I replied softly.

"At the crib? I thought you left for Atlanta."

"Uh, uh, yeah, I did but, uh, I'm home now."

"What's up? You all right, man?"

I lost it. "Mike, man, I caught Jennifer with another guy, man. Right there in my fucking face."

"What? No, man. When?"

"The other night. I went up there to surprise her, and she was getting out of the car with another dude."

"What!"

"Yeah, man, she was supposed to be in New York till Friday and I saw her ass getting out of the car with some nigga Thursday night when I came from the store."

"Aw, man, that's fucked up. I'm sorry about that, man. Hey, I'm on my way over."

"Noooo, I need to be alone right now, man. I don't want no company right now."

"No, man, I just want to make sure you're straight, that's all," he said.

"No. Not now, man. I want to be alone."

He paused for a moment. "Okay, I understand, man, no doubt. Well, hey, if you need to talk, you know I'm here. Just keep your head up, all right?"

"Yeah, I appreciate it, man. I'll holla at you later," I replied.

I hung up the phone and began to drink some more. A few hours later I passed out again. I woke up several times in the middle of the night and drank some more, only to fall asleep again. My stomach was beginning to burn from all of the alcohol I consumed without eating.

Jennifer continued to call throughout the night. In the back of my mind I started thinking some more crazy shit. What if I forgave her? She only made one mistake. We all deserved one more chance in life. Look what happened with me and Dana. But then another part of me thought if Jennifer was truly sorry and even cared she would be knocking down my door trying to apologize or trying to explain everything. But that was typical Jennifer, thinking I should run back to her. "Fuck her!" I shouted. "I can't believe I'm thinking like this. Take her back? I'll never go back 'cause it will never be the same. I'll always think about this shit," I muttered.

CHAPTER 16

Take it Like a Man

Sunday came and I was pretty much in the same shape, drinking and sleeping. I had to go to work the next day and knew I wasn't up for it. I left a message with the receptionist that I would be out for a few more days. I called my cousin in New Orleans and asked if I could stay at his crib for a while. He was an offshore seaman and was gone most of the time, so I thought it would be good for me to go and get my head right. I grabbed my things and headed to New Orleans. Since it was only a two-hour drive from Mobile I was there in no time. He left the key under the mat so when I got there I could let myself in. For the first couple of days I chilled the majority of the time at his place. Every once in a while I would get out and ride around the city or go to the park and get some fresh air. Still, I was hurting on the inside when I thought about Jennifer. I would find myself thinking and wondering what my life was going to be like without her. When thoughts like that ran through my mind I would feel the need to drink. While at the park, I grabbed my cell phone and called Mike.

"Hello," he answered.

"Hey, man," I said, hurt still evident in my voice.

"Man, you okay? Where are you? I been trying to reach you at home and on your cell phone," he said with concern.

"I'm just chilling in New Orleans for a minute, trying to get it together."

"Man, Jennifer has been calling here looking for you, all crying
and shit. She went by your apartment and you weren't there. Don't
you need to call her?"

"Call her? Man, fuck her. That bitch ain't shit. Fuck her. You tell
her to call that nigga she was with."

"Hey, I ain't trying to get in your business, but she said that it wasn't
what it looked like, and he was only giving her a ride from the airport
'cause—"

"Look, Mike, I know what I saw. She was supposed to be in New
York, but here she was, in Atlanta. Forget what she told you, man. I
ain't trying to hear that."

He paused for a moment. "Well, I guess I feel what you're saying,
man."

"Damn right. Anyway, I just called to let you know I was cool,
that's all."

"When are you coming back?" he asked.

"I don't know yet. I just need to clear my head."

"Okay, man. Well, just be safe."

"Yeah, I will. Later, man. Hey, and don't tell Jennifer shit about
where I am, man, 'cause, Mike, I swear if I see her I'll lose it. I'll—"

"You two don't need to be around each other, man, not like this."

I hung up and sat alone on the park bench. When I called my parents' house my dad answered the phone. Even though I was hurting,
I still kept my emotions together as I explained to him what had happened. Because my mother had stepped out, my dad said he would
explain everything to her. I was surprised he didn't give me any advice about my ordeal. Instead he just encouraged me to be strong
and take it day by day.

I didn't want to tell Rick what happened 'cause I knew what he
would say, and I wasn't in the mood for his shit either. Instead I just
spent the rest of the day chilling.

As the week went by my drinking increased and my patience de-
creased. I was still very much hurting inside. Instead of staying the
rest of the week in New Orleans, I decided to just go on home.

I got back late Friday night. When I got to my door, there were notes from Jennifer taped everywhere, begging me to call her. I grabbed each one, crumbled it up, and threw it over the balcony. I went inside and finally watched TV after going through a week of nothing but staring at the four walls. I checked my answering machine only to find that my mailbox was full. I went through each message one by one, deleting anyone who sounded like Jennifer at the first word. The last message was strange, though. It was from Mike wanting me to call him. His voice sounded really low, like he was upset or something. *No,* I thought, *I ain't calling him back. He probably wants to talk to me about this Jennifer crap.* Instead I grabbed the bottle of gin I still had on the counter and began drinking it. I sat there flipping through the TV while I got ripped. The gin had a different effect than the Hennessy. I was feeling crazy drunk, like I wanted to tear shit up. I started feeling really hyper and couldn't sit still in one place.

Since nothing was on, I decided to get up and take a hot shower to try and calm myself down and get comfortable. I ran the hot water and let it flow down my body, giving me a soothing massage as it relaxed me. When I got out I threw on some shorts, went to the bedroom, and lay across the bed still holding my bottle, taking a hit every now and then while getting madder by the minute thinking about how Jennifer had played me. I would reach over and pick up the phone, wanting to call her and cuss her ass out each time, but would just hang up. Instead I called Mike on his cell.

"Hey, man, what's up?"

"Yo, man, what's going on? You all right?" he asked.

"Yeah, I just wanted to let you know I'm home now, that's all."

"Oh, you are? 'Cause I need to talk to you."

"Look, Mike, I ain't trying to hear nothing Jennifer has to say, all right? Damn, I told you I was through with her ass, man."

"No, I'm not talking about her, man. I'm talking about Rick."

"Rick?"

"Yeah, Rick got fired from his job the other day, man."

"What? You lyin'."

"No, man, I'm on my way to pick him up now 'cause he's really down in the dumps. He has been sitting around his apartment all day pissed."

"Damn, when bad shit rains, it pours," I said in disgust.

"Yeah, well, anyway, I'm pulling up in his complex. Since you're home, is it cool to come up?" he asked.

I paused for a minute to think about that. I wasn't in the mood for company, especially to hear other people's problems since I had some of my own. But still, Rick and Mike were my best friends, and Rick needed us, so what the hell?

"Yeah, that's cool, man. I'll be here," I replied.

"Cool. We'll be over there in about thirty minutes."

"All right."

I hung up the phone with Mike and took me another hit of my gin and just lay back in my bed.

About an hour passed and I was awakened by a knock at my door. I struggled to get up since I was still buzzing and opened the door. Mike walked on in, but Rick was still getting out of the car. Mike walked straight to the den, looking around at my apartment in total confusion. Seconds later Rick appeared through the doorway.

"What's up, fellas?" I said as I walked into the kitchen.

Mike looked at Rick, who was looking around at my apartment with the same expression on his face.

"Damn, Troy. What's up with this? Your place looks like a pigpen," Mike said.

I looked around.

"C'mon, man. Clean your place up. You know you don't live like this."

I stood there and shook my head in disbelief myself.

"Man, look at you, hair all over your face, looking crazy, trash and shit piled up everywhere. Damn, dog, you gonna let a woman get you like this?" Mike said.

Rick looked at me, confused. "A woman? What woman?" he asked.

I looked at Mike and then at Rick.

"Well, yeah, man, me and Jennifer broke up."

"What?" Rick replied in disbelief. "What do you mean broke up? When did this happen?"

Mike just sat down in a corner while Rick and I talked.

"Well, I caught her with this guy last week."

"What, man? Where was I when this happened?" he asked.

"I don't know, man. Everything just happened so fast, and I just needed time for myself."

"Damn, that's fucked up, man. What did you do when you caught her?"

"Nothing. I cussed her out and left her with that guy she was with."

"Damn, man, that's really messed up," he said as he scratched his head in disbelief.

"Yeah," I said as I sat down on the right corner of the couch.

I really didn't want to have to tell Rick details and relive this entire ordeal all over again, so I just shifted everything over to him.

"So what's this about them firing you?" I asked.

"Oh, that," he replied. "Man, I don't know what happened. One minute I was working and the white girl I was telling you about came in my office late that afternoon. We started talking, you know, going back and forth with conversation, and the next thing you know she came around my desk and started rubbing me all between my legs and telling me how she wanted to kiss me down there, and one thing led to another."

"One thing led to another. What do you mean?" I asked.

"You know, she started giving me head, and the VP walked in."

"What? Head? You mean sucking your dick? Man, what the fuck is wrong with you? You lost your job over something stupid like that?" I said, laughing at him. "Man—"

Seeing this, Rick got pissed off. I could see it in his eyes that he didn't like my comment.

"I know I fucked up," he said defensively.

"Hell yeah, you fucked up. That's the craziest thing I've heard of in a long time. I told you your shit was gonna catch up with you," I said.

"You told me what, huh? Man, you didn't tell me shit," he replied as he looked at me with his face wrinkled in anger. "I know you ain't sitting there saying what you told me, 'cause I told you about this long-distance shit with Jennifer from the jump. Now look at your ass."

When he brought up Jennifer's name, it struck a nerve deep inside me that really pissed me off big time.

"Hold on, Rick. This is not about me right now, so slow your roll on my shit."

"No, it *is* about you. You sitting up there going off on me and mine. What about you and yours, sitting around looking all crazy, crib smelling like old-ass feet and shit? Who was it, huh? I bet it was one of the baseball players, wasn't it?"

I was so pissed off I couldn't speak.

"Wasn't it?" he asked again.

I turned and walked into the kitchen to get a drink.

"Yeah, I thought so," he said.

Mike sat there in silence as he watched us go back and forth. I just ignored him and tried to talk about something else, seeing that Rick and I had pissed each other off.

"So do y'all want a drink?" I asked nonchantlantly.

Mike shook his head.

Rick pulled out his own half-pint bottle he had in his back pocket. "I'm cool. Shit, I've been drinking all day. So what happened, Troy?" he asked as he took a sip of his liquor.

"Nothing, man, just leave it alone, all right?"

"Naw, what happened? You sitting here letting yourself go down over some bullshit you did to yourself. What kinda sense does that make? Me, I'm just celebrating, 'cause I'm moving on to bigger things now. Forget them crackers at that broke-ass bank. I don't need them. See, you need Jennifer. That's why you look and smell like shit. She probably was fucking around the whole time she was there," he said with a slight laugh.

That's when I'd had enough. I ran toward him in a rage. "Yo, man, fuck you! Fuck you, all right? How you gonna come in my place talking shit to me like that? I'll kick your motherfuckin' ass right now. I asked you twice to keep my shit out of your damn mouth."

"What!" Rick replied as he dropped his bottle and charged at me. We locked up, swinging and throwing each other across the

room, knocking tables and lamps to the floor. We both threw
punches, hitting each other all in the face and chest. Mike jumped
up, trying to break us apart, but we were locked too tight. Finally, I
took one big swing and hit Rick in the nose, causing him to stagger
backward. That was enough room for Mike to get between us and
break us up. Rick charged back in, swinging and cussing. Mike
grabbed him and pushed him toward the kitchen and held him
there. I rushed toward the kitchen, but Mike pushed me away, trying
to keep us from fighting again.

"Get back in there, Troy. What the fuck is wrong with you two?
You're supposed to be boys, and you're around here acting like little
bitches over some dumb shit."

"Forget that shit, Mike," I replied. "I told this Rick to leave me
alone about my business."

"Fuck you," Rick said angrily. "You weak-ass motherfucker. Let me
go, Mike."

"Naw, man, you two are boys. Just calm down," Mike said as he
held us apart.

"No, fuck him. I'm through with his weak ass. Let him sit around
here like a little-ass bitch and cry over his ho," Rick said.

I charged him again. This time Mike caught me as I was in the
middle of a swing that would have put Rick on his ass. As Mike
grabbed me, Rick swung and hit me in the side of the head near my
eye. From that punch I started seeing stars. I pushed Mike out of the
way, and Rick and I went at it again. We fell to the floor in the
kitchen still punching and choking each other. Mike ran in and
broke us apart for good. He pushed Rick outside and locked the
door, while I sat there on the kitchen floor trying to catch my
breath.

"Look, I'm taking his ass home. I can't believe this shit is happening like this between you two."

"Yeah, get him the hell out of here. Fuck that punk motherfucker." Mike grabbed his keys and headed out the door. I sat there
until I caught my breath, then got up and went into the bathroom to
look at myself in the mirror.

"Damn, this motherfucker hit me in my face, and I have to go to work on Monday." I looked down at my shirt and it was torn near the collar, right below the neck. My heart was still pounding from the fight because it had been a while since I had been in one.

My last fight with Rick was when we were kids wrestling over the new girl at the school. Needless to say Mike broke that one up too. This time was different though. Rick should have kept his mouth shut about me regardless of how true it was. I didn't need to hear that shit, not at the moment anyway. Forget Rick. I didn't need him. This was my situation. Let me deal with it. Besides, he had his own shit to deal with.

About an hour later Mike called.

"Yeah?" I said as I answered the phone.

"Hey, man, what the hell is wrong with you two? You're supposed to be boys, man, you know helping each other out, but instead y'all are acting like little kids."

"Noooo, he came into my spot talking shit. I asked him over and over to kill that shit, but he kept on."

"Yeah, Troy, but you know Rick, man. That's how he is."

"Forget that, Mike. I ain't trying to baby no grown-ass man. You should have told him he needed to chill out. Why you calling me talking like all this is on me?"

"All I'm saying is that Rick is Rick and he speaks before he thinks, but you, man, you're better than that. Look, just give him a few days. He'll be calling back."

"Mike, you don't understand, fuck that motherfucker. I ain't got nothing for him no more."

"What, man?" Mike replied, shocked.

"Yeah, that's right. Keep him from around me, man."

"See, that ain't even cool, Troy. We boys, and even though we say shit like that we don't mean it."

"No, we're not boys, we're men. You have to respect me like a man in my own place. If you were friends with me, you would have respect for me. He didn't, so to hell with it. I'm through with him, man."

"All right, all right, I see that right now is not a good time to talk to you, but just think about what I said and blow this shit off."

I exhaled out of disgust because it was obvious that Mike was not hearing me.

"Well, I'll call you tomorrow. Will you be at work?" he asked.

"Yeah, man."

"Okay, I'll hit you up there."

"Yeah."

I couldn't believe my life now. In two weeks I had lost my girl and one of my best friends.

It was Sunday night and I had to go to work with a bruised eye and swollen lip. How could I explain that shit?

Since I tossed and turned all night I decided to go in to work early on Monday. I rolled out of bed with a bad hangover. My ride was long and quiet. Since my breakup with Jennifer, I had no desire to listen to music. It just reminded me of her some way or another and how we used to be.

The streets were clear for the most part as the sun was starting to come up, making the outside world seem really creepy.

When I arrived at work I walked in and grabbed my mail before heading to my office. I really wasn't in the mood to be there, but since Dana was out of town I had to be. I was glad she was gone, because I wasn't in the mood for a lot of questions. She was the type who would want to know every detail.

I sat behind my desk and booted up my computer as I glanced over my papers and my mail. When my computer came up I started reading my e-mail. There were about ten e-mails from Jennifer almost back to back. Part of me became furious. How did she have the nerve to write me with all of the shit she had done? My heart was starting to beat fast, and I became short of breath I was so angry. I sat back in my chair and stared up at the ceiling trying to calm myself down and keep from throwing the computer off my desk. Instead, I just took a deep breath, sat up in my chair, and began deleting each e-mail one by one.

I got up from my desk and paced the room talking to myself, trying to calm down before people started coming into the office. I felt like I was out of control, which was not a good feeling at work.

I sat down at my desk again and got my Bible out of the drawer and started reading Psalm 37. I began reading my mother's favorite scriptures, Psalm 23, Psalm 20, Psalm 35. I asked God to give me strength and guide me down the righteous path.

As the day went by I think I worked maybe twenty minutes at the most. My focus just was not good. Since I took a short lunch I decided to leave work early and head to the gym where I could let off some of my anger and stress. It was close to four, so I figured the gym wouldn't be as crowded as usual. As I left my office, I quickly walked out with my head down, hoping no one would ask about my bruised eye.

When I got to the gym I changed into my workout clothes and went onto the basketball court and shot some hoops by myself for the first hour. I ran up and down the court like a madman, shooting jump shots and layups until I worked up a serious sweat. From there I went inside the weight room and did some bench presses and curls before hitting the indoor track. In doing all of this I was beginning to feel much better because I wasn't thinking about anything or anyone. I jogged about two miles and headed for the locker room to get my clothes. Instead of showering, I decided to go home and do it where I could relax the rest of the night.

I needed the workout. I was full of energy as I got in my car and headed home. I had even built up an appetite. On my way home I stopped by Subway and grabbed me a twelve-inch steak-and-cheese sandwich with the works, chips and a drink.

When I got home I jumped in the shower with the water steaming hot and just let it relax me. It felt so good that I just sat down in the bathtub and let the water just run all on my face and body.

I could feel the water stinging the cut under my mouth as it pierced my lips.

I sat there with my eyes closed as the visions of my fight with Rick went running through my head. I was in deep thought and it seemed like the fight was so real that I even threw a slight punch as I sat there deep in concentration. Back to my senses, I got out of the shower and walked into the den to eat my sandwich. I grabbed my soda and took a sip. Ahhh, it was terrible. I had left it on the table and the ice had melted, watering it down. Instead I went into the kitchen cabinet and got me a shot of gin.

Looking at the bottles and noticing that they were getting low, I made a mental note that I had to stop by the liquor store and restock my supply. I went back into the den and watched TV, only taking one bite out of my sandwich before throwing the rest of it away. My appetite was still shot to hell. All I wanted to do was get me a buzz so that I could drown in my misery.

CHAPTER 17

To Be or Not to Be

The rest of the week was pretty much the same. I went to work early and left early, went to the gym, headed home, and drank myself to sleep. Jennifer stopped sending me e-mails as of Thursday because all I kept doing was deleting them and not writing back. I was glad because it was hard to try to compose myself seeing her e-mails without wanting to lash out at her.

I was happy that the weekend had finally come. Now I could just sit at home and relax by myself with no interruptions. Mike called me that Friday night, but I didn't answer because I knew all he wanted to talk about was me squashing this shit with Rick, and I really didn't want to be bothered with that. Saturday morning Mike came by kinda early. He had just gotten off work and stopped by to check on me since I hadn't talked to him in a few days. I could tell that he'd had a rough night at work by the look in his bloodshot eyes. He sat there drinking coffee trying to stay awake.

"What's going on with you?" he asked as he sipped his coffee.

"Well, you know, just work, man, that's all."

"Just work, huh?"

"Yeah."

"I tried to call you but I got your machine, so I thought I'd come by to see if you were straight."

"Yeah, you know me, man, I'm cool."

"How are you really feeling, man? You know, under the circumstance?" he asked, trying to get deep inside my head.

"Cool, man. Like I said, I'm just taking it day by day, doing my thing. You know I ain't gonna let nothing keep me down. What about you and your family?"

"Oh, everybody's cool, man, just getting ready for the baby, that's all," he replied as a slight smile came across his face.

"Cool."

"I'm off tomorrow, so if you want to get out let me know. Maybe we can play a little golf or something," Mike said.

"Yeah, I'll let you know if I'm up for it, man."

"All right, let me know, but I'm out. I just wanted see if you were straight since I haven't heard from you in a few days."

"Well, that's nice looking out, but I'm good. Shit, you sure you can make it home after working all night?"

"Yeah, man, I'll make it," he said as he got up and headed out the door.

"All right, later, man."

Mike got in his car and headed home. As for me, I did my usual and chilled around the apartment. Later that day I got out and rented me a couple of movies from Blockbuster. I got a couple of comedies, *Kings of Comedy* and Chris Rock's *Never Scared,* to keep my spirits up throughout the day. I laughed from start to finish on both videos. I was really beginning to feel much better in a way. My appetite was beginning to get better, because all of a sudden I got hungry. I went into the kitchen and made a ham-and-cheese sandwich and ate it like it was a steak. It was so good that I was licking my fingers trying to get every crumb.

With my hunger satisfied, I went back into the den and watched the news. The next day Mike called me like he said, wanting to play some golf. Because I was feeling a little bit better, I agreed to meet him at the driving range to hit a few balls for a couple of hours. We met at Magnolia Springs Golf Course, a really exclusive club located in west Mobile often used by the LPGA.

Mike got there before me and was already hitting balls. I walked into the gift shop, bought some balls, and found a spot right next to him and began practicing my swing. For the most part we kept our attention on the game because there were other people around us who were practicing their swing before heading out on the course to play, so you had to be quiet out of respect.

I was hitting shots better and in a straight line exactly where I wanted them to go. I was in a zone, focused on nothing but my game, until I was distracted by Mike's cell phone. You would think he would have it on vibrate being on a golf course and all, but because he's a cop, he needed to make sure he heard it no matter what. It seemed like the phone rang every five minutes. He would answer it and cover his mouth as he talked. I knew something was going on by his expression and how he would look over at me from time to time as he talked. To get back in my zone, I moved down toward the end of the driving range to practice on another angle of the course.

Mike stayed behind and continued to talk on the phone, often looking in my direction. Several minutes later he started packing up his clubs and began walking toward me. Down to my last few balls, I was feeling a little worn out from swinging the different clubs. By the time he made it over to me, I was on my last ball.

"Hey, let's grab a couple of beers in the clubhouse," he suggested.

"Yeah, man, it's hot as hell out here. I could use a cold one," I replied as I hit the last ball.

I grabbed my clubs and we headed toward the clubhouse. Once inside we sat at the bar and watched the baseball game as we drank beer and talked. Mike was acting a little strange and nervous. He drank three beers back to back, often staring at the bottle and around the room.

Finally I just asked, "Mike, what's up, man? You're sittin' there all nervous and uncomfortable. What's on your mind?"

He nodded nervously as I spoke.

"Yeah, man, uh, I know how you feel about people all in your business and things, but Jennifer has been talking to my wife since the incident happened."

"Man, I don't want to hear—"

"Wait," he said as he cut me off. "It's not like that. My wife doesn't tell me what they talk about. All she said to me was to just talk to you because Jennifer really loves you and that—"

"Mike, trust me. I'm okay. That stuff between me and Jennifer is over, *over*. She is nothing to me anymore, man. I'm moving on with my life. I'm sick and tired of hearing her name right about now and how she loves me. It's over."

"That's 'cause you still love her, man. Just hear her out for a minute."

"Mike, I'm through with it, man, for good. Now if we're gonna hang out, let's talk about something else. If not, I'm going home, man."

"All I'm saying is this, Troy. No one's perfect. I never told anyone this, but I was in love just like you. I felt I had the perfect girl in my life. I put her on a pedestal equal to my mother. I bought her expensive things all the time. I felt like we complemented each other in everything we did together. Every holiday I would spend it with her family, not even considering spending time with mine.

"I thought it was real love, man. But one summer I had to go out of town and do an internship with the district attorney's office in Dallas, remember that?" I nodded. "Well, she had to stay in Mobile. It was hard to do, but I had to look out for my future. We talked every night I was gone. I would send her a card every now and then to let her know I was missing her and things. So one day she flew out to Dallas to surprise me on my birthday. I was lonely and was celebrating it by myself when I saw this girl that I was doing my intern with sitting by herself at this bar. We bought each other drinks and were laughing, having a good old time, until one thing led to another, and we ended up at my hotel in bed together. My girl came to the hotel and knocked on the door. Instead of me looking through the peephole, I just opened the door half naked, and she was standing there, her arms filled with gifts, balloons, and everything.

"When she looked in my eyes she knew something was wrong and stormed into the room and saw the girl lying in bed butt naked. She broke down crying and started having a fit. She screamed and yelled at me, grabbed the girl, and whipped her ass, then threw all of my gifts in my face and stormed out of the room. Needless to say, after that we broke up."

I looked over at him with a smirk. "What's the point of the story, Mike? You got some ass and got caught by your lady, big deal."

"Yeah, it was a big deal 'cause the one who caught me is now my wife. Yeah, we broke up 'cause I fucked up. But because I loved her I had to put those broken pieces back together. I'm not saying it's easy, all I'm saying is that it's possible. I know you still love Jennifer, and I know you still want her back. I'm not saying run back, I'm saying at least talk to her 'cause she's hurting. You have to understand to be understood, man."

"Yeah, okay, you said your piece. Can we talk about something else?" I said and I drank my beer.

"Okay, okay, I'll leave it alone then and say no more from now on."

"Good," I replied coldly.

CHAPTER 18

Still Standing

Monday was cool. I guess I was becoming my old self again, at least on the outside. When I got to the office, Dana was standing near the reception area looking like something out of a magazine. You could tell that California did her some good. She had this business suit on, and the skirt came a little above her knees. Her legs were nice and golden brown. Her hair was draped over her shoulders, and she had a glow that lit up the room. When she saw me enter the office, she turned and gave me a big smile as she walked toward me.

"Welcome back," I said. "How was your vacation?"

"It was great. I'll tell you all about it. Oh, and I have pictures too. I have to pick them up from the Photo Mart later today. How was your vacation?" she asked.

I quickly changed the subject. "Oh, uh, cool. So when did you get back?"

"I got back yesterday afternoon. Man, I was so tired I just crashed when I got home."

We started walking toward my office. When we got inside, I walked over to my coatrack to hang up my suit jacket.

"Daaamn," she said softly.

"What?" I replied as I quickly turned around.

"Damn, boy. What the hell happened to you while I was gone? You ain't got a tap of ass back there. Look at your pants sagging in the back. If I put a wallet in your back pocket, your pants would hit the floor," she said, laughing out loud.

I couldn't help but laugh, too, even though I was embarrassed. I guess I did lose a lot of weight not eating and all.

"What's up, Troy? You look all frail and stuff."

"Nothing. I've just been working out. Why, does it look bad?"

"Well, let's just say it's not becoming."

"Oh," I said as I walked to my desk, trying to shake off her comment. "I'm just trying to cut back a little, that's all. So, uh, you glad to be back?"

"Well, I guess. It did feel good seeing my family and all. But for the most part, yeah, I'm kinda glad to be back. You can only take home for so long and you're ready to leave."

"Yeah, I guess you're right about that."

"So, what's for lunch today? 'Cause you really need to eat," she said.

"Ha, I don't know yet. I may just work through lunch today."

"No, not today. Let's go out and get some seafood. Being in California I missed all the good seafood down here."

"I don't know yet."

"Aw, Troy, c'mon. Let's get out for lunch. The weather is so beautiful. We could eat outside on the patio and enjoy this beautiful weather. C'mon, man," she insisted.

"Well, okay. I guess we could go back to the Original Oyster House."

"No, they don't have a patio. Let's go to Copeland's. I want to get the lunch sampler platter. It's really good."

"Copeland's, huh?"

"Yeah. I've been thinking about Copeland's for about a week now."

"Yeah, okay, Copeland's is cool. Let's get together around eleven-thirty."

"Great," she replied as she got up out of her chair. "Hey, meet me in the break room, and I'll drive," she said as she walked out the door.

Dana was in a good mood, which put me in a good mood. She

had this real cheerful attitude that would brighten anyone's day. Lord knows I needed it.

For the rest of the morning I spent my time mostly answering e-mail from our clients. Often my mind would wander, and I would think about what Jennifer was doing. Then I would think about the night I saw her get out of that motherfucker's car and get pissed off. I would just shake my head, trying to snap myself back to reality and what was really going on.

When eleven-thirty came, Dana met me at my office door jingling her keys and smiling.

"Come on in," I said as I got up from my desk.

She walked in holding a gift. "I brought you something back from California," she said, walking close to my desk.

"Oh yeah? What is it?" I asked, surprised.

"Here. Open it up." She leaned over and placed the gift in my hand. I smiled as I began to unwrap it.

"I hope you like it," she said as I tore through the wrapping paper.

"Wow!" I said as I looked at the gift. It was two crystal picture frames. One was a five-by-seven and the other was eight-by-ten. You could tell they were expensive by the design. They both were clear crystal with frost covering each corner of the frames, and right at the bottom engraved into the crystal was the name *Jennifer*. I stared at the inscription for a minute before looking up at Dana.

"Well, do you like it? I had it made at this shop in downtown San Francisco."

"Yeah, it's beautiful, but—"

"But nothing, now you can put her picture in it and keep it on your desk. I know you get tired of trying to look at your woman in these wallet-size frames you have around your office," she said as she looked around. "Hey, what happened to your pictures?"

"Oh, uh, I took them home."

"Took them home?" she asked confused. "Oh."

"Yeah, uh, I, you know, just wanted to change things."

"Oh, okay. Well, it's your office. But anyway, do you really like the gift?"

"Yeah, I appreciate it, I really do."

"Good. So, are you about ready now?"

We left for Copeland's. I really appreciated what Dana did for me, but I just wasn't ready to talk about Jennifer and me. When we got to the restaurant, we saw a bunch of cars pulling up from all directions trying to get a parking space close to the front.

We parked in the back and went inside. There was about a fifteen-minute wait to be seated, so people stood outside waiting on their names to be called. Dana gave the hostess her name, and we walked over to the courtyard and took a seat on the bench. From where we sat, you could see the patio of the restaurant and all of the people sitting there.

"There's no way we'll be able to get a table out there," I said as I pointed to the patio.

"Yeah, I was just thinking the same thing," Dana replied, with a look of disappointment.

About twenty minutes later the hostess called Dana's name and escorted us to the first available seats. Wouldn't you know it? She put us at the table right next to where Jennifer and I had had our last dinner before she left for Atlanta. While Dana and I sat at our table I couldn't help but stare at the other table and remember how special that last dinner was and how beautiful Jennifer had looked sitting there.

Dana was just talking away. About what, I don't know, but she was going on about it. Finally I came back to earth and started looking over my menu.

"So what are you having?" she asked.

"Well, I think I'll just have an appetizer, like some shrimp or something. I'm not very hungry."

"What? Is that it? Man, I am starving right about now. I think I'm gonna get the lunch platter like I said earlier."

"The lunch platter. Wow, that's a lot of food."

"Uh-huh."

The waitress came over and took our drink order. "So what will you two have to drink today?"

Dana looked up. "I'll have sweet tea with a lot of ice and lemon."

The waitress looked over at me. "And you, sir?"

"I think I'll have the Long Island iced tea."

When Dana heard my order, her eyes opened wide. "Whaaat, what's up with the Long Island iced tea?"

"I don't know. I just need one right about now."

"I heard that," she said, laughing.

"So you're not gonna join me today?"

"Noooo. Not today. I have too much to do after work to be getting drunk."

"I'm not getting drunk. I just need to relax, that's all."

"Oh, is that what it is?"

"Yeah, just a drink to relax."

She responded to that by just staring at me, nodding.

The waitress came back with our drinks and took our food order. I grabbed my drink and quickly began drinking it. Dana just sat there and watched me with a puzzled look on her face.

"Why are you staring at me like that?" I asked as I put my glass back on the table.

"I don't know, you seem different."

"You mean weird, huh?"

"No, just different."

"How so?" I replied.

"Oh, nothing bad," she said, still staring. "Look, don't pay any attention to me. Maybe it's me."

"Yeah," I said nonchalantly. I finished my drink before our food came out. I noticed Dana still staring at me with a frown, like she was trying to figure me out. I didn't care, though, 'cause I was starting to feel a good buzz, and I just ignored everything else.

By the time the waitress came back I was ready for the second drink but decided not to because Dana was sitting there staring. Plus, I didn't want her asking questions.

I looked over at my plate and ate a couple of shrimp before sliding the plate away from me. Dana was all into her food. She had both elbows on the table with her head buried deep in her plate. I sat back in my chair watching and laughing to myself.

She continued to talk and eat as my mind started to wander again. I watched as other people stuffed food in their mouths, trying to hurry their meal to beat that lunch hour. Then there were others who sat at their tables trying to look important and shit, eating their food like they were sitting with the queen of England, all proper with their napkins stuffed in their shirts. I just laughed to myself, shaking my head, still buzzing from the Long Island iced tea.

I continued staring until my attention was shifted to a group of honeys from the reflection in the mirror behind Dana. They were all dressed in business attire with attitude in their eyes as they walked to their table. As they got closer, I recognized one of them. Seeing her, I felt my buzz starting to fade by the second. "Damn, that's Paula," I whispered to myself. She was one of Jennifer's good friends. They worked out at the gym a lot. She was a real ghetto bitch who loved to start shit. She was the last person I wanted to see, especially with all that had gone on. She didn't care much for me because she didn't like Rick and thought I was just like him, so she tried to keep shit going between Jennifer and me.

I just sat there stiff as a board following her with my eyes through the mirror as the hostess escorted them through the crowd. Paula casually looked around the restaurant as she continued on to her table before finally being seated. As she sat down she nonchalantly glanced in my direction. Damn, she had to pick the chair that faced me. Well, she really couldn't get a good look because my back was facing her, but I could see her clearly through the reflection in the mirror. I watched her grab her menu and look over it as she and her friends talked.

I looked back over at Dana, who was halfway finished with her lunch, as I tried to figure a way out the door without Paula seeing me. Don't get my wrong, I wasn't worried about Paula. It's just that I wasn't in the mood for any of her shit, especially around Dana.

I know, I thought, *I'll tell Dana that I have to go to the restroom when it's time to pay the bill and have her meet me outside at the truck. Yeah, that'll work.*

Finally Dana finished her lunch. She had been talking to me the whole time I had my eyes on Paula, but I wasn't paying her any attention. I would just nod and smile or something to make her think I was listening.

"*Ahhh*, that was good," she said, eating the last bite. "Hey, you barely touched your food. What's up?"

"Oh, uh, I'm not really hungry right now. I may just box it up and take it home."

"Okay, I know I enjoyed mine," she said as she sat back in her chair. "Oooh, I'm full. I sure could use a nap right about now."

"Uh, yeah," I replied, still looking at Paula through the reflection in the mirror.

"Well, are you ready to head on back to the office?" she asked.

"Okay, uh, hey, I have to go to the restroom, so why don't you pay the bill and I'll just meet you outside?"

"Oh, okay," she said as she reached for her purse.

I signaled for the waitress to bring us the bill and waited around so that I could give the money to Dana instead of just rushing off to the bathroom. The waitress brought us the bill, and I gave Dana thirty dollars to pay for the entire lunch.

"How much do I owe you for lunch?" she asked as she reached for the bill.

"Oh, nothing. Lunch was on me. Just give it to the waitress, and I'll meet you outside."

I waited on Dana to get up first to make it seem like she was alone. While she walked over to the waitress, I got up and headed for the restroom. While in the bathroom I just did my business and waited around to give Dana enough time to get to her truck. Moments later I came out of the bathroom and headed toward the door on the opposite side of the restaurant from where Paula was sitting. As I walked, I glanced over at her table and noticed that she was gone. Good, I thought. I quickly bypassed the hostess booth and walked out of the door, relieved Paula hadn't seen me. I stood outside looking for Dana so I could hurry up and get the hell outta there. Remembering we had parked in the back, I started walking along the side of the restaurant, hoping to catch Dana as she drove up. As soon as I turned the corner, I stopped in my tracks. There was Paula, standing there, on her cell phone. When she saw me, she gave me a look like she was going to rip my heart out or something. She quickly got off the phone.

"Well, well, well, I've been waiting to see you. I thought that was you I saw in there, but I wasn't too sure."

"See me? What do you need to see me for?" I replied sarcastically.

"You know damn well for what, nigga. For the way you did my girl."

"What!"

"You heard me. I said, for the way you did my girl," she said as the volume of her voice went up.

"Wait a minute, Paula. You need to check your tone, back off, and stay out of my business."

"Your business? Your business? You made this my business the day you treated my girl like she was some kind of ho or something."

I stood there shaking my head in frustration, trying to stay cool.

"And how you gonna embarrass her in front of all her neighbors and who knows who else was around? What kinda man are you?"

"Look, I ain't got time for this today. I'm not getting ready to go back and forth with you outside a restaurant like some schoolkid. What's done is done. She's happy and I'm happy, so fuck it."

"Fuck it! Fuck it! Is that all you got to say? After all she's given your sorry ass? Naw, fuck you!"

"What!"

"That's right, fuck you. I don't care who hears me, just like you didn't give a damn who heard you."

I took a real deep breath and turned around to walk off.

"Yeah, you better walk off, you sorry excuse for a man. Oh, don't think this is over. Now you got to deal with me. I'm gonna make your life a living hell. Trust me on that."

"Yeah, whatever, crazy-ass—"

"Oh, you haven't seen crazy yet. You haven't seen crazy yet. But you will. This ain't over, baby. Believe that," she interrupted.

Dana picked that moment to pull up next to me. Seeing this, Paula really started in.

"Oh, now I see what's going on. It wasn't Jennifer, it was your sorry ass," she shouted as I got into Dana's truck.

Dana looked at me with confusion as Paula kept shouting obscenities as she walked toward the truck.

"Dana, hurry up. Let's go," I said as I got inside. As Dana pulled off, Paula was standing in the middle of the parking lot still cussing and fussing. Dana looked in her rearview mirror as she exited.

"Damn, Troy, what was that all about?" she asked, looking at me strangely.

"Aw, it's not a big deal, just some crazy-ass honey I know talking a lot of shit, that's all. No big deal."

"What kinda shit? It's obvious that that girl was highly pissed off at you for something. What's up?"

I sat there staring out of the window in silence for a moment before responding. I was so pissed off at Paula that I was about ready to snap. I'd been holding all of this anger inside with no one in whom I really wanted to confide, but the episode with Paula today was the last straw. I looked over at Dana with a frown.

"Well, this is the deal, Dana," I said as I cleared my throat. "Jennifer and I broke up."

"What?" she exclaimed. "Why? What happened?"

"Well, uh, when I went to Atlanta I caught her with another guy."

"Oh, shit," she said in disbelief.

"Yeah. She told me she was flying in on Friday night, had me thinking she was still in New York, so I got there Thursday trying to set up something special for when she came home. Then later that night I caught her getting out of this guy's car."

"What! Damn. Who was it?"

"Hell, I don't know. Some wannabe baller in a BMW."

"Oooh, I am so sorry to hear that, Troy, but what does this have to do with that girl back there?"

"That girl is one of Jennifer's best friends."

"Oooh, now I see. But damn, are you okay? I know you must be devastated."

"Hell yeah, I'm okay. I just need time to get over this heartache. After that, I'll be straight."

"So that's why you're around here losing all that weight and removing all of her pictures in your office. Now I see. Man, I am truly sorry that you have to go through this. Is there anything I can do?"

"Naw, I'm cool."

"You sure?" she asked with concern.

"Yeah, I'm straight, but thanks anyway. I appreciate it though," I replied. When we made it back to work I went inside my office and closed my door to be alone. I couldn't believe that bitch Paula had stepped to me like that. It took all I had to keep from cussing her crazy ass out.

Throughout the day it was hard for me to concentrate without thinking about lunch. I got up from my desk and walked outside to cool off for a minute. *Damn that Paula,* I thought. *I bet she got on the phone and called Jennifer and told her that I was with another girl. So what? She has a new man, so what I do from here on out is my business. I wonder how long she has been fucking with that motherfucker.*

The more I thought, the angrier I got. I wanted to pick up the phone and call Mike and talk to him, but all he was going to say was that I should call Jennifer and talk about it. But forget that, I was through with her ass.

For the first time, I felt really alone. I felt like everyone was against me and I was left to deal with this heartache by myself. No matter what I did, I couldn't concentrate at work. *I just need to get out of here,* I thought. *Yeah, I'll go and tell the secretary that I'll be out of the office doing some research for this project and just go home for the rest of the day.*

I went back inside, grabbed my things, and headed toward the door. Before I left I gave the secretary my pager and cell phone number just in case someone needed to get in touch with me. I got to my car and headed straight to my apartment.

When I got inside, I went straight into the kitchen and made me a drink. The only thing left was the gin, so I grabbed the orange juice carton and the gin bottle and sat on the couch. By late evening I was lit. I sat back staring at the ceiling, going over my day in my head.

Dana called me later, concerned because I had left work early. We talked off and on throughout the night as I continued to drink myself crazy. She was very supportive of my feelings and the way I handled my situation with Jennifer. She didn't try to offer advice like everyone else. She mostly just listened while I got things off my chest. That night was the best I'd felt since all this happened. I was finally able to talk without interruption until I passed out holding the phone.

My days at work for the rest of the week were even better. Dana really turned out to be cool. She helped in every way I needed as a friend, which made things easy to deal with.

CHAPTER 19

Dryin' Out

Saturday came, and I was ready to hang out. Mike called and asked me to meet him at the gym to shoot some ball. It had been a while since we had a chance to hit the gym together, so I was ready.

I got to the gym early and hit the weights for a while to loosen up before Mike got there. By the time he showed up, people were starting to pick teams and begin playing. I'd finished my workout and was resting on the bench in the weight room as he walked through the door. We walked over onto the side of the court and watched the guys play until it was our turn to take on the winners. When their game ended, we along with two other guys teamed up and began to run the courts. We were out there for about thirty minutes as we took over the game, winning two in a row before taking a break.

Mike and I sat in the corner near the water fountain. He was trying to analyze our strategy for the next game, while I was trying to catch my breath from all that running from the last one. I guess drinking all that alcohol had started taking its toll on me. While I was sitting there catching my breath, Mike got up and walked inside the weight room to go to the bathroom. About ten minutes later the guys started filling the court, ready to play. While we waited on Mike, we just all passed the ball around taking turns shooting jump shots and stretching. Several minutes later, there was still no Mike. I trotted off the court to search for him so we could get the game started. When I got halfway to the door of the weight room, I stopped in my tracks. Mike was over near the aerobics room laughing and talking to Rick.

"What the hell is he doing here?" I said to myself.

Instead of going over there I just ran back on the court, picked another player, and began playing. We must have been out there for about fifteen minutes before Mike came running through the door of the gym. I guess he heard us playing and realized that we had started without him. As he walked the sidelines Rick was standing at the door leaning against it watching us play.

"Hey, what's up? Y'all couldn't wait till I came back to play?" Mike yelled on the court.

We stopped playing, and someone on the other team yelled out, "Your boy said to go on without you 'cause you were tied up."

"What! No, man, I was ready," Mike said, looking over at me.

I walked over to him.

"What the hell is Rick doing here, man?" I asked in frustration.

"Oh, I asked him to come out and shoot some hoops with me. What's wrong with that?" he replied.

"I know what you're trying to do, Mike. I told you I'm through fucking with him, man."

"C'mon, man, take the ball out so we can finish kicking that ass," someone shouted from the other team.

I looked over at their team. "A'ight, we ready," I said.

"Hey, can I get my spot back?" Mike asked, looking at the guy who replaced him.

"Yeah, cool, I got next anyway," the replacement said.

"Thanks, man," Mike said.

We were already down by four, and the other team needed two more points to win. Because we didn't start the game with Mike playing, we fell behind early. Mike got back on the court with us, and our teams went back and forth for another fifteen minutes before we finally lost. Mike, who was sort of pissed, walked off the court, heading in Rick's direction. I walked over to the other side of the court with the rest of our team and sat with them. I wasn't trying to act like a little bitch by not going over to Rick, I was just still pissed off at him, and I knew that if I had gone over there I would've snatched his ass up again. That's just the way I hold a grudge.

As I sat down I looked over at Mike and Rick from the corner of my eye and could tell that Rick was pissed off that I was at the gym too. I figured Mike was trying to get us in the same place to squash our little beef. But from the looks of things, Rick wasn't having that either. They talked for a few minutes, and Rick turned and walked out the door. Mike came back over to where I was and sat down next to me.

"What's up with that?" I asked.

"Nothing, man, just trying to get my boys to stop acting like two women and squash that silly shit between the two of you."

"Whatever. I told you I'm through with him, man," I said.

"Yeah, he's not having it either, so he just left."

"Good. Then there you have it."

Mike shook his head in disgust as he looked away.

Moments later my cell phone rang. I reached in my gym bag and grabbed it.

"Hello," I answered.

"Hey, what are you up to today?" Dana said.

"Hey," I replied, confused.

"I know you're wondering how I got your cell number."

"Well, yeah," I said.

"Well, the day you left early I asked the secretary if she had seen you and she said that you left for the day but could be reached on your cell or pager, so I got the number then. I hope you don't mind."

"No, it's cool."

"So what's up?" she asked.

"Nothing much, I just finished working out and shooting some ball, that's all. What's up with you?"

"Oh, I just left the mall and I'm on my way to the grocery store."

"Oh yeah?"

"Yeah. Really, I just called to see how your day was going and what you were up to."

"Oh, well, that's real thoughtful of you, but I'm cool."

"Well, what are your plans tonight?"

"You know, really, I don't have any. I may just cool out at the apartment or something."

"Well, I tell you what, I'll call you later and maybe we could shoot some pool or something downtown."

"Yeah, that's sounds good. Around what time?"

"I don't know yet but I'll call you later on," she said.

"Cool, that'll work," I replied.

"Okay, I'll talk to you later."

When I got off the phone Mike was staring in my grill.

"Why are you looking at me like that, man?" I asked.

"No reason, just trying to figure out what's up with you."

"What's up with me? Man, what the hell are you talking about now?" I asked, confused.

"Nothing," he said, shaking his head.

"No, tell me, man. It seems like everything I do now, you have something to say. If you must know, that was my friend from work, Dana. She wants to shoot some pool tonight. What's wrong with that?"

"I'm not saying anything is wrong with that. I don't give a care who you kickin' it with. I just think you're making a mistake with Jennifer, that's all."

"Oh Lawd, man, not that again. Can't we hang out once without you bringing up Rick or Jennifer's ass? I get tired of hearing that, man."

"All I'm saying is call Jennifer, man. Did you at least try to find out what happened that night?"

"What happened?" I replied. "Man, I know what happened. She lied and got caught, end of story."

"A'ight. A'ight. I hear you, man. Well, my wife said Jennifer had some of your things she needed to return."

"What?" I said.

"I guess Jennifer still has some of your clothes or something you had over there."

When he said that, a real sharp pain went through my body and burned the inside of my stomach. Instantly, I felt like I did the night I saw her with that guy. I began to frown from the pain. I guess this bad dream about Jennifer and me not being together was becoming more of a reality. Every time I thought I was over it, something was said that brought back the pain.

I guess it was over. Instead of an instant breakup, this shit was long and drawn out. I started to feel really depressed. I quickly got up and walked over to the weight room. Mike got up and followed me, still talking, but I was so caught up in my emotions I wasn't really hearing him.

"Hey," he said as I snapped out of my trance.

"Yeah. What's up?" I replied.

"Do you want to run another game with the guys?"

"Uh, naw, man, go ahead. I'm done for the day."

"Uh-huh. I know what's up. You over there thinking about what Jennifer said."

"Yeah, it made me think, I ain't gonna lie, but what's done is done. Yeah, tell her to mail me my shit back."

"Why don't you tell her? All you have to do is call."

"No, forget that. I ain't got nothing to say to her ass, nice or kind, so you'd better tell her."

"Okay," he said nonchalantly. "Well, I'll get the message to her. Hey, I'm gonna run another game. You still gonna sit this one out?"

"Yeah, uh, I think I'm gonna head on back to the crib."

"Okay, well, I'll hit you up later then."

"Cool," I said.

I walked to my car still torn. Mike was trying to screw with my head by bringing up Jennifer's name like that to see my emotions. It was tough, trying to hide them, because he caught me off guard. Now I felt even worse than before. I needed a drink and fast.

I got in my car and spun off. The first place I stopped was the liquor store. I got the biggest bottle of Hennessy I could find and headed straight home. Before I could even get in the apartment good I made me a drink. No ice, no nothing, just straight hot liquor. I drank three glasses in shots before I got up and went into the bathroom to shower. I stared down at the bottom of the tub as the water soothed me. I reached over to grab the soap out of the dish, but it was gone. I grabbed the liquid soap from the shower rack and began using it. As I showered I realized something. I looked back at the shower rack again. *This is the shower rack that Jennifer bought for me,* I thought. I reached over and snatched it off the showerhead, breaking the shower rack in two, before tossing it on the floor, as all the lotions and shampoo scattered everywhere. I got out of the shower, put on my bathrobe, and walked around my apartment gathering everything else that Jennifer bought for me and placed it all in bags to throw out. I threw out cologne, pajamas, T-shirts, dress shirts, then tied all the bags up and put them outside my door to throw in the Dumpster the next morning.

I went into the kitchen and made another drink before sitting down on the couch, staring into my glass thinking. Suddenly, I noticed the photo album on the coffee table directly in front of me. I quickly grabbed it, taking out her pictures, tearing all of them into pieces. It was like I was in a drunken rage. When I grabbed the very last picture I stared at it for a while. I started thinking long and hard to myself, *This is the girl I wanted to marry, spend the rest of my life with? I can't believe I was fooled for this long. Look at her with this innocent look on her face like she's some damn angel.* "Fuck you, Jennifer," I shouted as I ripped the picture into pieces and tossed it next to me. I got up and walked to my bedroom. I was so drunk that I walked to my bed and passed out.

The only thing that woke me up was the phone, which was in the bed next to me. Struggling to turn over, I grabbed it and looked at the caller ID. Damn, I thought, it was Dana. I forgot that she said she wanted to shoot some pool. I glanced over at the clock and noticed that it was six o'clock in the evening. I was still buzzing, and my mouth was kinda dry, so my voice sounded deeper than normal when I answered the phone.

"Hello," I said.

"Hey."

"What's up?"

"What's wrong with you?" she asked, concerned. "You sound like you're knocked out."

"Oh, uh, I was just lying here in the bed catnapping."

"Well, get up. I'm leaving home now and wanted to let you know that I'm coming to pick you up. How do I get to your apartment?"

"Hey, wait. I don't think I'm up for shooting pool tonight."

"What! C'mon, it'll be fun. Besides, you don't need to be at home drowning in misery. I'm not taking no for an answer, Troy, so how do I get to your apartment?" she insisted.

Taking a deep breath, I gave her directions.

"Okay, I'll see you soon."

"Damn," I yelled after I hung up the phone.

I got up and went into the bathroom to brush my teeth. I got dressed and started cleaning up the mess I had made in the den and put it in the trash I had outside.

Minutes later as I looked outside my window, I saw Dana getting out of her truck. She was looking good as hell as she walked up to my apartment door. She had on a pair of faded blue jeans that were kinda loose fitting but still accentuated her shape and a red sweatshirt that came down a little past her waist. I quickly walked into the back and put on my shoes before hearing the knock at the door. I opened it, and she stood there with a huge smile on her face.

"Hey," she said in an excited tone.

"What's up?" I replied, still sounding sluggish.

"So, are you ready?"

"Yeah. C'mon in."

I stepped aside and let her in. As she walked past me I could smell the sweet scent of her perfume.

"Have a seat. I'll be ready in a minute," I said as I walked into the back.

"Oh, take your time. I'm okay."

I went back into the bedroom and took one last look at myself. As I walked out of the room I noticed that I had left my drink on the nightstand. I leaned over, grabbed the glass, and gulped it down as I walked into the kitchen and put the glass in the sink. I reached in my pocket and grabbed some gum, then walked over to the door.

"Okay, let's be out," I said as I opened the door.

Dana got up, still excited, as we walked to her truck and headed out.

"So, where are we going to shoot pool?" I asked.

"Oh, I thought maybe we could go to Bumpers on the Beltline."

"Oh yeah," I replied. "I haven't been there in a while."

Bumpers was a cross between a sports bar and a pool hall. You could play games or you could sit at a table or the bar and just watch sports all night. It was a spot that me and the fellas used to hang out in back in the day. We parked, went inside, and got us a table and a couple of drinks. I got my usual Hennessy and Dana got some water with lemon.

"So, you're not drinking tonight, huh?" I asked.

"No, not right now anyway. When I kick your ass, I want to be sober."

"Oooh, kick my ass," I said, laughing. "Okay, let's do this. Allow me to rack them up first, because this will be the last time I have to do it."

"Ha, ha," she said, chuckling. "You think so, huh?"

"Oh yeah. Okay, go ahead and break," I said as I set the balls up on the table.

Dana chalked up her pool stick and leaned over to break. The attention in the room was all on her, as she bent over trying to get her stick aimed at the rack of balls. I think it was because her sweatshirt rose up her back, showing off some skin. But whatever it was had guys staring. After she got her aim together, she let go with a fierce shot. The balls scattered all around the table from her powerful break.

"Not bad," I said as I walked toward the table, "but you still didn't sink anything."

"That's okay, just play," she said.

I leaned over and sank a striped ball in the corner pocket. Then sank another in the opposite corner. As I walked to the other side of the table I glanced up at Dana, who had a look of disbelief in her eyes.

"Oh, don't give me that look," I said as I leaned over to take another shot.

"Shut up and just shoot the damn ball, boy," she said, smiling.

I leaned over and sank another shot as I set myself up for another corner shot. I leaned over and shot it but the ball stopped right at the edge of the pocket.

"Ha," she said. "Now it's my turn."

She walked over, took a shot, and sank a solid ball in the side pocket. Then she sank three balls in a row before missing. We went back and forth until finally I won. I could tell she couldn't take losing well because of the look in her eyes. Her face turned a little red as I talked trash to her as she racked the balls for the next game.

When I got ready to break she walked off from the table and up to the bar. I leaned over and broke the rack of balls, sinking one in the side pocket. When I looked up she was standing next to me with what looked like a glass of Long Island iced tea.

"Good shot," she said, looking over at me.

"Are you surprised?" I replied. "I'm getting ready to clear the table now."

"I hear ya talking. Just don't miss," she said as she took a gulp of her drink.

"Yeah, whatever," I said as I made another shot.

She walked back over to the chair and watched as I walked around trying to get the best angle for my shot. Finally, I missed, and we went back and forth again. I came out the winner for the second time. Dana really didn't like that, so as I continued to talk trash she walked away and ordered another drink.

When she got back she put her drink on the table and grabbed the rack to set up for the next game.

"Okay, rack 'em," I yelled as she leaned down to rack the balls again.

She looked up with a frown as she set up the balls. By the end of the night I ended up winning five games to her one. The only reason I lost was that I accidentally sank the eight ball in the middle of one of my shots. As the night continued, I was really feeling good. My buzz was on and Dana made good company, even though she was a sore loser. Instead of continuing to rub it in, I walked over to her with my hand extended to gesture a good game.

"Hey, that was fun," I said as we shook hands.

"Aw, you just were lucky tonight. I'll get you next time," she replied with a grin.

"For real, you play good," I said. "Hey, how good are you in hoops?" I asked with excitement.

"Hoops? You mean basketball? I'm no good at that," she said.

"Well, let's just play for fun and not get caught up in the competition thing then."

"Okay, that sounds cool."

As she got up from her chair, I noticed that she stumbled a little bit.

"Damn, girl, you all right?"

"Yeah, I'm all right. Just c'mon so I can kick your ass in this game," she said, laughing.

We walked over to the booth where the basketball games were and started playing. Actually, she was pretty good but I still had to whip that ass. By the end of the night we were both laughing at each other's drunken state. We walked over to the other side of the room where there were booths set up for eating and grabbed an order of wings. Dana ordered another glass of Long Island iced tea. Instead of my Hennessy, I ordered a glass of water. I figured I needed to bring down my buzz because from the looks of things, I would be the one driving.

It started getting really late and the place was about to close, so I got the keys from Dana, and we headed back to my place. By the time we got there Dana was already knocked out, sleeping kinda hard. I reached over and gently tapped her on the side of her face.

"Hey, we're here," I said as she struggled to get up.

Twisting and turning in her seat, she opened her eyes. "Um, where are we?" she asked.

"We're at my place. C'mon, get up."

"No. Let me just sleep here for a little while longer."

"Girl, c'mon and get your ass out of this truck," I said playfully as I continued to shake her.

She twisted and turned again before finally getting out. I walked over and helped her out as we walked up to my apartment. As soon as we got inside she walked toward the couch and threw herself across it. Shaking my head, I just walked into the back and started getting my bed ready for her to sleep in it since there was no way she was driving home.

By the time I returned to the den Dana had somehow rolled over on the floor. Laughing, I leaned over and helped her up and walked her into my bedroom, gently laying her in the bed and covering her up with blankets. I grabbed some extra pillows and went back into the den and passed out on the couch.

The next morning I got up and checked on Dana, who was still sleeping. I tiptoed inside to grab some clothes for after I showered, then walked into the bathroom and turned the water on so that it could get hot as I brushed my teeth. Minutes later I got in the shower. I closed my eyes as the hot, steamy beads ran down my body. I reached for the soap from the rack that hung from the showerhead, but I couldn't see with the water in my eyes. *I know it's right here,* I thought as I waved my hand around trying to locate it. Then I remembered I had thrown it out with the rest of the things Jennifer had given me. With that in mind I wiped my eyes and pulled back the shower curtain to get the soap from the dish near the sink. As I pulled the curtain back, there standing completely naked was Dana. Shocked, I jerked back with surprise.

"Hey, uh, what's up?" I asked as I stared directly at her.

Damn, was she fine! I mean fine. She stood there with one hand on her hip while the other hand was at her waist. I couldn't do anything but look her up and down. She had the sexiest, tightest body I'd ever imagined. The hair between her legs was neatly trimmed in a pathway to her spot. Instantly I got a hard-on. Without saying a word, she got in the shower with me and pulled me close, making our lips meet. She slowly slid her tongue into my mouth as we kissed with passion. Through the shower I could hear her moan with pleasure as the kiss got more intense. My hard-on began to throb at the sound.

She started kissing me on the side of my face, down to my neck, on to my chest, and worked her way down between my legs, kissing my inner thighs as she held my hard-on in her hand, gently stroking it. It was feeling so good that all I could do was stand there with my head back. When I felt her mouth slowly cover my tip, I looked down at her on her knees as her head moved slowly back and forth. The water from the shower drenched her hair. I closed my eyes tight, enjoying the motion of her tongue.

As I got into it I began to move my hips, taking in the pleasure. Out of the blue, she stopped. When I opened my eyes she was standing and staring me in the eye as water dripped from her face. She stepped out of the bathtub and walked toward the door. Her ass was so firm and round that it jiggled with each step. I was standing there watching as my hard-on tingled. She turned around at the door and gestured for me to follow her.

Without hesitation I got out of the tub and followed her down the hall to my room, still in a trance. When we got in bed, we quickly engaged in another kiss. This one was more intense than the other because I was on top of her, and my hard-on was pressed against her stomach, feeling her soft golden skin. Moments later she rolled me over on my back, spreading her legs open as she took her finger and rubbed across her wet kitty and traced it across my lips. "Um," I responded as she placed her finger in my mouth. I began to suck her finger, rolling it around my tongue as I watched her peanut-butter-brown nipples begin to harden.

I wanted her and bad. She had teased me long enough. I reached over and grabbed a condom out of my nightstand and quickly put it on. I climbed on her, guiding my hard-on straight inside her. She moaned as every inch of me went inside. I began to move slowly but deep as she moaned louder and louder, clenching my chest.

I rose up on my toes, looking down as I saw my hard-on go in and out of her kitty. Her body was so toned that you could see the firmness of her stomach as she tensed with desire. I started moving faster and harder as she began to yell out for more. I could tell Dana was feeling good, because I could feel her getting wetter by the minute. She began to yell out Spanish words as she grabbed my ass, pulling me in deeper. Her legs were resting on my shoulders. I could hear the sound of our bodies slapping together as we both moaned. Suddenly I felt myself about to explode. I started clenching my teeth together, moving faster and deeper. I could tell that she was reaching her point. She began to yell out louder, louder, and louder.

"Oh, *papi*. Oooh, *papi*, I-I-I'm coming, *papiiiiiii*," she said as her eyes rolled back.

I let out a loud grunt as I exploded with desire. Weak, I just collapsed on top of her as our hearts pounded against each other. "Damn, that was good," I whispered in her ear, still breathing hard.

"Oh yeah, I've wanted this for a long time," she replied.

I looked into her eyes and began to kiss her again. She relaxed, letting me take control until we slowly wound down.

Dana stayed with me pretty much the entire weekend. We didn't discuss anything about sex. We just did it, no questions asked. Each time it was better and better. It felt really good to be held and pampered.

By Monday we were both hard at work. We acted like professionals, trying not to give clues as to how deep our friendship had gotten. Throughout the week we attended meetings and even grabbed lunch together, still not talking about our intimacy. By the time the next weekend rolled around, I stayed at her apartment, still being romanced and catered to in a fashion unlike any that I had felt before.

By the following Monday, I was sick as a dog. I think I had come down with the flu or something, because my body just shut down. I had a stuffy head, runny nose, and my bones ached really bad. I tried to go to work, but Dana insisted that I stay at her place and just chill out. She came home for lunch and made me homemade chicken soup and gave me my medicine. When she got off work she rented movies and cuddled beside me in bed. She even went over to my apartment and got my mail and some extra cloths for me to wear. I couldn't believe how good she was to me. Not one time did I even dwell on Jennifer. I was feeling so good that none of that other shit even mattered, not Jennifer, not Rick, or anything. Right now it was all about me.

CHAPTER 20

Revenge

A few days had passed. I was feeling much better, and back at work. It was Thursday, which meant I only had one more day to the weekend. Mike had called a couple of times earlier that morning while I was in a meeting, trying to get together for lunch. I called him back to set up something but warned him not to pull any shit by bringing Rick along. As I walked out of my office to meet him I passed Dana in the hallway.

"Hey, where are you off to?" she asked.

"Oh, I'm gonna meet my boy Mike for lunch at Mammie's."

"Really? Oh, I thought we could maybe get something to eat and take it to the park today."

"Oh, uh, well, can I get a rain check? Maybe we can do it tomorrow or something?"

"Oh, well, yeah, that's fine," she said, with a disappointed expression. "Well, have a nice lunch."

"Okay, I'll get back with you later," I replied as I continued out the door. I left the office and made it over to Mammie's where Mike was sitting in the back corner waiting.

"Hey. What's up, Mike?" I said with my hand extended

"Mr. Sanders, what's up, man?"

"Just chillin', just chillin'. How's the wife and kids?" I asked.

"You should come over and find out."

"Yeah, you're right. Maybe one day next week or something when you're off."

"Yeah, right, man. You've been saying that same shit for weeks."

"I know, but I'm for real this time. So what's up, man, you know, with you?" I asked.

"Nothing, just trying to catch up with you to see what you're doing. You sitting here looking all happy and shit. What's up?"

"Nothing much, just moving on with my life and loving it."

"Bullshit, man. Who's the girl?"

"Aw, man, why's it gotta be like that?"

"'Cause I know your ass, man. Who is she?" he asked with a goofy look on his face.

"Nobody. It's all me realizing that I never should've left the game."

"Game? What game?" he asked, confused.

"The players game. I should have stayed in it no matter who I was with."

"What? Man, you're talking crazy now."

"No, I'm telling the truth, man. I finally realize it now."

"Now you sound like Rick's crazy ass."

I paused for a moment and just looked away. Instead of commenting, I just changed the subject.

"Yeah, so are you off this weekend?" I asked.

"Yeah, but starting next Monday I have to work the three-to-eleven shift."

"Damn. How do you put up with those hours, man?"

"Well, when you love what you do, it doesn't bother you."

"I heard that, man." I grabbed the menu and began looking it over.

As we continued to talk the waitress took our orders and brought us our food. It was good being back to my old self, talking shit with my boy about things like before. I was really feeling like a different person.

After lunch I headed back to the office where Dana and I worked on our new project. Dana was sitting behind her desk with her shoes off with those beautiful feet out in the open. I sat next to her staring at them occasionally as we continued to work. Like I said, she was strictly professional in the office, so no major flirting went on. We gave each other a look every now and then, but that was it until we left work.

That night I had dinner with her at her place. She made this Puerto Rican dish that was off the chain. It had chicken, rice, and beans, and a spicy gravy that you put over the rice. Later on that night we worked on a puzzle together, showered, and cuddled in bed until we both fell asleep.

I got up at around five o'clock the next morning because I had to go to my place and get a change of clothes. She slept peacefully as I tiptoed out of the room and out of the door. By the time I got to my apartment I had to use the bathroom something bad. I ran up to the door with my keys in hand trying to find the one for my locks. When I unlocked the first one, the door slightly opened by itself. *Hmm,* I thought, *that's strange.* I had made sure I locked both of my bolts before I left my apartment. I figured I'd forgotten to lock one of them when I rushed out of the apartment or something. Anyway, I darted into the bathroom and took a serious morning whiz before jumping in the shower. I then went inside my bedroom and grabbed a nice suit out of the closet and started getting dressed. While I was doing this, the phone rang. *Who could that be this early in the morning?* I thought.

"Hello," I answered as I buttoned my shirt.

"Hey, you left me kind of early today," Dana said, sounding half asleep.

"Yeah, I had to come home and get something to wear for work."

"Oh, well, why don't you bring some clothes over tonight so you won't have to get up so early? Besides, I really wanted you this morning. I'm lying here all hot and ready for you."

"Damn," I said as I thought about how good her sex was. "Well, I tell you what, maybe we could arrange something for this afternoon."

"Oooh, sounds good to me, baby," she replied, sounding sexy.

"Okay, it's set then. This afternoon at your place . . . Well, I'll see you at work in a few. Hey," I said before hanging up, "is it real hot?"

"Ooooh, *papi*," she said in a sexy voice. "It's sizzling."

"Damn," I said as my hard-on popped up. "Well, shit, I can't wait till lunch."

"Me either," she replied.

"All right, baby. See you at work. Hey, and wear some sexy under-wear today," I said, licking my lips as I envisioned her naked body.

"You got it, baby. Bye."

I hung up the phone with a hard-on strong enough to cut dia-monds. I still had a mental picture of how sexy Dana looked before I left. I finished getting dressed and made it to work. When I walked into my office, Dana came in behind me.

"Hey, I brought you the project release forms to sign so we can pass this on to the client."

Damn, still the professional, I thought. We had just gotten off the phone earlier that morning talking about sexing each other up and down, and she walked into my office like we just met or something. But I guess that's the way we needed to be to keep people out of our business.

"Oh, thanks," I replied as I grabbed the papers.

After I signed each document Dana walked out of my office and back to hers. For the remainder of the morning that's where I stayed, looking over project plans. When twelve o'clock came around, we both darted out the door five minutes apart and met at her place. By the time I walked through the door, I had already unbuttoned my shirt and unzipped my pants. We sexed everywhere we could think of, on the kitchen floor, in the bed, and even in the bathroom as she tried to comb her hair before going back to work. It was the bomb!

When we made it back to work things were back to normal, well, almost anyway. When I got back to my office, there was an envelope lying on my desk from Dana. When I reached inside, there was her bright red thong, which she had put on before we left her apartment. I couldn't do anything but smile as I rubbed it against my face, smelling the sweet scent of her perfume on the crotch of her thong. That shit made my day.

We spent the evening having dinner in bed. Dana cooked another delicious meal, but this time she put each dish on a plate and placed everything on a tray, which she put between us as we sat watching a Lifetime original movie. The room was filled with candlelight that set a sort of mellow mood. Every now and then she would slide her leg over and rub her soft toes against my leg.

After we got full, I carried the tray into the kitchen, got us some more wine, and headed back to the bedroom, trying to catch the end of a movie. When I walked through the bedroom door Dana was standing near her closet with her hands behind her back with a bright smile on her face.

"What are you up to?" I asked, smiling back at her.

"Well, nothing much. I have a surprise for you, being that your birthday is coming up in a few weeks."

"My birthday?" I said as my eyebrows shot up with surprise. "How did you know when my birthday was?"

"I have my ways, baby."

"Oh, you do, huh?" I replied.

"That's right," she said, walking toward me.

As she got closer I could see part of her breast showing through the side of her nightgown. She stopped in front of me and extended her arm.

"Well, surprise," she said as she looked in my eyes.

I reached for the envelope and opened it. "Wow, tickets to a cruise," I said, excited. "Aw, man, a cruise to Puerto Rico."

Dana's face turned red. "Do you like it?"

"Hell yeah," I said as I pulled her close to me.

"Good. I thought maybe we could get away for a few days, and this way you could meet some of my family."

"Hell yeah, I would love to. Thank you, Dana. No one has ever surprised me like this before. Thank you," I said as I walked her to the bed, taking off her gown. We embraced in another kiss that led to another night of sex. It felt like every time we made love was better than the last time.

That morning we both got up, jumped in the shower together, and headed to work. To keep from coming in at the same time I stopped at Krispy Kreme and bought the guys in my office doughnuts. I spent the remainder of the day upstairs in meetings with Mr. Ford. By the time I made it back to my office Dana had already left for the day. She left me a voice message that she was going to the gym to work out but that she would be home later that night. Still tired from the night before and from those boring-ass meetings throughout the day, I decided to go home and chill out in my own bed for a change.

When I got home I jumped in the shower and put on some shorts and a T-shirt and relaxed on the couch. I looked over at my answering machine and noticed the light flashing with two messages. One was from Mike and the second was from my mother telling me about dinner on Sunday. I got up and made myself a drink and read over my mail. When I opened my credit card statement, I noticed the dates on a couple of charges. It was the same night I caught Jennifer cheating on me. Still a bit frustrated, I tossed the statement aside and opened more mail. When I finished I called Dana, who was on her way home from the gym.

"Hey."

"How are you?" she asked.

"I'm cool, just chillin' right now, about to crash for the night."

"Already? You want me to come over?"

"Well, you're almost home so we can just get together tomorrow."

"Are you sure? 'Cause I can shower at your place and leave early in the morning to get some clothes."

"No, don't go through all that. We can just get together tomorrow. I'm kinda tired anyway."

"Well, okay. Have a good night, and I'll talk to you tomorrow."

"Okay," I replied as I hung up the phone, yawning.

I got up the next morning and got dressed for work for yet another day of long meetings with Mr. Ford and some of our support staff who were on-site from various locations to discuss a possible upgrade of our Billright software. Because I was the lead on these projects, it was mandatory that I attend. When I got outside to my car I noticed it leaning on one side. I walked around to the front passenger side and noticed that my tire was flat. *What the fuck is this?* I thought. I looked at the other cars around mine and noticed that they were flat as well. I glanced at my watch and realized I didn't have much time before my meeting with Mr. Ford and the clients. *Shit, I can't be late 'cause I'm the only one with the details of the project,* I thought as I walked around my car. Quickly I called Dana.

"Hello," she said softly.

"Hey. Are you up yet?" I asked nervously.

"Yeah, I'm up. Why?" she asked.

"Good, 'cause I need a ride to work bad. I have a meeting with Mr.

Ford in about thirty minutes. Can you help me out? Shit, I'll owe you big time for this," I said.

"What's wrong?" she asked

"I don't know. I have a flat tire and I don't have time to fix it and make the meeting."

"Sure," she said. "I'm on my way."

In what seemed like fifteen minutes Dana was there. I jumped in her truck, and we sped down the street, making it just in time for the meeting. When I got inside I was out of breath.

Mr. Ford looked concerned for a moment but smiled as he got up to greet me. "Good morning, Troy. Are you okay?"

"Yes, sir, just had some car trouble this morning and was rushing trying to get here on time."

He looked at his watch. I still had about five minutes before the meeting started. "You're fine. They're usually late anyway. Have a seat and let's discuss the details before the call," he said as he gathered his notes.

The meeting went fine up until the last hour. The clients didn't understand my explanation of our software and how effective the upgrade would be to their business. Before they spent any money on the upgrade, they insisted that I travel out to Orlando to give them a trial run. I was okay with it up until they mentioned the date, September 14, my birthday weekend, the same day Dana and I were supposed to go on our cruise. I tried to get them to change it, but that was the only time that was available.

Disappointed, I left the meeting and went straight to Dana's office to tell her the news. Her door was open, and she was standing up looking out the window. I knocked softly as I entered.

She turned around and greeted me with a smile. "Hey. How was your meeting? Did you make it on time?"

"Yeah, I made it," I replied with a somber look.

"What's wrong? Why the long face?" she asked as she walked toward her desk to sit down.

"Well, I got some bad news."

"Bad news? What bad news?" she asked, looking puzzled.

"Well, it's about the meeting. The client wants me to come to Orlando to give them a trial run of the new Billright upgrade."

"And so, what's so bad about that?"

"Well, the bad news is that it's on the same weekend as the cruise."

She stood and took a deep breath. "Well, can't they change it? Did you ask them if another day was possible?"

"I already tried to get them to do that."

"Well, why that weekend?" she asked.

"It's the only weekend they have available, and Mr. Ford really wants this deal."

Dana stood there staring at me as her face began to turn red as she spoke in Spanish. I knew she was cussing somebody's ass out, but it wasn't me.

"Hey, wait. Let's change the date and go the week before or the week after," I said.

"We can't do that," she replied. "I bought the tickets from a travel agent, and the purchase and the time are final."

"Well, we can do something else. I know, why don't you come with me and we can kick it in Orlando?"

"You won't have time to do anything but work, Troy. I don't want to just sit around in some hotel while you're out working and too tired to go anywhere. Just go on, and we'll get together when you come back. It's okay, I'll just have to plan something else, that's all," she said, deep in thought.

"Hey, don't sweat it. We'll just do something special before *and* after I get back, how's that?"

She smiled, nodding as she sat back in her chair.

After work Dana drove me back to my apartment. I went over to my car and changed my tire. It looked like someone had purposely cut it with a damn hunting knife or something. I was mad as hell because the tire cost sixty-five dollars.

As I began changing it something suddenly hit me. I slammed down the lug wrench and started cussing.

"What's wrong?" Dana asked.

"Nothing, nothing at all. I'm just mad as hell about my fucking tire."

"Well, it's just flat. It'll be all right, baby."

"Yeah, uh-huh," I said under my breath.

Dana stayed around as I mumbled to myself before she finally headed upstairs.

I finished changing the tire, went inside, and got in the shower to clean up a little. I was still hot because I knew it was no one but Paula's crazy ass who did this. It had to be. This had signs of her crazy ass written all over it. *That's all right, though, I'll get even with her*, I thought.

When I came out of the shower, Dana was standing in the kitchen with one of my T-shirts on that hung past her knees. Seeing this kinda eased my anger a little. She turned in my direction as I walked into the kitchen

"You cooled down enough to eat?" she asked.

"Yeah, I'm straight now. What's for dinner?"

"I just put together some hot wings and fries."

"Yeah, that's cool."

We sat down and ate together in complete silence as I thought more about Paula and how I was going to handle the situation.

CHAPTER 21

Table for Three

Sunday I had promised my mother I would come by since I had missed the last two hanging out with Dana. Nothing had changed though. The family was still the same and doing the same thing. My dad sat outside drinking his beer, talking shit with my uncles as usual, and my little cousins played in the backyard while my aunts and my mother prepared dinner.

I was outside with the guys listening to them talk about old times, when they played football against one another, and how they ran the ladies wild. I laughed at the old-ass lines they used to run on the women back in the day and how most of the women fell for them. Later I wandered off and watched as the kids played in the back. I sat down on one of the lawn chairs and let my mind kinda drift. I stared up at the clouds and watched as they slowly moved across the sky, still keeping their shape, and how the birds flew freely from place to place, not having a care in the world. The breeze, which was nice and gentle, moved the leaves at the top of the trees as though an invisible hand had combed through, caressing each one. My thoughts were interrupted by a touch on my shoulder, which startled me.

"Hey, son, what's up?" my dad asked as he pulled up a chair next to me.

"Oh, uh, nothing much, just sitting her thinking, that's all," I replied as I gathered myself.

"Yeah, I see. I asked your mama to back off from interfering with your personal life and let you handle your own business. She has been worried sick about you and Jennifer ever since you called that day. Is everything okay? You know, anything you want to talk about?"

I looked away. "No, not really. I was just thinking about how funny life is. You know, how one minute you feel like you're on top of the world and the next you're flat on your back, down and out."

"No, son, you're never down and out, just down. And if you're strong you won't be down for long. These are obstacles put in our lives to make us stronger. If I gave up every time something bad happened I don't know where I'd be right now."

I sat there nodding in agreement as he talked.

"You see, it wasn't easy getting—" he said but he was cut off by the ringing of my cell phone.

"Hold up for a minute, Dad," I said as I reached for my cell phone.

"Hello," I answered.

"Hey, what you doing?"

"Hey, Dana," I said with a smile. "I'm just chillin' over at my folks' place. What you up to?"

"I just got home from church and called to see if you wanted to grab some lunch or something, but I guess you already ate, huh?"

"Well, actually I haven't yet. I'm at my parents' house for Sunday dinner. Hey, why don't you come over and have dinner with us? This way you can get a chance to meet them."

"Well, are you sure it's okay?"

"Girl, yeah. They're cool. Just come on."

"Well, okay."

"Cool," I said.

I stayed on the phone another five minutes giving her directions. When I got off the phone my dad was staring oddly at me like he was trying to figure me out or something.

"Who is that you got coming over to my house, boy?" he joked.

"Oh, just a friend of mine, that's all," I replied nonchalantly.

"Female?"

"Yeah, a female. Why? What's up with that?"

"Nothing. Just asked."

"She's cool, Dad. We work together."

"Oh, but just a friend, huh?"

"Yep."

"Okay, I hear you, but just be careful with that friend stuff, especially when you work with them."

"What do you mean by that?" I asked.

"Oh, nothing. Just saying be careful, that's all."

"Uh-uh, what do you mean by that, Dad? We're just friends."

"Boy, I ain't no fool. I know what's going on here. All I'm saying is be careful. Right now your ass and your heart are in two different places. You need to put both of them in the same place."

"What do you mean by that? Like I said, we're just friends," I said, chuckling at his little saying.

"You'll figure it out one day," he said as he walked away.

My dad was full of old-ass sayings. Some of them made no sense to me whatsoever. I shook my head and sat back in my chair looking into the sky again.

About a half hour later, Dana arrived. I saw her coming up the driveway moving cautiously like she was unsure of the address. I walked up the driveway and met her as she parked. When she got out of the truck she was dressed sexy but appropriate with her jean shorts on. She brought a nice bottle of wine for dinner, which I thought was very cool. My uncles and cousins were staring her up and down as we walked inside the house.

I took her to the kitchen and introduced her to my mama, who was still cooking along with my aunts. My mama took one look at Dana and rolled her eyes at me. I could tell then that something wasn't right. I guess it was because I didn't tell her that Dana was coming, but whatever it was that bothered her she let me know with her eyes.

I introduced Dana, then grabbed the wine and put it in the fridge while they talked. Even though my mama seemed bothered, she didn't make Dana feel uncomfortable. Instead they laughed and talked for several minutes before I walked back over to them. I took Dana outside to introduce her to my dad and my uncles.

As we walked through the den Dana reached over and grabbed my hand as I escorted her out the back door. I looked back at my mama, who was standing there with a frown shaking her head. Ignoring the look, I just continued out the door.

The minute I introduced Dana to my dad they hit it off. Since he had been to California so many times they had a lot to talk about, which made Dana feel very comfortable. They were hitting it off so well that they left me there looking stupid.

I walked back inside to get a couple of sodas. My mama was standing near the refrigerator watching me as I got the sodas out of the fridge.

"So this is your new girl, huh?" she asked.

"What! Oh no, Mama, we're just friends."

"Come on, boy, I know better than that. I saw the way she reached over and grabbed your hand."

"Aw, Mama, that was nothing. That's how they do things in California."

"Troy, it's obvious that this girl has something else on her mind. So if you two are just friends, you better let her know it."

"Mama," I said, looking her in the eye, "it's cool. We're just good friends, that's all."

"Okay, okay, Troy. Your dad asked me to stay out of this. Just be careful, hear?"

"Yes, ma'am," I replied as I walked outside to join Dana.

When dinner was ready, we all sat down and ate. From time to time my mother would look over at Dana as she sat close to me. I could tell that my mother felt uncomfortable because she loved Jennifer so much that it was hard trying to adjust to someone new.

My dad was all in Dana's face making sure she had everything she needed to be comfortable. By Dana's expression I knew she felt at home. After dinner I walked Dana to her truck and she left. When I got back inside I was waiting on my mama's speech. She was standing there in the kitchen washing dishes with my aunts, still giving me crazy looks. I passed her and walked in the back to my old room and lay across the bed, still full from the big meal. Moments later she came in.

"Just friends, huh?" she said again as she walked in.

"Yeah, just friends, so don't give me a lecture, Mama."

"Oh, I didn't come to give you a lecture. She seems nice. I'm just saying there's something about her that doesn't feel right to me, that's all."

"Like what, Mama? She is very nice, polite, and a good friend. Stop trying to find the negative in her until you get to know her. You'll see she's cool. Besides, you said the same thing about Jennifer when you first met her."

"Yeah but—"

"Mama, Mama, it's okay. You think that I'm jumping back into something, but I'm not. I ain't trying to get serious with nobody. I'm just tired of being alone all the time, and Dana is a good friend I can talk to."

"Okay, okay, I'm just saying—"

My dad interrupted our conversation by bursting through the door to my room.

"I know you not in here giving this boy a hard time about that girl."

"No, we're just talking," Mama said.

"Yeah, whatever," he said, laughing. "C'mon out here. Everyone is getting ready to leave."

I got up and left with everybody else. If I didn't, I knew my mama would have interrogated me all night.

CHAPTER 22

Who's that Girl?

The time for my trip to Orlando finally arrived. I was still pissed off with the fact that I had to spend my birthday weekend working instead of going on the cruise.

Dana and I hung out the night before, but it still wasn't the same as a cruise. I drove myself to the airport so that I could park my car in a safe area instead of leaving it at my apartment complex to get vandalized again. On my way Mike called.

"Hey, man, what's up?" I said.

"Yo, what you got planned for your birthday?"

"Man, I'm on my way to Orlando on business."

"What?"

"Yeah, I got bullshitted on my birthday, man."

"Damn," he said. "I thought maybe we were gonna kick it or something."

"I wish, dog, but I'm headed to the airport right now."

"Well, let's do something when you get back."

"Sounds cool to me, man."

Mike paused for a moment. "Hey, I know you don't want to hear this but Jennifer called last night."

"Man, I don't want to hear—"

"Wait, hold up, Troy, let me finish," he said. "She'll be in Pensacola this weekend, and she had your things boxed up and wanted me to take them over to your place for her."

"Yeah, whatever, that's cool."

"And she also wanted to give you a present she bought you for your birthday."

"Hell no. Just tell her to bring me my things. She can keep her present. She might as well keep my clothes too. She had them for so long the shit is probably out of style by now anyway."

"Well, she's been gone since you two split up. She said she was trying to stay busy to keep from thinking about you."

"Yeah, right, and you believe that?" I asked.

"Oh, I don't give a damn. I got my wife. I'm just telling you what she said. She said that she has given up now because you won't even write her back. She said she has mailed you three letters in the past two weeks and you still haven't written her back."

"She's a damn lie, man. The only thing she sent me were e-mails and she sent me those when we first broke up. I never even seen no letters from her lying ass. If I had, I probably would've trashed them anyway."

"Well, like I said, I'm just telling you what she told me. Anyway, she'll be in Pensacola for about a week or so, and then she's moving to New York."

"Whatever, man. Look, I'm about to park so I'll hit you up when I get back."

"A'ight, man. Well, be safe."

"Yeah, later."

When I got off the phone with Mike I had a knot in my stomach. I grabbed my things out of the car and checked my bags. The first thing I looked for in the airport was the bar. Since I had about an hour before my plane left I sat there and had a few drinks. By the time I boarded the plane I had a nice buzz. I needed that to keep my mind off Jennifer and what Mike said, but it was hard. *Damn,* I thought. *She's moving to New York*. I began to feel empty inside. Thinking about that really fucked me up.

When I got to Orlando and checked in I went down to the hotel bar and had a few more drinks. Since it was Friday it was kind of packed. Most of the people there were on business too. I could tell because they came together in groups, some with their luggage still in hand.

As the night went on I met a few guys who worked for our office in Nevada. I remembered one of them from a conference some time the year before. His name was John. He was your typical computer programmer, with the long ponytail, square glasses, and white sneakers, which he wore with everything. He came over and introduced the rest of the guys with him and we all sat down and had a few drinks together, discussing business. Frankly, I was kinda bored but I played it off. They were all kinda nerdy, and we really didn't have much to talk about.

There was one brother in the group named Jessie who was cool. He worked for our office in Nevada too. I could tell he was bored 'cause all he did was look around the room, not paying any attention to what was being said at the table.

Later, he and I struck up a conversation, talking about the different honeys who walked into the bar. Jessie thought he was a real mack 'cause every time a honey would look our way he swore she was looking at him.

I found out that he was going to the same company as me the next day, Perl Industries. He was there for another project that screwed up his weekend, and he was doing everything he could to make the best of it. We talked for about an hour until this honey caught his eye and he left and sat with her. I got up and headed to my room and crashed for the night from all that drinking.

The next morning I got up and had breakfast. I took a cab over to Perl Industries and began working. It was my birthday, so I was rushing to finish so that I could leave early and hang out for a minute. When lunch came I was just about finished with my testing. I decided to grab a snack or something in the lunchroom downstairs. When I walked in, I saw Jessie sitting in a corner drinking coffee.

"Hey, what's up?" I asked.

"Oh, hey, man, I'm just chillin'," he replied as he sipped his coffee.

"Did you get with that honey last night?"

"No, man. She was married and shit and is in Orlando for her sorority convention. I talked to her for a few and then I went to my room and crashed."

"Man, I thought you were on it the way she was in your grill," I said, trying to fuck with his ego.

"Yeah, I could tell she wanted to be out, but, man, I wasn't trying to spend the whole night working on it, you know."

"Yeah, I feel that, man."

Suddenly my cell phone rang. "Hold up a minute," I said as I answered my phone. "Hello . . . Oh, hey, Dana. What's up?"

"Happy birthday," she said, all excited.

"Thank you, baby. I appreciate that. Yeah, today I'm another year older."

"That just means you're getting better," she said.

"You think?" I said with a chuckle.

"Oh yeah, I can't wait till you get back. I really miss you."

"Yeah, I miss you too. What are you doing tonight?" I asked.

"Well, really nothing. I think I may just stay home and read this book I bought."

"Okay. Well, I'm gonna try to hang out for a minute, but I'll call you later tonight."

"How is work going, by the way?" she asked.

"Oh, it's cool. I still think this shit could've waited till next week sometime, but fuck it, I'm here now."

"Yeah, I know. Well, okay, have fun tonight but not too much fun," she said firmly.

"Yeah, I'll do that," I replied as I laughed. "I'll call you later."

"Okay, bye."

When I got off the phone I had a little smile on my face at the thought of Dana calling me and wishing me a happy birthday. Minutes later it seemed like everyone in my family called. Jessie was sitting across from me looking at me, shaking his head and laughing at the things I was saying as each person called.

"Damn, man, you're popular today," he said, leaning over his empty coffee cup.

"Yeah, everybody's calling me wishing me a happy birthday."

"Oh, it's your birthday? Shit, it's on then. Let's hang out tonight. I know this live strip club downtown, man, with some bad honeys. You wanna be out?"

"Hell yeah," I replied, nodding.

"Well, hell, let me finish up here, and I'll meet you at the hotel bar at around six o'clock."

"Cool," I said as I got up from the table.

I went back into the computer lab and started working. I was excited about going to the strip club. I worked so fast that I was out of there by four o'clock and back in my room. Since we were probably gonna be out late I took a shower and lay down for about an hour.

At six o'clock I went down to the bar where Jessie was sitting waiting on me.

"You ready?" he said as he got up.

"Hell yeah," I replied.

"Let's be out," he said as we walked out the door.

We jumped in a cab and headed downtown. When we got to the club, there was a short line outside. The club was huge on the outside with neon lights flashing. The first thing I saw when we went inside were two girls dancing together over in a corner. They were feeling all over each other's titties and ass, licking their tongues out at the guys standing there with their money out. There were butt-naked women walking all around with no shame. They even had a few naked women serving drinks behind the bar.

We took a seat near the main stage of the club.

"So what do you think so far?" he asked with a grin.

"Wow, this looks like the spot," I replied as I continued to look around. "They got some fine women in here."

"Wait, my brother, you haven't seen nothing yet."

There were small stages on the side of the main one with women dancing and giving private dances. The fascinating thing about it was that the women were either black or mixed. All the women seemed to work out, 'cause their bodies were tight and firm. The main stage was empty. I guess it was still early and people were still lining up to come in. The waitress who served us even had a body. She was short with black hair and had the prettiest blue eyes I had ever seen. She brought us our drinks, while Jessie and I just sat back and watched as the men went crazy over the girls dancing on the side stages. I got up and tipped a couple of girls every now and then, just to get a closer look at their bodies. Jessie just sat there drinking.

"Hey, you not gonna get up and check out these fine-ass honeys, man?" I asked as I sat down.

"No. I ain't gonna waste my money on them. I'm gonna get my drink on and wait on the headliners to dance in about another hour or so."

"Oh, they got more honeys back there?"

"Hell yeah. Man, I'm telling you this is the spot. Pretty soon it'll be so packed in here you won't be able to move. So just hold on to your money and get your drink on. Get what you want. It's on me tonight."

"Cool," I said as I signaled for the waitress.

More people continued to come in. After about an hour and a half, the lights on the main stage came on. It looked almost like we were at a concert or something. People started walking closer to the stage as the deejay announced the first dancer. When the curtains opened, out came this beautiful chocolate honey. She had shiny, silky hair and a real firm ass. She came out dancing to Lil' Kim's "Magic Stick." She was shaking her ass and dancing like she was possessed or something. Jessie jumped up and ran over to the bar and got a stack of one-dollar bills and came back over to the table.

"Here you go, Troy. Let's head up to the stage." He handed me at least fifty dollars in ones.

"No, man. Keep this. I got some money," I said as I reached for my wallet.

"Shiit, man, I'm just buying the drinks. You on your own tipping these honeys," he said, laughing. "I just thought you needed some ones."

I laughed as I gave him two twenties and a ten. We walked up to the stage and watched as one honey after another came out dancing. It seemed like each one was prettier than the last.

I hate to say it but Jessie reminded me of Rick when it came to strip clubs. He was just throwing money at the honeys as they danced by.

All of a sudden this girl came out on Aaliyah's "I Care 4 You." She had the sexiest walk and the prettiest titties with big round nipples that pointed out. As she got closer I could see that she was the prettiest one in the club.

"Damn, she's fine," I shouted.

Jessie, who was reaching in his pocket, looked up.

"Man, do you see how beautiful she is?" I said. "Damn, look at that body."

When she got in front of us, I pulled out a wad of ones and just threw it in the air above her head and watched as the money fell like raindrops over her. Smiling, I looked over at Jessie, who was walking back to his seat. I watched as this girl lay on the floor with her legs wide open playing with herself as the crowd went wild. I didn't really get a good look at her until she threw her hair back, which shocked the hell out of me.

Damn, I thought, *she looks just like Dana*. I mean from head to toe. She could pass for Dana's twin.

After she finished dancing, I went back over to the table where Jessie was sitting with his drink in hand.

"Man, why did you leave? That honey was bad as hell. She reminded me of a girl back at home I've been kicking it with."

"Yeah, she reminded me of somebody, too," he said in a semilow tone.

"Oh yeah, one of your honeys at the crib?" I asked, smiling.

"Hell no. This crazy bitch wasn't my lady. We just worked together."

"Oh yeah?" I asked.

"Yeah," he said.

"Damn, man, you must really hate that honey to walk away from the stage while all that was on there."

He frowned and took another sip of his drink. Seeing this reaction, I got curious.

"So what happened, man? You make it seem like she was bad news or something," I said.

"Shiit, she was. Check it out, man. This guy at work met her through someone at our office. He was divorced so he was like 'cool, I'll hang out with her.' So they hooked up and went out for a few months, no big deal, then shit started getting serious on her part, and she was demanding all his time. Seeing this, he tried to back off and kinda cool out a little before it got out of hand. I was out of town working on a project, so he would tell me shit about her. You know, how nice and fine she was and things like that. So, man, all of a sudden she started changing. When he didn't return her phone calls she started really tripping. She started stalking him, calling his ex-wife, calling his parents and shit, cussing them out. She poured acid on his car, cut his tires even, called the police on him, and said that he whipped her ass."

"Damn, man, that's messed up," I said in amazement.

"That ain't all. His father just had heart surgery about a year before, and one time when she knew he was out of town, she got someone to call the house like they were the police at three in the morning and tell his parents that he was killed in a car wreck."

"What?" I asked in disbelief.

"Yeah, she had every piece of information on him, his Social Security number, his driver's license number, credit card numbers, and told them all that shit on the phone. Man, they had to rush his father to the hospital because after hearing that he had a mild heart attack and almost died."

I just sat there with a blank look on my face.

"That was the last straw, though. When he got back in town he went on her job, locked the door to her office, and kicked her ass all over the room. Because we all worked for the same company I saw her around but didn't actually know her until he started fucking with her. But, man, he whipped her ass so bad I thought he was going to kill her. It took about five people to kick her door in and get him off her. The police came and everything. Man, he whipped her ass so bad the judge locked him up for six months. He damn near lost everything he had because of her."

"Damn, man, that honey *was* crazy," I said.

"Damn right. That's why I walked away when that honey started dancing 'cause she looks just like her crazy ass. Man, my boy is still trying to bounce back behind that shit."

I shook my head in disbelief as I thought more about what Jessie said. He paused for a moment and took a sip of his drink. "I wonder whatever happened to her, man," he said under his breath. "I tell you what, he fucked her up in the end though. She has a scar directly under her chin where he kicked her in the face."

"Damn, he really did try to kill her, man."

He nodded as he looked for the waitress to get another drink. Minutes later Jessie kinda eased up a little. I think his buzz had really kicked in, and he was able to get back in the swing of things and enjoy the rest of the night. From that point we ordered one shot after another, toasting my birthday, until they cut us off at the bar.

We got in from the club around two in the morning. Jessie was fucked up and could barely walk. I drank so much I was buzzing too. I tried calling Dana in the cab, but no one answered her phone. She had called me earlier, but the music was so loud in the club that I missed her call.

Jessie staggered to his room and after a short struggle I made it to mine and just lay back in my bed with my eyes opened. As soon as I got comfortable, the alcohol started taking effect and everything around me began to spin out of control. I was buzzing so bad I started thinking about Jennifer and picked up my phone to call her but couldn't remember her number. I stared at the ceiling as it spun over my head until I finally fell asleep.

The next morning I woke up with a terrible headache, and my head was still spinning. I sat up, slowly rubbing my face before getting out of bed and out of my clothes, which smelled of cigarettes. I went into the bathroom and showered before getting dressed and going to work. Since it was my last day I took all my clothes with me so I could head straight to the airport when I finished. When I walked into the lab the smell of fresh coffee made me sick to my stomach, and it seemed like everyone had a cup. I worked in the downstairs lab where it was much quieter and where I could catnap a little every hour to get myself back on track.

By lunch I was starving and ready to put a little something in my stomach since I didn't eat breakfast. I headed down to the lunchroom where I ran into Jessie sitting at the same table as the day before having lunch.

"Hey, man, where you been? I went up to the lab looking for you," he said.

"Yeah, I went to the lab downstairs where it was more peaceful," I replied.

"Oh yeah, you were hungover, too, huh?" he asked, rubbing his head.

"Hell yeah. My head was killing me this morning, but last night was on."

"I told you, man," he said, laughing.

We sat there for a few minutes having lunch and jawing about the night before until I got up to head back to the lab to finish my testing. Before walking out of the lunchroom Jessie yelled out for me, stopping me in my tracks.

"Hey, Troy, hold up," he said as he walked out of the lunchroom, meeting up with me. "Here's my card. Hit me up sometime."

"Yeah, cool," I replied as I grabbed the card. "Maybe when I'm in Nevada we can hang out or something."

"No doubt, if you ever come to Nevada, it's on. It'll be like last night to the second power," he said as we slapped hands.

Later that evening I was on the plane heading back to Mobile. When I got to the airport I got in my car and drove home. I was glad to be there and couldn't wait to see Dana. A brother was feeling a little horny and ready for some serious sex. I called her, and she agreed to meet me at my apartment. I showered and waited on Dana to come over. I went to the kitchen, made me a drink, and relaxed in the den. Moments later, Dana came to the door struggling with several boxes. When I opened the door she rushed inside and set them on my kitchen counter. She then turned around with this big, beautiful smile and gave me a big hug and a kiss.

"Heeeey, I missed you so much," she said as she held me tight.

"Yeah, I missed you too," I said, rubbing up and down her back.

"I tried calling you several times last night, but you didn't answer. I got worried," she said.

"Oh, I was hanging out with one of the guys who was there on business, too, and didn't hear the phone ring."

"Well, did you have a good time?"

"Oh yeah, it was cool. We just hung out and had a few drinks downtown at this sports bar."

"Oh, that was nice. At least you got a chance to get out on your birthday."

"Yeah, it was fun."

She walked over to the kitchen counter and grabbed the presents, then guided me over to the couch.

"Well, happy birthday. Here are your presents," she said as she placed the boxes on the couch.

"Oooh, thanks baby," I said as I sat down and began opening them. There were three boxes. The first one was real long and kinda wide, wrapped in fancy paper like it was done professionally. When I got through the packaging I sat there amazed.

"Wow. Thanks, baby. This is nice," I said, excited.

Inside was a really nice black designer suit. It was neatly folded together to keep from getting wrinkled, so I just gently pulled all of the packaging off and stood up, holding it against my body.

"I hope you like it," she said, looking at my reaction.

"Like it? I love it. Wow, this is nice, baby. Thank you." I leaned over, giving her a kiss on the cheek.

"Try it on to see if it fits," she said as she cleared away the wrapping paper.

I tried on the coat, and it was a perfect fit. Dana sat back smiling as I walked to my bedroom to look in the mirror.

When I walked back into the den she was holding up the pants.

"Here, try these on, baby."

I took off the coat, and as I did I noticed the brand name on the inside near the buttons. *Wow, Versace,* I said to myself. *She paid some money for this.* I gave her the coat and tried on the pants. They, too, fit me to a tee. Dana reached down and handed me the other two boxes as I sat back down on the couch.

Since they were much smaller I opened them together. Again I was amazed. In one box there was a designer dress shirt with my initials on the cuffs, and in the second box there was a black-and-gray-striped Versace necktie that matched perfectly with the suit.

"Hey, baby. Thank you. This is very nice."

"Really?" she said with doubt in her voice.

"Yes. This suit is the bomb, truly."

"Well, I'm really glad you like it," she said as she sat back on the couch.

I began to gather up everything, neatly putting stuff back in the boxes before taking them to my room to hang up later. I walked into the kitchen to put some more ice in my drink.

"Oh, shit," Dana shouted as she dashed out the door.

"What!" I said but she didn't hear me.

I walked over to the door and saw Dana pulling bags out of her truck, before heading back to the apartment. When she walked inside she was frowning as she put the bags on the counter.

"What's wrong?" I asked as I walked to her.

"I stopped by Copeland's and got us dinner. But now it's cold and no good," she said, looking disappointed.

"What? Oh no, it's still good. Let's just heat it up in the oven. I'm sure it'll be okay."

"Yeah, but it's not the same."

"Wait a minute, watch this," I said as I got the food out and put it in serving dishes, placing them in the oven.

Dana had bought the big seafood platter that had everything on it. She reached in one of the bags and pulled out two bottles of wine, which were still cold, placing one in the fridge and the other on the counter, before she began setting the table for dinner.

When the food was ready, I placed everything on the table, opened the bottle of wine, and we had a nice quiet, romantic dinner. Everything was perfect. It was one of the best days of my life.

Later that night it got even better as we made passionate love until we both were exhausted and fell asleep in each other's arms.

While we slept, the phone rang at around two in the morning, waking us both up out of a deep sleep. Dana moved her head over on my chest as I answered the phone.

"Hello," I said in a sluggish tone.

No one said anything.

"Hello," I said a little louder.

"Troy," the voice said on the other end.

I paused for a minute, trying to catch the voice. It was Jennifer. I was so shocked I didn't know how to react. I lay there in silence as my heart started beating really fast and hard. Dana, who still had her head on my chest, felt this and sat straight up.

"Is everything okay?" she asked.

"Uh . . . I, uh, sorry, I didn't know you had company. I, uh, shouldn't have called. I, uh, just wanted to say happy birthday, that's all."

"Wait," I said as I got out of bed and walked toward the den. "I can't believe you would—"

"I'd better go," she said and hung up the phone.

I sat down on the couch staring at the phone pretty much in shock.

Hearing Jennifer's voice for the first time in months really fucked me up. I felt confused and angry at the same time. *Should I call her back?* I thought. *No, that's out. Well, what should I do? Lord, help me 'cause I feel all twisted inside. Why am I feeling like this? She's the one who cheated on me. The more I try to get this girl out of my mind, the more I realize I still love her. I need a drink.* I walked into the kitchen and grabbed the Hennessy.

As I took my first sip Dana came walking into the kitchen with my T-shirt on and hugged me from the back, kissing me on my neck. I quickly moved away from her and walked back into the bedroom.

"What's wrong with you?" she asked as she followed me.

"Nothing," I said softly as I got back into bed.

"Yes, something *is* wrong. What is it? Who was that on the phone? Did something happen to someone in your family?"

"No, Dana, nothing's wrong, okay?"

"Uh-uh, why are you acting strange then?" she asked as she reached out to hold me again.

"Dana, c'mon, please just chill and get back into bed, okay?" I replied as I rolled over on my side.

"Oh, so now I can't hold you? Who was that on the phone, Troy?" I just ignored her again and pulled the covers over me. "Troy," she said in a firm voice, "who was that on the phone?"

I lay there in bed with my eyes closed in deep thought as Dana walked out of the bedroom.

For a minute I enjoyed the peace and quiet until she came storming back in the room shouting at me from the top of her lungs.

"Is this why you're acting all crazy?" she said angrily.

I rolled over, facing her, shocked.

"Answer me, Troy. I looked at the caller ID. I know it was Jennifer."

"Look, don't trip, 'cause it ain't nothing," I replied nonchalantly.

"You're a lie. It *is* something. How long has this been going on?"

I ignored her.

"How long, Troy?" she asked as she threw the phone at me.

"Girl, what the hell is wrong with you?" I yelled.

"What the hell is wrong with you? What did she want?"

"What?"

"What did she want, Troy?"

"Girl, you better stop tripping and get back in this bed."

"No. Not until you talk to me about this shit."

"Ain't nothing to talk about, so get in bed."

"What do you mean ain't nothing to talk about? This bitch calls here in the middle of the night, waking me up, and has your heart beating like a damn drum. Then you sneak in the den to talk to her without telling me a thing. I think you better tell me something."

"Girl, I'm getting tired of this, now I told you it was nothing. Either get in this bed or take your ass home. I'm really not in the mood."

"What? What? I tell you what, I'll do just that. I'm gonna take my ass home," she said as ran into the den and gathered her things.

"Well, get the hell out then," I shouted.

As she got dressed she was still shouting obscenities, but I ignored her. She came back into the bedroom holding the suit she bought me, the extra bottle of wine, and what was left of the food.

"What?" I said as she stood there staring at me.

"Fuck you," she replied as she stormed out of the door, slamming it behind her. I could hear her outside as she sped off into the night. I didn't bother running out behind her, because I really wanted to be alone with my emotions, which were running wild. I just sat back in bed playing my conversation with Jennifer over and over in my head and thinking about the sound of her voice. I thought about how hurt she sounded as she heard Dana's voice in the background. I felt bad, because even though she hurt me, it was different than me hurting her.

In an instant, I realized something. I thought I still loved her. *But how could this be after all she's done to me?* I asked myself. *Well, do you really know if she cheated on you? Well, not really but before I end this, I need to find out once and for all so that I can finally have closure in my life. I can't move on until I know the truth about everything. I need to be sure.*

I got up and paced the floor with the phone in my hand, wanting to call. *I need to know for sure if she cheated,* I thought. But instead of calling I just got back in bed, sitting there the rest of the night contemplating.

CHAPTER 23

Right to Remain Silent

The next day Dana came in to work a little later than usual. Because I couldn't sleep, I got there around six o'clock and just closed my office door, trying to concentrate on work, but it was hard. Throughout the morning Dana and I passed each other in the hallway. I tried to at least speak, but she would look away and keep on walking.

After my last exhausting meeting I went to the break room to get a cup of water before going to my office. When I got to my office and opened the door Dana was sitting in my chair with her head down.

Before I could sit down, she stood up, leaning over my desk.

"Hey, you need to tell me what the deal is."

I walked back over to the door and closed it. "Hey, let's talk about it after work, okay? Now is not the time," I replied.

"No, I want to talk about this now," she said.

"Look, now is not the time. Wait till after work."

"No! I want to talk *now*," she said again firmly.

I could feel her getting more and more heated. Instead of pushing her buttons I suggested we go outside away from everyone in the office.

We both headed outside and sat in my car. Dana was pissed off, and her eyes were bloodshot.

"So what's up, Troy?" she asked.

"Damn, Dana, why are you acting like this at work?"

"'Cause I need to know where we stand, and I need to know *now*."

I paused for a minute as I gathered myself. "Well, Dana, I'm gonna be straight with you. I like our friendship and the way it was going, but I'm just not ready to settle down like you want."

"Friendship, is that what this was? Nigga, please. So you just used me to help you get over that bitch of yours, is that it?"

"No, it was nothing like that. You knew what I was dealing with when you met me. Don't sit there and act like you didn't."

"So what are you saying, motherfucka? Stop beating around the bush."

"I'm saying that if you can't be my friend, then maybe we need to chill."

"Oh, so you're saying if I don't continue to fuck you, then that's it, we're done."

"Well, no, you're taking it the wrong way."

"How else can I take it? Be a man for once and tell me."

"Look, take it like you want. Right now I just need some time to get my shit together, and if you can't understand that, then yeah, get the fuck on."

"You know what, fuck you," she said as she spit at me. I turned my head as the shit hit me all over my neck.

She opened my door, got out, and slammed it shut. I jumped out after her, wiping my neck as she trotted over to her truck. She got in, slammed the door, and sped off down the street. People who were outside stood there stunned as they watched us.

I turned and went back inside the building, stopping in the bathroom to clean myself up before going back to my office. As I sat behind my desk, I could see people whispering and pointing in my direction. Dana's little stunt was probably around the whole building. I was starting to get pissed off myself. I got up and walked back to my car and headed to the gym to cool off.

While at the gym I worked out with the weights and jogged a couple of miles to calm down. Since I had an extra change of clothes in my bag, I decided to shower at the gym to cool off from my intense workout.

When I got to my apartment I made myself a drink to calm me down some more. A few hours later I was buzzing, feeling good, and starting to think. I couldn't believe Dana was tripping like that. She knew what the deal was from the jump with me and her. *Then she spit on me. Hell no,* I thought.

After a couple more drinks, I found myself asleep on the recliner in the den. A short while later the phone rang, waking me up.

I knew who it was so I just let it ring. Drama always happened late at night when a person had a chance to think about all the shit that had happened during the day. I didn't have time for that, though, so I just lay back down. When my cell phone rang, I ignored that, too, and got up and went to bed.

I slept another good ten minutes, and the phone rang again. This time I was pissed because my sleep was completely broken.

"Hello!" I yelled in the phone.

"Hey, Troy. Troy, we had a boy."

It was Mike on the other end. Gail had just delivered their third child. He was so excited he could barely talk. I was completely up then and happy for him.

"Oh yeah? Where are you?" I asked.

"We're at Providence Hospital. She just had the baby about two hours ago," he said.

"Hey, well, let me get up. I'll see you in a few."

"Yeah. Okay, man. Hurry up so we can celebrate."

I got up and threw on some clothes and headed out the door. I made it to the hospital about thirty minutes later and saw Mike standing outside talking on his cell phone, still excited and smiling from ear to ear. I came up behind him as he continued his conversation. Seeing me he quickly got off the phone and walked up to me.

"Hey, man. Thanks for coming out. I tried to call Rick, but he's out of town."

I ignored that shit about Rick and shook Mike's hand to congratulate him.

"So let's go see your son, man," I said as we walked toward the elevator. We went to the nursery where you could see the babies through the window.

When we got there I knew which one was Mike's son right away. He looked just like him, nose and all, but not as chocolate yet.

"Mike, man, you can't deny this one. He looks just like your ugly ass, and he's big too."

"I know, man," Mike replied, still grinning as he slapped hands with me.

"How much did he weigh?" I asked.

"I think eight pounds, six ounces or something like that."

"Oh, okay. How's Gail?"

"Oh, she's cool, man. She's in her room resting. C'mon, let's go see her."

"Where are the girls?" I asked as we walked to Gail's room.

"Oh, Gail's friend is with them downstairs in the waiting area."

We went in to see Gail, who was half asleep. I walked over and gave her a big kiss on the cheek and congratulated her. She smiled as she went in and out of sleep. I stayed a little while longer as other family members started coming up to see little Michael Smith Jr.

Mike was a little preoccupied, so I decided to leave.

"Hey, man, I see you have your family here, so I'm out," I said as I walked toward the door.

"No, man. Hold up," he said as he continued to hug his cousins as they came in.

"Go ahead, man. It's cool. I'll call you tomorrow."

"Wait. Let me walk out with you 'cause I have to check on the girls."

"Hey, don't worry about it. I'll see if they need anything. Go ahead and just chill with your family."

"Oh, thanks, man. Call me on my cell if they need me for something," he said as he walked me to the door.

I got on the elevator and headed back downstairs to the lobby. When the elevator door opened I could hear the sound of the TV down the hall. I followed the sound all the way into the corner room near the back of the hospital. When I walked inside the waiting room, my heart dropped as I came to a halt.

Jennifer was sitting there watching the kids for Gail and Mike. The girls were both asleep on pallets next to her. As I stood at the door in shock, Jennifer turned in my direction. When she saw me, her eyes opened wide and her mouth dropped like she had seen a ghost. We stared at each other like we were both in a trance. My heart was beating so fast my whole body trembled. I was at a loss for words. Jennifer slowly got up from her chair and started walking out of the other door leading to the bathroom.

What should I do? I thought She was looking more beautiful than ever. She had cut her hair really short, kinda like Halle Berry's. It seemed like everything was moving in slow motion. I was still at a loss for words as she kept getting closer and closer to the bathroom. Just as she reached out to open the door, I called for her.

"Jennifer, wait!"

She stopped in her tracks, turned around, and looked at me as tears flowed down her cheeks. She started shaking her head slowly as she wiped her eyes.

"No, Troy. I can't do this. I can't do this at all," she said as she broke down, crying. I walked slowly over to her, still nervous.

"Uh . . . well, I can't lie. I don't know what to say right now because this is awkward for me too."

Still she remained silent. I reached over and wiped her eyes as the tears continued to flow.

She looked up at me. "Troy, I never cheated on you. I promise, I never cheated on you." All I could do was bite down on my lip real hard. "I know you have someone else now, but I just needed for you to know that I never cheated on you in any kinda way." I couldn't say a word. I didn't know what to say or do. She turned away. "Please just go," she said as she walked back over to where the girls were sleeping.

Stunned, I just walked outside to my car and sat there for a while. I was hurting really bad inside. For some reason, I believed her. The look she gave me when she spoke was that of complete sincerity. But I know what I saw that night. I remember everything like it was yesterday. *What should I do?* I thought. I wanted to go back inside, but I didn't know what to say. Instead I started my car and headed home.

CHAPTER 24

Moment of Truth

Itossed and turned for all of what was left of the night. When I got to work the next morning Dana was standing outside the break room talking to some women as I passed her by. She gave me a real evil look, turned her head, and continued with her conversation. I was so caught up about seeing Jennifer that it didn't really faze me how she was acting. I just kept walking right past her ass and into my office, closing the door behind me.

I checked my e-mail, then started my projects. Throughout the day I would see Dana pass my office. I'd never seen her go by that many times. She was smiling, being her old self, like nothing even happened. It was like she had two different personalities. One was sweet and innocent, and the other was that of a mean-ass bitch. But every time she went by I just ignored her crazy ass. Shit, I never made a commitment to her. All we shared was friendship, two adults having a good time.

Sitting behind my desk I must've written Jennifer about ten e-mails, but when it came time to send them, I deleted them all. Something about them didn't seem right. I didn't want to seem like I was begging her to come back. I just wanted us to meet up somewhere and talk. Maybe I could call Mike to help me out.

I looked at my watch. He was probably still sleeping from being up all night. I sat there for a moment, thinking. "Forget it. I'll just call her," I said.

I got my cell phone and started dialing. With each digit I hit, the more nervous I started to feel. I really got nervous when it rang.

"Hello," she answered softly.

I paused for a moment and cleared my throat.

"Hello," she said again.

"Uh, hey, Jennifer, it's me."

She paused. "Troy," she replied, surprised.

"Yeah, uh, it's me. Hey, sorry to bother you and everything, but I was wondering if we could meet up somewhere today or tonight or something."

She paused again, longer than the first time.

"Are you still there?" I asked.

"Troy, I don't know if I can do that."

"I just need to talk to you about all of this. C'mon, just five minutes of your time is all I'm asking for." I could hear as her voice began to tremble.

"Does it matter now, Troy? It's obvious you've moved on with your life. What's left to talk about? I explained everything to you in my letters, and you still ignored me. Then I took a chance on calling you, and you had a female there with you, so what's the use now?"

"Letters? What letters are you talking about? I never received any letters from you," I said.

"I sent you so many letters over the past few months and not one time did you even bother to respond to them. Besides, I've gotten over a lot of stuff since then and can't go back to it again."

"Wait, let's just meet for five minutes. That's all I'm asking for."

"Troy, I'm on my way back to Atlanta. I can't."

"C'mon, Jennifer, please. I need to talk to you."

"We can talk now," she replied.

"No, I need to see you in person. I can't do it over the phone."

"I don't know if I can do that, Troy."

"Just five minutes, Jennifer. That's all."

She paused. "Well, I'll be in town next Friday for one day. If I can, I'll stop by then. But I won't make you any promises."

"Fair enough," I said.

I was still nervous when we got off the phone, and it was really hard for me to keep my mind on my work. *I need a few days off or something to clear my head, 'cause right now I can't concentrate,* I thought.

I got up and checked the log at the receptionist's desk to see if there were days I could take off. As I looked at the sheet, I noticed that Dana was scheduled to be off for a few days starting the next day, which meant that someone had to be here to work on our projects. At first I was pissed but I dealt with it. Just the fact that I wasn't going to see her was good enough for me, so with that in mind I just headed back to my office.

The next day at work was peaceful and stress-free. No Dana, no drama, just some quiet time for me to work and get my head together for when Jennifer came.

Every time I thought about what I was going to say, I started getting butterflies like she was standing directly in front of me. It felt like I was meeting her again for the first time. Well, I knew one thing, this time it would be different. I was just gonna lay down all my cards and see what happened.

When I got home at the end of the day, I opened the door to a horrible smell. It was so horrible that I had to open my windows to air the place out. The shit made me sick to my stomach. I started looking around each room, trying to see what the hell was smelling so bad. I looked in the closets, under the bed, all in the bathroom, and even in the den until I finally found it. There was a dead rat, mouse, or whatever the fuck it was that was in the bottom broiler of my oven. I don't know how the fuck it got there but it was horrible. Even though the oven was off, the heat from the gas sent the stench all around the apartment and had my entire place smelling like shit. I immediately called the leasing office, pissed, because if they had a rodent problem, they needed to do something about the shit. All the money I was kicking out for a decent place and I had shit like this happening.

As soon as I called they sent a man over to spray the place down. They also sent a local cleaning crew over to clean my carpet, wipe down my walls, and even clean and disinfect my kitchen. It took them more than four hours to get things smelling halfway decent. In the meantime I left and washed some clothes so that I could at least have something to wear to work the next day. By the time I got back, it was late and I was too sick on the stomach to eat, so I showered and headed to bed.

I woke up the next day and was starving. I got up and shut some of the windows that were left open to dry the carpet, which was still kinda damp from the cleaning. For the most part, everything smelled fresh. I went into the kitchen and made a bowl of cereal before work. I was so hungry that I fixed a super-duper bowl to chow down on.

As the cereal hit the bottom of my stomach, I could hear it growl with relief it was so empty. By the third spoonful the sweetness of the cereal turned bitter. When I looked down in the bowl I could see tiny milk bubbles everywhere. With a mouthful of cereal I jumped up, ran to the kitchen, and spit it out in the sink. I walked back over to the table, puzzled, and stirred the cereal around. The shit started to suds up into even more bubbles. *What the hell is this?* I wondered. I walked over and opened the refrigerator to check the milk, but it wasn't supposed to go bad for another week. Still puzzled, I checked the cereal but it was fine too. I grabbed the milk, smelled it, and then shook it up really good and opened the top. The entire milk jug was thick and sudsy. I walked over to the sink and poured the rest of it down the drain. I grabbed my bowl and did the same. As I rinsed the bowl out I looked over at my liquid detergent and noticed that it was almost empty. *Hold up,* I thought, *I just bought this last week.* The first person I thought about was Dana. She probably did this shit before she stormed out the other night. It had to have been her. After her spitting in my face, I wouldn't put it past her. I was just glad she was out of my life and I wouldn't have to deal with this shit again.

When I got to work, I sat back in my chair thinking about Jennifer. Old feelings started coming back and I began to miss her more. I closed my eyes, envisioning how I used to hold her in bed, kissing and caressing her body right before we made love. How she used to rub my chest and reach down to put me inside her. Just as I was about to envision the good part, my cell phone rang. I was so deep in thought it startled me.

I reached for my phone. "Hello," I said.

"You need to come and get your shit from my place," Dana said angrily.

"What?" I replied.

"I said you need to come get your shit."

"What are you talking about?" I asked.

"Your shirts, your pants, and your shitty-ass drawers. I'll put them outside on the doorstep in a trash bag and you can get them."

"Yeah, whatever, just leave the bag there, and I'll pick it up later."

"Well, if you're not here by Saturday, I'm throwing this shit in the trash."

"Yeah, whatever."

"Fuck you, fuck you, you stupid mother—"

I hung the phone up.

The phone rang several times after that, but I didn't answer.

I was convinced from that moment that Dana was a serious nutcase. I tried to envision Jennifer and me together again, but after talking to Dana I just couldn't concentrate.

Late Thursday night Jennifer called. We set up a time of seventhirty Friday to meet at my place. My heart was pounding nervously about seeing her. After all that I'd been through lately, I wasn't sure about too much. It seemed like all the honeys I had dogged out, messed over, lied to, and cheated on had come back to haunt me. Karma's a bitch, and I was about to come face-to-face with my future Friday night, and find out what change I was going to have to make in my life with or without Jennifer.

All that night I tossed and turned. I couldn't wait to see Jennifer, but at the same time I was scared that whatever relationship we'd had might come to an end.

Friday morning I got up and cleaned up a little around the place. I really didn't go all out and set some kind of mood, because I didn't know what to expect. I did get a nice bottle of merlot and chilled it in the refrigerator, but that was about it.

As the day went on, I could hear the rain start to come down real heavy, which made everything outside look real gray and dreary. This put me in the mood to drink and relax a little.

I was sweaty and needed to freshen up before she got there. As my buzz kicked in I relaxed under the water as it washed the scum from my body while I went through in my mind what I wanted to say to her.

In the middle of my shower the phone rang, breaking my flow. I jumped out and ran to answer it, hoping to get to it before the caller hung up. By the time I got there it was too late. I looked at the caller ID and it read *Private Caller*. *Damn*, I thought, *I hope that wasn't Jennifer calling to tell me she was on her way.*

I looked over at the clock, and it read ten minutes to seven, so I still had enough time to get dressed and fix myself up little. I had walked back into the bathroom when I heard a knock at the door.

Still dripping from the shower, I nervously grabbed my towel wrap and proceeded to the door. *She's early for a change. Maybe that's a good sign*, I thought. But still I didn't want her to see me half naked. Rushing to get myself together, I cracked opened the door to let her in. As I did, the door was forced open. Since I was still dripping wet it caught me off guard and I staggered back.

When the door completely opened, standing there wearing a baseball hat, old jeans, and T-shirt was Dana. She had a trash bag in her hand as she stood there staring at me.

"Girl, what the hell is your problem?" I yelled.

"You, you're my problem," she said as she barged in. "Didn't I tell you to come and get this shit?"

"What? Girl, you better get your crazy ass outta my crib."

She threw the bag across my den, knocking down my lamp as my clothes scattered.

I grabbed her by the arm to put her out, and she began wrestling with me, kicking and scratching.

"Let me go," she kept screaming.

"Shut up, and get the hell outta here," I yelled as I tried to push her out the door.

I had one hand on her and my other hand was holding my towel wrap to keep it from coming off. I didn't want to be too aggressive because I knew I would be going to jail that night, so I just kept on trying to push her out the door.

Suddenly Dana starting kicking at me wildly and caught me in the balls. I felt the pain as it streaked through my body. I dropped to one knee as she darted off into my bedroom.

"What bitch do you have in here, huh? Where is she, mother-fucker? C'mon on out, bitch. I know your ass is in here hiding," she kept yelling.

I quickly caught my breath and darted into the bedroom after her. This time I was pissed. I grabbed her from behind and picked her off the floor, body-slamming her on the bed.

She was lying facedown kicking and screaming as I sat on top of her.

"Get off me! Get the hell off me!" she screamed as I held her down. She started spitting wildly everywhere.

I grabbed her by her head and stuffed her face into the pillow to shut her up, but she still kicked her legs around, trying to get away.

When I let her face up, all she could do was try to catch her breath. When she started to scream and yell again I stuffed her head back down. I wasn't trying to kill her. I just wanted her to quiet down enough for me to throw her ass out. Dana started crying as she struggled for air, so I turned her over, facing me. My towel wrap had completely unraveled, and I was sitting on her butt naked. She started whimpering. Her arms grew weak and her strength was almost gone.

"What the hell is wrong with you? Didn't I tell you to leave me the fuck alone?" I yelled.

As I continued to yell at Dana, out of nowhere Jennifer appeared at my bedroom door. She stood there with her mouth wide open and her eyes full of tears. I was so shocked all I could do was look at her.

I jumped up and ran toward her, grabbing my towel wrap, trying to put it on me. She backed up and quickly started for the door.

"Jennifer, wait!" I yelled as I ran after her.

"No, no, leave me alone," she yelled back as she continued on.

I grabbed her by her arm right as she got to the door. "Hold up, please!" I said.

"No, I'm leaving. I don't know what is going on, but I'm getting the fuck out of here," she replied as tears flowed down her face.

She tried to turn around again, but I grabbed her hand, accidentally knocking her keys and purse to the floor as she tried to get out the door. As I reached down to pick them up, I saw Dana charging at me with one of my dress shoes in her hand with the heel pointing at my face. I ran toward her, grabbing her arm as she swung. I knocked us both to the floor, and I landed on top of her. I could hear the breath leave her body as my weight fell on her. I looked back, but Jennifer was gone. I got up and ran to the door, and I could see her as she ran for my car in the pouring rain. I still had her keys in my hand, and her purse was on the floor next to Dana.

Jennifer opened my car door and got inside. I looked on the counter and realized that she had taken my keys and was about to drive off. Since I couldn't catch her before she took off, I ran to my bedroom and put on the first thing I saw lying across on my chair. Dana was still lying on the floor in the fetal position, holding her ribs and whimpering, as I dashed past her. By the time I got outside, Jennifer was gone. I jumped in her car and started behind her. When I caught up to her, she was at a red light getting ready to turn. I sped up, flashing my high beams so she could see me. The rain was so heavy that it was hard to see clearly.

When I got up to the corner to turn I could see Jennifer weaving on the road in front of me like she was struggling to maintain control. I sped up, gaining on her. She turned another corner just up ahead to get to the main street. As the car turned, it spun out of control, missing a van that was parked on the side street. As it continued to spin, the right front and back tires flew off, causing the car to tilt on the left side. My heart was pounding a mile a minute. A car that just missed her lost control and was heading toward me. I tried to dodge it by driving off the road, still trying to focus on Jennifer. All I could see was an eighteen-wheeler coming down the main street at full speed, heading straight for her. I tried to get back on the road, but I lost control and was headed for a tree. The last thing I heard before everything went dark was a loud crash.

I was awakened by a voice that sounded like it was coming out of a tunnel as it echoed in my ears. My upper body was hot, and I could feel pain in my ribs and shoulders. My eyes were still closed, and I heard the faded voices around me. As I slowly tried to open my eyes I could feel each one sting with every movement. My heart began to beat extremely fast as I remembered the last thing I saw before blacking out. I finally managed to open my eyes. They still burned, but I was able to see more clearly. I could see people standing around me as well as red and blue flashing from a police car. I tried to say something, but nothing would come out of my mouth. I tried to get up, but the people around me held me down. I struggled to speak, but still I couldn't talk. I wanted to check on Jennifer, but no one would let me get up.

I wiggled around, fighting the pain as it shot through my body. I looked down at my legs as the paramedics examined my body and people held me down. I tried to call out for Jennifer, but no one could hear me. I could feel someone wiping my face as I continued to struggle to get up. When I looked up, Mike, dressed in his policeman's uniform, was holding me down as he wiped my face and neck. I could see the bloody towel as he tried to find a cleaner part to wipe off my face. I tried to call out to him, but he didn't hear me either. He kept his eyes off me and continued to wipe the blood from around my face and eyes. I moved my head, still trying to get his attention, until finally he looked into my eyes. I moved my lips again, but he looked away. As I was lifted up and put on a gurney I was able to look over the people standing around me. When I focused, I saw two bodies lying near the accident with sheets over them saturated with blood. My heart starting beating faster and harder as I took a deep breath. Mike stood in my way, blocking my view as I struggled to speak. I found the strength to yell from my heart.

"Jennifer! Jennifer! Oh my God, noooooo. Jennifer!"

I could see Mike wiping his eyes as he turned away. I tried to reach in Jennifer's direction as I was wheeled to the ambulance. I didn't want to go. I yelled and yelled until they shut the doors and took off down the street.

I woke up to a roomful of people sitting around my bed in tears. My mother was holding my hand and machines were connected to all parts of my body. I had just enough strength to look around the room. Suddenly, I remembered what I had seen in the middle of the street. Tears began to flow down my cheeks as I called out for my mother. Seeing me struggle with words, she leaned over to me.

"Jen-Jennifer," I whispered.

"Jennifer," she replied as she squeezed my hand a little tighter. "She's, she's in surgery, baby."

Not believing her, I shook my head. I knew she was just saying that to keep me calm, but I knew what I saw.

"Jennifer," I whispered firmly.

"I know, I know. She's in surgery, baby."

I began to feel pain in my arms. I tightened my face to fight the hurt. I looked over and saw my father sitting in the corner with his Bible in his hand reading scriptures. I saw my uncles and aunts standing up looking at me lying in the bed, all wiping their eyes. I knew something was wrong, but they wouldn't tell me.

I lay back and stared up at the ceiling as tears continued to slowly flow out of the corners of my eyes.

My mind was still focused on Jennifer. I guess the medicine started kicking in again, because as I was looking up at the ceiling, it slowly became a blur right before my eyes.

When I woke again, Mike was standing over me. My mother and father were still there sitting in their same spots. I was more conscious than before and was able to communicate better.

"Mama," I cried out.

She leaned over, again still holding my hand. "Yes, baby?" she said rubbing my hand.

"Where is Jennifer?" I asked again.

Before she could answer, the doctor came in to examine me. "Hi, Troy. You feeling okay?"

I kept staring at my mother, waiting on a response, as the doctor continued examining me.

"You suffered two bruised ribs, a mild cut on the top of your head, and a broken arm. Your kidneys were bruised, so your back may be sore for a while, but for the most part, you were lucky. I would like to keep you here overnight to monitor your kidneys and after that you should be able to go home and rest."

"What about Jennifer?" I asked, looking over at him.

He paused and looked over at my mother, then back at me. "Well, Troy, she just got out of surgery." My heart was beating like ceremonial drums as he continued, "She suffered severe head, neck, and back injuries. We have her in intensive care right now."

"Will she be okay, Doctor?" my mother asked.

"Well, she has severe swelling on the brain and is in a coma. We've done all that we can as doctors. Right now, all we can do is pray that the swelling goes down."

"And if not?" my dad asked.

"Well, it doesn't look good," the doctor said calmly.

"What are her chances?" my mother asked.

"Well, not very good right now, but like I said, we just have to pray the swelling goes down before we do anything else at this point."

Hearing this news was the worst thing that I'd ever heard in my life. I couldn't believe this was happening. I felt helpless because I was confined to the bed and couldn't see Jennifer or be there to comfort her. The drugs I was on made me feel like my emotions were compressed or something, because I was lying there like a zombie.

Mike pulled up a chair and sat next to me. "Hey, man," he said with sadness in his eyes. I turned and looked over at him. "Uh . . . just hang in there, okay? Just keep praying, man, okay? I'll be right here if you need anything."

I nodded. As I looked in Mike's direction, I could see the door behind him open.

Rick walked in, and hurt and sorrow were in his eyes as he slowly walked over to the bed. He stood there looking at me, trying to find the right words to say but struggling. I reached out, and he walked closer and grabbed my hand as he broke down in tears. All this time we had been acting like little kids about things when deep down inside we still had love for each other. He was still struggling to speak, so I said, "Hey, man, I'm sorry."

"No, man. It was me. I was wrong with the way I came at you. You're my boy no matter what, and I let you down as a friend," he replied as he wiped his eyes.

"No, man. It's cool. We were both upset. I just hope everything is cool now."

"Yeah, dog. You my boy and I love you, man."

I nodded.

As we talked, Jennifer's parents came into the room to check on me. Her mother came over to the bed and kissed me on the forehead. Seeing her mother reminded me of how beautiful Jennifer was.

Everyone sat in the room talking and praying. I just closed my eyes and listened to the powerful words spoken to God.

My mother would check on Jennifer and give me reports on her. Every time she came back into the room I would get nervous because I didn't know what kind of news she had for me.

CHAPTER 25

Can I Get a Witness?

Two days later, I was released from the hospital. I was able to walk on my own, but the doctor insisted that I had to be wheeled out. I didn't want to go home, though. I asked to be taken to intensive care to be with Jennifer. At first my parents felt I needed to go home, but when they realized I wasn't having that, they left it alone.

When I got to the intensive care unit, I saw all of her friends and family in the waiting room gathered around in prayer or in silence. Paula gave me a look like she wanted to tear me apart. I could also feel the hatred in the room from other people in Jennifer's family, but I didn't care. I needed to be there with her. I wanted to be by her side every step of the way.

We all had to look through a glass window because only doctors and nurses were allowed in her room, but what I saw was devastating. Jennifer had tubes running in and out of her mouth, her arms, and all sorts of things connected to her chest to monitor her.

I watched as her chest rose and fell from the breathing machine. I tried so hard to be strong, but I couldn't. I was looking at my heart and soul, my life, my soul mate lying in bed fighting for her life over something I did. She was in there because of me. I couldn't do anything but pray. I asked God to please heal her. I sat there full of hatred for myself about what I'd done. Everything I had done wrong shouldn't affect her life like it was. Jennifer never hurt anyone. All she wanted was a chance at life and a family, but I took that away from her. I kept saying that over and over, hoping this would get God to bring her back.

Two days had passed, and things didn't look good for Jennifer. The longer she stayed in her coma, the worse her condition would be if she ever came out of it. I was as nervous as ever. I think I prayed every five minutes that things would get better, but they didn't.

Finally the doctors let us go into her room. I tried as hard as I could to go in there to be with her. Her face was still swollen and bruised from the accident. I leaned over and gave her a kiss on her bruised cheek. It was the first time in months that I had a chance to put my lips on her. Her parents stood over her still praying and talking to her, trying to give her strength to pull through. I rubbed her hands and said my own prayers for her. My eyes were getting heavier by the minute as I fought to keep them open, but the medicine I had taken made me sleepy.

I stayed in the room with Jennifer as long as I could, but the pain just seemed to get worse for me. I walked out and sat down in the waiting room, but it was hard for me to get comfortable. It was even harder on the cots that were given to us, so I was allowed to sleep in a hospital bed in the next room because of my condition.

Seeing that I was struggling to stay awake, Jennifer's dad suggested that I get into bed to get some sleep, promising they would let me know if anything changed with her condition. I shook my head. I needed to be there for whatever happened.

I did manage to doze off for a while but was awakened by the voices of Mike and Rick as they came in. Rick stood by the window to look in on Jennifer while Mike went over to my parents. Jennifer's parents had gone to the lounge to get some much-needed rest, so my parents stayed instead.

Mike sat down between my parents as they talked, and from my mother's reaction something wasn't right. I saw my mother jump up from her chair, walking off, shaking her head. My dad looked over at me and turned away. Struggling to get up, I walked over to where they were to find out what was going on, but they cut off the conversation when they saw me.

"What's wrong?" I asked. "Is something wrong with Jennifer?"

My mother walked over to me. "No, nothing's wrong," she said.

"Yes, there is, Mama. What is it?"

"Nothing, baby. Everything is fine," she said as she kissed me on the cheek.

Suddenly we heard the monitors beeping out of control in Jennifer's room. Jennifer's body was going into convulsions like she was having a seizure or something. The nurse monitoring her called out some codes on the intercom as doctors and nurses ran to her room. My dad called Jennifer's parents and told them what was going on, and they came running from the lounge. I moved as quickly as I could to the window, but one of the nurses pulled the curtains and shut the door. My heart began racing, and I started feeling numb. My mother grabbed her Bible and started praying out loud. Jennifer's parents embraced each other as Jennifer's mom cried out for her. Mike and Rick grabbed my father's hand, and they started praying silently. I was talking to myself, asking Jennifer to just hang on. "Come on, baby. Please, just fight. Don't give up."

Twenty minutes later, the doctor came out of Jennifer's room with a somber look. We all stood there anticipating the worst, but praying for the best. As he walked up, Jennifer's mother shouted, "Oh no! What happened to my baby? Please help her, Doctor."

He paused for a moment. "We were able keep her stable for now. We just need for her to be strong."

"What happened?" I asked.

"Well, she—"

Jennifer's mother began to yell at me. "What happened? What happened? She was fucking around with you, that's what happened. You should be in there instead of my baby. I told her not to come home for you. You should be in there, not her," she said hysterically.

Jennifer's dad held her mother and walked her away as she continued to yell and scream at me. I stood there not saying a word because in my heart I felt she was right. I should be the one in there instead of Jennifer. I caused all of this shit.

My mother came over to me and held me.

"Baby, she doesn't mean that. She's just scared, like we all are right now. Just keep on praying for Jennifer, okay? Just keep on praying," she said.

I walked off, shaking my head, and sat down near Mike as tears began to form.

"I did this to her, man. She's in there because of me. If she dies, I don't know what I'll do," I said.

Mike looked over at me. "Hey, don't do this to yourself. You didn't do this, man."

"Yes, I did. I asked her to come back when I should have gone to Atlanta to talk to her or something. I put her in this hospital, man. I don't care what nobody says."

Mike paused and took a deep breath. "Look, I need to talk to you about something, but I don't know if I should. I have to tell Jennifer's parents, too, because something happened that you had no control over."

I looked at Mike and frowned. "What are you talking about, man?"

"Well, uh, it seems that the car Jennifer was driving was tampered with."

"Tampered with?" I said. "What do you mean tampered with? Man, stop beating around the bush and get to the fucking point."

"Well, at the scene, the tires were off."

"Yeah," I said, "when she turned the corner I saw two tires come off."

"Yeah, that's because someone unscrewed all the nuts off the wheels to your car. In other words, someone deliberately tried to fuck you up. That's why she lost control," he said.

"What?"

"Yeah, man. The investigation guys said that your car tires rolled completely off your car."

"Oh no," I shouted. "I'm gonna kill that crazy-ass bitch."

"What?" he replied.

"I'm gonna kill her, man. I know she did this shit."

"Who, Troy?" he asked.

"No, don't worry about that. I'll take care of her myself," I said as I tried to get up.

"No, let us handle this, man. Don't get yourself in trouble over some dumb shit. Let me go downtown and see what I can do. Just tell me who she is."

"Hell no. Forget that," I shouted. Mike and Rick caught up with me as I struggled down the hallway, trying to leave to find Dana.

"Man, where do you think you're going?" Mike asked, walking toward me.

I ignored him as I kept on limping down the hallway.

My parents saw me and came up behind us.

"What's going on here?" my dad asked.

"Nothing. Nothing's going on. I'll be right back," I replied.

"I told him what happened with his car and now he's about to go out and do something crazy," Mike said.

"He's not going anywhere," my mother said as she walked up to me.

I just kept walking in silence.

"Who is she, Troy?" Mike asked.

"Who are you talking about, Mike?" my mother asked.

"Troy won't tell me the girl's name he thinks did this."

"Think nothing. I know she did this. I'm gonna take care of this myself," I said.

"You talking about Dana Suarway or whatever her name is?" my mother said.

"Who?" Mike asked, looking confused.

"Some girl he works with or something. Did she do this, Troy?" she asked firmly.

I ignored her as I struggled to make it out the door.

"Boy, listen to me," my mother shouted. "Is she the one who did this?"

I stopped and looked at her. "Yeah, Mama. She did this."

"Well, sit your ass down and let Mike handle this," she shouted.

"Oh, the girl you were talking about at the gym?" Mike asked, looking surprised.

"Yeah, that's the same one, man."

I looked over at Mike, still pissed off. My arm was hurting and my ribs were throbbing. I gave him all of the information I had on Dana and he wrote down every detail before heading to the police station. I was in so much pain that I had to be wheeled to the waiting room again. I was angrier than ever. I felt helpless just sitting there doing nothing.

Later on that night Jennifer's parents came into the waiting room and stood by the door. I turned my back to them and directed my attention to watching Jennifer through the window. Moments later I felt a hand touch my back.

"Troy." When I turned around, Jennifer's mother was standing in front of me.

"Troy, I'm sorry. I didn't mean to lash out at you like that. I know you wouldn't do anything to hurt my baby. I hope you can understand that I was upset. Mike told us what happened, and I guess I just lashed out at you. I'm so sorry," she replied as she reached out for me.

I grabbed her hand and we hugged. She walked over to my parents and sat next to them as she hugged my mother.

About an hour later, my parents went into the waiting room to get some sleep. Rick was sitting next to me half asleep in one of the chairs. I was still boiling with anger and hatred for Dana and felt I had to get out of the hospital and do something about it. I couldn't walk out on my own, though; I needed some help. I looked over at Rick and gently touched his shoulder.

"Hey, man," I said in a whisper. He turned over to the other side, still asleep. I leaned over and nudged him a little harder.

"Hey, Rick, man, wake up."

"Yeah, man? What's up?" he asked sleepily.

"I need you to do me a favor on the real," I said.

"Yeah? What's up, man? What you need?"

"I need you to take me over to Dana's house."

"What?" he said in disbelief.

"Yeah, man. I'm gonna get that bitch for this shit."

"Man, you talking crazy. Leave that bitch alone and let Mike handle that shit."

"Look, man, I need you on this," I said desperately.

"Troy, listen to me. Ain't shit you can do. Your ass is broke up enough as it is. Just sit here and be with your girl, man. That's what you need to be worried about."

"What?" I replied, confused.

"Yeah, man, that's right. Don't go and get yourself in trouble with that girl, man. Now you know normally I would be down for that shit, but right now you need to be here so when your girl pulls through, the first thing she sees is you, that's what's real. So c'mon and let Mike handle it, man."

I looked away and put my head down. Rick did make sense in a way, and I could tell that he was sincere. No matter how much I wanted to kill Dana, I still needed to be there for Jennifer, no matter what.

Later that evening I sat in the room with Jennifer. There was something about that night that was different than any other when I was in the room with her. I had prayed so much that I felt like I didn't know what else to say. I looked over at her and grabbed her hand. I remembered I never apologized to her for the way I had acted that night in Atlanta. As I began to open my heart to her, Mike came to the door.

"Troy," he whispered.

I looked up as he gestured for me. I walked over to him and he directed me to an empty room across the hall. When I got inside I saw two police officers standing there with a box on the table. He reached in the box and pulled out a stack of five-by-seven pictures and handed them to me.

"What's this?" I asked with a puzzled look.

"Look at this shit, man," he said.

I looked through the pictures one by one. It was pictures of letters from Jennifer addressed to me, a set of keys labeled with my name, as well as other things of mine.

"Where did you get this?" I asked.

"Man, you won't believe this. We got a search warrant and searched Dana's apartment today. This girl was obsessed with you and everyone she fell in love with. She had your name written next to hers on papers with hearts around them, she had all of the mail that Jennifer sent you stacked together, and she had the dates she went into your house and what she did while she was there. We even found the nuts she unscrewed from your car. Check this out, when we ran a check on her we found that this is not the first time she has done shit like this. She did the same thing in San Francisco with someone else at her job. We spoke to her manager in California and found out that instead of firing her they just transferred her to the office here to keep her away from that guy."

"Well, did you arrest her ass yet?" I asked.

"Yeah, we arrested her when we entered with the search warrant. Another thing, she filed a charge against you for domestic violence. Here are the photos of what she claimed to be her injuries."

"What?" I said as I looked at the photos.

There were pictures of her stomach with bruises where I fell on top of her. There were other pictures of her face and neck.

"Don't worry, man, that shit won't stick. After the district attorney gets a look at this shit they'll see that she's crazy."

"Why didn't they arrest her before, man?" I asked.

"Well, in looking at her record, we found that the guy who she was messing around with beat her ass and got charged with domestic violence. The report stated that he came on the job and then locked himself inside an office with her and kicked her ass, almost killing her."

"Damn," I said, shaking my head in disbelief. "Man, you know what, this story sounds familiar. When I was in Orlando this guy told the same shit happened at one of our partner companies. I wonder if this is the same crazy bitch."

"I don't know," he said.

I looked at the photos again. *Damn, that's the scar under her chin Jessie was talking about,* I thought. "Well, I'm about to find out," I said as I pulled out my wallet.

I grabbed my cell phone and looked for the card Jessie had given me before I left and called him. He remembered me right away. I explained everything that had happened. He was shocked and even more pissed off about this entire episode. I gave the phone to Mike as he wrote down every detail Jessie could provide that would help us. Jessie explained how he didn't really know about her transfer because the company kept everything confidential. It seemed because Dana was assaulted at work, she and the company filed charges against the other guy, Cirrus was his name. Later that year Jessie transferred to Nevada and had been there since.

Before getting off the phone he made me promise to let him know about all of the legal proceedings so he could come down and possibly testify, and I agreed.

"Well, it's true, man," Mike said, "and with what we have on her ass now, she's gonna do some time for this."

I nodded in disgust. As I sat down at the table I looked at the stack of pictures and grabbed a handful.

"I wish I could have read her letters," I said.

"Yeah, I know, but we had to take them in as evidence," Mike replied.

At that time the other two officers put the pictures in the box and left the room. Mike reached in his back pocket and pulled out a white envelope. "Hey, man, here you go. I thought you'd want to have it."

He had one of Jennifer's letters and placed it on the table next to me. I looked at him as a smile covered my face.

"They won't miss it," he said.

Before he left he looked back at me as I began opening the letter.

"Hey, don't worry, man, we got her ass this time."

"Okay, thanks, man," I replied, still in shock.

I walked back into Jennifer's room and sat next to her with the letter in my hand.

"So this is the mail you sent me, huh?" I said. "Well, I never had a chance to read it, so I'll read it now." I began reading the letter out loud. In it Jennifer explained everything in detail that I didn't bother to listen to before. She said that I was the most important thing in her life, and that no matter what I believed or what I saw, it was far from the truth. She felt our love was strong enough to endure some hard times like the distance we had until I was able to move there. With the time she had alone, she wanted to use it to her advantage to make a better life for the both of us. She never questioned me in anything I did because she truly believed in me and knew that I would never do anything to hurt her.

She went on to say how she tried to come home and explain

everything to me in person but couldn't because her job had her traveling all the time this was going on between us. After that her only possible resource was e-mail or by mailing a letter since I wouldn't return her calls.

She went on to explain what had happened that night. Her meetings were canceled in New York that Thursday and she was able to catch an earlier flight home. Rhonda, who dropped her off, was supposed to pick her up at the airport that night but couldn't. Rhonda was at the hospital with Robert, who they found out was gay and HIV positive. He had suffered a stroke because of his illness. Rhonda had her cousin pick up Jennifer, and they stopped by her apartment to drop off her luggage before heading to the hospital.

You never gave me a chance to say a word, she wrote. *Instead you treated me like scum on the street. You probably don't believe me now anyway, but it's the honest-to-God truth, something I'll put my life on. I was trying to be there for Robert like he was for me as a friend and nothing more. You never gave any of my friends a chance to get to know you. It's like you wanted me all to yourself and couldn't trust the fact that I do have male friends and that's all they are to me, friends.*

She explained how losing me was like losing her life and that from that point on her life was nothing. The job, the city, the money were nothing without me to share them with.

I paused, putting my head down as I folded the letter. I couldn't read any more because it hurt so much inside. All I could do was look at her lying there with only machines keeping her alive and continue to blame myself.

"Please, baby, get up. Please get up," I pleaded as tears began to flow down my cheeks. "I love you, baby. I can't think of tomorrow or the next day, because it hurts to know that you might not be there with me. God, help me. I'm so sorry for everything I've done to hurt her. Please, God, please, God, give her strength."

Jennifer's mother came in and saw how I was losing control and wrapped her arms around me.

"Come on, Troy, let's go outside and get some fresh air," she said.

"No, no, I can't leave her. I need to be here for her."

"Just for a little while, okay? Let's just get some air," she insisted.

"I'm sorry, I'm so sorry. I know you hate me. I'm so sorry," I said as tears poured out of my eyes. "I love her more than anything in the world, Lord, please help her. Please, Jesus," I cried.

Jennifer's mother grabbed me by the hand as I continued to lose it and walked me outside.

CHAPTER 26

A Moment of Silence

While outside I sat on one of the benches and rested my head on a table. We stayed out there for about thirty minutes praying and reciting scriptures. Suddenly, Rick came running outside calling for us to come back in.

"I think Jennifer is having another seizure," he shouted.

Her mother grabbed my hand, pulling me inside, but I refused. I had a numbness inside that had me in a state of shock. Jennifer's mom ran inside behind Rick while I got up and walked off. I didn't know where I was going, I just walked around the hospital in complete silence. I had made my peace with God and Jennifer, so I was prepared for anything.

Before I realized it twenty minutes had passed. When I turned around I could see the hospital in front of me like it was miles away. I began walking back, still feeling empty. As I made it to the door I took a deep breath and walked inside toward the waiting room. Instead of coming in the back way like before I came in from the front entrance. When I turned the corner I saw everyone gathered together crying and hugging. Then I knew it was over. I knew I had lost the only love I had ever known because of my foolishness. I was trying to be so hard that I didn't give time or effort to Jennifer when she needed it most. I gritted my teeth and walked forward. When I looked into the intensive care room, it was empty. They had already moved her body.

Seeing me come in, my mother ran to me in tears. "Troy, where have you been? We've looked all over for you. Jennifer is—"

I cut her off and hugged her as I got weak in the knees.

"No, Mama, don't say it," I cried. "Please don't say it."

"Troy, listen to me," she shouted. "Jennifer is out of her coma. We thought it was another seizure, but it wasn't. She just went into shock coming out of her coma. The doctor said that the swelling went down and took her back for further examination. He said that the worst part is over. She's gonna make it, son."

My body felt so weak that I slumped over on my mom as she struggled to hold me up. I couldn't believe what I had just heard. Was I dreaming? *Is this true?* I thought.

Rick ran over to me and hugged me as we both stood there in tears. I hurried over to Jennifer's parents and hugged them, too, along with Jennifer's friend Paula and Jennifer's family members, who were inside.

I couldn't believe it. It was a miracle. God answered my prayers. He brought Jennifer back.

I walked over into the corner and began to praise his name.

"Thank you, Jesus," I shouted.

Hours later Jennifer was brought out and was put back into intensive care. No one was allowed back there because she had to be closely monitored again.

Mike came running into the hospital with a huge smile, hugging everyone he saw. "Rick called me on my cell phone and told me the news. Where's Troy?" he shouted, almost out of breath.

I stood from the crowd and looked at him as I nodded my head.

He walked over to me and gave me a hug, repeating over and over, "Thank you, Jesus."

Three days later Jennifer was conscious. When the doctors thought she was strong enough to talk, her parents went in first to see her while I waited outside. I was still nervous because I didn't know how she was going to react to seeing me after everything that had happened. Really it didn't matter, as long as she was alive and well, that's all I wanted.

More and more people came to see her. When I looked in the lounge I saw people from her job, more family members, old church members, basically everyone who knew Jennifer was at the hospital. When her parents came out of the room they gave me the signal to go on in. I was so nervous that a lump formed in my throat and I began to shake.

When I got inside, there was a doctor still in her room examining her. I slowly walked up to her bed. It was so good to see her beautiful eyes again. When Jennifer saw me, a tear fell from her left eye. I stood there not knowing how to react. With the little strength she had, Jennifer tried to reach out to me. I gently grabbed her hand as she tried to squeeze mine tight. I leaned over her and kissed her on her cheek.

"I love you, Jennifer. I love you so much. I thought I lost you again."

Tears began to fall from her eyes as she put on that half smile that I loved so much.

"I promise I will never leave you again ever. I promise I will take care of you for the rest of your life, okay? I love you," I said as I continued to gently kiss her cheek.

"I . . . love . . . yo-you t-t-t-too," she said, struggling with her words.

"Shhhh, save your strength, baby," I said as I gently stroked her face.

I stayed another five minutes, then left because she was so weak and needed her rest. For the most part I just wanted her to know that I would be there when she needed me. When I left the room I walked outside to get some air. I saw Mike and Rick coming from the parking lot and started walking toward them.

"Hey, what's up?" I asked.

"Nothing much," Mike replied. "How is Jennifer?"

"She's doing fine. I just left her room a minute ago."

"So she's conscious?" Rick asked.

"Yeah, but it's hard for her to talk right now because she's so weak."

"Yeah, I'm just glad she conscious, man," he said as we slapped hands.

"Yeah, man," I said.

"Oh yeah," Mike said. "Dana had her bond hearing this morning."

"For real?" I said, surprised. "Good. I hope that crazy bitch rots in jail."

"Yeah, when the judge denied bond, they said that she was kicking and yelling so wildly they had to hog-tie her ass to get her outta there."

I shook my head in disgust. "Yeah, I'm just glad she's off the street," I said.

"Hell yeah," Rick said.

We walked over to a table and sat down.

"So what about you? How is your arm and ribs, man?" Rick asked.

"Still a little sore, but I'm cool. I just have to keep this cast on for a few weeks. So what's been up with you lately?"

"Man, I've been just chillin', coming to grips with myself. I had a chance to take a good look in the mirror and decided I really need to get my life together," Rick said.

"Good. I think I really learned a serious lesson these past few days, man," I said. "Life is truly what you make of it. If you do good, life is good, but if you constantly screw up, you're gonna get screwed in the end."

"You got that right," Mike said.

The three of us sat there talking about old times for most of the evening.

CHAPTER 27

Say No More

The next day Dana was officially fired from her job. I finally went home for the first time in about a week to the mess that was made in my apartment that night of the accident. My mother and my aunts came over and helped me clean up. When I first walked in, I relived that night in my mind like it had just happened moments before. *It's hard to believe that I was caught up in some shit like that,* I thought.

I went to the hospital a couple of days later and sat with Jennifer until the doctors came in. Since all kinds of tests had to be run on her, I decided to go home and get some much-needed rest. Each day I visited, Jennifer was more coherent than before and her condition was getting better. She had been moved into a private room with a great view of the city on the seventh floor near the elevators. When I walked in, her room was filled with flowers, stuffed animals, and get-well cards. I added to the flowers by ordering a huge bouquet of roses.

Most of the tubes had been taken out of her except the one that was monitoring her vital signs. Her parents were sitting with her while the doctor ran his daily test to make sure her functions were still normal.

"How's everything, Doc?" I asked as I watched him examine her.

"Well, everything seems to be normal so far. She's recovering really well."

"Really?" I replied with happiness in my voice.

"Yeah, if she stays normal, it won't be long before she is released."

I smiled as I walked over to look out of the window. As I did, I heard the most beautiful sound.

"Troy," Jennifer said in a soft voice.

I turned around, and she was looking in my direction with her beautiful eyes wide open. I walked over to her with a big smile, showing all my teeth.

"Hey, baby," I said, kneeling. "How are you feeling?"

"I feel extremely tired, but I'm better now that you're here," she said. "My parents told me how you stayed with me."

"Yeah, I'm never gonna leave you again, I promise. Never again, okay?"

She smiled as tears formed in her eyes.

"How are you doing?" she asked softly.

"Oh, I'm doing fine. I'll be okay."

"Good, 'cause you can't hold me if your arm is banged up," she said, smiling.

I laughed as tears filled my eyes. "You don't hate me, do you?" I asked seriously.

"No. I know I put my work before you. I'm—"

"No, no, no, don't say you're sorry. It was me and my stubbornness that messed us up. I should have trusted you. It was all—"

"Troy, please, let's not talk about that, okay? You're here and I'm here. That's all that matters."

I nodded as I leaned over and kissed her on the cheek. The doctor finished examining her and started walking toward the door. Jennifer's mom got up and met him before walking out.

"So what's next, Doctor?" she asked.

"Well, in looking at the X-rays, I can tell her brain is back to its normal size, but because she suffered spinal injuries, she will have to go through therapy to strengthen her legs again. But for the most part I think she will fully recover."

"Really?" her mom said, excited.

"Yeah, I think so. She was very lucky, Mrs. Stevens, very lucky."

"Well, Doctor, once you let God take over, nothing is impossible," Mrs. Stevens said.

"You're right, Mrs. Stevens. You're absolutely right about that," he replied as he turned and walked out of the room.

"Thank you, Jesus," Jennifer's mom shouted. "God is good."

We all watched as she praised God. I must say, that moment changed my life completely. Seeing God's miracle touched my heart in a way that I can't describe. All I know is that I felt the power of the Holy Spirit in that room.

Weeks passed and Jennifer was released from the hospital and stayed with me so that she could attend her therapy. She was confined to a wheelchair until she was strong enough to walk again. She had to go to therapy three times a week, and I was there with her every day. Her firm put her up for junior partner and told her to take as much time off as she needed until she felt she was ready to handle the cases. I started back to work again, too, and was welcomed back with an office party thrown by Mr. Ford. As I walked to my office I glanced over to the one Dana used to occupy. I felt strange at first, but after I went inside and started on my new projects, I was back to my old self again.

I met the guys at Mammie's like always where we laughed and joked through lunch. I guess you could say things were back to normal. Well, almost back to normal. Rick had kept everyone in suspense about his whereabouts for the last few weeks. He said he wanted to surprise us later with his reasons for being away.

Jennifer and I patched things up completely and carried on our plans to live in Atlanta together. This time, though, we agreed that we would be husband and wife when we did move. Yep, we made it official, as soon as she was able to walk down the aisle, we would get married and move to Atlanta. Mr. Ford hooked up a position for me with our other firm, and I could start as soon as Jennifer and I were ready to move.

Mike was ready to take on a better-paying job since he had three kids, and he knew Mobile wasn't going to get it for him. Jennifer got him hooked up with the DA's office in Atlanta as one of the chief investigators while he applied for law school.

After two months of rigorous therapy, Jennifer was ready to make the walk of her life. She still had a slight limp but insisted that she was ready. We were both excited as we prepared for our day. We sent out invitations to our family and friends all over the country. We spared no expense because to us this was a blessing from God to be getting married. She insisted on having the wedding in Mobile because it was home to her, even though Pensacola was only a short drive away for her family and friends.

The night before the wedding the guys threw me the best bachelor party I had ever been to. Mike and Rick rounded up all of my friends and male cousins and threw a nice bash at this really nice frat house owned by Kappa Alpha Psi. There was no alcohol, no strippers, and no music, just a whole lot of pool, dominoes, and spades being played with old friends. It was a special moment for me to receive the love from all the fellas.

The wedding was at Mt. Zion Baptist Church. All the groomsmen were in the back waiting on the people to arrive. I was a nervous wreck as I paced the floor with sweat running down my face. Mike was sitting in the corner calm and cool reading a paper, tripping off the way I was acting.

"Calm down, man. You gonna walk a hole in your shoes," he said.

"Man, I'm just ready for this to be over so I can get to the good part," I joked.

"Man, this *is* the good part. Trust me," he said.

I laughed as I kept on pacing.

"Hey, where is Rick, man? He was supposed to be here thirty minutes ago," I said as I looked at my watch.

"Man, you know Rick. He'll be here. He said he had a surprise for us or something."

"Well, I hope he hurries up," I said.

About five minutes later, Rick came in through the back door.

"Man, where have you been?" I asked.

"Oh, I had to stop and pick up someone first," he replied, smiling.

"What are you smiling about, man?" Mike asked as he folded up his paper.

"Come outside. I want you to see why I've been out of pocket for the last few weeks."

We followed Rick outside to the back of the church. When we turned the corner we got the shock of our lives. Rick was standing there with Gina, the woman from Atlanta we had met when we moved Jennifer up there. I was really shocked 'cause this wasn't like Rick. Mike was standing there with his mouth wide open. Gina was really looking good. Rick was standing there smiling from ear to ear as he stood next to her.

"Hey, guys," Gina said with a big, beautiful smile on her face as she hugged Mike and me.

"Hey, girl," I said. "It's been a long time. How are you doing? You look good."

"Thanks, I've been doing good. What about you guys?" she asked, "Especially you, Troy? Rick told me about what happened."

I smiled. "Well, I'm truly doing great now and will be even better in a few minutes. I'm glad you could make it."

"Thanks. I'm really excited for you two. I wish you nothing but the best."

"Well, thanks, Gina," I said.

"This is great. I was wondering what happened to my boy since he was missing so much," Mike said.

Rick laughed. "Shiiit, man, I'm doing great."

"Hey," I said, "man, we outside a church."

"Oops," he said, "my bad."

"Still the same ol' Rick," I said, laughing. "Well, we better get inside so we can get this show on the road. Gina, I'll see you later, and tell your girls I said hello."

"Okay, congratulations again," she said as she walked off.

"Okay, baby. I'll see you later," Rick said as Gina walked away. "You sure you don't need me to walk you inside?"

Gina shook her head as she continued to the front of the church. We all turned and walked inside.

"Rick, when did you two hook up like that?" I asked.

"Man, when I was down and out, Gina was there for me through it all, encouraging me, praying with me over the phone, just being a good friend. No matter how I treated her she would call just to say hello and that she was thinking about me. Then when I lost my job she flew me to Atlanta just to get away for a while. She took me to her church, introduced me to her family and friends, you know, made me feel special. Not one time was it ever about money or what I could do for her. It was about one friend being there for another. Then one day, it hit me that I was falling for her. So from that point on we got serious. I helped her with her business ideas and fronted her the cash for a management company."

"Management company," I said. "Man, that's great."

"Yeah, I borrowed money from my investments and helped jump-start the business, and now she or should I say we are managing a couple of businesses in Atlanta.

"What do you mean, we?" Mike asked.

"Just what I said. We have an office in Atlanta."

"So are you moving up there?" I asked.

"Yeah, man. You don't think I'd let my boys leave me here, do you?" he said, smiling.

We all laughed and gave each other a group hug as the wedding planner came in and gave us the cue that the wedding was about to start.

All of the groomsmen lined up outside. I came in from the side entrance and stood at the front of the church. The church was filled to capacity. I was so nervous that my hands were starting to sweat. I looked over at my mother, who was staring at me, wiping her eyes. Minutes later the music started and everyone watched as the groomsmen and bridesmaids walked into the church in pairs. My dad, who was my best man, stood by my side the whole way. When everyone came in and got into position, there was a moment of silence as we all prepared for Jennifer. As the music played everyone in the church stood and positioned themselves to get a clear view.

When the church doors opened I saw the most beautiful sight I have ever seen. It was like the gates of heaven opened and standing there was one of God's angels. All I heard were the *oohs* and *ahs* from the people in the church. I turned in Jennifer's direction and prepared to receive her as my wife. The cameras started flashing all at once as Jennifer got ready to walk down the aisle. The music continued as she started toward me. As she began to move forward, her first step was kinda hard for her. Her leg buckled as she held on to her father. The second step, however, was a little bit smoother, and she continued, gradually pacing herself. People were in tears as they saw her struggle to make it up the aisle despite her injury. I wanted to run out and grab her other arm and help her make it without the pain that she was going through, but I had promised her no matter how difficult it was for her, she was going to do it on her own. She continued, step by step by step, at a slow and careful pace.

When she made it to the altar I received her from her father. She grabbed my arm and held on as tight as she could as tears of happiness flowed from her eyes. We both listened intently as the preacher explained the meaning of marriage and our pledge of love for each other.

"The rings please," the preacher said.

Jennifer grabbed the wedding band and held it to my finger.

"I, Jennifer Monique Stevens, take you, Troy Julian Sanders, to be my lawfully wedded husband, secure in the knowledge that you will be my constant companion and faithful partner throughout our lives, and to be my one and only true love. I promise in the presence of God and everyone in attendance to stay with you as your faithful wife in joy and in sorrow, as well as through good times and in bad, in sickness and in health. I promise to love and cherish you for as long as we both shall live."

I watched as Jennifer put the ring on my finger as the tears poured from my eyes. I grabbed the wedding ring, then Jennifer's right hand as we stared in each other's eyes. As I looked at her, my mind flashed to that night when I almost lost her. I tried to hold back the tears, but I couldn't. The church was quiet as everyone looked at me. I took a deep breath as my words began to flow. "Uh, today is a miracle from God. And in front of God and all of these witnesses, I vow my love to you.

"Jennifer Monique Stevens, today and forever I promise to give you the very best of me and to ask of you no more than you can give me. I vow this day to respect you as your own person and to realize that your desires and needs are no less important than my own. I vow to share with you my time and my attention and to bring joy, strength, and imagination to our marriage. I vow to keep myself open and faithful to you and to let you see through the window of my world into my innermost thoughts and feelings, secrets and dreams. I vow to grow together and be willing to face any changes to keep our marriage alive. I vow to always love you in good times and in bad, with all that I have to give in the only way I know how, completely and forever, until death do us part."

When I finished, Jennifer wiped the tears from my eyes. The preacher looked at me and then at the congregation.

"I now pronounce you husband and wife. You may kiss your bride."

We embraced in a kiss that felt better than any joy I've ever felt before in my life. We turned and faced the congregation of people as they stood applauding.

"Ladies and gentlemen, I would like to introduce to you Mr. and Mrs. Troy Julian Sanders" the preacher said.

Months later we all were settled in Atlanta. We all bought houses nearby but in different neighborhoods. Mike and his family were doing really well, adjusting to the new city. Rick had settled down and was planning to propose to Gina around the first of the year. As for Jennifer and me, well, she was back hard at work and I was enjoying my job as well. The doctors released her from her therapy and she was getting around pretty much the way she was before, just with a little caution. Oh yeah, because we had such an exciting honeymoon, we were expecting our first child in September.

THE JUMP OFF

DOUG DIXON

ABOUT THE GUIDE

The suggested questions are intended to enhance
your group's reading of this book by Doug Dixon.

DISCUSSION QUESTIONS

1. What do you think of the characters Troy, Mike, and Rick, and which one would you date and why?

2. What do you think of Mike and Rick as a friend?

3. Do you agree with Jennifer's decision to move? If not, why?

4. How would you react to Jennifer's decision to move if you were Troy?

5. What do you think of Troy and Jennifer as a couple?

6. Do you agree with the way Troy confronted Jennifer about her alleged infidelity? If not, how would you have approached it?

7. What were your thoughts of Dana?

8. Do you agree with Troy's decision to confide in Dana about his personal life?

9. What is crossing the line when it comes to friendship at the workplace between men and women?

10. If you were Dana, how would you have handled your friendship with Troy?

11. After an ordeal like the one Jennifer went through in her accident, would you have stayed with Troy? If not, why?

12. How did you feel about the way the book ended?